# GENUINE DECEIT

To Cindy,

Enjoy the adventure! -

Best wishes,

# GENUINE DECEIT

*A Suspense Novel*

## Joy York

ISBN: 978-1-7370528-1-4 (paperback)
ISBN: 978-1-7370528-0-7 (ebook)

Editing by Kathryn J. Jones
Cover Design by Berge Design

In memory of Mama Leavie, my beloved grandmother, for her legacy of storytelling, and my mother for inspiring me to write.

# Chapter 1

If he didn't find it soon, all bets were off. Regardless of his instructions, he'd have to take matters into his own hands. He wasn't sure how long he'd searched the house, but he knew she could be home any minute. Anger burned inside him as he looked down at the fake turquoise jewelry in his trembling hands, then threw it to the floor with the rest of the worthless junk in the jewelry box.

Drawing in a deep breath to calm his racing heart, he surveyed the destruction he had left on the room. All the drawers from the mirrored dresser and chest of drawers lay upside down, contents strewn across the floor. The boxes from the top of the closet were emptied and scattered. The drawers to the bedside tables leaned against the far wall, where he had flung them in frustration. He had even ripped the mattress and covers off the bed when it occurred to him that she might have cleverly hidden it between the mattress and box springs. Nothing.

"Shit! Shit! Shit! Where is it?" he growled. He felt a wave of nausea and the beginnings of a headache. He needed a hit. Bad. But first he had to complete this job. If he didn't find it, he wouldn't be able to pay back the money he owed, and his life would be worthless. Probably dead within 24 hours.

"Think! Think!" he pounded his fist against his temple as if he could knock some sense into his head. "It has to be here somewhere." Staring at the cheap paintings hanging on the walls sparked an idea. There could be a hidden wall safe. Within seconds, he pulled down and discarded the paintings, the last one suffering his wrath with a foot through the middle of the canvas. No safe.

He had concentrated his efforts in the master bedroom, assuming that the old lady would have kept anything expensive in her room. From the looks of the tired, outdated house, it didn't make sense that she owned anything of value, but he was positive he had the right address … well, almost positive. He had parked his car a couple of streets over to avoid it being noticed. Bad Idea. After cutting through a few backyards, he found himself turned around and for a while lost his bearing in the dark. It was already going to be difficult to get out of the house before she got home, and now he had the added worry that he was in the wrong one.

"No! It can't be. White brick, dammit! It's a fuckin' white brick house!"

Anxiety clouded his judgment. "You got to keep your shit together, man," he muttered to himself, wiping beads of sweat.

He had this one last chance to wipe his debt clean. The instructions were simple. Find it and leave no trace you were ever there. *Well, I've already fucked up the last part,* he thought, looking around the room at the chaos he'd created. He hoped all would be forgiven once he delivered the prize.

*What if she has it with her? Wouldn't be my damn fault,* he tried to rationalize. But as soon as it crossed his mind, he knew that wouldn't mean shit to his creditor, who had zero tolerance. One way or another, he was going to find it if he had to tear the whole house apart, piece by piece. Just when he decided to search another room, he heard the faint sound of a door closing somewhere in the house. He froze.

*Shit! The old lady is home!* Sliding his hand into his hoodie pouch, he wrapped his fingers around his weapon reassuringly. It gave him a sense of power. His heart sped up as the adrenalin kicked in. A few seconds later, he heard glasses clinking. *Definitely home.* He smiled, realizing it might be to his advantage. If he could get her to talk, fine. If not, screw her.

Stepping as quietly as he could, he inched his way out of the bedroom and down the hall. When his foot hit a squeaky board, he stopped. The sounds still coming from the kitchen assured him he hadn't been detected. As he made his way through the darkened house, carefully stepping past the living room furniture cloaked in shadows, he could feel his muscles tighten in anticipation of the upcoming confrontation.

The light filtering in from the kitchen door illuminated the heavy oak table in the dining room, making it easier for him to follow an unobstructed path, but he didn't notice a chair sitting skewed from the table. His boot hit a chair leg, creating the unmistakable sound of wood scraping against a hard surface. He heard the old lady scream and a glass crashing to the floor.

*What if she called the cops? It would only take one touch on speed dial.*

When he made it to the kitchen, he watched her fling open the door to the garage and just missed grabbing her as she stumbled down the stairs into the dark. The dim light coming from the kitchen was barely enough to see her shadow cut left in front of the car and into shadows. He fumbled to find a light switch before remembering the miniature penlight he'd stuffed into his jeans pocket. With shaking hands, he pulled it out and almost dropped it as he flipped it on.

In the wobbly beam of the penlight, he saw the old lady frantically trying to unlock the door to the outside.

"Stop! Turn around and get away from the door!" he barked. Despite his warnings, she ignored him, continuing her attempts to escape.

"Oh, God. Oh, God. Please help me," he heard her mutter.

*The crazy bitch won't look at me. Probably already called the cops.* Fueled by rage, he reached her within seconds, grabbing her by the shoulders and shaking her hard. The old lady lost her balance, her knees hitting the door she'd tried so hard to open and her head cracking against the glass window.

She gasped, trying to speak, but no words came out.

"Tell me where it is!" he demanded.

"I ... I d...don't kn..." she choked.

She was useless to him. Because of her, he was a dead man.

With one swift motion, the blade in his hand sliced across her throat. Her lips sputtered noiselessly, her shoulders slumped, and her head fell forward.

# Chapter 2

Unable to force herself out of the car, Reagan Asher stared at the faded white ranch-style home where her grandmother was found murdered less than 24 hours before. Snow from a recent storm remained in patches around the yard, giving the scene an uncharacteristically frosty chill. Everything about the house looked different … felt different, empty and detached. She could hardly believe that less than two months ago, when she visited during the Christmas holidays, it had been her sanctuary.

The only outward difference was the neon-yellow crime scene tape slapped across the front door, making it look like a second-rate CSI set. Nonetheless, it was still the same house her grandparents had purchased over 40 years ago in the small bedroom community of Lancashire, Ohio, nestled between Cleveland and Akron. The one she had called home for most of her life. The most significant difference — her grandmother was dead. A shiver crept up her spine and her heart clutched tightly in her chest.

Reagan cleared her thoughts and pushed the emotions down deep inside, then opened the car door.

"Where are you going?" Mattie asked indignantly from the driver's seat.

"Inside to wait for Detective Kowalski," Reagan answered with resignation. "I told him I'd meet him here at 3 o'clock for an interview and walk-through, and I'm not bailing on him. The sooner he has the information he needs from me, the faster he'll be able to find Nana's … whoever killed her." She could barely comprehend those words, let alone speak them. So far, she had been able to keep her tears in check. Losing her composure would only make her best friend feel worse about leaving.

"There is no way you're going into that house alone!" Mattie slammed her hand on the steering wheel. "Damn! I wish I didn't have this Parent/Teacher Day hanging over my head or you know I'd do this with you. I'm so sorry, Reagan. I don't have any way to reschedule those parents at the last minute." Mattie wiped a tear from her cheek. Nana had been like a grandmother to her too.

Reagan reached for her hand and squeezed. "Stop feeling guilty. It's not your fault. You already left work to pick me up at the airport, plus you and Josh gave me a place to stay. That's more than enough."

"But that detective is already 20 minutes late. Let me drop you by our house, and you can relax for the rest of the afternoon. He obviously doesn't respect your time, so why should you care about his? You can do this tomorrow when I can get off work."

"I'm fine. Honestly. I'm sure an emergency of some kind came up, and he'll be here any minute." Reagan glanced back at the taped barrier on the front door. "It's too cold to wait outside, so I'll sit quietly in the living room and won't touch a thing. Now go before you face the wrath of an angry parent." Then to reassure Mattie, Reagan leaned over the console and threw her arms around her friend.

"Thank you," she whispered in Mattie's ear. "For everything this will entail. I don't know what I would do without you. You're all I have left."

"I love you. You know that, right?" Reagan nodded, feeling the tears she refused to shed sting the backs of her eyes.

Mattie held her tighter. "You stand your ground with that detective like you do with those alpha egomaniacs you work with every day. I'm sure that detective has other cases but finding Nana's killer needs to be his top priority. We expect results! And soon! And he'd better not be late to another appointment or I'll personally kick his butt!"

Reagan rolled her eyes and smiled at her overprotective friend as she waved goodbye. That was Mattie, a take-charge, "in your face" kind of woman. She had been fighting Reagan's battles since elementary school and couldn't seem to turn it off. The truth was Reagan was grateful that Mattie always had her back. It hurt like hell to watch her drive away when she needed her so badly.

With a trembling hand, Reagan fumbled around in her handbag until she found the house key, then took a deep breath. She slid the key into place and slowly turned it until she heard the lock click. It required every ounce of courage she could muster to push open the door, slip under the yellow tape, and step inside. Despite the early morning call from the detective about Nana's death, Reagan couldn't help but hold out a sliver of hope that it had all been some kind of a terrible mistake. A part of her expected to find Nana relaxing in her lounge chair, a blanket tucked around her, watching television and laughing about the absurdity of the misunderstanding.

Instead, to her surprise, Reagan found the living room as neat and tidy as always with the handwoven afghan Nana had made for her lying on the well-worn cornflower-blue sofa. The TV remote and a drink coaster were strategically placed on the end table next to Nana's chair for easy access, and a romance novel lay open face down on the coffee table, as if awaiting her grandmother's nightly fantasy escape. Everything reflected the illusion of normalcy.

Clutching the afghan to her chest, Reagan sat on the sofa, leaned her head back and let fond memories fill her mind. She could almost pretend Nana was bustling around the kitchen eager to hear about her day at school. *How did you do on your math test? Is Ms. McCleary still taking away cell phones before class? Has that cute Conner Thornhill asked you to prom yet? When is the next parents meeting for the soccer team?* Even the memories of Nana's nagging to do her homework or to turn down her music brought a welcome feeling of warmth. She squeezed her watery eyes shut as regret washed over her. Nana had begged her to move home after she graduated six years ago with her MBA from Purdue, but Reagan had instead accepted an offer for her dream job in Chicago. *Could I have somehow prevented this if I had come back home?*

Reagan wasn't sure how long she'd sat on the sofa or if she had nodded off and begun to dream, when a loud bang startled her upright. Assuming it was Detective Kowalski, she quickly made her way to the front door and peered through the peephole. No one was there. It must have been a dream.

"Where the hell are you?" she muttered to herself as she sat back down. The detective had been vague on the phone about the circumstances of Nana's murder. He may have mentioned burglary, but in her state of shock, she could hardly catch everything he said. The one thing she did remember clearly, his insistence that she meet him at her grandmother's home at 3 p.m. Checking her cell, she realized he was 40 minutes late.

Three rapid pounding sounds sent Reagan instantly to her feet. The noise seemed to come from the back bedrooms, and this time it wasn't a dream or her imagination. Every nerve in her body screamed on heightened alert. Until that moment, the possibility of the murderer returning to the house had not occurred to her. It wasn't in her nature to overreact and mentally go to the worst-case scenario, but the past few hours had knocked her off balance, so she wasn't exactly herself. She took a calming breath as Nana's favorite saying, "Don't borrow trouble," popped into her head. *It's nothing. Probably the ancient heater. Nothing to worry about. There's police tape on the door, for gosh sakes.*

Determined not to let irrational fear paralyze her, Reagan decided to investigate what caused the noise and prove to herself there was a logical explanation. On the off chance her fears were well founded, she approached with caution. Silently creeping down the hall, avoiding the creaky floorboards, she peered into all the rooms with open doors, stopping at the only one that was closed, Nana's room. She pressed her ear to the door to listen. Nothing. Bracing her shoulders and steeling her back, she slowly reached for the door handle, but just before she turned the knob, an image flashed in her mind of a masked gunman. She drew her hand back swiftly. Woefully unprepared for that scenario, she decided further exploration was a matter left for the truant detective.

As she turned back toward the living room, the sound of a window slamming shut reverberated through the house. A terrified scream escaped her lips as she fled down the hall, through the living room, and into a hard body, her forward momentum sending them both crashing to the floor in a heap of tangled limbs. As she lay on top of a large muscular chest, startled pale blue eyes bore into hers. It took a few moments for her brain to engage, and she momentarily relaxed when she remembered she was expecting the detective.

"D...D...Detective K...Kowalski?" she panted, trying to catch her breath as the two stared at each other, nose to nose, their mouths so close they were exchanging the same air.

He scrunched his forehead in confusion, then narrowed his eyes. "No, I'm not Detective ..."

That was all Reagan needed to hear for blind terror to kick her self-preservation instincts into high gear, and her fists flew with wild abandon at the stranger. Within seconds, the solidly built man caught her wrists securely in his hands to stop her tirade and rolled over on top of her, supporting his weight on his forearms.

"Hey now …" he began.

"Let me go! Get your hands off me!" Reagan screamed and bucked, trying to free herself from his grasp. "The police will be here any minute!" she yelled as loud as she could. When she tried to knee him in the groin, he lowered his weight over her legs enough to still her lower body. "Help! Help! Someone help me! Please!"

"Whoa! Whoa! Whoa! Whoa! Watch the knee. I might want to procreate at some point in my life. Calm down! I'm not going to hurt you!" he implored, but his entreaties fell on deaf ears. She continued to struggle.

"Get your hands off me!" She writhed and thrashed to get out from under him, but she might as well have been attempting to move a Mack truck. He had her completely immobile.

"If you stop struggling and trying to maim me, I'll let you go," he said, trying to reason with her.

"Why would I do that?" she said through gritted teeth. "You broke into my grandmother's house!"

"I didn't break in. The front door was wide open. I'm not a threat to you, so please stop fighting me. Okay?" His blue eyes pierced her green ones with an intensity that pleaded with her to believe him, but after Nana's violent death, her trust would have to be earned. Besides, he could break her like a twig without even using a weapon.

Ssssurrre," she said sarcastically.

He groaned and twisted his lips, seeming to consider his options. "You're not very convincing, but I'm choosing to believe you." Gradually loosening his grip on her wrists, he quickly rolled away and jumped to his feet in one fluid motion.

It took a few seconds to get the feeling back into her legs before she scrambled to her feet. Taking in his 6-foot-plus height and muscular frame made her painfully aware of her physical vulnerability. Rushing over to an end table, she grabbed a tall brass lamp and yanked the cord out of the socket. She confidently held her makeshift weapon over her shoulder like a baseball bat.

"Get out of my house!" she commanded, hands visibly trembling.

The man stared at her, lips turned up in the most irritating smirk. With his palms held up in a nonthreatening way, he said, "You honestly think I'm going to stand here quietly while you beat me senseless with a lamp?" He shook his head. "No good deed goes unpunished." Then he calmly walked over to her and with a quick flick of his wrist effortlessly took it out of her hands.

"Hey, give that back!" She'd been told her icy glare could cut iron, but it didn't appear to faze him one bit.

"Not giving it back to a loose cannon," he said, placing it back on the table. "Since I already proved the lamp is useless, can we please give up the whole 'kill me with a random household item' thing?"

Exasperated, she yelled, "Who the hell are you and what are you doing in my grandmother's house?"

He closed his eyes and breathed for a moment before opening them again, then gave her a look that said, *I'd rather be anywhere but here.* It occurred to her that she might be able to annoy him into leaving.

Pointing to his chest, he spoke to her so slowly he might as well have been instructing a kindergarten class. Reagan was so aggravated by his condescension, she ended up focusing on his asshole tone rather than his words.

"I … am … Aiden … Rannell. Josh …is … my … brother." The only word she actually heard was "Josh," which got her attention.

"W...w...what? You're who?" She backed up a few feet to collect herself. "Give me … a … se...cond."

While her heart rate began to stabilize, she took in his now relaxed stance. She noted that he wasn't acting like he wanted to kill her.

"Okay, now repeat what you just said. You know, after you broke in and attacked me."

"Attacked you? I think you've got that backward, missy. You are the one who plowed into me. Are you Reagan?"

"I am." *How the heck does he know who I am?*

He stuck out a hand in an attempt at greeting, but she ignored it. He shook his head and retracted his arm to his side.

"Aiden Rannell. Josh's brother, Mattie's brother-in-law? Ever heard of me?" As she continued to eye him suspiciously, he reached in his back pocket to pull out his wallet. Reagan instinctively backed up a few more steps. He flipped his wallet open and carefully handed it to her. "Military ID, Driver's license. Credit card. Take your pick."

Reagan's nerves were so frayed she had to read the information twice for her brain to interpret what it said. He was the brother of her best friend Mattie's husband.

The light went on. "Oh. Got it. Sure, I've heard of you! You scared the crap out of me!" she scolded, then pushed on his chest for emphasis. He grinned and held up his hands in surrender.

"The feeling is mutual. I thought I was back in combat duty."

"Not funny," she said in a deadpan tone.

"Scaring you was never my intent. Mattie asked me to come over, because she didn't want you to be alone in the house with some 'asshole detective,' her words, not mine. She told me you had a meeting at 3 to do a walk-through with him, and she couldn't make it. My flight was delayed so I'm late. When I got here, the front door was open, so I ducked under the yellow tape and came on in, which by the way is probably a felony or something that would get me arrested. Alias, I'd do just about anything for Mattie. Anyway, the next thing I know, I've got a half-crazed, hysterical woman beating on me. Not usually how I like those things to go when I'm flat on my back." He broke into a broad, mischievous smile.

Knowing now that he was only there to help her at Mattie's request, Reagan refrained from giving in to her overwhelming desire to punch him and his cocky attitude. "I guess I should apologize," she said begrudgingly, then extended her hand. "Let's try this again. Reagan, a complete idiot. Thank you for coming to my rescue."

He took her small hand in his and frowned. "Rescue? Why do you need rescuing? Where's the detective?"

"Late or he stood me up. While I was waiting, I thought I heard someone in my grandmother's bedroom and decided to investigate. When I got outside the door, my better judgment took over. I realized it was reckless of me to wander around a crime scene, but I could have sworn I heard a window slam. That's when I got spooked. More than likely, it was the heat kicking on."

"Probably best that you didn't check it out. It's doubtful the police have figured out what happened yet. Besides, as I said, the front door was open."

"You mean unlocked?" she corrected.

"I mean wide open," he said, motioning to the door.

"Wow. I shut it when I came in. Huh?" She stopped there, not wanting to say more. She'd already made a fool of herself and didn't want to make it worse.

"What happened to your grandmother was horrendous. I'm so sorry for your loss."

Reagan swallowed a lump in her throat. "Thank you. It still hasn't sunk in."

"The circumstances would make anyone jumpy. Mattie's worried about you. I take it she didn't mention that I was coming to town?"

"She didn't. Would you like to have a seat?" She walked to the sofa.

"Thanks, but I'd feel better if I took a look around, just in case the door wasn't opened by accident."

"If you think it's necessary, but what would you do if you found somebody?"

He opened his jacket to reveal a gun tucked neatly in a holster against his waist. "Don't take chances."

Her mouth formed a perfect "O."

"Point me to where you thought you heard the noise."

"It's at the end of the hall on the left."

Before he took a step, someone knocked twice on the front door. Reagan jerked around in surprise. Aiden motioned her behind him, pulled his coat aside resting his hand on his weapon, then carefully opened the door. Reagan peeked around his arm, using his body as a shield.

"Ah, you must be the incredibly late detective," Aiden said with a grin.

# Chapter 3

Detective Brad Kowalski was an attractive, clean-cut guy in his mid-30s with sandy-blond hair and deep-set brown eyes. He expressed genuine remorse for being late, explaining that he had been stuck in court testifying in a vehicular homicide case. Reagan decided to give him the benefit of the doubt and to reserve judgment on his abilities to effectively identify Nana's killer.

Aiden wasted no time advising the detective of Reagan's concerns about an intruder, prompting the detective to remand them to the living room while he searched the house. After 10 minutes of sitting impatiently on the sofa waiting for the detective to finish his inspection, they were startled by a loud sound coming from the back of the house. Aiden jumped to his feet.

"That's exactly what I heard right before I ran into you," Reagan whispered.

"Everything all right, Detective?" Aiden called.

"Yeah," he called back. "Be there in a few minutes."

"What do you think he found?" Reagan asked. Aiden shrugged and shook his head. "He might have gotten a phone call and needed some privacy."

He was obviously trying to make her feel better, but she knew Aiden didn't believe his own words.

Fifteen minutes later, Detective Kowalski was back, looking grim. He slid his cell phone into his coat pocket.

"Was that the sound you heard?" he asked Reagan.

"Exactly."

"Someone was definitely in the house, though it doesn't appear they had much time to look around or do whatever they intended to do. I compared the room in its current condition to the crime scene photos I had on my phone from the initial investigation of the scene. Someone may have broken in before you got here and fled sometime after you entered the home."

Reagan's hands flew to her mouth. She had prayed it had been her overactive imagination, and the fact that she had been only one turn of the doorknob away from walking into that room made her feel sick.

Aiden, looking concerned, put his hand on her shoulder. "You okay?"

She glanced up at him and nodded yes, but her brain screamed no. Nothing was okay.

"How do you know for sure someone was in there?" Aiden asked.

"The screen has been cut and the window pried open with something strong enough to splinter the wood. Possibly a crowbar. The lock on the window was busted. I opened and closed it hard to see if the sound matched what Ms. Asher heard earlier. There are also fresh muddy boot prints on the carpet under the windowsill, but they don't go any farther into the room. Someone from the crime lab is on the way over to check for fingerprints and make a cast of the boot prints outside the window. We still have a key we got from the next-door neighbor if we need to get back in the house. My guess is the perp assumed the house was empty. He must have heard Ms. Asher and fled."

"Thank God I didn't go in that room," she breathed.

"What about the open front door?" Aiden asked.

"There could have been a partner, but we don't know for sure. Most likely the latch didn't catch when Ms. Asher closed the door. We'll check for prints just in case."

Reagan gulped. None of the scenarios sounded good.

After the detective finished investigating the second break-in, they all settled at the dining room table to begin the interview. Despite Detective Kowalski's request for Aiden to give them some privacy, she insisted he stay. She wanted someone there who was on her side, and since Mattie couldn't be there, Aiden would have to do. He may not like her after the earlier incident, but everything she'd ever heard about him from Josh and Mattie led her to believe he was a good guy. She'd just have to trust him until he proved her wrong.

Reagan nervously kneaded her forearms with her thumbs. "Do you have any idea who killed my grandmother?"

"Not yet. There are still a lot of unknowns at this point. The fact that someone may have come back a second time is troubling. Although it's possible that whoever broke in today could be unrelated to the original crime, it's not likely. Only desperate people enter a home marked with crime-scene tape. Please make sure you are never in this house alone until we have our perps in custody."

"Count on that," Aiden said before Reagan had a chance to respond.

Reagan studied Aiden for a minute wondering if he was her self-designated protector but kept her thoughts to herself. Maybe that was a result of his military background. She was too grateful to have him there to question his motives.

"You seemed deliberately vague on the phone. Can you tell me exactly what happened to my grandmother?"

Aiden sat at the end of the table next to Reagan, his arms crossed over his chest in observation mode. Detective Kowalski sat directly across from her with an iPad and stylus in front of him. Reagan snuck a glance at the top of the electronic pad that read, *Homicide-Fiona A. Burke Moran. Age 73. Lancashire, Ohio.*

"There are not a lot of facts in evidence at this point, Ms. Asher, but I will share with you what I can. First, I need to get some basic information from you."

"What do you want to know?"

"Tell me a little about Mrs. Moran's job, her friends, hobbies, that sort of thing."

Reagan paused for a few seconds to collect her thoughts, slipping into her business persona. It was the only way she knew how to get through this invasion into their personal lives.

"My grandmother is a … was a retired nurse who worked part time at the Lancashire Community Hospital. She volunteered at the Fairview Nursing Home on the weekends that she didn't have to work. Nana, that's what I called her, regularly attended St. Michael's Catholic Church for years and was active with the women's groups."

"I understand you were raised by Mrs. Moran. Are your parents still in the picture?"

Reagan wondered where he had gotten his information and why it was relevant. It was a painful subject for her, but she guessed it couldn't be avoided. She cleared her throat and swallowed hard.

"My parents divorced when I was a child. A year later, my mother … committed suicide. I was 7 years old at the time." She heard Aiden gasp, a common reaction among the few people she'd told. She struggled to keep her voice even. Having to say it out loud reminded her just how truly alone she was.

"Your father is Stuart Alan Asher?"

"Yes."

Reagan realized she hadn't called her dad yet, not that he would necessarily care about Nana's death. He had divorced her mother, Claire, 24 years ago, when Reagan was only 6. Since then, he had been mostly absent from her life. After he left, he took a job in Washington state. Oddly, she had never realized there were any problems between her parents … no screaming or yelling. Of course, as a child she probably wouldn't have noticed any other signs. A few months after her father moved to Spokane, his former secretary, Carol something, packed up to join him. They were married within a year. *What a cliché*, she thought. They never had any kids of their own, but he sure didn't have any problem raising her two kids from a previous marriage. The bitterness she felt then hadn't abated.

Reagan's grandfather died of a heart attack when she was 3 years old, so she didn't remember him very well. Just the smell of cherry pipe tobacco. Because of the sudden financial strain his death left on Nana, Reagan's parents moved in to help out until Nana got back on her feet, or that was what she was told. They ended up staying. After three years of living with Nana, her dad was gone, and a year later, her mother was dead. Nana became her legal guardian, and Reagan had lived with her until she left for college. The first few years after her mother's death had been a dark time in Reagan's life, but her Nana and her best friend, Mattie, who lived down the street from Nana at the time, pulled her through it.

From Reagan's point of view, her mother hadn't thought she was worth living for and her father hadn't thought she was worth sticking around for. Instead of her father growing closer to her after her mother's death, he pulled further away. She visited him twice during the first couple of years after he moved, but then he became the occasional phone call and greeting card dad. Reagan couldn't help but blame him in part for what her mother had done, and maybe he put some of the responsibility on himself. He invited her out to Washington several times over the years, but she never took the invitation too seriously. Long distance seemed to be their friend.

"How was your grandmother's relationship with her son-in-law after your mother's divorce? Any resentment? Did your father get along with her?"

"Wait. What?" Reagan asked, stunned, her voice a few octaves above normal range. "Don't you think 24 years is a bit long for my father to hold some kind of a grudge against my grandmother?" Reagan could feel her face flush as she dug her nails into her palms. It was an absurd notion that her father had anything to do with it.

Detective Kowalski reached across the table to touch her hand in a soothing gesture but caught himself and awkwardly pulled back. Reagan involuntarily flinched.

"Please don't read anything into my inquiry, Ms. Asher. These are all standard background questions to determine Mrs. Moran's routine, the people she interacted with and their relationships. It wasn't intended to upset you or accuse anyone of anything."

*These are questions he has to ask,* she told herself. She nodded her understanding.

"If there was any animosity between my father and my grandmother, I assure you it would have manifested itself years ago. Since he had a job already lined up, he obviously had been planning to leave for some time, and Nana seemed to be happy he was gone. The front door had barely slammed shut before she was pulling his pictures out of the frames. As far as my mother's death, my grandmother never told me if she held him responsible … I think she partially blamed herself for not recognizing the severity of Momma's depression. The last time my parents saw each other was when they signed their divorce papers. As far as I know, my grandmother saw him three times after that: at my high school and college graduations, and when I received my MBA."

"Was Mrs. Moran seeing anyone? A boyfriend maybe?"

Reagan furrowed her brows. "Not that I'm aware of. Although I encouraged her to date, I don't think she ever did. She seemed content to be without a man in her life."

"And you live and work in Chicago?"

"I do."

"And where are you employed?"

"I'm the Assistant Director of Human Resources for Rothman-Morgan Chemical Corporation U.S. Division in Chicago. Been there for the past seven years."

"When was the last time you saw your grandmother?"

"Two months ago, during the Christmas holidays."

"And did she seem worried about anything?"

"She was perfectly fine. I would have noticed if anything was off."

"How was Mrs. Moran's financial situation?" he asked, studying her closely.

"Things were often a bit tight when I lived with her, but we seemed to do okay. I earned scholarships and took out student loans to pay for college, which are all paid off. Nana never mentioned any financial issues after I left home, but she always lived frugally."

"Did she own many valuables?"

Reagan sat back and waved her hand in a wide circle over her head, pointing her finger. "Look around, Detective. This home is over 40 years old. It's never been remodeled and has had the same furniture for as long as I can remember. The only things of value Nana owned, other than her 8-year-old car, were her laptop and television, both of which were gifts from me. Not sure how much the house is worth, but it can't be a lot. It's outdated for today's market and needs lots of repairs."

"Life Insurance policy?"

"No idea. She never discussed it with me."

"Did she have any brothers or sisters?"

"They were all much older and are deceased. I'm all she had left."

"And yet she didn't discuss any of her finances with you?" the detective asked.

Reagan wasn't sure what he was implying, but she didn't like it. "She did not."

Detective Kowalski sighed and shifted uncomfortably. Most of his questions didn't seem to be getting him any closer to finding Nana's killer.

"What about jewelry?" he asked.

She thought for a few seconds recalling Nana's love for colorful, chunky costume jewelry. The louder, the better.

"Nothing of any real value. She had a wedding band with a tiny diamond, but I doubt it's worth much. It's been sitting in her jewelry box since my grandfather passed away. Most of the jewelry she owned might be considered 'shiny baubles'… the metal painted gold or silver and the stones made of glass or p…plastic." The words caught in her throat.

*Why didn't I ever buy her anything nicer?* Reagan admonished herself. *I make a good salary. I could have afforded it. Nana sacrificed everything for me. Did without. Now it's too late.*

"I know this is uncomfortable, but did she have any enemies that you're aware of? Someone who gave her a hard time — maybe at work, or a neighbor?"

"Not that she ever mentioned. I can ask my best friend, Mattie Rannell. She saw my grandmother weekly. Nana babysat for her 5-year-old daughter, Ellie, a couple of days a week."

"I see." He looked over at Aiden and raised his eyebrows. "Isn't that your last name? Rannell? Your wife?"

"Sister-in-law. She's married to my brother, Josh." The detective stared at Aiden for a beat and turned back to Reagan.

"I've never known Nana to hold a grudge or have any major disagreement with anyone. She and my mother were quite opposite from the stereotypical redheads you hear about with hot tempers." Reagan chewed her bottom lip nervously, trying not to show her impatience. "Now, Detective Kowalski, will you please tell me what happened to my grandmother?"

The detective flipped his fingers through a few screens on his notepad until he found what he was looking for, leaned back and sighed. "I have to warn you, Ms. Asher, the details are very disturbing and, as much as loved ones want to know, it never makes them feel any better. Mostly worse." He paused as if he were waiting for Reagan to change her mind, but she remained silent.

"We're speculating that Mrs. Moran arrived home from her shift at the hospital while her house was being burglarized but can't totally rule out the possibility that she was followed home. Her handbag and lunchbox were on the kitchen table, the garage door to the kitchen was open, and she was still wearing her coat. There was a broken glass on the floor in front of the sink, which might indicate she was getting a drink and was startled when she realized someone was in the house. Maybe she saw him or heard a noise, then tried to flee through the garage. We're going on that assumption because there were no signs of a struggle in the home. It appears she was trying to exit through the side door in the garage when she was attacked. More than likely it was a male, although we can't be sure. There could've been more than one assailant, but the evidence doesn't point either way."

Reagan wrapped her arms around herself while Aiden reached over and lightly held one of her hands. That small act of compassion almost undid her. Although she and Aiden had just met and knew of each other only through Josh and Mattie, he offered her genuine comfort that she appreciated.

Reagan cringed at the thought of Nana being attacked while trying to escape. The terror she must have felt. If only Reagan had insisted on having an alarm system installed, the police might have arrived in time.

"How do you know it was a burglary and not just some random act of violence?" Aiden asked.

"The condition of the home," Detective Kowalski said. "We can't be sure what is missing until Ms. Asher walks through and gives us a list." He turned to Reagan. "If Mrs. Moran had a laptop as you mentioned, we didn't find it, but an expensive television is still on the wall in the living room. A bit confusing unless the intruder was interrupted or simply ran out of time."

"I wondered about the television," Reagan said. The more she learned, the tighter her chest clenched.

"Mrs. Moran's bedroom was the only room ransacked. We aren't sure why, unless they were looking for something specific."

Reagan shook her head. It made no sense.

"W…why would he kill her?" Reagan asked. "Why not just run? It's not like she had a weapon."

"That's a good question. Maybe he didn't want to be identified or perhaps it was personal. The fact that his search began in her bedroom leads us to believe he was looking for something specific. All of his focus was there. Maybe he confronted her, and she ran."

"Oh my God," Reagan whispered. She couldn't help but visualize the scene in her head.

"How did he get in?" Aiden asked.

"The back door in the far corner of the living room has scratches around the latch. The lock's pretty flimsy. A 10-year-old kid could have used a credit card to get in if the deadbolt wasn't engaged."

Reagan's mouth dropped open, and she shot daggers at the detective.

"Sorry. That was thoughtless of me. It's just these older homes aren't always as secure as they should be. If the deadbolt had been engaged, he probably would have broken a window instead. I'm not laying blame here, nor should you, but I would recommend you reinforce the house."

His words only added to Reagan's all-consuming guilt. *Why hadn't she realized that herself?*

"Did Mrs. Moran take prescription medication of any kind?" the detective asked.

"Blood pressure medicine."

"Any kind of anxiety meds or narcotics you're aware of?"

Reagan raised her brows. *Was he suggesting she had a drug problem?* Before she could voice her indignation, the detective clarified why he asked the question.

"Not implying anything, Ms. Asher. Many older adults take narcotics for anxiety, pain killers for arthritis, and medicines for their heart — drugs that are in high demand on the streets. Seniors, especially those who live alone, are often preyed upon for those kinds of drugs. We can't rule out that the motive may have been narcotics. Mrs. Moran was a nurse; she would've had more access than most."

Reagan had to admit it made sense.

"As I said, my grandmother took blood pressure medicine, that's all."

"Have there been other burglaries in the neighborhood?" Aiden asked.

"Other than a few bored teens smashing mailboxes, we haven't had any trouble in this neighborhood for years." He scrolled through his electronic notes. "Mrs. Lucy Langston, her next-door neighbor, said she heard Mrs. Moran's car pull in the garage around 10 p.m., but never heard anything else."

The arrival of a two-person forensic team gave Reagan a much-needed emotional break. While the detective escorted them to her grandmother's bedroom to retrieve evidence on today's break-in, she and Aiden sat in uncomfortable silence. Reagan felt her interview had been a waste of time. Not one piece of information she provided could possibly help the detective find Nana's murderer.

The detective returned 45 minutes later with the crime scene investigators trailing behind him. They explained they would take another 30 minutes outside the house and then would be on their way.

"Are you finished investigating my grandmother's home now? I'd like to get things in order for her funeral."

"The only thing left before I release it is the walk-through with you, if that's still convenient. And your permission to revisit the scene if necessary."

"That's not a problem. Oh, is there any reason I can't use my grandmother's car while I'm here?"

"Afraid it won't be available for a few more days. Forensics took it. We wanted to make sure no one was hiding in her backseat when she left work," he explained. "It's not likely, but we haven't ruled it out.

Reagan quivered at the image of Nana driving home with a gun to her head.

"Detective Kowalski, do I need to identify her b…body?" Reagan asked, dreading the answer.

"Not necessary. Her personal physician, Dr. Maxwell, did that for us. Mrs. Langston suggested it to save you the anguish, and we weren't sure how quickly you would get here from Chicago. We'll contact you as soon as we can release her to the funeral home.

"How did my grandmother die?" Reagan had put off asking the question because she wasn't sure she wanted the answer.

The detective rubbed a hand under his chin and stared at the ceiling for a few seconds before he met her eyes. "Sure you want the details?"

Reagan nodded.

"Her throat was cut." Reagan focused on his Adam's apple, which bobbed when he swallowed. "Although the coroner hasn't done an autopsy yet, it appears her assailant came from behind. It probably happened quickly, and I doubt she saw it coming. We aren't releasing that information to the public."

Reagan felt as if every ounce of air had been sucked out of her lungs. A sudden lightheadedness forced her to grip the edge of the table to keep from falling out of her chair. Images of Nana lying on the cold cement garage floor bleeding, dying alone, swirled in her head.

"You okay?" Thankfully, Aiden's voice pulled her out of the dark thoughts and back to the task at hand. She refused to let her emotions swamp her. She nodded.

"Do you need a minute before we begin our walk-through?" the detective asked.

Reagan steeled her resolve. "Let's get started."

# Chapter 4

Aiden watched closely as Reagan surveyed the damage done to her grandmother's bedroom, the only room apparently searched to any degree. Bewilderment was written all over her lovely face. He shared her confusion. Virtually nothing in the nondescript home was worth stealing.

Although he had never met Reagan before, he'd heard enough about her over the years to feel he already knew her. Josh and Mattie considered her part of the family; therefore, out of loyalty to them, he would too. He had promised Mattie he would help Reagan in any way he could, and he didn't take that responsibility lightly. The last 12 years in the Navy had made it difficult, if not impossible, for him to be there for his family. He missed weddings, birthdays, graduations, funerals, holidays, and not once had his family made him feel guilty. They had always given him their complete support, showing nothing but pride in his service to his country. This was his first opportunity to prove his commitment to them, so whatever Reagan needed, he would step up.

Looking around the ransacked room, he saw that the drawers from the dresser, chest, and bedside tables had been pulled all the way out, their contents dumped on the floor. The bedcovers were stripped and wadded in a ball. Reading glasses, tissues, a Bible, magazines, buttons, and framed family photos lay scattered about. A carved wooden jewelry box had been turned upside down and emptied in a heap, costume bracelets, necklaces, and cocktail rings tangled together on the worn beige carpet. The fresh muddy boot prints by the window reminded Aiden that the danger from whoever killed Reagan's grandmother was not over.

After Reagan verified that the only missing items were her grandmother's diamond engagement ring and the laptop, Detective Kowalski left with a promise to be in touch soon. He removed the crime scene tape from the door before he left.

Reagan's calm demeanor had slipped the moment she walked into her grandmother's bedroom. The sight of the desecration of her Nana's personal items had drained all the color from her face. Watching her struggle to mask her grief felt like an intrusion into her own personal hell, but Aiden had no intention of leaving her to deal with it on her own. It was ingrained in his nature to protect, and that's what he intended to do.

Reagan stood in front of her grandmother's dresser mirror rubbing her face with her hands when their eyes locked in the reflection. There were no tears, but her face and neck were flushed. She smiled apologetically.

"I know I'm a blotchy mess. Always happens when I'm under stress." She shrugged offhandedly like it was no big deal.

Despite her pale skin and the dark shadows under her almond-shaped, emerald eyes, she was absolutely stunning. Tall and slim with straight dark chocolate hair that fell just below her shoulders, she was a natural, understated beauty. Shaking his head, he mentally admonished himself for taking notice of her appearance. It was irrelevant. He was there strictly for support.

"You're entitled to grieve, but I think you'd feel better if we moved out of this room." He offered her his hand, and she politely took it, allowing him to lead her into the living room where they settled on the sofa. Reagan instinctively gathered the afghan to her chest. *A security blanket or was she cold?* he wondered.

An awkward silence fell between them for a few minutes until she spoke.

"You've been in the service for a while, haven't you?" The neutral topic flooded him with relief.

"I was. Resigned my commission a few months ago. It was time for me to find a different life."

"Really? You've been in in the military for like forever, haven't you? Didn't you do some kind of secret spy stuff?"

He rolled his eyes and grinned. "Secret spy, huh? What tales has Mattie been spinning? Navy Seal."

"So, what did you do first when you got out? Anything wild and crazy?"

"Pretty tame, I'm afraid, which was what I was going for. The first two months I laid on the beach in Florida and did a little deep-sea fishing. Sort of decompressing. Chase Scranton, a buddy of mine, owns a condo on Marco Island. He and Owen Walton, both retired Seals, started an international security company last year. It designs and provides security protocols for companies expanding into developing nations. The business has really taken off, so they offered me a job and a partnership. My parents and Josh aren't happy with me right now. I'll be traveling about 90% of the year. They were hoping for me to settle into a nice 9-to-5 job. Don't see that happening. I've spent the last 12 years in a state of continued flux with the Seals. Afraid I'd get bored staying in the same place for too long."

"I love your mom, but she has a stubborn streak," Reagan chuckled. "How did you get her off your back?"

He flashed her a knowing smile. "We compromised. Last week, I signed a contract on a condo in Beachwood. It gives me a home base near family, which appeases them, and I have a property investment. I'll furnish it and stick to short-term leases, probably three to six months at a time, until I get a gauge on my actual travel time. When I work on a project, my living expenses will be covered by the clients, so it's a win-win. The family feels better knowing I have a tie to the community, and I can do my own thing with less guilt. Josh and Mattie have been putting me up for the last couple of weeks, until I could find a place, buy some furniture, and locate a reliable renter. Now that I have all my loose ends tied up in Virginia, I'm hoping to get things set up in my new home within the next few weeks."

"You're staying with Josh and Mattie too. I had no idea." He detected worry lines around her eyes.

"That was by design. Mattie predicted you'd want to move to a hotel so you wouldn't inconvenience anyone."

"She knows me too well. I hate to put them out."

"You'll break her heart if you don't stay. Once she makes up her mind, it's a done deal. She wants to fix everything for you, sometimes whether you need it or not. She found my condo and picked out most of my furniture. Don't get me wrong, I appreciate what she's done for me. I'm just glad I liked what she selected. Sometimes it's hard to convey my point of view when she has other ideas."

Reagan laughed. "That's Mattie, all right."

"Their four-bedroom home has plenty of room, but if it makes you uncomfortable for me to be there, I'll move to a motel."

"Not necessary." She waved her hand for emphasis.

Aiden had been silently debating with himself whether he should bring up what happened last Saturday. It had been nagging at him ever since he heard about the attack on Mrs. Moran, hoping his actions hadn't been a catalyst in her murder. Unable to ignore the guilt eating at him, he decided to come clean and let the chips fall where they may.

"I've had a few things on my mind, and I hope you won't mind if I ask you a few questions," he asked.

She gave him a quizzical look. "Sure."

"Are you positive your grandmother didn't have any jewelry that might have been valuable?"

She raised her eyebrows. "Why would I lie? What motive could I possibly have?"

"I'm not suggesting you'd lie, but you haven't lived here in years. Maybe she bought something you were unaware of … splurged a little on herself?" He tried to be as tactful as possible.

"Nana never spent money on herself. Not that she attempted to play the martyr, she just didn't have the desire for expensive things. She barely spoke to me for weeks after I bought her that television."

"Maybe she purchased something at a garage sale not realizing its value?" He was racking his brain for explanations.

"To my knowledge, Nana never went to a garage sale. What exactly are you getting at?" He could see a flush of pink appear on her neck, slowly moving up to her face. Defensiveness.

"Before you pull out the claws, let me explain to you what happened last Saturday, and why I'm asking these questions."

Reagan narrowed her eyes and folded her arms across her chest. "I'm listening."

*Nothing like keeping an open mind,* he thought, but what he said was, "It's kind of a long story, so please give me an opportunity to get through it."

"I said I'm listening," was her sing-song response.

He ran his hand over his chin and sighed.

"Last Saturday, Josh and Mattie made plans to meet some friends in downtown Cleveland for lunch and a matinee. They forgot Ellie had been invited to a birthday party at one of those indoor playground places at the same time, so I agreed to drop her off and pick her up. Afterwards, I would bring her here to stay with your grandmother until Mattie and Josh picked her up in the evening. I couldn't keep her myself, because I had to catch a 5 o'clock flight to Virginia.

"On the drive over, I noticed Ellie playing with a tarnished gold ring with a huge green stone. It was too big for her, so she had wrapped tape around it to make it stay on her finger. I asked her where she got it, thinking maybe she took it out of her mother's jewelry box. Ellie told me it was 'princess' jewelry that your grandmother let her wear when she was babysitting her. She admitted she had failed to ask for permission to take it home but assured me she would be returning it to your grandmother. To make sure she didn't lose it in the meantime, I suggested she let me hold it for her until she was ready to leave the party."

"This is going somewhere, right?" Reagan drummed her fingers in exaggerated impatience on the coffee table.

He arched a brow. "Patience isn't really one of your virtues, is it?"

She sneered half-heartedly, and he continued.

"While I grabbed a quick burger at a local pub, I pulled the ring out of my pocket and looked it over. Honestly, I was a little suspicious of where Ellie had gotten it. She's been known to stretch the truth to avoid discipline. At first, I thought the gold was peeling off, but on closer scrutiny, I realized it appeared more antique and ornate. The square emerald-like stone wasn't dark like what you usually see on cut-glass jewelry; it was a much lighter color. The center stone was surrounded by what appeared to be diamonds. It reminded me of something similar I had seen when I was in Iraq. A small band of terrorists we captured had a stash of stolen antique jewelry on them, and some pieces we found out later were from as early as the 13th century. The cut of the jewels was less refined than you'd find today, and the colors weren't as brilliant and polished. We thought they were fakes and were totally shocked when an expert authenticated them as genuine precious stones and extremely valuable."

"Maybe I was bored," Aiden continued, "but my curiosity got the best of me. On my way back to the party, I decided to stop at a jewelry store in a strip mall to alleviate my concerns."

"You're kidding."

He shook his head. "Nope. When a salesman offered to help me, I handed him the ring and asked if he could tell me if it had any value. He took it in the backroom to let the owner have a look at it. When he came back, he confirmed my suspicions. His boss verified the ring has genuine precious stones. The emerald could be somewhere between 8 to 9 carats, and each of the diamonds surrounding it at least one carat, although one was missing. He recommended I find an expert in period jewelry to get an appraisal."

Finally finished, Aiden waited for her reaction.

Reagan twisted her lips. "Let me get this straight. You took my grandmother's fake ring into a jewelry store, and they told you it was real?" Her words dripped with sarcasm.

"Yes, ma'am. That about sums it up. It sounds kind of crazy when you say it like that, but I was afraid it might be more valuable than your grandmother realized. The salesman told me his boss suggested it could be worth over $50,000. Probably a lot more depending on how old it was, but I would need to show provenance to get a reputable jeweler to buy it. He recommended an auction to receive the best price."

Aiden could tell by Reagan's expression that she thought he had lost his mind.

"Where is the ring now?" she asked, matter of fact.

"That's why I was so worried when I heard what happened to your grandmother. After I introduced myself to her when I dropped Ellie off, I explained that Ellie had taken the ring home without asking permission, assuming it was play jewelry. After relaying the story of my visit to the jewelry store, I apologized that Ellie had taken it without asking."

"And what did Nana say?"

"She told me how much she appreciated my concern and the trouble I'd gone to by taking it to the jewelry store, but they were obviously 'pulling my leg.' The ring was only cut-glass, and you and your friends played with it when you were little girls. Then she handed it back to Ellie and told her to ask for permission the next time if she wanted to take it home. I was speechless."

Reagan's expression was devoid of emotion. Ever since Mattie called him that morning with the terrible news, he had worried that somehow he had been responsible for others knowing about the ring, and how that might have led to the robbery and subsequent murder.

"Please say something," he appealed to her.

"I agree with Nana. They played a joke on you. Did you talk to an actual gemologist?"

"Well … no, but the salesman said he spoke to the owner whom I assumed would know what he was talking about. I'm not sure what his credentials were. What would be the benefit in deceiving me?" He watched while she mulled it over.

"Maybe it was a game to them. Who knows, but I assure you the ring isn't real."

"I don't understand why you don't believe me," he said.

Reagan stared at him with frustration. Suddenly her eyes went wide, and she lightly hit her forehead with her palm as if an idea had just popped into her head.

"Come with me. I'll prove to you that it's only junky jewelry." Aiden followed as she rushed out of the room and down the hall to her childhood bedroom. She knelt in front of an antique wooden chest that sat at the foot of her bed. She flipped the lid open and removed the top tray that was neatly sectioned off with an assortment of tiny boxes, knickknacks, and memorabilia. He watched over her shoulder as she pulled out a square boot-sized box covered with metallic-pink wrapping paper and cut-out red hearts. Neatly printed in a child's handwriting with a bold red marker were the words *My Princess Box*.

Reagan set the box on the bed and took off the lid. Inside was an array of colorful necklaces, bracelets, and assorted jewelry like the one Ellie had taken. She pulled the larger pieces out in handfuls and lay them on the comforter. In the bottom of the box was an assortment of smaller pieces: jeweled hair pins, barrettes, chains, earrings, and rings. After she dug around for a few seconds, she held up the emerald and diamond ring. He recognized it immediately.

"Is this the one?" she asked, holding it in the palm of her hand.

Aiden took it from her. "It is. There's the missing diamond," he pointed out.

"You see, Aiden. This is my princess jewelry. It's a beautiful array of antique-looking costume jewelry I used to play dress-up with when I was a little girl."

Reagan rummaged through the pile until she found a diamond and sapphire tiara. Apparently evoking a special memory, it brought a delicate smile to her face, and she placed it on top of her head. She walked to her dresser where several small, framed photographs were displayed, selected one and handed it to Aiden. In the picture, Reagan, wearing a frilly, blue party dress, sat in front of a birthday cake with five candles, while two women on each side of her glowed with pride. The older woman was a much younger Nana; the younger had to be Reagan's mother, Claire. Both women had bright round, green eyes, soft delicate facial features, and curly, flaming red hair. They could have been sisters. Though Reagan had her mother's emerald eyes, Aiden assumed her more classic facial features and much darker straight hair were inherited from her father, who was absent from the picture. To accessorize her outfit, Reagan wore an elaborate diamond and sapphire necklace with the matching tiara that now sat on her head. The other young girls at the party were also adorned with jeweled necklaces and earrings.

"I see you needed to establish yourself as royalty," he said with a wry smile.

She laughed, holding her chin up high. "You got that right. My friends could play with whatever they wanted, but the tiara was all mine! Princess Reagan." She flung one side of her hair over her shoulder for emphasis.

"And a cute one at that," he chuckled.

"You wouldn't say that if my mouth were open. I'd lost most of my front teeth. It was a good time for the tooth fairy, but not so much for the fair maiden."

Aiden looked closely at the picture. "Is that Mattie sitting next to you?"

Reagan scanned the photo. "It is, and if you look at her hand holding the pink cup, you can see the ring that's causing all the fuss."

A quick glance confirmed she was right. It was the emerald and diamond ring. Then something caught his eye in the pile of princess loot, and he picked up an emerald and diamond interlaced antique-gold necklace and compared the stones to the ring.

"What are you looking for?"

"Similarities in design."

"You're taking this too far, Aiden. It's all just colored glass and painted antique-gold jewelry. I've had it for as long as I can remember. You don't understand. Mattie and I dressed up with necklaces, bracelets, earrings, and hair barrettes to have tea parties in the backyard where we made mud pies, for gosh sakes! Sometimes we were so dirty, Nana hosed us off before we came back in the house. Do you honestly believe anyone in their right mind would give kids real jewelry to abuse or lose, and leave it stored in a decorated boot box? Ellie plays with it now. Nana should have given it to her a long time ago. She probably kept it around so Ellie would have something to do when she came over."

"What if your Nana had no idea of the true value of the jewelry? Look closely at this emerald and diamond necklace. It has the same type of gold settings. And the cuts of the stones are similar." He held them up for her to inspect.

"So what?"

"You don't want to believe it, and I know it sounds absurd, but the jeweler wasn't playing a joke on me. This ring is real. I'm deadly serious, and I'm starting to believe the necklace is too. What if all of these pieces are genuine?"

Reagan slowly shook her head, searching his face for some sign that he was making fun of her gullibility, but his expression betrayed nothing.

He picked up the other pieces and scrutinized them closely, then compared the diamond and sapphire necklace to the tiara. He handed them to her.

"See the similarities in color and design?"

"I admit they appear to be in the same style, but perhaps all this jewelry was made by the same manufacturer."

"Have you always had these pieces or were others added to your collection over the years?"

She bounced her index finger against her chin in mock concentration. "Let's see. I broke the clasp on a couple of necklaces. Most of the stones fell out of a red and green bracelet, so Nana threw those away. Then Mattie and I left two rhinestone rings underneath the merry-go-round while we played on the jungle gym and forgot about them. They were gone when we went back the next day. The rest I've had as long as I can remember."

Aiden burst out laughing.

"What's so funny?"

"Who knows how many thousands of dollars you may have thrown in the trash or lost in a mud pie?"

"You're honestly saying you think they are ..." She stopped, shaking her head.

"Genuine?" He held up some of the jewelry in his fist. "I'm no expert by any means, but these pieces appear to have come from the same time period."

Reagan sat stunned. He could see her certainty waning as the logic of his argument began to take hold, and it was terrifying her. "It ... it just can't be. No way in hell."

"Any idea where this jewelry came from?"

She slowly shook her head. "My guess would be a store that sells cheap stuff."

"I think we need to find someone reputable who can authenticate the jewelry," Aiden suggested. "If it's as valuable as I think it is, and someone knows about it or at least the ring, then you could be in real danger. My God, Reagan, someone broke in today. With crime scene tape on the damn door. That's ballsy. We need to call Detective Kowalski and let him know about these jewels. I'm sure he can recommend a jeweler you could trust. He could also get protection for the house."

"No!" Reagan blurted.

"No? Why not?" Aiden was incredulous that she wasn't more concerned about her safety.

Reagan leaned over and grabbed his hands firmly in hers, meeting his eyes. "Please, just listen for a minute." She paused to collect her thoughts, but never lost eye contact. "First of all, I think you're totally off the mark on this, but I'll get them appraised if you insist. These stones are worthless, and I'm sure that will be proven as soon as they are examined. I know we should call the detective about your trip to the jewelry store, and that would be the smartest and the safest thing to do, but I just need a little time to get my head around this. You can tell from the picture and the location of the jewelry that it has been treated for years with little importance to anyone but a little girl and her friends. If by some miracle they are real, it does leave lots of unanswered questions that I'd like to find the answers to before this all reflects negatively on my family's memory. Can't you see ... even when you told her the truth about just one ring, Nana dismissed it as a joke. She put the ring back in the same box it's been stored in for over 20 years."

"What exactly are you afraid of?" Aiden's whole military career had been a series of operations to serve and protect the interest of his country. Accurate intel was one of the critical elements to the success of his team's mission. Withholding vital information from the police who were trying to find her grandmother's killer went against every instinct he had.

"Aiden, think about it for a minute. We are obviously not people with the means to afford expensive jewelry, which begs the question, how in hell did we come into possession of thousands of dollars worth of jewelry? Where did it come from? Was it stolen? There are two questionable deaths in my family. My mother's suicide and my grandmother's murder. Throw in the possibility of a decades-old jewelry theft, and it's a media headline in the making. This is totally blowing me away. I just want a chance to make some sense of it. I've already lost my family. If by some minute chance you are right about this, it could completely destroy what is left of my life." She tightened her grip on his hands and pleaded with worried eyes. "Please, Aiden.

Will you help me? You've raised enough doubt in my mind that I simply can't ignore the possibility."

Aiden had the impression not many people got to see Reagan's vulnerable side. She had not once shed a tear during the interview with the detective, the walk-through of her murdered grandmother's home, or the discovery that a second break-in happened while she was alone in the house. Except for the involuntary flushing of her face, she had maintained her professional control, occasionally masking her emotions with anger or a snarky comeback. The momentary dropping of the shield she used to protect herself gave him a little more insight into the woman Mattie and Josh loved.

"Losing your mother that way, and now your grandmother ... I can't imagine ..." She let go of his hands and stiffened her back, visibly distancing herself from her emotions.

"My mother was a long time ago. Not many people know about it. It's a guaranteed mood killer when people find out, so I keep that part of my life to myself. I've moved on."

"You don't have to talk about it. You already have enough on your plate."

"Might as well get used to it. The investigation into Nana's death has already brought those painful memories to the forefront. Losing Momma a year after my father left was like a double punch. Since then, he's been mostly absent from my life. You can see why Nana meant so much to me. She was literally the only family I had left who gave a damn about me. Please don't get all weird. It was a long time ago."

Aiden understood what she meant about the media having a field day with speculations about her family tragedy. Could he justify putting her through that if it wasn't necessary? He did have some time before he started his consulting job, though it felt like an impossible task to find answers from a trail that had been cold for decades. Reagan had to be around 30, same age as Mattie, and she had been playing with her princess jewelry at least since she was 5 years old. It was going to be hard to find anyone with information about the jewelry. If her father had been out of the picture for years, he probably couldn't shed much light on the subject. Aiden was no detective, but he decided he would at least try to help Reagan figure out the jewelry's origin.

"Well?" she prompted.

"I promised Mattie I'd help you, so I will. It's going to be tough, and we might not find anything."

"I'm aware."

"If we are going to go down this road, let me make something perfectly clear. If we find out the stones are real, and we don't find any logical explanation for why your family was in possession of them, I'm going to have to insist we notify the authorities. I will not sacrifice your safety. Agreed?"

"Agreed," she said, though her quick response held no conviction.

"We need to decide what to do with the jewelry until we get it checked out," Aiden said.

"Can't we leave it where it is? I mean nobody's disturbed it thus far."

"The house has already been broken in to twice. We can't take any chances." The thought that his visit to the jewelry store may have brought this chaos on her family still consumed him with guilt. He scrubbed his hand over his face.

Reagan gently laid her hand on his forearm. "What's going through your head?"

He hesitated before he answered. "I'm still afraid that because of my meddling, someone at least knows about the emerald and diamond ring. Anyone at that jewelry store could have overheard my conversation with the salesman and followed me back here when I dropped off Ellie. I'm not quite sure why you're not holding me responsible for your grandmother's death."

Reagan cocked her head to one side and studied him. Her face softened.

"I could try to convince myself you're responsible, but I don't think it would make me feel any better. You were only looking out for my grandmother's best interest. How could you possibly know someone with malicious intent would be lurking around, if that's even what happened? It could have been a random break-in. Too many unknowns to place blame."

Aiden's face relaxed. Her understanding was more than he felt he deserved, but she was right. He couldn't be sure he'd been the spark that had put the tragedy in motion.

"That's all true, but somewhere along the way, someone knew about this jewelry. They could have been here today. Thank God whoever it was didn't try to confront you. Next time, I'm guessing they'll do a more thorough search."

"We can't take it with us. I don't want to bring any harm to Mattie, Josh, and Ellie," Reagan said. "Now that I think about it, maybe we shouldn't mention this to them until we know for sure what we're dealing with."

Aiden cringed at the thought of keeping something so vital from his brother. He promised himself he would hold off long enough to have the jewels checked, but that was it. He looked at his watch. "If the banks weren't closed, I'd suggest you get a safe deposit box to secure it."

Reagan rubbed her fingertips over her lips absently, then paused as if searching her memory for something.

"What?" Aiden asked.

"I think Nana had a safe deposit box at her bank. Maybe I could use that."

He shook his head. "Not unless your name is on the account too, otherwise the bank won't let you in it without a court order or proof of power of attorney. Did she ever discuss any of this with you? What she wanted to happen after she was gone? A will? Attorney? Finances?"

Reagan shrugged. "Whenever she tried, I refused to consider the possibility of losing her. Foolish of me, I know. If I didn't face it, how could it happen? I would have accused anyone else of being childish and unprepared for the future."

"It's understandable."

"Would you mind if we took a few minutes to look through her files? Maybe I'll find a will or the name of an attorney. At least a starting point."

"If she had a will, there's a likelihood that she made you executor since you are her only family."

Reagan rubbed her hands nervously across her knees. "This is a lot to take in."

He didn't know what to say. Nothing seemed appropriate.

His cellphone rang. "Hey, Mattie. What's up?"

# Chapter 5

Aiden assured Mattie they would be back for dinner by 7 p.m. He hoped that would give them time to come up with a place to hide the jewelry and look for any pertinent information Reagan would need to begin settling her grandmother's affairs.

They started in the small guest bedroom that had been converted into an office/craft room. Reagan took a seat in a rickety, wooden rolling chair in front of a huge walnut antique desk and began searching through the top drawer, while Aiden sat cross-legged on the floor in front of a rusty, two-drawer aluminum file cabinet.

"Looks like her most current files are in these drawers or at least the past two years. Your grandmother kept them organized by category, month, and year. If you're named the executor, you're going to have to go through all of this for financial liabilities against the estate, but for now, I'll just look for relevant things."

They had both searched silently for about 30 minutes when Reagan started laughing. "Pretty slick, Nana."

Aiden peered up from a stack of papers. "Find something?"

She held up a long flat key.

"Looks just like the key to a safe deposit box. Where was it hidden?"

"In a cassette case with a strip of masking tape that said *Heart of Gold* by Neil Young. Tomorrow I'll ask someone at her bank what I need to do to get in it."

"Good idea. At least you know there's another place to look for important documents. See an attorney card?"

She frowned and shook her head.

Rolling the chair out of the way, Reagan sat on the floor next to Aiden. "Anything helpful in the file cabinet?"

"Unfortunately, no mention of an attorney or a will, but you might want to look at these bank statements. Did you know your name is on all of her accounts?"

"What? You're kidding?"

Aiden handed her an envelope from the bank addressed to Fiona Burke Moran. Reagan K. Asher was listed underneath.

She wrinkled her forehead. "Absolutely no idea," she breathed.

"Do you ever remember signing any bank papers?" Aiden asked. "They would have to have your approval to add you to her account."

"Not since I opened an account when I left for college." Reagan thought for a few seconds. "I gave Nana access to my checking account so she could make deposits and monitor my balance while I was away at Purdue. Nothing since then. That account has been closed since I moved to Chicago years ago."

"Your grandmother probably added you to her checking and savings accounts at the same time. She either forgot to take you off or she left you on her accounts on purpose with future needs in mind."

"I'm shocked. Obviously, you know more about Nana's finances than I do. How much is in her accounts?"

"Didn't want to snoop."

"Go ahead. I trust you."

He fished out the most current statement. "As of this past January, she had $21,246.23 in her checking and $65,746. 86 in her savings account." He handed her the statement.

"My gosh! That's a lot more than I expected. I guess her thriftiness paid off."

"If she put your name on her bank accounts, there is a good chance that she put it on her safe deposit box too. Maybe she wanted to make it easier for you to manage things when the time came."

Reagan's eyes met his. He could see the pain. All the "should haves" and "would haves." He was familiar with the feelings. When you lose someone close to you, there are almost always regrets.

Aiden looked at his watch. "We better get moving or we're going to be late, and Mattie's going to be pissed at me. Now we need to find a place to hide your 'princess' jewelry." He did the finger quotes for emphasis.

They spent the next 10 minutes searching the small home, but Aiden couldn't come up with a single hiding place that wouldn't appear obvious. Feeling frustrated, he suggested they head to the kitchen to get a glass of water and regroup.

"What's in that room?" Aiden asked, pointing to a door off the kitchen.

"The laundry room. Maybe we could hide it in the washer or dryer?" Reagan suggested. She stepped inside and set the box of jewelry on top of the washer lid.

Aiden walked in behind her. "Too visible." He noticed another smaller door on the back wall next to the dryer. "What's in there?"

"It's a mechanical closet. The heating and air conditioning units."

Aiden opened the door and had to duck his head to step inside. The space was barely big enough for a repairman to work.

"I'll need a screwdriver, some electrical tape, and a flashlight," he said.

"You're going to hide them in the air conditioner?"

"The only other alternative is to find a place under the house in the crawl space, which I really don't want to do. If there's any room in the AC, it's the best I can come up with tonight."

Reagan hesitated. "The tools … are in the garage. That's where N…Nana was …" Aiden instantly understood.

"Just point me in the direction of the toolbox," he said quickly. She opened the door to the garage and pointed toward the far corner, then quickly stepped back into the kitchen. Within a couple of minutes, Aiden returned with the tools he needed.

Reagan leaned against the dryer as she watched him take the front panel off the AC and fiddle around inside the metal casing. Lying on the floor on his back, with his legs partially in the laundry room, he held a flashlight in one hand and stuck the other hand up inside the unit. His face contorted as he struggled to reach or remove something.

"Shit! I need two hands. Do you think you could hold the flashlight for me so I can see inside this unit? There's not much room in here, but there's something blocking a cubbyhole that might be a perfect place to conceal the box."

"Got it." She stepped over his legs into the cramped space, then let her back slide down the wall until she was squatting over his prone body. "Where do you want me?"

"If you can wedge yourself next to me, I'll hand you the flashlight."

"You're kidding, right?" she said, looking at the space with barely enough room for her feet, let alone her butt. "If you turn sideways, I might have enough room, otherwise I'll be sitting on your chest."

Aiden smiled at the thought and scrunched himself closer to the AC unit until her hips were nestled snuggly against his. He fought to ignore the warm sensation of her closeness. She reached for the flashlight, which illuminated the object from a better angle. Now he could see some sort of a container taped in the upper far corner of the unit. After he worked it for a couple of minutes, the mystery item finally broke free, sending him backwards. His head banged on the linoleum floor.

"Shit!"

"You all right?"

"Yeah." He winced as he rubbed the back of his head and slowly sat up. He was holding a square object, about 12 inches long and 5 inches deep, covered in faded-gray electrical tape.

"What do you suppose that is?" Reagan asked. "A part for the air conditioner?"

"Don't know, but it's been in there for a while."

He set the box-like container on his lap and struggled to pull off the old tape. After a few strips were torn away, they began to see what looked like an old plastic storage container. Reagan leaned over him for a better view.

"Doesn't look like an air conditioning part," Aiden observed. "A repairman would never put all this tape around something he needed to easily access."

Reagan took it from his hands and carefully pulled the rest of the tape until it was completely uncovered. They stared at the once see-through, now cloudy, yellowed plastic container.

"I'm afraid to open it," she said cautiously. He gave her a reassuring smile.

"It can't be that bad. Who knows how many years it's been wedged up in this old air conditioning unit. It's still tightly sealed, so there can't be any critters in it. Alive, anyway. I'm guessing it's pretty safe."

Reagan rolled her eyes and slowly began to work the lid off. When the contents were revealed, they both stared in wonder.

"What the heck?" Reagan gasped.

"Of all the things I expected, this wasn't even in the same hemisphere," Aiden said, sounding amused.

The container held two pieces of decorative plastic fruit, an orange and a banana.

"Are you seeing the same thing I'm seeing?" Reagan asked. "Plastic fruit? Does this not seem bizarre to you?"

He looked at her with a twinkle in his blue eyes. "What? Would you have preferred grapes? Pomegranates? Perhaps a kumquat?" She playfully smacked him on his arm and picked up the orange. When she turned it over, she felt something move inside.

"It's not empty." Putting the orange to her ear, she shook it and heard it rattle softly.

Aiden reached for the banana. "May I?"

"Sure. Why not?"

Closely examining it, he moved it back and forth in his hand. He felt the weight shift. "There's something in this one too."

He ran his finger along a line around the middle of the banana and gently pulled on both ends. To his amazement, small beads tumbled into his lap and pooled in the creases of his jeans where his legs were squeezed together. When he shifted to get a better look, many of the beads rolled down his joined legs and spilled out into the laundry room. Aiden scooped a few into his palm for a closer inspection. Reagan flashed the beam on his hand as Aiden gently rolled them over under the light.

"What do you think?" Reagan whispered as if, somehow, she could be overheard.

Aiden took his time picking up one bead after the other, examining them in detail.

"They're pearls."

She looked at him skeptically, then gathered a handful to make her own assessment.

"How can you say that? They aren't even white. They're painted gray, see?"

Aiden used his finger to roll the beads around in Reagan's palm. "See how these are tinted with different colored hues? This one's tinted blue, here's a pink one, and this one's kind of greenish."

"Just shows you how bad the paint job was. They couldn't even get the colors right," she said.

"I'm no expert, but they look like black pearls to me."

"Really? I thought black pearls were a myth to make pirate's treasure sound more interesting," she said playfully, not taking him seriously.

"They are not a myth, I assure you. These have a dark iridescence about them … exactly like black pearls. My dad bought my mom a black pearl and diamond necklace for their anniversary when he was on a business trip in Germany. It cost him a small fortune. The unique thing I remember about it was, even though it looked gray, you could see blue and silver hues when it was under different types of lighting. I thought it was cool, so I Googled it. Each stone is supposed to have its own unique colors."

Reagan shook her head with impatience. "Just stop it, Aiden. Why do you insist on making something out of nothing? These are not genuine pearls. They are clearly painted beads. That's all they are!" She glared at him.

Aiden tried to remain calm despite his irritation. She was dealing with a lot, and he wanted to respect that.

"I know this isn't the answer you want to hear, but think about it for a minute," he said, maintaining an even tone. "Why would someone hide painted beads in the air conditioner if they weren't valuable?"

Reagan didn't answer, probably because she couldn't come up with a plausible explanation. Instead, she carefully picked up the plastic orange and held it over the container while she pulled it apart. She gasped as a couple of handfuls of sparkling diamonds tumbled out.

"What the fuck?" Aiden shouted in disbelief. He felt Reagan's body go rigid against him. "I guess those aren't real diamonds either, because everyone stores rhinestones and painted beads in their ventilation systems." He bit his tongue after the caustic words were already out of his mouth. "I'm sorry, Reagan. That was uncalled for."

She didn't acknowledge his comment or his apology. He doubted she even heard him. Her emerald, green eyes were laser-focused on the diamonds, her face drained of all color.

"Oh, God," she mumbled to herself.

"Reagan?"

She took a deep breath and met his eyes. "Just give me a minute. I'll be right back," she said, as she shoved the container into Aiden's hands and scrambled over his legs to get to the door. The jerking movement sent the black pearls that were balancing on his legs scattering in all directions.

Seconds later, he heard footsteps down the back hall and a door close.

Deciding to give Reagan a few minutes to process, Aiden scooped up the pearls, digging many of them out from under mechanical equipment, and secured the front panel of the AC unit the way he had found it.

When he located her, she was sitting on her childhood bed, staring at nothing, deep in thought.

"May I come in?" he asked softly from the doorway but didn't wait for an answer. He had half expected this to be the last straw that broke her composure, envisioning her crumpled on the floor in tears, but that wasn't the case. *You are made of sterner stuff, Ms. Asher.* He walked over to the bed, putting the container of gems and the "princess box" on the bed beside her.

Turning to meet his gaze, she spoke with confidence. "I know this looks bad, Aiden. Real bad, but I swear to you on my life … I know *nothing* about any of this."

He opened his mouth to speak, then stopped. *Why would she feel the need to defend herself?* It was obvious she was just as shocked and baffled as he was. Something he said must have made her feel that he doubted her integrity and that made him feel awful. Sometimes his sarcasm got the best of him. Hanging 24/7 around guys with no filter would do that.

"Don't you think that if I had any knowledge those gems existed, I would never have let you go digging around my grandmother's house? You can tell this box hadn't been opened since the Stone Age … well, not that long, but a lot of years." She picked up the faded plastic container and shook it at him. "I'm sure a few of those babies would have financed my whole friggin' college education."

"You don't have to justify yourself to me. I believe you, Reagan, and I apologize for whatever I said or did that made you feel I questioned your honesty."

"Thank you. I'm not sure I would have believed you if our situations were reversed, but it means a lot considering you don't even know me. But I promise you, I'm going to get to the bottom of it no matter who gets hurt."

She glanced away for a few minutes, then turned back to face him, her face hard and full of determination. "Now what?"

"The immediate problem is finding a safe place to stash these gems and the jewelry for the night. Seems I'm not the first person to think of the air conditioner as a hiding place. You know, now that we've found these diamonds and pearls, it lends more credibility to my theory that the jewelry is genuine."

"I know, and it's all so mind-boggling."

"Try not to worry about it tonight. I promise I'll do my best to help figure this out," he assured her.

Reagan placed her hands firmly on his forearms to gain his full attention, her eyes sincere.

"Please believe that Nana couldn't have had any knowledge of these gems. Why would she have lived on a shoestring budget all these years if she had all this wealth at her disposal? None of it makes sense."

"I believe you. There is nothing in your actions or your grandmother's that could possibly lead me to think otherwise. But I have to be honest with you about the seriousness of this — somebody somewhere knows about these jewels. They didn't just materialize out of thin air. When I saw those diamonds, my heart dropped in my stomach. There's a lot of money at stake, and whoever put this stuff here is not going to let it go. The safest thing we can do is call Detective Kowalski and turn all this over to him." He heard her sharp intake of breath.

"I know that's what I should do, but you know why I don't want to do that yet. If we could just have a few days to try to figure this out without dragging Nana's name through the newspapers. People would speculate we are all a bunch of jewel thieves. Whether we find anything out or not, I promise I'll call Detective Kowalski."

Aiden sighed, knowing full well what he was going to do, despite the fact that he shouldn't. He was going to help her. Not just because of his promise to Mattie and Josh to watch out for her, but because he wanted to help ease the sense of utter aloneness she was feeling.

"If you've made up your mind, I won't try to talk you out of it. I do have a suggestion for where we could store them. After I signed the contract to purchase the condo, I rented a storage unit to keep my belongings until the move-in date. There's not much in it right now, just what I could fit in my car. It's not too far from here, so we can stop by there on the way to Josh and Mattie's house. I'll give you my keys to it if it makes you feel better."

"Sounds like our best option. And no. Keep the keys. And thank you," she said earnestly.

"I'll temporarily secure the broken window in your grandmother's room. That hopefully will discourage anyone from breaking in again, then we can be on our way."

# Chapter 6

Reagan had always felt welcome in the Rannells' traditional two-story brick home with the bright burgundy-red door and the neatly trimmed front yard. Josh had done quite well in pharmaceutical sales, allowing them to purchase their spacious home in the nearby affluent neighborhood of Claremont two years ago. Just the sight of it caused Reagan's tense muscles to relax.

"Reagan! Reagan!" Ellie screamed, leaping into her arms.

"I missed you so much, Sweetie!" Reagan said, hugging her goddaughter tightly to her chest and swinging her from side to side.

"We were about to give up on you guys. That detective must've taken his sweet time going through the house," Mattie said, greeting them at the door.

Reagan put Ellie down and ruffled her long, ash-blond curls. She was an adorable child who had a perfect blend of her parents' good looks, inheriting Mattie's big brown eyes and Josh's wavy blond hair. Mattie had always reminded Reagan of an ancient Greek seductress with her long black hair, flawless olive complexion, and voluptuous body. When people saw her with Josh, who was tall, slim, fair-skinned, and blue-eyed, the contrast usually made them do a double take.

"Go sit at the table, and I'll be right there. Then you can tell me all about your day," Reagan told Ellie.

"Okay, but Mommy says I have to wash my hands first!" She scampered off to the bathroom.

"It'd be best to blame the detective," Aiden whispered in Reagan's ear as he took her coat. She gave him a knowing smile.

"Sorry to be so late. The detective got caught up in court and put everything way behind schedule. You should have started without us," Reagan said, motioning to the dinner table.

"It's my fault too," Aiden said, sharing the blame. "I wanted to make sure the house was secure."

Mattie met Aiden with a hug. "Thanks for helping Reagan today. I really appreciate it. Since I couldn't be there, I felt so much better knowing someone I trust was in Reagan's corner."

"Not a problem," Aiden said, winking at Reagan.

"How was your trip? Get all your business taken care of in Virginia?" Josh asked.

"The loose ends are finally wrapped up, and I should be receiving most of my possessions within a couple of weeks. Still no idea about the closing date for the condo, so everything may have to go into storage."

"So, tell us what happened with the detective's visit," Josh said, settling into his seat at the head of the table.

Ellie skipped back into the room and held out her hands for her daddy to inspect. "All clean!"

Josh pulled her in for a kiss on her cheek. "Great job, Pumpkin. Now let's fill that little belly!" She giggled and wiggled out of his arms and into the seat next to him.

"I'll update you guys after dinner," Reagan said, tilting her head toward Ellie.

The conversation remained light as they shared vegetable lasagna, salad, and garlic bread. Reagan struggled to focus, her mind drifting back to the murder, the jewels, and so many unanswered questions. She felt as if she had stepped into an episode of *Stranger Things*, but the monsters were real.

Now that Nana was gone, Mattie and Josh were the closest thing she had to family, and she was grateful for their love and support.

Reagan hadn't quite gotten a clear read on Aiden yet. He seemed like a good guy, a bit arrogant, but she mostly trusted him. He had stood by her, lending support during her interactions with Detective Kowalski, and had remained calm and level-headed as he helped her navigate through the discovery of the gems in the AC unit. She could tell he was a strict rules person, probably from all the years of following orders in the Navy. Hopefully, he would keep his word and not go running to the police at the first opportunity.

As Reagan sat at the dinner table, she couldn't help but appraise the brothers as they sat next to each other. They both had pale, crystal blue eyes, and they certainly were both handsome but in totally different ways. Josh was classically good-looking and exuded charm, while Aiden was more angular and rugged. Their personalities were a sharp contrast as well. Josh was gregarious and outgoing, compared to Aiden who was more serious with a quick, dry wit. Josh was an immaculately dressed executive type whose only outdoor activity was golf. Aiden on the other hand seemed to be a more athletic, outdoorsy type of guy. His years in the military certainly explained his well-toned physique.

Asking Aiden to help her decipher the jewelry mystery had been extremely selfish on her part. He had his own challenges with getting settled in a new home, new job, and starting a totally different kind of life, but she really didn't have any other options. Getting Josh or Mattie involved could be dangerous, something Aiden was more prepared to deal with. There was no way she would let any of the ugliness near Ellie.

After the dishes were washed and Ellie was safely tucked in bed, the adults relaxed in front of the fire with copper mugs of Moscow mules.

"Tell us about your visit with the detective today," Mattie encouraged.

Reagan walked them through the entire afternoon, leaving out anything to do with the jewelry, gems, and break-in. Aiden apparently didn't agree with the last omission, because he barreled right in.

"Someone broke into the house just before Reagan arrived today, so I don't think it's safe…"

"What?" Mattie interrupted, jumping to her feet. She narrowed her eyes at Reagan. "Why didn't you call me immediately?" Josh grabbed her arm and pulled her back down on the sofa.

"Calm down, Mama Bear. Let Aiden tell us what happened before you go all ballistic on Reagan."

Aiden held his hand up. "It's been handled, and no one was hurt. They ran out when they heard Reagan in the house. I was there within minutes, and the detective wasn't far behind. Kowalski seems to think they were looking for something specific, because everything was focused on Mrs. Moran's bedroom. Someone took a real chance coming back to a house with crime scene tape plastered across the front door. That's why I'm going to spend the next few days helping Reagan get the place in order and her grandmother's finances settled," he explained. "I don't think it's safe for Reagan to be there alone."

Mattie looked suspiciously at Aiden and Reagan. "Well, you two seem to have hit it off quite well."

Reagan ignored the hints of jealously. Mattie had always been her protector, and Reagan knew she felt replaced, but it couldn't be helped. She wasn't putting Mattie at risk.

"Aiden was extremely helpful when the detective was there, and he offered good suggestions for figuring out Nana's final wishes."

"Y…you know. I can take some time off work," Mattie said, her voice breaking.

Aiden interjected to help ease the tension. "Fortunately, I won't be starting my job for a couple of weeks, so I'm the ideal solution." Mattie's face fell.

"Can I at least help you with the funeral arrangements?" she asked.

Reagan got up off the sofa where she was sitting next to Aiden and walked to Mattie's chair, throwing her arms around her neck.

"How could I get through any of this without you?" Reagan said, nestling herself on the arm of the chair.

"The whole thing is crazy," Josh said. "I for one am glad Aiden's going to be there with Reagan and not you, Babe. What's the plan for tomorrow?"

"Until the coroner releases Nana's body, I'm on hold with funeral arrangements, so I thought I'd begin by going to the bank to check into her financial situation. We found a key to Nana's safe deposit box. That will be the first order of business. Surprisingly, my name is on her accounts. Hopefully, I can get into it without a court order. Finding a will would be helpful."

"What about the house? Have you decided what you want to do with it?" Mattie asked.

Reagan swallowed hard. "Sell it. Doesn't feel like home anymore. Now it's a reminder of things I want to forget." She and Aiden exchanged looks.

"Have you heard from Tyler?" Mattie asked.

"Not yet, but he travels out of town on short notice a lot."

"Have you checked your phone? I tried to call you several times today and finally called Aiden because you never answered."

"Really?" Reagan got up and found her handbag. "It's dead. Must have forgotten to plug it in last night and never even thought to check the charge level." She pulled a charger out of her bag and plugged her cellphone into a wall socket. After a few seconds, it began a succession of pings.

"Wow. Tyler tried to call me at least 20 times, and his wasn't the only call I missed. Sorry everyone, but I need to return some of these. I also need to call Dad. Not sure if he would care about Nana's death, but it seems appropriate to tell him. Mattie, thank you for a lovely dinner," she said, hugging her. "Goodnight, Josh … Aiden, I really appreciate you being there today." She tried her best to let her tone express the depth of her gratitude.

"No problem. Still want to leave about 8:30 to get to the bank by 9?"

"Sounds good," she said with a wave as she ran up the stairs.

When she reached the top step, she heard Aiden ask, "Who's Tyler?" and she smiled.

When she got to her room, Reagan called Tyler, deciding to wait to talk to her dad. He picked up on the first ring.

"Reagan! I've been worried sick. I'm so sorry to hear about your grandmother. How are you doing?" It was comforting to hear his voice, but she knew she was going to have to filter her responses. The last thing he needed was to get sucked into her giant mess.

"I guess I'm okay. It's been an emotional rollercoaster."

"I can't imagine and feel like a total jerk for not calling sooner. One of our divisional managers got sick, so I had to hop a plane early yesterday morning to fill in at a conference in Dallas. I shot off a quick email to let you know I'd be back to Chicago late this afternoon. When I couldn't reach you today, I called your office. Your assistant told me what happened."

"Afraid I haven't been operating on all cylinders. My phone died sometime today, and it never occurred to me to check my email."

"Can you tell me a little about what's going on?" he asked.

Reagan spent the next 20 minutes filling him in on the day's activities, minus any mention of the jewels. Tyler totally caught her off guard. He expressed more emotions to her than he had the entire six months they had been dating. It felt quite wonderful to realize she was more important to him than she imagined. Maybe, she thought, this was a turning point in their relationship.

Reagan met Tyler Hamilton at a charity fundraiser, and they had an immediate physical attraction to one another. With his aristocratic good looks, beautiful hazel eyes, and midnight-black hair, he was hard to resist. She hadn't been able to keep her eyes off of him, nor could he keep his eyes off her. To complete the package, he dressed in the latest designer fashion trends, having plenty of money to finance his style preferences. As suave and cultured as he appeared, he was a complete computer nerd at heart, a shy, reserved, and extremely intelligent techie.

Although Tyler and Reagan never actually defined their relationship as exclusive, she hadn't gone out with anyone since they began dating. She never mentioned it to him, but she had seen a picture of him the month before in the society pages of the newspaper. He had a gorgeous blonde on his arm at an art gallery opening. It had hurt her pride, but it also signaled her to keep her options open. They usually went out once or twice a week, staying overnight at either her downtown condo or his penthouse apartment. His sincere concern tonight warmed her heart.

"I want to be there for you. It took some arranging at work, but I'm catching a flight to Cleveland tomorrow and should be there by mid-afternoon if that works for you. Don't worry about picking me up, I'll get a rental. Just need your address."

Reagan squeezed her eyes shut while her thoughts raced. *Oh shit! He can't come tomorrow. How can I possibly explain the jewels? Or the possible danger? Or why Aiden is helping me and not him? The fewer people involved, the better.*

"Tyler, that is so nice of you, and I can't tell you how much it means to me to have your support … but …"

"But what?" She heard the tension in his voice. "You don't want me to come? I can't let you go through this alone."

"It's not that ... I would love to see you ... I miss you. It's just the police are still investigating the house and ... they haven't even released my grandmother's ... I can't even plan the funeral yet. All I can do right now is work on getting her finances in order and go through her personal belongings. It's ... so hard for me right now."

"Putting additional stress on you was never my intent. How I can help, Baby?"

"I'm so grateful, but there's nothing you can really do right now. Maybe when it's time to make the funeral arrangements. Would it be too much to ask if you could wait?" She wasn't sure that was even a good idea, but felt she had to let him know he was important to her.

"If that's what you think is best, but you can't possibly be in that house alone after what happened. I'll arrange a security ..." She knew where that was going, and she quickly cut him off.

"Thank you, but it's not necessary. Mattie's brother-in-law, who is ex-military, volunteered to help guard the house when I'm there." She didn't want to lie, but she also didn't want to tell the whole truth, so again she went with a partial. She was going to have to keep her stories straight.

"Another guy, huh? Should I be jealous?"

Reagan tried to read his tone, not sure if he was kidding, but she had to defuse his suspicions. The reality of the good-looking ex-Navy Seal would not go over well with him, so she ad-libbed.

"He's been in the service a long, long time. Mostly in the Middle East. Still carries a gun everywhere he goes. All military, if you know what I mean. He probably sleeps in his camos with an AK-47 under his pillow," she laughed nervously. She bet Aiden would be furious at her description of him. She had just implied he was just short of living off the grid on K rations in a bunker in the wilderness of North Dakota, waiting for the zombie apocalypse. She felt a wave of guilt, but she pushed it aside. She would mentally beat herself up later.

He chuckled. "Then make sure he doesn't shoot you by mistake."

"I'll duck if bullets start to fly. It means so much to me that you care. Just hearing your voice brightens my miserable day." She sighed deeply. Crisis temporarily averted.

"I'll call you tomorrow to check in. If you need anything at all, I'm here. Dad's jet is always fueled and ready to go within a couple of hours. I miss you, Baby." Tyler rarely used terms of endearment, but his use of them that night, when she had deceived him about what was really going on in her life, made her stomach churn. Had she misjudged his level of commitment to their relationship?

"Me too. Goodnight."

The phone call confused her, but she couldn't allow herself to get dragged down that rabbit hole when she had too much to fret about already. Deciding to compartmentalize her feelings as she always did when she didn't want to deal with them, she tried to fall sleep.

# Chapter 7

It was a long night of tossing and turning, barely closing her eyes. Reagan couldn't wrap her head around all the bizarre things that had happened in the past couple of days. It felt as if she had woken up in someone else's life and didn't know how to find her way back to her own.

She had always prided herself on her ability to plan and organize her life to meet her goals, both professional and personal. Being well prepared and having a back-up plan were key elements to her success. Reagan took risks when necessary, but when she did, the obstacles were anticipated, alternatives calculated, and the results deemed acceptable.

Her childhood had been spent at the mercy of her parents' selfish choices, and she had suffered the consequences. When she became an adult with her own resources, she promised herself she would never again be a victim of others' bad decisions. Now, here she was again, wrapped up emotionally, and this time legally, in a tragic situation created by the actions of others, left to sort out the confusion. As upset and discombobulated as she felt, she was certain of one thing, her grandmother would be just as baffled. Nana had always been honest and straightforward, an example Reagan lived by. That was why she felt awful about keeping the jewels a secret from Mattie, Josh, and Tyler, but their safety had to take precedence. She had already lost more than she could bear.

When Aiden insisted the jewelry she had worn and played with as a child was genuine, she truly believed he was mistaken. She had given in to hiding it and agreed to authenticate the jewels mainly because of his misplaced sense of guilt over Nana's death. Finding the diamonds and black pearls hidden in the air conditioning unit had been a hard dose of reality. It threw her off kilter, and she hadn't been able to right herself. The implications of what it could mean racked her to her core.

By 8 a.m., Reagan was showered and conservatively dressed as always in a cream-colored silk blouse and black pencil skirt. When she walked in the kitchen, Aiden sat at the table engrossed in his iPhone. He was dressed casually in a sweater and a pair of well-worn denim jeans. Since he had already eaten, Reagan grabbed a travel mug of coffee and a granola bar to have on the way.

After a quick trip to the storage locker to pick up the jewels and stuff them in one of Aiden's faded-navy backpacks, they arrived at the bank just after opening. A smartly dressed young man looked up from his work as they approached his desk.

"Excuse me. I hope I'm not interrupting," Reagan said with friendly confidence. "My name is Reagan Asher, and this is my friend, Aiden Rannell."

"Not at all. Good morning. I'm Seth Johnson," he said, smiling broadly and extending his hand in greeting. Reagan's hand met his in a firm grip. "How may I assist you today?"

"My grandmother, Fiona Moran, died recently, and I need to get into her safe deposit box. My name is on a couple of her accounts here, so I hoped it might include her safe box as well. This is the key," she said, holding it up, "but I'm not sure about the box number."

"I'm sorry for your loss," Seth said kindly. "I'd be happy to help you any way I can. If you could give me some details and your driver's license, we can pull up the account." Reagan provided the necessary information.

"You are correct. Your name is on the safe deposit box," he confirmed. Reagan sighed with relief. "For future reference, the number is 268. Would you like a room to privately view the contents?"

"Please."

Within minutes, she and Aiden were sitting at a small wooden table pushed against the wall in a room the size of a mini walk-in closet, staring down at a metal box just large enough to hold legal documents. Aiden placed his backpack on the table.

"Here goes," Reagan said under her breath.

In the box, they found a stack of loose papers, file folders, and legal documents that Reagan spread out on the table. Among them: the deed to the house, title and bill of sale for the car, death certificates for Reagan's grandfather and mother, her mother and grandmother's marriage licenses, her mother's divorce papers, insurance papers, and two manila folders filled with various papers and old receipts. When she found her grandfather and grandmother's wills, her hands began to tremble.

"May I?" Aiden asked, holding out his hand, sensing her discomfort. She flashed him a grateful look, then patiently waited as he reviewed each document.

"Mr. Moran's will is pretty straightforward. He left everything to your grandmother. Notarized in 1986, it lists property, cash, assets, personal belongings, things like that. Your grandmother's will is a bit more detailed. It was also written in 1986, but a codicil was added in 1990."

"That was the year my grandfather died."

"That makes sense. Your mother's name was Claire, right?" She nodded. "Your grandmother split her estate 50/50 between you and your mother with the exception of her personal effects," Aiden explained. "All her personal belongings were left to you."

"Really? I wonder why."

"Not to be insensitive, but did your grandmother and mother have a good relationship?"

"I'm not really sure how to answer that. It's been so long ago. I was young when Momma died."

Aiden quickly put his hand over hers and lightly squeezed. "That was a thoughtless question. I apologize." Her sad eyes met his, and she forced a smile.

"Not necessary. With everything that's happened, I guess I should look at my life from all angles and figure out if I missed something. To be honest, Nana was a controlling force in our lives for as long as I can remember. After my parents moved us into her house, I remember her using the phrase 'it's my house' a lot when she was upset with my parents. I don't think Daddy was especially happy about it, but Momma always went along to avoid an argument. Now that I think about it, since they moved in to help Nana out financially, that was a rather selfish thing for Nana to do.

"I loved Nana dearly, but she had a big personality. Momma was more reserved. Guess you could say Nana overshadowed her. After Daddy left, Momma hardly ever left the house. Didn't have any friends that I can remember. She was tired a lot and always seemed to be sleeping. I've tried to piece things together over the years. I believe she battled depression. People often mistake it for apathy. It may have started before Daddy left. I remember them arguing because she wouldn't go see a doctor. Momma always refused. Said she needed some rest."

"The symptoms seem right. A lot of people struggle with depression but won't seek help. I'm sure she loved you. Maybe your grandmother wanted to leave you half of what she had in case your mother couldn't take care of you."

Reagan looked at Aiden and smiled, appreciating his reassurance.

"Do you want to take this with us and look through the contents more thoroughly when we get to your Nana's house?"

"Good idea. Let's take everything," she said, stacking the papers into a pile. "Ready to put the jewels in the safe deposit box?"

"Sure, but I think we should keep at least one diamond, one pearl, and one of the pieces of jewelry to authenticate — maybe the sapphire and diamond necklace. If those items are genuine, then there's an excellent chance the others are too. I searched online last night and found a reputable jewelry appraiser in Cleveland. He's highly regarded."

"When do you want to go see him?" Reagan asked.

"Hope you don't mind, but I left a voicemail last night asking to set up an appointment for tomorrow at noon. He confirmed it this morning. If you can't make it, I'll reschedule."

"That's fine. Thanks for taking the initiative to make it happen. The sooner we know what we actually have, the better."

"I may sound paranoid, but I gave him fake names and used a burner phone to call him this morning so it can't be traced back to either one of us. I had some disposable phones left over from when I was overseas."

Her eyes widened. "You're really that worried?"

"We have no idea what we're dealing with or who's aware those jewels exist. When it's that kind of money at stake, there's no telling what lengths people are willing to go to get their hands on it. That includes killing, stealing, and paying people off to get private information. The

GPS in phones and cars can be tracked. We'll take my truck since you and I have no prior history together. Just being cautious. You say the word, and we'll call Detective Kowalski and dump all of it in his lap. I'd prefer it, actually."

"Just a few days. That's all I'm asking," she reminded him.

"All right then, but ..." He reached in the backpack and pulled out a handful of the jewelry and held it up over the too small safe deposit box. "We're going to need a bigger box."

# Chapter 8

As Aiden pulled out of the bank parking lot, Reagan's cell phone rang. She quickly reached in her handbag and said hello.

"Ms. Asher, it's Detective Kowalski. I'm afraid I have some bad news about Mrs. Moran's home."

Reagan glanced at Aiden wide-eyed. "What now, Detective?"

"Put it on speaker," mouthed Aiden. She did.

"Someone broke into Mrs. Moran's home again … sometime during the evening. One of the neighbors heard loud banging coming from inside the house and called the police around 2 a.m. There is some pretty serious damage. It's becoming more apparent that they are searching for something specific. Probably the work of more than one person judging by the level of destruction.

"Destruction? Exactly what does that mean?" Reagan's voice rose a few octaves.

"It's best if you see for yourself. The crime scene investigators have been here for the last few hours. How soon can you get here? We're hoping you can help make some sense of this."

"We're about 20 minutes away," Aiden said.

"I can be there …" Reagan began.

"Yeah, I heard. Mr. Rannell is still with you?" Detective Kowalski said.

"He is," she said, wondering how it was any of his business. "We'll be there in a few minutes, Detective." She quickly hit the end button and threw her phone in her handbag.

"Do you think the man who killed Nana came back last night?" she asked.

"Someone is desperate to find something, whether it was someone from the jewelry store or the owner of the gems we found. That AC unit looked old. Do you remember when your grandmother last replaced it? I'm trying to get a feel for how long those gems have been hidden in there."

"Not sure it's ever been replaced. We mostly used box fans when I was growing up because Nana said air conditioners were too expensive to run. They didn't have one when my mother was growing up, so it was probably installed sometime after she went to college."

"Sounds like your grandmother was budget conscious. That means those gems could've been there a really long time. I'm guessing at least 25 years. It's rare for an AC unit to last that long. The energy efficiency must be crap if it still runs. You'll need to replace it before you sell the house, but that's a discussion for another time."

Detective Kowalski's warning did not adequately prepare Reagan for the shock of seeing her childhood home in shambles. As she stepped over debris, she fought to retain her self-control. Most of the walls in the living room, dining room, and kitchen had at least three huge holes where the dry wall had been busted open. A sledgehammer, tire iron, mallet, and other assorted tools scattered around were evidence of the hasty retreat of the perpetrators. Chunks of plaster, broken picture frames, an overturned bookcase, and sliced-open furniture cushions littered the rooms. The refrigerator had been emptied and thrown face-down on the kitchen floor, its contents tossed around the room and the back pried open with a crowbar that was still protruding. The destruction ended at two floor-to-ceiling holes in the front of the hall.

"This is as far as they got," Detective Kowalski said, pointing to the wall. "We're assuming they heard the police sirens and fled. The responding officers called for backup, and the neighborhood and surrounding areas were searched, but without any kind of description of the perps or vehicles, it was fruitless. They left a black bag on the floor of the dining room. Nothing in it. Must have been caught by surprise, or I'm sure they wouldn't have left all these expense tools."

Reagan stood dumbfounded, surveying the damage. This had been her home. It held all her memories … good and bad. Until Aiden questioned her when they were discussing Nana's will, she had forgotten about the growing tension she noticed between her grandmother and her parents. More so with her dad. Her mom mostly retreated into her shell.

Reagan's memory flashed back to the day her father left. The house had seemed uncharacteristically quiet that early Saturday morning, so she peeked out of her bedroom door to see if anyone was up and stirring. She saw her father wearing a gray suit, unusual for a Saturday. He rolled two large blue suitcases down the hall toward her mother who stood at the front door, a vacant look on her face. He stopped directly in front of her and waited, as if he expected her to say something. Maybe stop him. Their eyes held for a long moment, and they appeared to be having a silent conversation that nobody else was privy to except them. Then without uttering a word, she robotically opened the door and watched him get into a waiting cab. Her face reflected no emotion.

There were no tears. No explanations. No goodbye for his daughter. Reagan guessed she wasn't worth remembering. Her daddy had walked out of their lives and never came back. She cried herself to sleep that night, but she was sure no one else did.

Reagan's mother never offered a reason for his departure or spoke of him again. It was Nana who explained that her parents were divorcing, and her father was moving to the other side of the country. Things didn't change much after that. Nana got her ready for school every morning, took her to play dates, played games with her, and made sure she went to Sunday school every week like always. Her momma read books, blankly watched television, and slept. It wasn't long before she rarely left her bed.

One chilly, wet October afternoon, Reagan sat excitedly on the school bus. She couldn't wait to tell her mother and Nana about her idea for a Halloween costume. When she stepped off the bus, she thought it odd that her mother wasn't at the corner to meet her as she did every afternoon when Nana was at work. The bus driver noticed Reagan standing there perplexed and offered to watch her get safely to her front door.

A familiar disappointment filled her heart when she found her mother sound asleep in her cover-tousled bed. Reagan debated waking her; after all, she really wanted to share her idea, and Nana wouldn't be home for another couple of hours. Deciding to risk her mother's crankiness, Reagan called out to her a few times, but got no response. She studied her mother's beautiful face as she slept, thinking she looked like Sleeping Beauty, so lovely and peaceful with pale white porcelain skin. Reagan secretly hoped that one day she would be as pretty as her mother. That's when the idea came to her. If she woke her mother with a kiss, maybe she wouldn't be too upset at being disturbed. When her lips touched her mother's cheek, a shriek caught in her throat. Her momma's skin was ice cold. Aware something was terribly wrong, Reagan dialed 911 as Nana had taught her. The rest — ambulances, fire trucks, policemen, neighbors huddled around the front yard — was a blur. From that day forward, it had been just Nana and her.

"Reagan?" she heard Aiden call her name as if he were at the end of a tunnel.

"Ms. Asher?"

Her vision began to narrow, and she felt weightless, as if she was drifting above herself. The people speaking to her sounded far away. As her legs began to give way, strong arms slid around her waist and behind her knees, lifting her off her feet. Then everything went black.

---

As Aiden gently laid Reagan on her childhood bed, Detective Kowalski placed a wet cloth on her forehead. Fortunately, that room had been untouched by the intruders. While the detective had gone to get the washcloth, Aiden took a quick peek in the chest at the foot of the bed that had once held the jewelry. Nothing appeared disturbed. Apparently, the thieves hadn't made it past the hall.

"Should I call an ambulance?" the detective asked Aiden.

Before he could answer, Reagan's eyes fluttered open. "N...no. I'm ... fine," she said groggily. She tried to get up, but Aiden placed his hand firmly against her shoulder.

"You just blacked out," Aiden said, stroking her hand. "Give yourself a few minutes to get your equilibrium back. It's been a lot to absorb."

"Oh, my God. I'm so embarrassed. I have never fainted in my life." Reagan covered her face with her hands.

"Anyone would have a tough time with what you've faced these past few days," Aiden said.

Detective Kowalski walked to the door and motioned for Aiden to follow. They stood facing each other in the living room, Aiden patiently waiting for the detective to say what was on his mind.

"Are you sure we shouldn't call the paramedics?" Detective Kowalski asked in a low tone.

"Don't think it's necessary, but it's your call. If you walked into your family home where your grandmother's throat had been sliced open and saw the place torn to pieces, you might react similarly, maybe worse."

"Guess you're right. But I've got to say, I'm stumped. This family isn't wealthy. Nothing about their lifestyle begins to explain what someone would be looking for. I made some calls this morning hoping to find out if the history of the house could shed any light on motive. The Morans purchased the house in 1974. The original owners were a pastor and his wife. They sold the house after they were transferred to a church in Cincinnati three years after they built it. Today they live in a modest retirement home in central Florida. A dead end.

"My first impression was a junkie looking for drugs or electronics who might have panicked when Mrs. Moran came home. But when somebody comes back with a demolition crew to take the place apart, that speaks to a different story entirely. It indicates something extremely valuable or important to someone. I know you said you just met Ms. Asher, but do you have any ideas at all?"

Aiden hated lying, so he decided to stick to the truth as much as possible. He chose his words carefully. He resented being put in that position because it went against everything he stood for.

"I very recently met Mrs. Moran and only spent a short time with her, but she seemed to be a caring and hardworking lady. She babysat for my 5-year-old niece, Ellie. Mrs. Moran always kept her entertained. Ellie particularly loved to play with her costume jewelry. I was concerned when Ellie brought a ring home with her, but Mrs. Moran assured me she had nothing of value and not to worry about it. Mattie, who's married to my brother Josh, used to live down the street from here when she and Reagan were growing up. Mrs. Moran was like a second grandmother to her, so Mattie knows the family well. These are not people of wealth or intrigue. Whatever the thieves are looking for, my guess is that Mrs. Moran had no knowledge of it. It did occur to me that someone who knows the family could have stored something here for safekeeping without her knowledge."

"That's a thought. We're checking out some of her neighbors and close contacts. I'll probably be in touch with Mrs. Rannell soon. Ms. Asher mentioned that she was going through her grandmother's belongings. Do you know if she found anything significant? A will? If she had a safe deposit box, it may hold something of value that the perps assumed was in the house."

Again, Aiden chose the truth as the best option. Besides, it wouldn't be hard for the detective to find out he and Reagan had gone to the bank to review the contents of Mrs. Moran's safe deposit box that morning. Might as well be upfront.

"As a matter of fact, we found both. We found a key to a safe deposit box in Mrs. Moran's desk last night. Unbeknownst to Reagan, her name was on the account. We had just looked over the contents at the bank this morning when you called. There was nothing in the safe deposit box a thief would find valuable. No jewelry, bonds, cash, or anything close. Mostly important documents, but we didn't have a chance to review them." He didn't mention they had taken the contents with them, because they hadn't had an opportunity to study everything thoroughly.

"Did you find a will?" Detective Kowalski asked.

"We did."

"Who benefits?"

"That's an interesting way of putting it, detective. I can't see any benefit in Mrs. Moran's death at all." Aiden's tone was laced with sarcasm.

"Poor choice of words, but you know what I mean."

"If you're asking who inherits this vast estate," Aiden said, waving his arms through the air, "Reagan, but from the looks of Mrs. Moran's bank statements, I wouldn't call it particularly substantial."

"What about an insurance policy?"

"We didn't have time to study the documents, but you are way off base if you think Reagan had anything to do with this," Aiden said, losing patience. "You do realize Mrs. Moran was her only remaining relative who gave a shit about her. I'm guessing Ms. Asher is far better off financially than her grandmother was."

"We're just excluding the people closest to our victim," Detective Kowalski said dismissively. Aiden didn't comment.

"Obviously, Ms. Asher didn't stay here last night."

"And thank God she didn't," Aiden said. The detective nodded in agreement.

Aiden's eye caught movement down the hall. Reagan was leaning outside the door to her room, eavesdropping.

"Just for my records, is there a personal relationship between you and Ms. Asher?"

Aiden saw Reagan's eyes narrow.

"You mean personal as in we've had family connections for years or personal as in, am I sleeping with her?" The detective was fishing.

"Merely establishing relationships to the victim."

"Hmmm," Aiden sighed. He suspected the detective had a personal interest of his own in Reagan. "We met yesterday for the first time. I believe she has a boyfriend in Chicago, though …Tyler something. You should ask her if you're interested."

Before the detective could respond, he was interrupted by one of the crime scene investigators.

"Excuse me, Detective Kowalski. We've got everything we need. Unless you have anything else, we're headed to the lab."

Reagan slipped back into her room.

"Fine. Give me a call if you identify any of the fingerprints." The investigator nodded and followed his team out the door.

"If you don't need anything else, I think I'd better check on Reagan," Aiden said.

Detective Kowalski looked at his watch. "I'll be back in the office after 4. If Ms. Asher feels up to it, have her call me. I have more questions. Tell her that I'll have a patrol car cruising the area just in case our perps return. We still have an extra key to Mrs. Moran's house. If it's okay with Ms. Asher, I'd like to make it available to the officers patrolling the area in case of an emergency."

"That's probably a good idea. I'll have her contact you." He watched Detective Kowalski open the door and flip the lock on as he left. It seemed like a useless effort since the house had already been broken into three times in the last two days.

When Aiden returned to the bedroom, Reagan was staring at the ceiling.

"You think they were looking for the jewels?" she asked, not meeting his eyes.

"Maybe, but why after all of this time?"

"I've wondered that myself." She propped herself up on her elbow and turned to face him. "Maybe my grandmother's murder stirred it all up somehow."

Aiden sat on the bed beside her.

"I have a hard time believing you could forget where you stashed millions of dollars' worth of jewels."

She considered that point, looking directly into his eyes. "They could have been in prison and just got released. Or maybe someone died without telling others involved with the theft where they were hidden."

"That's a thought. You said you played with the jewelry pieces when you were a kid, so let's assume you've had them for at least 25 years, maybe more. I can't believe the gems in the air conditioning unit are not related somehow, so we'll estimate the same time frame for them. It's feasible that someone could go to prison for 25 to 30 years, especially if it was armed robbery. On their first attempt to retrieve the jewels, your grandmother could have surprised them, resulting in her death. They may be panicking now, fearing the house could be renovated or sold. That would explain the reckless behavior."

"What if my grandmother found the jewelry somewhere in the house years ago and assumed it was fake, so she gave it to me to play dress-up?"

"Seems logical. There could also be more than one group of interested parties looking for the gems, which is even more disturbing. Remember the thieves didn't know where to look. Whoever hid the diamonds and pearls in the AC would have looked there first. You do realize the police could probably get fingerprints off of the container and the tape the gems were wrapped in, don't you?" He said the last part with a bit of annoyance in his tone.

Reagan's face flushed. Swallowing hard, she turned back to face him. "Thanks for keeping quiet. I understand what a terrible position I've put you in, but I need some time to figure things out."

"We still have the container and the tape, so when you do decide to tell Detective Kowalski, we can say we just found them. Did you want to take some time and go through the contents of the safe deposit box? We can go back to Josh and Mattie's if you'd feel more comfortable."

"We left your backpack in the car."

"You're right. Stay right here." He pointed to the floor to indicate exactly right here. She rolled her eyes.

He ran out to the car and grabbed his backpack. When he returned, Reagan was gone.

"Shit! That woman is too damn stubborn for her own good." He mumbled with irritation. "Reagan! Reagan!" he called.

"The utility room."

Aiden was there within seconds, almost breaking his neck when he slipped on melted ice cream.

"I guess you missed the 'stay here' part."

Her brow furrowed, and her lips pursed. "As much as I appreciate everything you've done for me, let me explain one thing … I don't react well to demands. As a matter of fact, I have been known to turn into an obstinate bitch who feels compelled to do the exact opposite. Childish, I admit, but it's how I've survived in a male-dominated company." Aiden grinned at her candidness.

"Good to know, but how can I know you're safe if you wander off without telling me? Not 24 hours ago, a possible murderer broke into this house while you sat on the living room sofa. I don't think my concern is unfounded."

"Point made, but please change your approach."

"Note taken. Now, why are we in the utility room?"

"I wanted to make sure no one looked in the AC unit. And by the way, they didn't. Totally untouched."

"Good catch. Whoever was doing the searching didn't know to look there."

"Maybe it was someone from the jewelry store after all, looking for that emerald ring," Reagan suggested.

"I don't think they would tear up the house with a sledgehammer to find something as small as a ring. The robbery and murder were highly publicized in the news, so they knowingly took a huge risk."

"What if several people committed the original robbery, but only one of them knew where the jewels were hidden, then got caught by the police? If he was going to jail, he would want to ensure he got his share when he got out ... or maybe he died before he got out of prison and never told anyone the exact location." Reagan's imagination was running wild.

"Or he confessed on his last dying breath, and someone is trying to claim the loot," Aiden said, tongue in cheek.

"Loot? What is this, a 1930s James Cagney movie?"

"You've watched James Cagney? Wasn't that before your time, or are you older than you look?"

"Nana loved old movies. We rented them every Friday night until I was in high school and actually got a life." Aiden couldn't imagine a time when she didn't have an active social life.

"Well, one thing's for sure, whoever broke in didn't have a clue where to look," he confirmed.

Aiden pulled the contents of the safe deposit box out of his backpack and spread them out on the comforter in related piles. The first thing Reagan picked up was the life insurance policy. Aiden peered over her shoulder.

Reagan K. Asher was the sole beneficiary of Fiona Moran's $50,000 life insurance policy. Her grandmother had kept a small ledger listing the date and check numbers of every payment she had made over the years. With a dazed expression, Reagan laid the papers on her lap, her face drained of color. She slid off the edge of the bed and landed on the worn, pale blue shag carpet and buried her head between her knees. Seeing her shoulders tremble, Aiden eased down beside her.

Remembering she was virtually alone in the world, he acted on instinct and awkwardly pulled her into his arms. He was surprised when she snuggled against his chest. As he softly stroked her hair, his embrace seemed to give her permission to let go. And she did —

into full-blown, gut-wrenching sobs. His small gesture of compassion sparked the release she so desperately needed.

Aiden wasn't sure how long she stayed in his arms, the dampness from her tears seeping through his sweater. When he heard her steady breathing, he tried to move her onto the bed, but her eyes popped open in alarm.

"You okay?" he asked, using his free hand to reach the nightstand for a tissue, folding it into her hand.

She blotted her eyes, sniffed, and gazed up at him. "I'm so sorry ... and a complete mess. You had no idea what you were getting yourself into when you walked in my front door."

He stared down at her and tenderly pulled away wet strands of hair clinging to her cheeks. "Maybe a bit of a mess, but still a cute one — if you look past the red blotches. There's one there, and there, and there," he said playfully, as he lightly touched different places her face with his fingertips.

She smacked him in the chest. "Please stop trying to make me feel better."

"By all means, I'll go back to being a controlling ass." She rewarded him with another swat for his sarcasm.

Chuckling, he stood up and offered her a hand. "Do you want to finish going through these papers or call it a day?"

"Let's get this done so I can move on."

The rest of the papers were the normal important documents that people tuck away for safekeeping, nothing that referred to the jewelry or gems. Reagan's real disappointment was the absence of any reference to her Nana's final wishes.

"I think I'm ready to pack this all up for the day. What do you think?"

"Good idea. Hungry?" Aiden asked. "It's after 1."

"Not really, but I guess I should eat something, or Mattie will nag me all evening. Can you hand me the backpack? I don't want to leave anything important in the house."

Reagan stacked up all the papers and legal documents while Aiden held the bag open.

"What's that?" he asked.

"What?"

"There's something stuck to the back of the papers in your hand."

Reagan turned the papers over and noticed a photo stuck to the back. She held it up so they could both see. It was a well-worn color Polaroid of a handsome young man with dark, wavy hair who appeared to be in his middle to late teens. He wore a white polo shirt with navy slacks, and a huge grin was plastered on his face. It was difficult to tell the age of the photo because it appeared to be water damaged. There was an arm around his neck, but you couldn't tell who it belonged to because the picture had been cut in half. Nothing was written on the back, nor did it have a date.

"Huh? Wonder who that is." Reagan said.

"You don't recognize him?" Aiden asked. "He looks Middle Eastern."

"He does, doesn't he? Never seen him before."

"The arm around his neck looks small and delicate, definitely female. Maybe he was mad at the mystery girl and cut her out of the picture," Aiden suggested. "Maybe a friend of your mother's."

"That's hardly likely. My mother told me my grandfather wasn't very open-minded. He didn't like her to have 'non-white' friends. I remember Momma telling me about his bigotry and how important it was for me to accept people of all cultures. Anyway, I can't imagine why the picture would be in Nana's safe deposit box."

"Could it be a friend of hers?"

"Doubtful. Nana went to an all-girl Catholic school. Her family was extremely strict. My grandfather was the first and only man she ever dated."

"It was probably in a drawer somewhere with other pictures and got stuck to something," Aiden suggested.

"Maybe. When I searched Nana's desk for the safe deposit box key, there were pictures of Momma and some of her friends that I'd never seen. I'll put this picture on top of the desk to remind me to check it out later. Right now, there are too many other things to worry about."

"Sounds like a plan," Aiden agreed.

She put her hand lightly on his forearm. "I don't think I could handle this without you. I …" There was anguish in her voice.

"We'll figure this out together. Every step of the way."

Reagan cocked her head to one side. "Funny. Feels like I've known you for a lot longer than a couple of days. Know what I mean?"

"I do," he nodded, his eyes warm and sincere. *Exactly what you mean,* he thought. Their gaze held just a little too long for a newly established friendship, but before he had time to analyze what it might mean, they were interrupted by banging on the front door. Aiden instinctively reached into his holster and pulled out his 9mm.

"Are you expecting anyone?" he whispered. She shook her head.

"I'll see who it is. Why don't you take the picture into the office before we forget it? It might be important." Grabbing the picture and the backpack, she ran to the office while he headed for the front door.

"Can I help you?" he called through the door.

"Got a call from Mrs. Moran last week about repairing a light fixture. It was scheduled for today. Is she home?"

Aiden detected a thick accent but couldn't distinguish it through the door. He glanced over his shoulder at Reagan who had crept up behind him. She shrugged and shook her head. He looked through the peephole on the door. The man on the doorstep was probably in his late 50s, a little less than average height, and stocky with short-cropped black hair. He wore a navy-blue uniformed shirt and pants without a business logo of any kind.

Aiden motioned for Reagan to take a look. She peered out for a couple of seconds and jumped back as if he could see her through the door.

"No idea," she mouthed.

"Stay behind me. Don't worry, I'm not going to let him inside," he whispered.

Aiden opened the door just enough to check the guy out without allowing him to see inside the house, his foot and knee firmly planted against the door to prevent a forced entry, his gun hidden at his side.

"Who do you work for?" Aiden asked, scanning the street for a company vehicle or possible partners.

"Frank's Electric Repair."

"Your name?"

"Arturo Fuentes. I have a tight schedule today, so if you don't need me, I will be on my way."

"Do you know which light fixture you were supposed to work on?" Aiden asked.

"Just go where the boss tells me." *In other words, no.*

"Ms. Moran no longer needs your services. By the way, where's your van?" Aiden asked.

"Down the block. Wrote down the wrong house number. I'll call the office and cancel the service ticket. Have a good day," he said and hurried away.

Aiden watched until he was out of sight, then closed the door without noticing that Reagan had crept closer to him.

"Do you suspect he's one of the guys who broke in?" Reagan said into his ear, causing him to almost jump out of his skin. "Scared you, didn't I?"

He flashed her a crooked grin. "And I was beginning to think you had no sense of humor, but today you've proved me wrong." She looked pleased with herself. "But let me give you a valuable piece of advice. Never surprise anyone holding a loaded gun."

"Got it. Now what do you think about our repairman? Was he Hispanic?"

"Don't think so. He gave me a Hispanic name, but his accent and features are definitely Middle Eastern. I believe he wanted us to think he was Hispanic, although I'm not sure why."

Aiden walked outside the door to see if he could catch a look at what the man was driving. A few minutes later, a Frank's Electric Repair van drove right past the front of the house. Arturo Fuentes waved at them.

"He wanted us to see his van," Aiden said.

"Why would that be important?"

"Doesn't want to arouse suspicion. Probably because I asked about it. When he left here, he walked in the direction toward the entrance of the neighborhood. He could have gotten in his vehicle and driven out. Instead, he drove back this way so we could see he was legit. I doubt he realized he's headed into a dead-end." Sure enough, a few minutes later, the van passed in front of the house again, going the opposite direction.

Aiden put his gun back in its holster and pulled his cell from his pocket. "I'm going to make sure there really is a Frank's Electric Repair. Could be a ruse."

A Google search easily found the business. When he called the number, the receptionist was quite helpful. There was in fact an Arturo Fuentes working for Frank's Electric Repair, but he was on vacation in Mexico and would not be returning for a couple of weeks.

"It sounds like our guy is an imposter. Probably stole the truck. That begs the question, who the hell is the guy pretending to be Arturo Fuentes and why did he come here? My truck is out front, so he knew someone was home."

"Could that be the guy who killed Nana?" She looked at him expectantly.

"Reagan, you know I can't answer that."

# Chapter 9

Aiden lightly held her shoulders as she searched his eyes. He felt totally inadequate not having the answers she desperately needed. Every new revelation seemed to prompt more questions, leaving Reagan more bewildered and off-center. Her tormented expression pleading with him to right the situation stabbed his gut.

"I'm doing my best, Reagan," he murmured, trying to reassure her she wasn't alone.

Her pupils dilated into black pools that eclipsed all but traces of her expressive emerald, green irises. Her gaze held him mesmerized, moving from one eye to the other. Neither of them moved or broke the trance.

Reagan caught him off guard when she stood on her tiptoes, slid her arms around his neck and gently pulled him to her, tentatively brushing her lips lightly across his. As he closed the tenuous gap between them, a surge of heat and an urgent need spread through him with a yearning he hadn't felt in a long time. His moral compass screamed it was a really bad idea, but he couldn't help but open his mouth to meet her tongue with passion and deepen the kiss with a level of ferocity that suddenly consumed him. With one hand he pulled her closer to his body, while the other became entwined in her luscious dark hair that felt like spun silk on his fingertips. Her kisses became so intense and demanding, he could barely catch his breath. Desire ignited through his every pore as her hands lightly moved down his neck and rubbed seductively up and down his solid chest. Without warning, she abruptly pulled away. He stared at her cautiously waiting for the regret and awkwardness to hit her, but instead she grabbed his hand and dragged him down the hall to her bedroom. He hadn't seen that coming, but it gave him the break he needed to regain his common sense.

No matter how badly he wanted her, he had to put a stop to it before it went any further. Because of the tumultuous circumstances of their meeting, he had forced himself not to hold any romantic notions about their relationship. But he had to admit that his desire for her had been on the periphery of his mind. Reagan had experienced tremendous loss, and he happened to be the man she had chosen to fill the void. He couldn't deny the palpable chemistry between them. She was beautiful, smart, and sexy, but also emotionally vulnerable. He would not take advantage of the situation. The fact that she had a boyfriend in Chicago was further proof she wasn't thinking clearly. He admonished himself for not pulling away immediately.

As Reagan pulled him through the door and slammed it behind him, Aiden struggled to find the words that would gracefully end the trajectory they were on without destroying her self-esteem. She wasn't thinking this through, and apparently neither was he. With both hands on his chest, she shoved him backward onto the bed, falling on top of him, her mouth seeking and finding his. A guttural groan escaped his throat, but he forced himself to roll over on his side, gently holding her at arm's length. His hand caught hers as she began to unbutton her silk blouse.

"Reagan, we can't …" he said, as he sat up facing her.

She looked confused. "Did I misread our attraction?" she asked, sounding wounded.

Aiden knew he had to tread carefully. All he really wanted to do was breathe in her delicate floral scent, explore the soft crevices of her body, and get lost in her luxurious hair, but that wasn't what she needed.

Reagan scooted to the side of the bed, buttoning her blouse back up, her head down. "I'm sorry. I just assumed …"

Aiden immediately jumped off the bed and knelt on the floor in front of her, linking her fingers with his. He lifted her chin, forcing her to meet his eyes.

"You are one of the most exquisitely beautiful and desirable women I've ever known. I'll admit that I've been drawn to you since the first time we met, but I have refused to let myself think about a sexual relationship because of the emotional land mines you're navigating right now." He stroked her cheek and followed her jawline to her lips.

"B…but?" her voice quivered.

"But … I would be the biggest asshole on the planet. You have suffered some huge traumas. Your emotions are all over the place."

"You would regret sleeping with me?"

"Not a chance, but I'm afraid you would regret sleeping with me, and I couldn't live with that. I want to devour you more than anything, but I have to be sure you're doing it because you want to be with me, not to fill the emptiness consuming you. If your boyfriend were here, I'm afraid you'd feel differently. You don't seem to be the kind of woman who takes sex or cheating lightly."

Her expression became defiant. "First of all, I don't cheat. Tyler and I have never had an agreement to be exclusive. He sees other women. The damn pictures were in the newspaper."

"The newspaper?"

"Society stuff. His family is a pretty big deal, so I guess he is too."

"Ohhhhh."

"And as to your other point, you've never taken sex lightly?" she asked, raising her eyebrows. "Had a one-night stand?"

"Sure I have … but Reagan, you're not a one-night kind of woman." He placed his hands on her cheeks and brushed a soft kiss on her forehead.

She gently broke their connection. "Too bad. I really like you," she said, touching his bottom lip with her fingertips.

"Let's give ourselves some time to figure out just how much that is."

"Will you give me a few minutes?" she asked, falling back on the bed and turning over on her side, almost in a fetal position.

"I'll be in the living room."

When he got to the door, he glanced back. Sunlight beamed through the windows, reflecting deep scarlet highlights dancing across her dark chocolate hair like flames. It was shimmering radiance. He'd been all over the world, but he'd never seen hair color like that.

As he waited by the living room windows watching the wind rustle the tree branches, deep in thought, Reagan came up behind him.

"Ready to get something to eat? It's almost 2," she said with a casual tone that seemed to erase the previous tension.

Before he could answer, they heard a loud pounding on the door.

"Reagan! Are you here?" Mattie yelled, then continued to almost beat the door down.

Aiden threw the door open.

"What's wrong?" he asked, pulling her inside and closing the door behind her.

"I'm fine, but where's Reagan?" Mattie asked frantically. "I've been trying to call her for the past two hours."

Reagan stepped out from behind him. "Right here."

"You scared me to death!" Mattie shouted, hands on hips.

"Aren't you supposed to be at work?" Reagan asked.

"I was, but when the detective called me because he couldn't reach either one of you, I freaked out! What the hell is going on?"

Reagan realized she had left her phone in Aiden's truck, and he had put his cell on silent when they were at the bank. They apologized to Mattie that neither could have heard the calls.

"You said the detective called you. What did he want?" Aiden asked. "We just saw him not long ago."

"When he couldn't get in touch with you guys, he called me. He said the house had been vandalized, but I had no idea it was this bad. He wanted to notify you that the coroner released Nana's body today. I gave him the name of the funeral home you selected so he could contact them to arrange for a pick-up time."

"Thank you," Reagan said. "That should have been me."

"Not to worry, we have an appointment with the funeral director as soon as we can get there."

Reagan turned and looked at Aiden.

"Go ahead," he said. "I'll lock up the house. The detective gave me some yellow crime scene tape to put across the doors to hopefully discourage another break-in. If you want to give me the backpack, I'll take it back to the house and leave it in your room."

Reagan handed it over to him. "Thank you for *everything*," she said.

# Chapter 10

Aiden felt lucky to be alone in the house. It gave him an opportunity to look around without Reagan feeling he was prying more deeply into her personal life. He also needed to make a few calls.

First, he called Detective Kowalski to tell him about the visit from the repairman. He detailed his call to Frank's Electric Repair to verify that Arturo Fuentes did in fact work there but was out of the country on vacation. The detective followed up with his own call to the owner, Frank Sanders, and learned that Arturo was a highly regarded full-time employee, so much so that he was assigned his own company van. Arturo emigrated from Mexico over 20 years ago. He and his wife, who was also an emigrant, received their U.S. citizenship eight years prior. Arturo had bragged to his co-workers for months about his upcoming trip to Mexico for his cousin's wedding, so there was no doubt in the owner's mind that Arturo left the country with his wife and two children.

Detective Kowalski suggested that whoever was interested in the house stole the truck and used it as a cover. The thief must have found Arturo's information on the registration in the glove compartment. To confirm that the man who came to the house was not Arturo Fuentes, the detective texted a copy of his driver's license to Aiden. It was not.

Aiden went back to Reagan's room and sat down on the bed. He needed some quiet time to mull everything over. Grabbing the backpack, he decided to give the papers another glance. He wasn't sure what he was looking for, but he felt he had to get a better feel for the family history to try to make sense of what was happening. The gems had obviously been tucked in the AC for a long time. Whoever might have known about them was a big unknown but almost certainly had ties to the family's past. Aiden strongly believed that the owners of the jewelry Reagan played dress-up with as a child had no idea of the true value. There had to be a connection somewhere.

Separating the papers into piles by category of documents, he picked up the legal ones and sorted them by year chronologically. The oldest document was a birth certificate for Fiona Aileen Burke, who was born on February 17, 1946. Next was the marriage certificate of Fiona to Daniel D. Moran on June 6, 1964. She was 18 years old at the time; he was 26. Claire Renee Moran, Reagan's mother, was born two years later, July 10, 1966. The marriage certificate for Claire and Stuart Alan Asher was dated November 4, 1986. There was no birth certificate for Reagan, but a confirmation certificate said she was born May 1, 1987.

Aiden rubbed his chin. "Well, well. I wonder if Reagan knows she was a preemie … or maybe that was the reason for the marriage."

*Could that be why the marriage didn't last? If Claire married the man who got her pregnant, and she never loved him, that could make for a miserable life,* he reasoned. It would help explain a lot of the heartache in the family but not the jewels.

Nothing else stuck out in the papers, so he headed to the office. Reagan had mentioned there were pictures in the desk that she wanted to go through later. Aiden wanted to take a few minutes to see if anything in the photos jumped out at him.

He found the torn picture of the teenage boy from the safe deposit box lying in the center of the desk. He wasn't sure whether it being kept in a secure location held any significance, but he wanted to find out. In the bottom left drawer were two photo boxes, one marked "Claire" and the other "Reagan." He began with Reagan's.

What an adorable child Reagan had been, he thought smiling to himself. Her hair had lightened a little over the years from her childhood jet black to a dark chocolate with scarlet highlights. There were pictures of Reagan with her mother and father, but they all seemed posed, completely opposite from the silly and hammed-up images of his own family.

Claire had been a lovely child too, with long, curly bright red hair like Fiona's. She appeared to have been a happy kid, because she grinned and confidently posed in all the pictures from toddler age through her high school years.

He thumbed through the school pictures kids usually exchange trying to find the same boy. A photo of Claire with a Middle Eastern boy and girl caught his eye. They sat on three separate swings in a park or maybe a school yard, hands stretched out and clasped, Claire in the middle. They appeared to be in their mid-teens. There were numerous pictures chronicling the three of them through their teenage years at sporting events, outdoor activities, and high school graduation festivities. In several of the pictures, Claire stood a bit closer or had her arms locked with the teenage boy. Curiosity grew as he searched for names. He found a message on the back of one picture. Claire was all smiles posed in the middle while the boy and girl each kissed her cheeks. "Me with Darius and Rosana. Love Forever!"

Aiden sat back in his chair and studied the pictures. Darius and Rosana had similar facial characteristics and were probably brother and sister. They both had a darker tan skin tone. He thought about Reagan's comments about her grandfather being a bigot. He compared all the pictures of Darius to the photo of the boy they found in the safe deposit box. Although the features were definitely similar, the water damage made it impossible to be sure if they were the same boy, but what were the chances that a prejudiced father would allow his daughter to have more than two Middle Eastern friends? *What did "love forever" mean? Were they all best friends, or had Claire been in love with the teenage boy?*

As he compared the pictures of Darius and the mystery boy, he glanced at a framed picture of Reagan on the wall. It was one of those professional pictures, with elaborate poses and props, that high school students have taken their senior year. Reagan sat on an ivory laced-iron bench under a dogwood tree with white blooms, sun beams highlighting the scarlet red in her long dark hair. Her emerald eyes sparkled, and her full, mauve-colored lips held a lighthearted smile. As he stared at the picture, something nagged at him. He held up a picture of Claire to Reagan's photo on the wall. Except for the eye color, they looked nothing alike. Not even their stature. Claire was petite and curvy, while Reagan was tall and slim.

*Who does she look like?* he asked himself. He quickly pulled out one of the photos with Reagan's dad. As a young man, Stuart Asher had boy-next-door good looks with his golden blond hair, deep-set hazel eyes, and angular face. No visible resemblance to Reagan whatsoever. *How does a blond-haired dad and a red-haired mom have a child with dark chocolate hair?* He didn't know much about genetics, but it didn't seem to fit.

A wild idea popped in his head. Holding a picture of Darius to Reagan's, he swallowed hard when he began noticing similarities. The skin coloring was wrong, so was the contrast of her green eyes to his brown. What was remarkable were the similarities of the tall and slim body types, almond-shaped eyes, full wide mouths, straight classic noses, and the structure of their cheekbones. His thoughts ran rampant. *Could Darius possibly be Reagan's father? Two conflicting cultures their parents would never accept? Was Stuart a clueless patsy or did he willingly come to Claire's rescue? Maybe Stuart and Claire Asher could no longer live with the lie, resulting in divorce and eventually Claire's suicide. It would certainly explain her father's indifference and her mother's depression. Stuart may not have even known until Reagan was born.*

It was a can of worms he had no right to open even if it were true. Could Reagan have a family somewhere she knew nothing about? Would she hate him for suggesting the whole scenario and destroying everything she thought she knew about her family? More than likely, it was his imagination run amok.

"Besides, they always shoot the messenger," he mumbled to himself. "And what does this have to do with the jewels?" His cell rang.

# Chapter 11

The morning sun had disappeared and was replaced by low-hanging gray clouds. Ice pellets began to ping off the windshield as Reagan and Mattie climbed into Mattie's metallic blue Lexus SUV.

"I'll drive," Reagan offered, making her way to the driver's side. "It will give me something to do, and you can give me the scoop on Aiden."

Mattie laughed. "You mean besides the fact that he's hot as hell? I dearly love him like a brother. On the rare occasions he's on leave, he spends most of his time with us. He never wants to make extra work for me while he's here, so he helps clean the house, offers to cook, grocery shops while we're at work ... even babysits Ellie so Josh and I can go out on dates. Ellie adores him. He spoils her worse than her grandparents."

Reagan nervously maneuvered her way out of the neighborhood, keeping an eye out for the white electric repair van while also trying to focus on the worsening weather that now had sleet collecting on the wipers and covering the roadway.

"What about his love life?" Reagan risked a quick glance at her friend.

"I'll share as much as I know, but just remember you've got a great guy of your own at home."

"Mattie ..."

"No current girlfriend. He was engaged several years back. I'm not sure who broke it off, but he's never said an unkind word about her. She was gorgeous, rich, and a well-educated Southern belle. Never had a broken fingernail or a hair out of place. Josh and I only met her a couple of times, and as much as I wanted to hate her perfect ass, I couldn't. She was a real sweetheart. As far as I know, there hasn't been anyone else. Why are you so interested?"

"Aiden has been a huge support for me in dealing with the aftermath of Nana's death. And he seems to genuinely care. I know you asked him to be there while I did the interview with the detective, but he didn't have to get involved with everything else. As wild as it sounds, I feel like we've known each other for years."

"Probably because you've heard us talk about him for the past 10 years. I'll admit a man that handsome and sincere is hard to resist. Josh and I could tell you guys had an instant chemistry. Just be careful. He does have his jerky moments. Not to mention, he'll be traipsing all over the world for God knows how much of his time with that new job he's so excited about. Besides, you are dealing with a lot of shit right now, and I hate to say it, but your modus operandi is to shove everything down deep and pretend it's not there. When it finally makes its way to the surface, you totally shut down. According to Josh, Aiden's never been a player, but he's had his share of women. I can't help but worry that someone I love will get hurt."

"Me or him?"

"Either. Both." Mattie shrugged.

"I appreciate your concern, but I could really use his help."

"All righty then. I'll back off."

After a trip to the drive-through at McDonald's, Reagan was ready to face the funeral arrangements. It crossed her mind that she had promised Tyler she would let him help, but there was nothing she could do at that point. She would call him later and explain. Besides, having him there after what happened with Aiden would be beyond awkward. Her feelings were a jumbled mess, and she didn't feel like trying to dissect them.

Bromberg Funeral Home was a white, two-story colonial-style house set back off the road on a quiet street at the edge of Lancashire. Reagan pulled into the front parking lot, which was covered with ice and newly fallen snow. The lot was empty except for one car parked directly in front of the building.

"Park as close to the door as you can," Mattie said. "I forgot my boots today."

Just as Reagan veered left through the parking lot toward the building, "Bam!" They were rammed from behind with a force that sent the car sliding. The seatbelt tightened around Reagan's shoulder, slamming her head hard against the headrest, while Mattie screamed at the top of her lungs and tried uselessly to grab the dashboard. Reagan, staving off panic, instinctively turned the wheel in the direction they were moving until they finally stopped about 40 feet away from the impact, facing toward the black van that hit them.

"Oh, God! Are you all right?" Reagan asked, frantically reaching for Mattie's arm.

"Scared the crap out of me, but I think I'm fine. My limbs seem to still be intact," she said as she flailed her arms around. "Who's the idiot that hit us?"

Reagan fumbled to unlatch her seat belt and took a deep breath to compose herself. "Not sure. They probably made that turn into the driveway too fast and slid into us when they tried to apply their brakes. There's a layer of ice under the snow. I'll go find out if anyone is hurt. It's probably one of the funeral home vans. Are you sure you aren't hurt?"

"Just shook up. I'll call the police to make an accident report," Mattie said, pulling her cell out of her handbag. "They didn't hit hard enough to deploy the air bags, so maybe the car will still drive."

After taking a couple of moments to calm her nerves, Reagan got out of the car and carefully walked toward the van. The sleet had turned to large snowflakes that were coming down so hard the windshield of the black van was almost covered, making it impossible to see the occupants. When she reached the driver's window, there was no one in the front seat. She assumed they must have gone to the back to check their cargo, which she hoped didn't involve a toppled-over coffin with a dead body. A shiver went up her spine at the thought.

When she reached the back of the van, the tinted rear doors windows made it impossible for her to see inside, so she knocked.

"Hello. Anybody in there? Are you hurt?" Receiving no response, she put her ear to the glass. Nothing. The driver had disappeared into thin air. She decided to go back to the car to get paper and pen to write down the tag number, but just as she turned to leave, she heard the backdoor latch click open.

"Wanted to make sure you were ..." Reagan's words were stopped short when a gloved hand shot out of the door and painfully clasped her forearm. Before she could respond or even get a look at him, a dark cloth sack was slid over her head, drowning her in darkness. Panicking, she could barely comprehend what was happening. As she gasped for air and reached up to remove whatever was covering her face, rough hands grabbed her around the waist and threw her hard against the side of the van. Her right cheekbone smashed against frigid metal while her hands were pulled tightly behind her back. When the shock subsided enough for her to put two coherent thoughts together, she realized someone was trying to abduct her.

She let out a piercing scream and struggled to free her hands while kicking blindly at her attacker. Her tight pencil skirt and the ice under her boots made maneuvering difficult, but she fought frantically to get away. As one of her heals slipped out from under her, it forced her weight to drop, loosening her right hand from his grip. Taking advantage of the brief reprieve, she swung her arm up and over her shoulder in an attempt to scratch his eyes, but her fingers clutched only a knit face mask instead of bare skin. Not to be deterred, she continued to claw at his face until two of her fingers slipped through a hole into wetness. Ignoring the churn in her stomach from the realization she was touching the monster's saliva, she dug both fingernails into his lips until she heard his angry groan, and his head yanked out of her reach.

His arm tightened around her waist, pulling her snug against his chest. His hot breath on her neck sent cold shivers down her spine.

"You bitch! Stop struggling before I break your arm," the man threatened in a thick accent.

"Let me go, you bastard!" she yelled, squirming to get loose. She slammed her head backward with all her might, trying to smash his nose, but the shift of her weight threw them off balance, and they fell hard on to the icy pavement. A sharp pain seared through her elbow. Her attacker quickly flipped her over facedown, securing her with a knee in her back and one hand wrapped around her neck. Melted ice seeped through the cloth over her head and burned her cheek as she gasped for air. Oh, God, please don't let me die, she prayed, tears stinging her eyes.

"Move again and I will snap your neck!" he said between clinched teeth.

"Not in this lifetime, you asshole!" It was Mattie's voice, flooding Reagan with hope. She wasn't alone.

Reagan was unable to see, but she could hear. A loud "crack," groaning, scuffling, and then her neck was free from the man's clutches. She sucked in a deep breath, rolled over on her back, and yanked the hood off. It took a few seconds to adjust to the light, but when she did, she wasn't sure if she should laugh or cry. Mattie had a flashlight in one hand and Josh's aluminum racquetball racquet in the other. Alternating hands, she was beating her attacker, who wore a black ski mask. Somehow, Mattie had caught him by surprise, gaining the advantage. Reagan's captor was lying on the ground, hands over his face to protect himself, while Mattie stood over him swinging her weapons, one after the other.

Reagan shakily reached up to clasp the door handle of the van to help pull herself to her feet. Mattie quickly glanced over to make sure she was able to stand. That small distraction allowed the masked man to grab the end of the racket and jerk it loose from her grip. Reagan promptly wrapped her fingers around Mattie's and maneuvered her out of the man's reach before he could strike her.

Anger outweighing her common sense, Mattie struggled to break loose. "Let me go, Reagan. I'm going to kill that son of a bitch! His balls are going to be stuck so far down his throat, he'll have to shit them out to ever see them again!" The man literally growled at her as he tried to stand but, lucky for them, slipped back down on his butt.

"We're leaving now! He may be armed!" Reagan yelled and pointed Mattie in the direction of the building.

"Aaaah!" Mattie screeched in frustration.

They ran toward the funeral home, hand in hand, barely able to maintain traction on the snow and ice. When they heard the van rev to life, they increased their speed. A quick glance confirmed the van was headed toward them, not away. It was critical to make it to the steps of the porch just beyond the curb or he would run them down. An older gray Cadillac was parked near the door. Reagan prayed someone was inside who could help them until the police arrived.

Pumped with panic and adrenalin, they had just reached the Cadillac when the van drew close on their heels.

"Jump on the car," Reagan screamed at a wide-eyed Mattie.

Still clutching Reagan's left hand, Mattie dipped her chin in confirmation. With the help of their forward motion, Reagan swung Mattie around in front of her giving her the momentum she needed to dive across the hood of the car, Reagan following close behind. They easily glided across the snow-covered metal and landed in a pile of limbs on the opposite side, the van barely missing them as it scraped along the side of the car, then crashed into the office sign. Reagan scrambled to her feet and heaved Mattie up by her coat. There was no time to check for injuries. As the van backed up, they ran full speed up the stairs and burst through the front door.

Inside, Reagan suddenly stopped, momentarily stunned as the overwhelming floral scent transported her back to another terrifying time, another emotionally crippling funeral. Her mother lying peacefully in a white satin bed where she would sleep for eternity with not one bothersome thought for the daughter she left behind.

"Reagan!" Mattie startled her out of her memory. "We've got to get moving. I think I saw a gun."

"S…s…sorry." She rubbed her face and shook it off.

Mattie flung open the first door. It was an empty office. They ran farther down the hall, past viewing rooms and a small chapel until they found themselves in a reception area.

"Can I help you?" asked a gentle male voice.

Reagan clutched her chest. When she turned around, a middle-aged man in a tweed sport coat was smiling at them.

"Mr. Bromberg?" Mattie cried out.

"I am. And you both appear to be in distress," he said calmly. Reagan figured he was used to distraught people coming through his doors every day, just not for the same reason.

"A man in a black van tried to run us down," Mattie said frantically. "He sideswiped the car out front and ran over your sign. I called the police, but they haven't come … I mean it was just for an accident, but that guy is dangerous."

They heard a door open and slammed closed.

"My Lord. Let's get to my office immediately," Mr. Bromberg said, motioning the way.

"But he has a gun," Reagan said.

"We can lock the door, and I have outdoor cameras to watch for the police."

They were relieved when it turned out to be a police officer at the front door responding to the accident. The black van had disappeared, but the evidence remained in the banged-up Cadillac and the splintered sign.

# Chapter 12

Reagan listened patiently as Mattie gave her account of the events to the responding officers. Mattie's first call, while Reagan was on her way to the van, was to notify the police about the accident. The second call had been to Josh to tell him what happened and let him know they might need a ride home if the car wouldn't start. It didn't. While Josh was lecturing Mattie on how to drive on ice (she hadn't gotten around to telling him she wasn't behind the wheel), she turned on the windshield wipers to clear the snow so she could keep an eye on Reagan. That's when she saw a man push Reagan against the side of the van. At first, Mattie thought she might be hallucinating, maybe even in shock, but a second look assured her that what she saw was real. Springing into action, she searched the car for a potential weapon, while Josh, oblivious to the danger, continued to talk to dead air. The only items of possible use were a heavy-duty flashlight in the console and Josh's racquetball racket in the backseat. By that time, she could hear Reagan screaming. Mattie threw down her phone and jumped out of the car, totally forgetting about Josh.

One of the officers called an ambulance to have Reagan and Mattie checked out. The EMT's arrived within 10 minutes. Reagan had minor injuries: a badly scraped elbow, bruises on her arms, neck and back, and a swollen cheek. Luckily, her knit hat had helped protect her head. Mattie had a few scratches from colliding with the hood ornament when she slid over the top of the Cadillac. Both declined to go to the local hospital emergency room for more thorough exams.

Reports were filled out, pictures taken, paint chips collected, and DNA swabbed from Reagan's fingernails and neck. Her blood ran cold at the very thought of the man's skin under her fingernails and the feel of his hands on her body.

When Detective Kowalski pulled up in his Charger, the CSI team were already in the process of packing up. He spent a few minutes reviewing the evidence and shaking his head. Reagan knew from his scowl as he walked toward them that she was about to receive a tongue-lashing. When he stopped in front of her, he crossed his arms across his chest.

"This can't be a coincidence. What are you not telling me, Ms. Asher? What is this really about? Who are these people and what do they want from you?"

Reagan's defenses immediately went up. She didn't like his condescending tone or the fact that he didn't bother to ask if she or Mattie were physically okay.

"Detective Kowalski, I assure you that if I knew who these people were, you'd be the first to know. What do they want from me? I have no idea. I do know that a black van rear-ended us. We came here to make funeral arrangements for my grandmother. It was sleeting and snowing, and it's not unusual to have a fender bender in this kind of weather, so no red flags went up. I assumed the van belonged to the funeral home. As I told the officers, our attacker wore a ski mask, and he had a foreign accent."

"Was it the same man who came to Mrs. Moran's home presenting himself to be Arturo Fuentes?" he asked.

"I don't think so. The vans were different colors, and this man was taller and seemed a bit younger, though I never got a look at anything other than a little skin on his neck."

Mattie interrupted, coming to her defense. "Reagan is the victim here. Find out who is after her and who killed her grandmother! That's your job, not hers!"

"I'm trying to do just that, Mrs. Rannell, but I have to have all the facts to do it properly."

A pang of guilt hit Reagan. She was keeping valuable information from the man, but she couldn't bring herself to reveal it yet.

"Josh is here," Mattie said, nodding toward his car as it entered the parking lot. Reagan sighed in relief. "He doesn't look happy. I'd better go explain before he comes unglued. I'll stop by my SUV and grab our handbags. See you in a few." Mattie rushed off to do damage control.

"If you don't mind, Detective, I have a splitting headache and every inch of my body aches. You can call me tomorrow. I'm leaving," Reagan declared.

As she walked away, the detective called after her. "Ms. Asher." She stopped and turned to face him. "It would be easier to find your grandmother's killer if I didn't have one hand tied behind my back."

Her face fell as his words hit their mark.

Back at the Rannell home, Aiden was impatiently pacing the kitchen. Reagan observed that both men's faces were flushed as she and Mattie recounted the entire events of the afternoon.

Reagan wasn't sure how long Aiden would let her keep her secret, especially now that his family was also at risk. "Where's Ellie?" she asked.

"I called and arranged for her to go home with her best friend Megan," Josh said, grabbing a beer out of the wine and beer cooler under the counter. "I'm supposed to pick her up around 7. After considering the escalation of this situation, I think we should ask if she can stay for a few nights. We're all pretty shook up right now. Ellie will surely pick up on the tension."

"Agreed," said Mattie. "It was hard enough for her to learn about Nana's death, and I don't want to risk any more trauma. Bree and Camden Yeager, Megan's parents, are good friends of ours. They won't mind. We've kept Megan many times while Bree and Cam were on vacation or wanted a night out. They've done the same for us. I'm going upstairs to change and give them a call."

"As soon as I get moved into my new condo, you'll have me as an option too," Aiden called after her.

"Reagan, would you like a glass of wine or a stiff drink?" Josh asked.

"I'll get it. And if you guys don't mind, I'm going to take myself and my glass upstairs to shower and change clothes. I can't wait to get that man's scent off of me." The thought made her skin prick.

"I made some calls on your behalf today. I'll walk up with you and give you an update," Aiden said, getting up from his stool.

Reagan sat on the bed in the guest room and put her head in her hands. "I never meant to bring this chaos and danger to Mattie and Josh. For God's sake, they can't even bring Ellie home."

Aiden sat next to her. "It's not your fault."

"Of course it is. If I had let you call the police when we first discovered those gems, none of this would have happened."

"We still don't know for sure if they are after the jewels, but if they are, they must think you know something about them."

"I can't stay here. I'm putting all of you in danger. It's best if I go to a motel tonight."

"Not tonight. Please. The idiot who attacked you today was an amateur. Your attempted kidnapping is already on the news. It won't be long before the reporters make the connection between you and the murder of your grandmother. There will probably be reporters camped out at your grandmother's home by morning."

"What makes you think the guy's an amateur?"

"I'm guessing he followed you from your grandmother's house, saw an opportunity to grab you in a deserted parking lot and took it. He threw a bag over your head but didn't bother to put a gag in your mouth. A professional would've brought a drug to knock you out, some zip ties to bind your hands and feet, and wouldn't have done it in front of a witness. You said his skin was under your fingernails. If he's in the system, the police should know who he is pretty quick."

"Because the guy didn't have experience at kidnapping, I don't have a right to be scared out of my mind?"

"Hell, no! Inexperienced people can often be more dangerous because they're unpredictable and easily panicked. I don't want you to overreact and put yourself in more danger. They aren't likely to try anything with the police and reporters circling this attempted kidnapping story. We have an appointment with the appraiser tomorrow at noon. At least stay tonight. Once we're sure about the authenticity of the jewels, we need to give that information to the police. They need all the tools available to find those guys. You don't want to drag your grandmother's memory through this, but that's our only option. I won't put my family in the crosshairs of those thugs. If you decide to go to a hotel, I'll go with you. You are not going to be left alone until this is resolved."

She squeezed his hand. "You're bossy."

"Just worried about everyone's safety."

"Thank you. You've been beyond patient with me."

"No problem." He stood up and pulled her to her feet. "Now, I'll let you get cleaned up. Pizza sound good?"

"Fine with me. I'm almost too tired to eat, but I'll feel better once I get a hot shower. Every time I think of that man's hands on me I ..."

Aiden drew her to his chest, wrapping her in his arms. "Shhh. You're safe now. Try to put it out of your mind. I'll call our order in. Hopefully, Mattie and Josh don't insist on something weird like pineapple pesto with tofu," he laughed.

With a shuddering breath, she whispered, "Thank you." She regretted the absence of his embrace the moment he released her and walked out the door.

# Chapter 13

When Aiden returned to the kitchen, he found Josh sitting alone at the breakfast bar, his face in his hands. Aiden knew Josh was totally bewildered, unable to make sense of what had happened to Reagan and his wife. Even though Aiden didn't have any idea who was behind the break-ins and attacks on Reagan, he had an excellent idea of the why, and he couldn't help but feel responsible. Keeping his brother in the dark about the jewels he and Reagan had found put them all in a dangerous situation. If he had given Josh a heads-up, they both could have figured out an effective way of keeping everyone safe. Josh must be livid, and Aiden held himself accountable for what had happened to Mattie and Reagan. As soon as Reagan got downstairs, he would come clean to Josh and Mattie about everything. His brother had a right to know, especially now that it affected the life of his family.

Aiden put his hand affectionately on Josh's shoulder. "How ya holding up, buddy?"

Josh slowly lifted his head, his eyes pleading with Aiden and desperation in his voice. "What the hell's going on? I don't understand any of this shit. Why would someone want to kidnap Reagan or try to run her down? I realized he was aiming for Mattie too, but it makes more sense that Reagan was the intended target. Is he going to make another attempt? Does he know Reagan's staying here? Where we live?" He grabbed Aiden's forearm in a vise grip. "I'm scared out of my fucking mind for my family ... and that includes Reagan, but bro ..."

Aiden sat down beside him, trying to keep his voice calm. "Where's Mattie?"

"She took some clothes to Ellie. Bree and Cam agreed to let her spend a few days with them until we sort all this shit out." He took a swig of beer. When he turned back to Aiden, his face was etched in pain. Josh made no attempt to mask his emotions, which was rare. "I hate sending my baby girl away, but I don't know what else to do.

We want to help Reagan, but we're also concerned about protecting Ellie."

"Reagan wants to move to a hotel tomorrow. I talked her out of going tonight. The thought of her driving around alone looking for a place to stay after what she's been through today is ludicrous, but if you think it's for the best, I'll go with her."

"My wife and baby have to come first. We're not going to abandon Reagan, but we have to figure out the best way to handle this."

"Abandoning who?" Mattie said, as she came in from the garage. "You'd better not be talking about Reagan, because she's like family. We're all she's got."

"What's going on? Has something else happened?" Reagan asked, taking a seat across from Aiden.

"We were just …" Mattie was interrupted when someone's cell phone rang. "Not my ring tone."

"It's mine." Reagan said. "Mattie, it's right behind you on the counter. Mind handing it to me?"

"Course not," Mattie said. When she reached behind her back to grab Reagan's leather bag, it slipped from her hands and flipped upside-down, spilling the contents on the kitchen floor.

"Sorry, Reagan. I'm such a klutz." Mattie bent down to pick up the assorted items as Reagan rushed around the breakfast bar to help. Aiden caught her panicked expression as she tried to snatch the envelope out of Mattie's hand.

"No worries, I've got it," Mattie said, but when she attempted to put the envelope back into Reagan's handbag, the flap opened and the jewels tumbled to the floor. Aiden watched Josh's wide eyes track the black pearl rolling toward him, until he caught it with the toe of his shoe.

"What's this?" Josh asked, scooping it up and turning it over in his palm. He held it up to the light, then turned his attention to Reagan. "I've seen something similar before but can't remember where."

Reagan's face turned bright pink, and she looked tongue-tied. Mattie calmly picked up the sapphire necklace and the single diamond that landed under a chair and held them in each of her hands. Josh walked over to her to inspect the jewels, then eyed Reagan quizzically.

"What the hell is this, Reagan?" Josh asked, taking the diamond from Mattie's open palm and holding it in front of her face. Reagan looked like a doe caught in the sights of a hunter's rifle. This was exactly what Aiden had feared. He rubbed his hand down his face and silently swore at the ceiling. Josh would never forgive him.

Mattie quickly came to her defense. "This necklace is part of Reagan's 'princess jewelry' collection. Ellie plays with it all the time. She's brought it home a bunch of times. Don't you recognize it? I've never seen the other two pieces, though," she said, scrutinizing the gems in Josh's hand. "Probably came out of one of the settings. They're pretty." She picked up the diamond. "This almost looks real."

"Yeah, it does," Josh said, narrowing his eyes. Reagan and Aiden exchanged looks.

He couldn't stay silent any longer. "That's because they probably are genuine," Aiden breathed.

"What are you talking about?" Mattie laughed. "Don't be ridiculous. Reagan and I played with this necklace and many other similar pieces of jewelry our whole childhood. At one point, there was a ruby and rhinestone necklace like this one, but we lost it at a sleepover at a friend's birthday party. We suspected she stole it, but Nana told us not to worry about it, because there were plenty of other pieces for us to play with. It wasn't worth ruining a friendship over."

The doorbell chimed.

"That's the pizza. I'll get it. You guys get settled. I have a feeling it's going to be a long discussion," Aiden said, knowing the brief reprieve would give him a chance to get his thoughts together.

They sat at the table with paper plates, pizza, and beer, the diamond, pearl, and necklace in the center of everything.

Aiden began with the Saturday he took Ellie to the birthday party. He explained what happened when he took the ring to the jewelry store. Mattie remembered him telling her that Ellie had taken the ring without permission from Nana. Aiden went on to explain that once Nana had assured him the ring had no value, he had forgotten about it … until she was murdered. Mattie and Josh sat in stunned silence, as Aiden brought them up to date on the events related to the gems.

"What the fuck, Aiden?" Josh jumped up, paced around the kitchen, kneading his scalp.

"I know. I know." Aiden pinched the bridge of his nose.

"It's my fault, not Aiden's. I should have told you guys from the beginning. I begged him not to say anything until we knew for sure what we were dealing with," Reagan said, grabbing Mattie's hand. "It never occurred to me that someone would actually come after me."

"You're my fuckin' brother, Aiden."

"Josh, the gems haven't even been authenticated. We won't know for sure until we get these samples appraised tomorrow." Aiden knew his attempt to justify his actions was lame.

"That's bullshit, and you know it. A jeweler already told you the ring was genuine, which is a good indication all the other supposed 'princess jewelry' is real too. And I'd say it's a good assumption that no one would hide fake diamonds and pearls in an HVAC unit for the hell of it."

Aiden nervously ran his hands through his hair. He'd screwed up, and he knew it. For once in his life, he had put compassion over common sense, and it had backfired on him. He was a Seal for God's sake, and there was no excuse for it. "You're right. It's my mistake. Should have told you immediately."

"Please forgive me," Reagan pleaded. "Aiden wanted to call the police right away and tell you both. I begged him not to. I … I didn't want to believe anyone in my family could be involved in this. Now, I don't know, and you're all in jeopardy." Aiden read the panic in her eyes. She was truly terrified for their lives and also that she might have lost the only remaining family she could count on.

"Don't call the detective until you talk to the appraiser," Mattie declared.

Everyone turned to her in surprise.

"Yeah. You should have told us, but at this point what difference does it make to wait one more day? Nana couldn't have done this," Mattie said with assurance. "I mean really … the woman washed and reused paper plates. Does that sound like someone who was sitting on millions of dollars in jewels?" Josh looked skeptical, his faith in Nana obviously not as solid as Mattie's.

"What time are you supposed to meet with the appraiser?" Josh asked with irritation.

"Tomorrow at noon," Aiden confirmed.

"Reagan and I have an appointment at the funeral home tomorrow at 9," Mattie said. "Aiden can pick Reagan up there, and you guys can make it to your appointment. When you get back, we'll decided what to tell the detective. Everyone agree?" she asked in her usual take-charge way.

"Whatever you want, Josh. It's your call," Aiden said, intentionally directing his response to his brother. "I'll call the detective now if you think it's best."

Josh blew out a breath and shook his head. "I hate this shit!" He kneaded his temples. Finally, his face fell in resignation. "Okay. I'll drop Reagan and Mattie off at the funeral home. Afterwards, you can pick up Reagan, and I'll take Mattie to work. But let's get one thing straight. Neither of them is ever left alone. Period."

"Don't you think that's a little extreme?" Mattie asked.

"Take it or leave it. Or I call Detective Kowalski myself right fuckin' now!"

Everyone agreed.

For the rest of the evening, Mattie sat in the lounge chair cuddled on Josh's lap, while Reagan and Aiden sat on the sofa. They watched a series of comedy shows until Mattie couldn't keep her eyes open, and she and Josh went to bed.

When Aiden heard Reagan's soft breathing, he realized he was the only one watching an old episode of *Seinfeld*. He turned off the television and gingerly picked her up. She woke up in his arms as he ascended the stairs.

"I can walk," she said sleepily.

"Why? When you've already got a ride?" he replied. She put her head against his shoulder and shut her eyes.

Aiden gently placed Reagan on the bed, her head settling into a fluffy down pillow. As he tucked a blanket around her, dark eyelashes fluttered open and deep green pools captured his gaze.

"Sleep tight, Reagan," he whispered, kissing her on the tip of her nose.

"Stay with me," she answered softly. "Please don't leave me alone."

He stood frozen, his conscience battling his heart. It was wrong on so many levels. She was scared. Insecure. Lonely. Confused. All the ingredients that led to bad decisions and lots of regret. He couldn't trust himself with her. The chemistry between them was insane. *Maybe I could just lie down until she falls asleep.*

"Just for a few minutes," he tentatively agreed, crawling on the bed and snuggling against her.

After a few minutes, she turned over to face him, running her fingertips lightly over the stubble on his chin. "Cuddling wasn't exactly what I had in mind. Can't we lose ourselves for one night?" Her eyes pleaded. "I really like you, Aiden. And I trust you. And ... I don't want to feel numb anymore."

He drank in her exquisite face, enticing lips, alluring eyes, and succumbed. His resolve broken; all vestiges of chivalry gone the second his lips gently met hers. He was spellbound. Each kiss became deeper, more fervid. Electrical currents pulsed through every fiber of his skin as her fingers explored his body and he caressed hers. Intoxicated from her essence, dizzy from her natural fragrance, he had only one desire, to be closer to her. When he tugged off his clothes as she shed hers, they were barely able to keep their hands off each other. It was as if they feared the invisible twine tethering them might somehow break if either let go for even a second. They quickly became entangled in an intimate reverie, a desire that consumed them. The ecstasy and total abandon left Aiden dazed and completely mystified how he could be so completely enthralled by a woman he had just met.

# Chapter 14

Reagan awoke with a start, disoriented. It took a few seconds to get her bearings, but the warm nestling against her back awakened the memory of the most intimate and intense moments of her life. His even breathing against her neck made her smile. She wondered if it had been the same for him.

She lifted her head to read the digits on the clock radio on the bedside table … 6:14. Aiden stirred. Warm lips lightly kissed across her shoulders. His firm hand slid around her waist, pulling her tighter against his chest. She released a long sigh.

"Good morning, princess," he whispered in her ear.

"Princess?"

"Regal. Classy. Graceful. Beautiful." He kissed her neck lightly with each pronouncement. "Besides, you're the only woman I've ever met who owns a tiara."

She chuckled and turned over to face him. "My dad used to call me that too, for the very same reason. I haven't been anyone's princess in a long time."

"Would you prefer I not?" He lightly nuzzled her ear lobe.

She grinned. "It's okay. I like reclaiming my title."

"How'd you sleep?"

"Wonderfully, when I was finally able to sleep." Her face flushed.

He snickered against her hair. "I hope you aren't complaining. You'll crush my ego."

"Hardly. Last night was amazing, but I need to shower and get dressed. You should get back to your room before Mattie wakes up."

"Are you sure about that?" he cooed.

Thirty minutes later, Reagan kissed Aiden at the door and watched him walk down the hall. He met Josh coming out of the master bedroom. Reagan ducked back in her room but left the door cracked open enough to hear their exchange. Sure, it was eavesdropping, but she couldn't help wondering what Josh thought about them sleeping together.

"The walk of shame, huh? Thought those days were over," Josh grinned, patting Aiden on the back.

"Very funny. You the bed-check police?"

"Not me. It's Mama Bear you have to worry about," Josh said, motioning his thumb over his shoulder. "And don't tell her I said that. She won't appreciate my humor."

Aiden shook his head. "Then don't tell her."

"Mattie has radar. She'll figure it out after one look at Reagan. Those two have a psychic connection. It's creepy sometimes."

"For my sake, I hope not. I'll see you downstairs. Going to grab a quick shower."

Josh put his hand on Aiden's arm to stop him and spoke with concern in his voice. "Aiden, you know I love Reagan to death, and she's like family to us, but believe it or not, it's you I'm worried about. She's just about everything a guy could want in a woman, but seriously, man … are you sure you know what you're doing? She has a boyfriend in Chicago."

Aiden shrugged off Josh's hand. "Maybe not for long. Besides, she said it wasn't exclusive."

"Don't want to see you get hurt," Josh said, lowering his voice.

Reagan strained to hear.

"Why do you assume it'll be me, little brother?"

"I'm not saying Tyler won't get hurt too. It's just that … well … Reagan seems to have trouble with commitment. I've never known her to be in a relationship for more than a few months, and some of those guys were pretty destroyed. She's always the one to break it off. Mattie says she's afraid to lose someone else she cares about, so she avoids getting too close. Don't get me wrong, I want her to find happiness, but I don't want you to become a casualty if she's not ready. And suppose it does work out? You're going to hop on a plane and be out of the country for eight to ten months of the year with your new job. Just another person she cares about leaving her to cope with all this shit by herself. You need to think this through, man, because I'm not seeing a good ending for anyone."

Reagan felt an invisible punch to her gut. It wasn't as if Mattie hadn't said the same thing to her. What stung the most was that Josh believed he had to warn Aiden that she wasn't a woman he could count on long term. Throw in the probability that Tyler would consider her a cheater, and she looked like a complete floozy … not marriage material. *Maybe he's right. What exactly am I doing?*

Swallowing down the hurt, she closed the door, not waiting to hear Aiden's answer.

From the first moment they met, Reagan believed Tyler had the potential to be "the one." He was smart, handsome, sophisticated, and well established in his career. Despite his father being an obscenely wealthy New York investment banker, she admired Tyler for being a success based on his own merits. If he found out about last night with Aiden, she knew in her heart that he would be devastated.

She marveled that she could be attracted to two completely different types of men. With Tyler, it had been an immediate physical attraction. With Aiden, it had been an instant mental one, though she couldn't deny his rugged physical appeal. Aiden had a genuineness about him. She felt as if she had known him all her life. Their intense chemistry had snuck up on her, catching her completely off guard. But she had to admit to herself, when she got too close and let people in too deep, they left her. Her grandfather. Her father. Her mother. And now Nana. The loss of her father in some ways hurt the most. He had a choice. Josh was right about her. How could she risk that kind of pain again?

# Chapter 15

Mr. Bromberg handled the arrangements for Nana's funeral with professionalism and compassion. Because of the violent circumstances surrounding her death, Reagan decided a short visitation and graveside service with immediate family and friends would be appropriate. The last thing she wanted was intrusive media or curiosity seekers.

Aiden drove his truck into the parking lot at 10:30, Josh following behind in his blue Mercedes to pick up Mattie. After waving goodbye, Reagan took off her wool dress coat and laid it in the backseat of Aiden's truck. She dusted snow off her tall suede boots and straightened her wool houndstooth skirt before buckling her seatbelt.

Once settled, she gave Aiden a tentative smile, her mind still lingering on the conversation she had overheard that morning.

"Hey. Thanks for picking me up," Reagan said.

"No problem. I know you think I'm paranoid, but just to be on the safe side, I would appreciate your help in keeping an eye out for a tail on us."

"Sure. I'll keep an eye on my rearview mirror, but I hope you're being overly cautious."

"Me too. So how did it go?" he asked, starting the engine.

"Mr. Bromberg assures me he has it all covered. That's all I could ask for."

As he pulled onto the street, Aiden asked, "Is there anything you'd like to talk about?"

Reagan wasn't sure if he was referring to the funeral plans, their night together, or the cool way she had greeted everyone at breakfast. Mattie asked several times what was wrong, but she insisted it was merely the daunting tasks of the day. Mattie sensed there was more, but thankfully let it drop.

"Not that I can think of," she lied. She regretted not waiting to hear how Aiden responded to Josh when he brought up her "lack of commitment." It had nagged at her all morning. If it appeared she was playing around with two men at the same time, that had never been her intent. She couldn't explain why she was drawn to Aiden, or why she had overtly pursued him. *Would I feel differently if Tyler were here?*

"You've been quiet since I left your room this morning." He reached over the console and took her hand in his.

"There are a lot of things going on at once, Aiden. You were right when you said my emotions were all over the place. I need to mentally regroup for a bit. Can you understand?"

His face showed no emotion. "Of course. You can have all the space you need." His response, as cryptic as hers was to him, unsettled her.

———————————

Aiden didn't know what to make of Reagan's sudden change in attitude. Last night, they could barely keep their hands off each other, then "poof" it all disappeared when he left her room, as if a spell had been broken. Maybe Josh was right: she wanted to avoid commitment, and he wasn't in a position to make one. Then there was her boyfriend, who Aiden had totally discounted. He should have listened to his instincts.

The appraiser's office was in a strip mall between a tax office and a dry cleaner. Aiden parked by the street away from the businesses, so his truck could not be seen by outdoor cameras.

Mr. Dunbar, the appraiser, was somewhere in his early 70s with dyed, light brown wavy hair and not a single strand of gray. He extended his slim, bony fingers in greeting to Aiden and nodded with a pleasant smile to Reagan. His sparsely decorated office had none of the display cases of jewelry and antiques that Aiden had expected.

Aiden introduced himself as Tim Blankenship and Reagan as his fiancée, Sarah Chapman, both from Ashtabula. He told Mr. Dunbar that his grandmother recently died, leaving him three pieces of jewelry in her safe deposit box. He was in Cleveland settling her estate and wanted to get an idea of the value of the items, if they were even real.

Mr. Dunbar advised them that he didn't feel comfortable giving them a general appraisal for authenticity rather than taking his time to do a more thorough written one. He cautioned that whomever they end up selling to would insist upon a written appraisal from a certified gemologist, not just his unsubstantiated opinion. Aiden told him he appreciated his concern, but that selling wasn't his motivation. He was looking only for an estimated value.

Mr. Dunbar took his time and tested each item separately while he and Reagan waited impatiently. Several times Aiden had to put his hand on her bouncing knee. Their anxiety rose every time Mr. Dunbar took a piece to the back room, wondering if he was checking the item against a stolen list or calling the police.

The final results were astounding.

The diamond was deemed exquisite. It was 4.3 carats. The color rating was a D or colorless, which was the rarest and most expensive. The clarity was IF or flawless, with no blemishes, specks, or inclusions when put up to a 10x magnification, also the highest rating. The cut was round with the polish, cut, and symmetry excellent. He appraised the diamond at $45,000. Aiden couldn't help but mentally calculate a rough estimate of the value of the other 100 or so diamonds. Reagan almost choked on her tongue when she asked, "For one diamond?"

The bead was a black pearl as Aiden predicted. Mr. Dunbar declared it charcoal gray with silver and pink hues. With an x-ray machine, he determined that it was a natural pearl, and he showed them the film that verified there was no irritant in the middle, which would have indicated it was a less expensive cultured pearl. Mr. Dunbar also told them that it was probably a Tahitian black pearl and that its size — approximately18.5 mm — was on the large size for a black pearl. He said it was as close to perfectly round as he had ever seen. The surface was virtually flawless. He explained the luster was the way the light glowed and reflected off the layers of the pearl. The light reflected undertones of pink, silver, and even a little blue, creating a beautiful iridescence. For the right buyer, he guessed the value between $10,000 to $15,000, but noted they weren't as popular as other stones.

The last item, the sapphire and diamond necklace, truly astonished Mr. Dunbar. From that point on, the appraiser's demeanor changed. He viewed them with suspicion and began probing for more information about the origin of the necklace. He clearly doubted Aiden's entire reason for being there. When he took the necklace into the backroom for an extended length of time, Aiden fully expected to see the FBI come storming through the door.

"You're absolutely sure you have no idea where your grandmother acquired this necklace?" he asked again as soon as he returned. His eyes narrowed on Aiden as if daring him to lie to his face.

"Absolutely none," Aiden responded with certainty. "Can you tell me anything about it? Are the setting and stones genuine or are they cut glass?"

"Oh, it's quite genuine, Mr. Blankenship. Although I am not an expert in period jewelry by any means, I will give you some general observations."

The sapphires ranged in sizes up to 10 carats and the diamonds varied between 3 to 5 carats. He advised that a true appraisal of the necklace by an expert would cost a minimum of $5,000, maybe more due to the time and research required. The gold itself was 18k. The unique thing was the age, which Mr. Dunbar didn't have the equipment or resources to determine. His guess was somewhere between the 13th to 17th centuries. In other words, priceless. He noted he had seen a similar style in a museum in Paris years ago.

Mr. Dunbar's behavior toward them changed so dramatically that Aiden could almost see frost coming out of his mouth. That was the cue Aiden needed to get the hell out of there. Reagan must have sensed it as well because she stood up, took the necklace from Mr. Dunbar's hand, and dropped it in the envelope in her handbag. Aiden followed suit, thanking the appraiser for his help and shoving $500 cash in his hand without waiting for a receipt. He struggled to calmly walk out the door rather than grab Reagan's hand and make a run for it.

# Chapter 16

Neither spoke as they briskly walked through the parking lot, Aiden holding Reagan's elbow to steady her on the slippery surface of unplowed snow and slush. He looked back several times to make sure Mr. Dunbar wasn't writing down his license plate number. Quickly turning over the engine, he drove onto the street, keeping an eye out for anyone following them. Traffic was terrible on good days, but when the snowfall was heavy, it was a nightmare.

"Feel like talking?" Aiden asked, as he maneuvered up the interstate ramp.

"You mean about how Mr. Dunbar thinks we're jewel thieves? Or that he implied the necklace could have come from Europe?"

"I'm really not concerned about what he thinks about us, unless he has hidden cameras and goes to the police before we have a chance to talk to Kowalski. It might give the detective the impression we have connections to the jewels and therefore may have had a motive for your grandmother's murder."

Reagan gasped and reached for his forearm. "That never occurred to me! Surely you don't think that about me. That I asked you not to tell the police because I'm hiding something."

Briefly glancing her way, he caught her truly horrified expression.

"No, Reagan. I don't think you are involved with those jewels in any way." He couldn't tell her it had never crossed his mind, because when they first found them, for few brief seconds it had. But when he weighed the modest means she had grown up with, it made absolutely no sense.

"As for Mr. Dunbar's suggestion that he had seen something similar in a museum in Paris, it brought something to mind worth exploring. Do you know where your grandfather was stationed in the Army?"

She leaned her elbow on the console and turned to face him. He glanced her way long enough to see her eyes narrow. With a clipped tone, she asked, "How did you know my grandfather was in the Army?"

His initial reaction was to respond with the same curt tone; after all, she was the one who had asked for his help. Mentally counting to 10 to suppress his irritation, he chose a calmer route.

"There was a letter from the Veterans Administration in your grandmother's file cabinet. I'd forgotten about it. And no, I didn't read the letter. It was none of my business."

She let out an audible sigh of understanding and settled back into her seat. "Nana told me my grandfather never talked about his six years in the Army, but she wasn't really interested in hearing about it anyway. He served before they were married. Grandpa was eight years older. She was only 18 when they got married. I'm not sure where he was stationed, but I know he was in Germany at some point. Do you think he could have stolen and smuggled those jewels back with him when he came home? Oh, God!"

"Don't jump to conclusions. There's no proof, especially if you look at their lifestyle. No offense, but don't you think if they were rolling in diamonds, they would have sold a few and upgraded the neighborhood at bit?" His attempt at levity missed its mark.

Reagan took a deep, shaky breath. "I'm so confused. The very reason we moved in with Nana was because she couldn't financially support herself after my grandfather died. She wasn't working at the time."

"Why don't you put it out of your mind for a while? None of this is your fault." Aiden reached for her hand, but she pulled it back, clutching her fist to her chest as if he had burned her skin. The rejection hurt, but he tried not to take it personally.

If the snowfall accumulation hadn't made the drive so treacherous, he would have pulled off at the nearest exit to have a face-to-face conversation. Now that the gravity of the situation had been confirmed, Reagan was having a rough time accepting the implications of what it all might mean.

"I've really screwed up, Aiden," she said in a barely audible whisper. He didn't respond. Didn't feel she wanted him to. She had to work through her emotions.

"You were right. I should have called the police as soon as we found those gems in the air conditioner. I've impeded the investigation this whole time by not allowing myself to believe what was happening. Those jewels were so far removed from my life, they couldn't have anything to do with me or my family. It's embarrassing to admit I've been in denial. If the police had known what they were dealing with, they could have broadened their search ... maybe even internationally."

Another quick glance. She was twisting a strand of her hair. He spoke to her in a calm, soothing voice.

"Take some deep breaths, Reagan. Watch the snow falling out the window and let your mind go blank."

She was second-guessing everything now and piling more guilt on her already overly full plate. There was no doubt that after confirming the authenticity of the jewels, things got real. With Reagan in possession of millions of dollars' worth of jewels, she was a huge target. As critical as it was to deal with the situation, he had to get her in the right head space.

When she spoke again, her voice was so strained, he could barely hear her over the windshield wipers.

"What the hell was going on in my own home?"

"All we can do is move forward. Stop beating yourself up."

She sighed deeply. "Will this nightmare ever end?"

Thirty minutes later, Aiden pulled into a shopping center on the east side of Cleveland and parked in front of a two-story, old fashioned-looking theatre next to a Mexican restaurant.

"What are we doing here?" she asked.

"Going to the movies," he said, as if it was a perfectly normal thing to do.

Reagan threw up her hands in disbelief. "Are you insane? My life is breaking into pieces. Someone tried to kill me. We're in the middle of a snowstorm, and you want to go to the movies?" Her tone was incredulous.

"Welcome to your brief reprieve," he said. "You can't make rational decisions when you're in a tailspin. I remember you told me that you and Nana used to watch old movies together." Her hand flew to her mouth, and tears of happiness glistened in her beautiful green eyes. She nodded.

"Well, this is the closest classic theatre I could fine, so we're going to spend a few hours watching old films and forget about this shit for a while." He flashed her a charming smile.

"Really? Did you plan this before we left the house?" He gave her a wink. "You were preparing for my reaction to the outcome of our appointment, weren't you?"

"Figured a distraction wouldn't be a bad thing for either of us. We can grab something to eat, then find ourselves a nice comfy seat in the back of the balcony and relax. If I play my cards right, I was hoping I might get to second base." She burst out laughing and hugged his neck.

After a leisurely lunch and two Doris Day and Rock Hudson movies, they were on the road headed back to Mattie and Josh's house by 5:30 p.m. For a short time, they had been like any other couple enjoying a carefree afternoon on their first official date.

Aiden decided to broach the subject he had been putting off all day. "This afternoon was a great escape, and as much as I don't want to taint it, I have to ask. What happened this morning after I left your room? You were visibly upset at breakfast. It usually takes me a little longer than a couple of hours to screw things up."

She twisted her lips to one side, obviously debating whether she was going to tell him or not. "I heard you talking to Josh. He warned you about my … uh … lack of commitment."

"I see."

"Apparently, I'm a love 'em and leave 'em kind of woman. Best to stay away from me." Her eyes were downcast, avoiding eye contact.

"Then you heard what I said, right?"

She shook her head. "Didn't want to hear you say it out loud. It wasn't hard to get the picture." She nervously ran her fingers through her hair. "Besides, it seemed to be a fair assessment."

"Truth be told, I haven't been the best at commitment myself. I'm 34 years old and I've had only one serious relationship. In my late 20s, I was engaged. We met in Amsterdam when I was on leave. Her name was Kate, and I thought I was in love with her. Gorgeous. Intelligent. Sophisticated. Delightfully positive personality. She was getting her doctorate in architecture. I was stationed in Afghanistan when we met.

We managed a long-distance relationship for three years. Her parents planned an elaborate wedding in Charleston, South Carolina, where she grew up. An emergency came up, and my leave got canceled." He stopped, reliving the moments.

"Did she get mad and break up?"

"Her parents were a lot more upset than she was. She wanted to fly to Afghanistan and find someone to marry us. Her exact words were, 'I'd go to the ends of the earth to marry you.' That's when I realized … I wouldn't do the same for her. Though I had nothing to do with it, canceling the wedding was an unexpected relief. I felt like a totally dishonest shit when it occurred to me that I wanted to love somebody the way she loved me — if I was even capable of it. Regardless, it wasn't fair to either of us, so I broke it off."

"Sounds like the right decision."

"Not what her dad thought. He is a powerful man. Gave me fair warning never to step foot in South Carolina if I ever wanted to see the light of day again. So, you see my track record is suspect as well, and I've never had to deal with the losses you have. I'm not going to try to label it, but you and I have had some sort of connection I can't exactly explain. Neither of our circumstances are the best right now for a relationship and there is the whole long-distance thing, but I wouldn't mind seeing where it goes." Out of the corner of his eye, he watched her wring her hands.

"I know what you mean. I feel drawn to you, but …Tyler. Not sure where he fits, if he still does. Apparently, he feels our relationship is more exclusive than I do. I mean, we've never actually said those words, but I'm pretty sure he would feel I've cheated on him. Josh's conversation with you this morning reminded me just how awful I am. You suggested things might feel differently between us if Tyler were here. I don't know for sure because he's not. When I'm with you, I want to crawl into your arms, but I'm not sure if those feeling are real or induced by a sense of loss. A need to feel safe. Do you understand?"

"I get it. You have to figure that out on your own without any pressure from me. We can't move forward until you know how you feel about him. We're beyond casual sex. I know it's been a zero-to-90 kind of thing, but if you want to explore what this is between us, you have to be all in. If you decide this isn't what you want, I promise you I'll still see this situation through. Can you live with that?"

"That's fair." They rode in silence the rest of the way home.

# Chapter 17

Moonlight reflected off the ice crystals formed by the afternoon snowfall and the extreme drop in temperature, making the whole neighborhood look like a winter wonderland. As amazing as their afternoon had been, Reagan sighed with relief when they arrived safely at Mattie and Josh's house. Tired, hungry, and in need of a hot shower, she couldn't wait to get inside. Aiden gave her a chaste kiss before he unlocked the front door. Neither of them wanted to endure a lecture from Mattie.

After handing her coat to Aiden to hang in the hall closet, Reagan headed to the kitchen. She froze in the doorway when she saw Tyler sitting at the breakfast bar with Josh, a glass of red wine in hand, as if it were the most natural thing in the world. Her mouth fell open and words stuck in her throat. Mattie jumped off her stool. Tyler flashed a wide grin and stood. Josh swallowed so hard it looked like he was trying to force down a hairball. Then Aiden appeared, took one long look at Tyler, and eyed Reagan with a *"Who the hell is that?"* question on his face.

"Tyler," Reagan barely croaked, blushing a deep crimson.

"Tyler?" Aiden repeated, dumbstruck.

"Reagan!" Mattie exclaimed, meeting her at the door, then throwing her arms around her neck as if they hadn't seen each other in years. "I would've told you if you'd bothered to call me back," she whispered. What she said out loud was, "Tyler's here! Yay!"

As Tyler moved toward her with open arms, Reagan struggled to make her feet move. She hesitated when the thought occurred to her that she might smell like Aiden's cologne. Their afternoon had been pretty tame, a few kisses and a little hand-holding, but the guilt from the previous night in the face of Tyler's sudden appearance washed over her like a bucket of ice water. As he stepped closer, she awkwardly opened her arms to accept his hug. She was caught off guard when he pulled her into a passionate kiss that lasted longer than was appropriate for an audience. It felt different. Uncomfortable. The thought of Aiden watching made her cringe. When Tyler finally pulled away, she could feel the hot burn of embarrassment on her cheeks.

"Are you okay, baby? You don't look well." His fingertips lightly touched the black and purple bruise on her cheek.

"Just tired. It's been a long day." Reagan couldn't bring herself to look at Aiden, but she could feel his eyes boring into her back. "Would you mind if I ran up and got a quick shower before we catch up? I'm sure I'll feel much better."

He traced her jaw with his fingers and held her chin. "Want me to join you?" His voice was suggestive. Everyone heard it. She didn't have to see Aiden to know he was fuming. Judging her.

*Oh, dear God, please just melt me into the cracks of the wood floor right now. I deserve it. Tyler's staking his claim. Of course he is because he immediately sensed something between Aiden and me.*

"I won't be long," was all she could manage before she practically ran out of the room, filled with shame over the disaster she had made of her life.

Mattie caught up with her on the stairs and whispered, "As soon as Tyler showed up, Josh changed the sheets on your bed. From the look on your face, I just figured out why. Two great guys? What's a girl to do?" Reagan knew that Mattie's intention was only good-natured ribbing, but she was dying from humiliation.

"Don't, Mattie. Not now," she said as she stumbled up the stairs.

Tyler was waiting in Reagan's room when she returned from the shower wrapped in a terrycloth robe, her hair in a towel on top of her head. He met her just inside the door pulling her to his chest, kissing her deeply. She squirmed under his touch. *This feels so wrong. Is it guilt? Or have my feelings changed?* Her head was so muddled she couldn't be sure of anything.

"I've missed you so much," he breathed in her ear. "Feeling better?"

"A little," she lied.

"Does the bruise still hurt?"

"A bit tender."

"I should have been here for you," he said, nibbling her neck.

He untied her robe and slipped his arms around her waist, pulling her against him for another kiss. Her body's response to his familiar touch, his warmth, and his undeniable sex appeal only confused her more. Easing out of his embrace, she refastened her robe.

"Can we just talk, Tyler? It's all been too much. I…I'm sorry." She choked back a sob and fought back tears. He took her hands in his and met her eyes.

"Shh, baby. Don't feel bad. It was unfair of me. You just feel so good in my arms. We'll have plenty of time for that later."

Regrets swallowed her whole. *Has he been hiding the true depth of his feelings? Or have I refused to see it?*

Reagan released his hands and sat on the bed. "Mattie told me she explained what's been happening. I know I should have been the one to tell you, but the last thing I wanted to do was put you in danger too."

Tyler sat down in a beige overstuffed chair in the corner of the room facing her, putting some distance between them. He crossed one leg over his knee and rested his elbows on the arms of the chair, his fingers intertwined on his lap.

His face tensed. "Yeah. I have to admit I was pretty pissed."

"You're not anymore?"

"Let's just say I was reserving judgment until you had an opportunity to explain, which I might add has not been easy. You don't seem to have trouble sharing your problems with Aiden. Who, by the way, is absolutely nothing like you led me to believe. Why would you involve him in all this, a virtual stranger, and not me?"

"He was there when most of it happened, and he had a gun to keep me safe." It was the best she could come up with.

"I'm perfectly capable of protecting you with a gun, or at the very least I could have gotten a security detail."

She was shocked. "I thought you hated guns."

"I hate violence, and Chicago has more than its share. My family is wealthy, so I've always been a target. Seems there are many details you've left out." She averted her eyes to avoid facing his judgment.

"I didn't know at the time I was going to need protection. And maybe if you communicated with me more, I would've known to ask for your help." He was the injured party, and she had no right to be defensive. "Let's not argue. Aiden and I had never met before this week. Mattie sent him over to help me when I was meeting with the detective handling Nana's case. She was worried about me. At the time, I didn't realize there was any real threat."

"Turns out she had good reason to be concerned." He leaned forward with his forearms on his knees. "Why did you make Aiden out to be some half-crazed retired military zealot? Did you think I'd be jealous of you spending time with a guy who looks like he stepped off the screen of a GI Joe movie?"

*That comment alone should have answered your question,* she thought.

She took a deep breath to collect her thoughts. "At first I thought he was a pushy jerk … and maybe I was a little concerned you might not appreciate him helping me. But then I realized he was a good guy. If it weren't for him, I never would've found the gems, which we just confirmed are genuine, by the way."

"From what Josh and Mattie told me about finding them in your grandmother's air conditioner, that doesn't surprise me. What about the jewelry? That genuine too?"

She nodded. "I assure you if anyone in my house knew that jewelry was real, they sure as hell wouldn't have given it to me to play with."

"Probably not," he agreed. He quietly held her gaze for a few minutes before he spoke again.

"Why, Reagan? Why didn't you trust me with any of this? Your friends told me completely by accident, assuming you would have confided in me. Imagine their surprise when they realized you hadn't."

She blew out a breath and slid off the bed onto the floor in resignation. "If you come sit with me, I'll tell you everything." She patted the carpet beside her. "Please."

Tyler hesitated, fighting his feelings of hurt and anger, but finally relocated himself cross-legged in front of her on the floor. Resting her hands on his knees, Reagan took him through the timeline of events and the emotional upheavals that went with them, minus her intimate relationship with Aiden. Tyler listened without interruption. Finally, he stood up and offered her his hand. She stared at him, frozen with indecision. He moved to the bed and motioned for her to join him.

He sensed her reticence. "All I want is to hold you. I've never pressured you to do anything you weren't comfortable with, and I am not going to start now." She crawled up beside him, resting her head on his chest. He gently stroked her hair as he wrapped his arms tightly around her. A sense of warmth, peace, and normalcy ran through her as she snuggled closer, wishing all the madness and uncertainty would go away, but something had shifted in her feelings for him. She just wasn't exactly sure what had changed.

"I didn't mean to lose my temper," he said softly, twirling a strand of her hair around his finger. "It wouldn't have bothered me so much if I didn't love you."

Her breath caught. Squeezing her eyes shut, she unsuccessfully fought back tears. There was absolutely nothing he could have said that would have made her feel more worthless than she did at that moment.

—

# Chapter 18

Reagan and Tyler were asleep when Mattie knocked on the door and told them to get dressed. Detective Kowalski was at the front door demanding to see her. She couldn't imagine what could be so important that required rousting her out of bed at 1:15 a.m. She threw on the closest things she could find, a pair of faded jeans and a sweatshirt. Tyler, on the other hand, fished through his suitcase and pulled out a black Givenchy sweater and khaki slacks. When he slipped on a pair of Tom Ford loafers, she shook her head.

"Really? That's what you're putting on in the middle of the night?" she asked. He shrugged nonchalantly.

*I shouldn't be surprised,* she thought. *Tyler doesn't even own a pair of old sweatpants.* It hadn't occurred to her until that moment how pretentious it might seem to her friends.

When they got downstairs, everyone was seated around the dining room table with Detective Kowalski and an older man in his 50s with short, salt-and-pepper hair. Detective Kowalski introduced him as Detective Ray Hilliard.

"What's this about?" Reagan asked.

Detective Kowalski cleared his throat and began. "We believe we have identified the man who murdered Mrs. Moran."

"Thank God," Reagan gasped.

The detective continued. "As part of our investigation, we interviewed persons with prior arrests for burglary in surrounding areas. We concentrated on those individuals who have been convicted of violent crimes. It eventually led us to a man named Justin Pane.

"Pane had a history of drug addiction and an arrest record for possession and distribution, domestic battery, a couple of petty thefts, but no B & E's. Another suspect we interviewed gave us Pane's name. Said Pane had been working for a jewel fence from Youngstown to pay off a large debt. The guy suggested Pane might have gotten in over his head, because he'd heard Pane had been roughed up pretty bad.

"When Detective Hilliard and I paid Mr. Pane a visit, his injuries were so severe that he was completely unresponsive. Since he was still on probation, he had begged his wife not to take him to the hospital. Once we got his wife talking, we realized there was a good chance he was our perp. She claimed her husband had screwed up a job he'd taken from a man named Gabe Ledbetter. Pane owed Ledbetter a lot of money, and taking the job was his way to get out from under it. At first, we didn't find her credible, but when she described the house on Larkin Drive, we took notice. I asked her to tell me something that hadn't already been reported by the media. That's when she described exactly how Mrs. Moran was killed, which was never released."

Reagan felt a shiver of goosebumps creep up her arms. Tyler shifted her closer to him. When she glanced across the table, she saw Aiden's jaw tense at the intimate gesture.

"Did he confess?" Mattie asked.

"Unfortunately, he never gained consciousness. Died around 2 o'clock this afternoon. Mrs. Pane decided it was in her best interest to tell us all she knew. It's all hearsay, but it rings true. Apparently, the way she explained it, her husband was one day away from having every bone in his body broken if he didn't come up with the money he owed Ledbetter, so Pane jumped at the chance to pay off his debt. A man had contacted Ledbetter offering to sell him a diamond-and-precious-stone ring that he claimed had been appraised at $80,000. The seller had texted Ledbetter a picture of a ring, but Ledbetter, who's been on the FBI's radar for years, was afraid it was a setup. When Ledbetter asked how the guy came into possession of the ring, the seller said he didn't have it in hand at that time but could easily obtain it."

As Detective Kowalski spoke, his gaze flicked from person to person. Suddenly he leaned forward with his elbows on the table and focused his full attention on Josh.

"Do you know what else he said, Mr. Rannell?" Josh, mesmerized, said nothing. "He said his daughter had been to this woman's home numerous times. Matter of fact, the woman sometimes babysat for her. He didn't think the lady had any idea of the value of the ring because she let his daughter take it home to play with on more than one occasion. It wouldn't be hard for his daughter to bring it home again, and the lady would probably never realize it was gone. All he had to do was instruct his 5-year-old daughter to pocket it. He implied there could be more where that came from. Ledbetter didn't believe him. Needed more proof the man was legit. The seller revealed the street the lady lived on … Larkin Drive, and another little tidbit … she was a nurse who worked at a local hospital."

Josh started to sweat under the intense scrutiny of Detective Kowalski, who was implying he had something to do with Nana's death, which Reagan knew was absurd. Josh sat paralyzed, his face ashen. Reagan and Mattie exchanged horrified glances, both stunned by the implications of the detective's words.

"Since Larkin Drive is only 10 blocks in length, it didn't take long for Mr. Ledbetter's scouts to figure out who the nurse was and where she lived, so he no longer needed the middleman." His eyes remained locked on Josh, scrutinizing his every move, pausing for effect. "If the ring turned out to be real, Ledbetter would have the money all for himself. If not, no harm done. That's why he sent Pane to find the ring and report back if there was more jewelry. Pane was instructed to take nothing except the ring. If he found it, his debt would be paid in full. If it was all a hoax, it would buy him another 24 hours to come up with the money he owed. Pane was desperate and was counting on finding that ring because, according to his wife, no matter how much extra time Ledbetter gave him, they would never be able to scrape together what was owed.

"Pane was so hopped up on heroin he didn't hear Mrs. Moran enter the home until it was too late. Panicked. You know the rest. He never found the ring. Knowing Ledbetter was going to kill him, he grabbed a couple of items hoping to sell them and get out of town."

No one said a word. The silence in the room was deafening. Reagan heard his words, but they weren't registering in her brain. Detective Kowalski appeared to be accusing Josh of getting Ellie to steal Nana's ring so he could sell it to a fence. That couldn't be right. Josh would never do such a thing. She looked over at him and could see his distress. Then she remembered Aiden taking the ring to a jeweler. He could come under suspicion too. Her cheeks felt hot and a dizziness came over her. Things had gotten so screwed up. All because she insisted on keeping quiet about the jewels. She tried to stand, but the blood rushed out of her head, causing her to sit back down abruptly.

"You all right?" Tyler asked, steadying her with his arms.

"Fine. Please don't make a fuss," she said brushing him away.

"It's late, I know, but Mr. Rannell, we'd like you to come to the station with us," Detective Hilliard said.

"What?" Mattie asked. "Why?"

"Stop, Mattie. I can speak for myself. I have never contacted this Ledbetter person, nor have I ever heard of him until tonight. My daughter, Ellie, has been playing with Mrs. Moran's princess jewelry for years. She has even brought some of the pieces home, but I assure you it never occurred to any of us that some of it could possibly be real."

"Do you have a photo of the ring?" Reagan asked. She wasn't sure why it popped into her head, but it seemed important.

"I do. We found it on Pane's burner phone."

The detective pulled his cell phone out of his pocket and flipped through until he found the picture. He handed his cell to Reagan, with Tyler looking on. Aiden leaned over the table anticipating the worst. She gave him a slight smile and showed it to Josh. It was the sapphire ring surrounded by diamonds, her favorite ring that matched the tiara. Reagan felt a small burden lift from her heart. It wasn't the emerald ring Aiden had taken to the jewelry store. Both rings were safely stored in the safe deposit box with the other jewels.

Mattie reached for the phone and viewed the photo. "Ellie has never brought that ring home. She likes the green one with the rhinestones."

Aiden took the cellphone from Mattie's hands as it made its way around the table. Reagan watched his face momentarily relax.

"We can talk about it at the station," Detective Kowalski said, standing up. "Mrs. Moran babysat for your daughter, and she brought jewelry home. Not a lot of people fit that scenario, Mr. Rannell."

"Wait a damn minute!" Aiden stood up almost knocking his chair over. "Josh had nothing to do with this! You believe the word of some dead junkie's wife over my brother? Did that Pane guy have an accent? Because the guy who attempted to kidnap Reagan did. So did the fake repairman who came to the Moran house. Sounds to me like you've got the wrong guy."

Detective Kowalski stood up to meet Aiden eye to eye. "We aren't sure if Mr. Pane is connected to the kidnapping of Ms. Asher or not, but we will find out. It could be completely unrelated."

"How could it not be related?" Reagan asked. "I don't even live here."

"The kidnapping is a separate issue until we have evidence linking the two events," Detective Hilliard interjected. "The point is, Mrs. Pane knew details about your family's interactions with Mrs. Moran that a stranger wouldn't be privy to. It's certainly enough to take Mr. Rannell downtown for questioning."

Tyler motioned for Josh to lean toward him. With Reagan sandwiched between them, he whispered, "You need to be honest with me, Josh. Do you or your wife have anything to hide regarding this jewelry or the death of Mrs. Moran?" Reagan sat back in her chair in disbelief. What the heck, Tyler? She punched his arm in frustration, but he shook her off.

Josh whispered back, indignantly. "Absolutely not. This is all bullshit!"

Tyler stood up and stuck his hand out to Josh. "Give me a dollar." Josh looked at him like he was out of his mind. "You don't have a dollar?" Tyler furrowed his brow.

Exasperated, Josh fished around in his jeans pocket and pulled out a five. "That's all I've got on me."

"We need to go, Mr. Rannell," Detective Hilliard said, coming around the table.

"My client isn't going anywhere tonight, Detective," Tyler said firmly.

"We don't need your permission to take him in and hold him for 48 hours," Detective Kowalski said. "Who the hell do you think you are?"

"As of now, I am Mr. Rannell's attorney." He reached in his back pocket, pulled out his wallet and flipped his ID at the detectives. "I am licensed to practice law in 14 states, and Ohio is one of them. I can have my office fax you my credentials in the morning if you like."

Everyone gasped, but no one was more surprised than Reagan. That was one detail he had failed to mention. The two detectives stared at Tyler.

"You can take him in and hold him, that's true, but I assure you he will not utter one word in response to your questions, I'll make sure of it. And don't interpret that to imply Mr. Rannell has anything to hide. It's more in response to you guys rustling everyone out of bed in the middle of the night to intimidate and illicit a confession of some sort.

"It has come to my attention that Reagan Asher and Aiden Rannell have recently uncovered some things in Mrs. Moran's home that may be helpful to your investigation. They had already made plans to contact you first thing in the morning, but now we will have to adjust that to, let's say, 11 o'clock. I would make it earlier, but since it's past 2 a.m., we're going to need a little sleep. If you decide to take Josh in tonight, all the parties at this table will retain attorneys and you won't get jack-shit from anyone. The questioning is over." He gave them a tight-lipped frown and crossed his arms to punctuate his words. "And by the way, your hearsay information from the wife of a murderer and a heroin addict with an extensive record would never get you a warrant, let alone be admissible in court. You and I both know it. What's it going to be, Detective?"

Detective Kowalski ran his fingers over his face and rubbed his chin, trying to determine if Tyler was bluffing. Detective Hilliard, probably hardened by years of similar grandstanding, shrugged, shook his head and shuffled his feet.

"I assure you we want to cooperate with your investigation, and I think you'll find our meeting in the morning very enlightening," Tyler said firmly. "So, if there are no objections, we'll see you at Mrs. Moran's home at 11."

The detectives looked at each other, communicating in some unspoken cop code, and decided the offer on the table was more productive than taking Josh in for questioning. Picking up their coats, they headed to the door. Detective Kowalski stopped and turned around.

"We'll be there. I'll check you out first thing in the morning, Mr. Hamilton. And let me warn you, this had better not be a ploy of some kind to prevent us from taking Mr. Rannell into custody. You won't like the consequences."

Tyler smirked. "By the way, Detective, you may want to bring a couple of forensic guys, and we'll need a gemologist."

Kowalski's expression was priceless.

# Chapter 19

The anxiety level in the room dropped dramatically the minute the door closed behind the detectives. Mattie threw her arms around Tyler's neck in gratitude for rescuing Josh from a trip to the police station.

Josh patted Tyler on the back. "Don't know how to thank you for that, Tyler. If you weren't here, I'd be spending the night in jail."

"Glad I could help."

Aiden offered Tyler his hand. "Thanks, man," he said sincerely. "Of all the scenarios I've played out in my head as to where this investigation was headed, Josh being under suspicion was not in the ballpark."

Reagan grabbed Tyler's arm, jerking him around to face her with fury in her eyes. "Why didn't you tell me you were an attorney? How could I possibly not know that about you after six months?"

"Don't be upset, baby. Can't you just be happy I saved your friend an overnight stay in a jail cell? It's just something I'm licensed to do, it's not my primary job."

"You're not in computer programming?" Josh asked. "What kind of lawyer are you?"

"An intellectual property attorney and, yes, my company develops computer programs. My title is VP of Development, mostly leading project teams that develop software, but I'm also a part owner. Being an attorney comes in handy with the legal aspects. When I went to Harvard, I started out in criminal law, but halfway through, I decided it wasn't a good fit."

Turning to Josh, he said, "You need to contact a good attorney first thing in the morning. Depending on what they find tomorrow, they may end up questioning you anyway."

"Why?" Josh asked, incredulous. "I've got nothing to hide."

"Innocence doesn't preclude the police from arresting you if they have enough circumstantial evidence. They just have to prove it in court, but in the meantime, lives can be ruined, financial resources drained, jobs lost, relationships tested, reputations destroyed. You get the picture."

"I'll get a referral in the morning from the attorney who handles my business dealings. What I don't understand is how they came up with that story. I've never known a fence in my life, and as for the ring, it never occurred to any of us that Ellie might be playing with genuine precious stones."

"The police sometimes get bits and pieces of a story. Then they look for suspects and possible motives. Sometimes they concoct scenarios that could fit. They try it out on a suspect and see if anything shakes loose. I'm pretty sure they found the man who attacked Reagan's grandmother, and the wife probably provided some information about the jewelry fence. The rest could be a distortion of the facts to do a little fishing. It sounds to me like they'd like to nail that guy in Youngstown too."

"But what about the sapphire ring he had a picture of?" Reagan asked. "It looks just like one of the rings in my play jewelry collection. It's with the rest of the jewelry in the safe deposit box."

"If the picture matches one of the rings in your jewelry collection, it lends credibility to the theory that someone was trying to steal it from your grandmother and sell it. The piece is unique, so it can't be a coincidence," Tyler said. "Someone who had access to your grandmother's home must have seen it. Could've been a neighbor, co-worker, or service worker. Maybe they came across it at some point and took it. Got it appraised and was too afraid to fence it themselves. Josh was an easy target because of his access to the home."

To Josh, he added, "The detectives probably fabricated the rest to intimidate you into confessing. First, it's all hearsay. Second, that Pane guy was a drug addict. Not reliable. Probably why he's dead. It appears he made a mess of things and brought undue attention to himself, and the fence — that Ledbetter guy — didn't want any of it leading back to him."

"This is a fuckin' nightmare," Josh said, rubbing the back of his neck.

"Actually, I think it'd be a good idea for all of you to retain an attorney. You too, Reagan. You guys have no idea where those gems and the jewelry came from, and none of you want to get caught in the crosshairs if it turns out to be stolen. If the police can't identify the origin, it becomes Reagan's property through possession and inheritance. You'll need an attorney to help establish ownership. Then Uncle Sam's going to want his share, but that's a tax attorney's problem."

"My head is spinning," Reagan said. "I can't believe Nana knew anything about it."

"If she did, she could have been in denial," Tyler suggested. "If it's out of sight, it's out of mind."

Aiden hated to admit it, but he'd thought the same thing. It took the cool pragmatic observations of an attorney to lay it out.

Reagan looked up at Tyler with surprise. "Are you saying my grandfather may have had something to do with this?"

"I'm not trying to hurt you, baby, but somebody's responsible, and it's not you. It was hidden in your grandparents' home. No way around that. If your father was responsible, I can't imagine he would have left without it. It'd be a serious mistake not to consider all of the options," Tyler said, stroking her hair.

Aiden cleared his throat. He had no intention of standing around any longer watching Tyler fawn over Reagan. "We can hash this out in the morning. I'm going back to bed." He was proud of himself for resisting the temptation to childishly stomp up the stairs in frustration.

The last thoughts he had before he fell into a restless sleep was how Reagan could switch her feelings on and off so easily. The realization that he had been a placeholder burned.

The next morning Aiden showered, dressed, and headed downstairs. It was just after 7. The house was silent. The heavenly aroma wafting from the automatic coffeemaker was a welcome greeting. Selecting an Ohio State University mug from the cabinet, he filled it up with caffeine and took a seat at the bar.

"Hope you don't mind sharing that pot."

The voice caught Aiden by surprise, shaking him from his thoughts. Tyler, dressed elegantly in a navy Burberry sweater and gray wool slacks that probably cost as much as Aiden's new monthly mortgage payment, poured himself a cup of coffee.

"Not at all. That's what it's there for," Aiden said, trying to sound pleasant.

After offering to top-off Aiden's coffee, Tyler joined him at the breakfast bar. "Am I interrupting?" Tyler asked. "You appeared deep in thought."

"Contemplating what a cluster-fuck this is."

Tyler raised his mug. "Couldn't have put it more succinctly myself."

Aiden decided to put feelings aside and pick this guy's brain. He was smart and obviously had Reagan's best interests at heart. Maybe he could add a fresh perspective.

"Putting the pieces together after some 20 years has been a challenge to say the least," Aiden said, rubbing his face. "After her husband died, Reagan's grandmother lived paycheck to paycheck on a nurse's salary and a small veteran's pension. I'm not sure if there was a child support check for Reagan or not. I didn't go that far back in the records, but maybe I should have. It occurred to me her grandfather, who was stationed overseas, could have gotten involved in something illegal."

"Has Reagan talked to her father?" Tyler asked. "Surely, he would have taken the gems with him if he were involved, but maybe he knows something. Reagan said her parents divorced when she was young, but that's all I really know."

"She's probably seen him a handful of times since her parents split. He remarried years ago. Lives in Washington state. I'm with you on that. Can't see him walking away from what could be millions."

"Agreed."

"Her father may not have known the period jewelry was genuine, but he did know it existed. There's a picture on the wall in Reagan's old room of a birthday party when she's 5 years old, and she's wearing a friggin' diamond and sapphire tiara. Imagine how much that sucker is worth. The other kids, including Mattie, are all decked out in jewels. It's mind-blowing when you think about it."

"Maybe her father realized they were real at some point but didn't want to go to jail for someone else's crime?" Tyler suggested.

"If that's true, then maybe Reagan's mother figured it out too. Might be why she committed suicide. Reagan always suspected the divorce w..."

"What?" Tyler came off his stool, his eyes wide. "Reagan's mother killed herself?"

Aiden did a silent *Oh shit*! Reagan was going to be pissed.

"Man, I'm sorry. I had no idea you didn't know."

"How long ago?" Tyler asked in almost a whisper as he sat back down.

"A year or so after her father left. Seven years old, I think. Did you know she had passed?"

"Yeah, but not when or how. Reagan clammed up. I thought it was too painful." Tyler rested his chin on his hand and retreated into thought. After a few minutes of silence, he said, "Someone needs to talk to her father. He was the only one around at the time. Maybe he can shed some light on this shit-show. Old family secrets have a way of working their way back to the surface, and Reagan seems to be the one suffering the brunt of them."

"You're right about that," Aiden said.

Tyler chuckled. Then he set down his mug and looked Aiden directly in the eyes, not with malice or animosity, but acceptance. "It just occurred to me that my girlfriend has confided more to you in a few days about her personal life than she has to me in six months."

Aiden was speechless. He opened his mouth but couldn't think of anything appropriate to say.

"I didn't say that to make you feel uncomfortable. Just a statement of fact."

Aiden finally found his voice. "Don't judge her too harshly, Tyler. She lost her mother and father years ago, and the only family who stuck by her was brutally murdered. She obviously keeps a shell around herself so no one can get close enough to hurt her again. I just happened to be there when her emotions were raw and exposed."

"Maybe some of it is my fault too. I haven't been the most forthcoming myself. There's no doubt Reagan's gone through a tremendous loss, and I understand people seek comfort when those things happened. I should've been here for her. But there's no denying that she cares about you, I'm not blind. I just need to figure out if it's circumstantial — or more. Reagan's a beautiful woman, inside and out. Not going to ask her if anything's happened between the two of you, because I don't want to know. I'm in love with her and not planning on giving her up without a fight."

Aiden, surprised by his candidness, said, "That's up to her."

Mattie bounded into the kitchen in a t-shirt and a pair of black yoga pants.

"Good morning, gentlemen. Any coffee left?"

He wasn't sure what she had overheard, but Aiden was thankful for the interruption.

# Chapter 20

A CSI van and two patrol cars were parked in front of the Moran home when Reagan and Tyler arrived in his rental. Josh, Mattie, and Aiden followed in a black Mercedes belonging to their new attorney, Ethan Rowling. Ethan had been following the case in the papers and jumped at the chance to help Josh. Mattie suspected the publicity might have been his motivation, but he had a good reputation.

Detective Kowalski was literally tapping his foot against the hardwood floors when they arrived, his irritation evident. Detective Hilliard led everyone to the dining room, the space with the least amount of debris.

Reagan was grateful when Aiden took the lead, relaying the events from the first day they met. He reminded Detective Kowalski about his conversation with Mrs. Moran that one of the rings Ellie had taken home might be more valuable than she thought, and how she had dismissed him as being mistaken. Because of his prior experience with stolen period jewelry in Iraq, he hadn't been able to let it go. After the additional break-ins in Mrs. Moran's home, Aiden began to wonder if his original assessment of the ring had been correct. When he voiced his concern to Reagan, she showed him her entire collection of princess jewelry she had played with since childhood. To alleviate his concerns, she agreed to get it appraised. It had been evening, so they decided they should find a more secure place to hide the jewelry until they could get it to a safe deposit box at the bank and locate a jeweler. With little storage space in the house, Aiden suggested the air conditioning unit as an unlikely but secure place. That's where they found the diamonds and black pearls. He ended with the trip to Cleveland to see Mr. Dunbar, who verified that samples of the period jewelry and gems were authentic and extremely valuable. That implied that the rest of the jewelry was more than likely genuine as well. Realizing it may have been the motivation for the murder of Mrs. Moran and the attempted kidnapping of Reagan, they made plans to contact the police. The police showed up at their door the night before they got the chance.

"Where are the gems and the jewelry now?" Detective Hilliard asked.

"In a safe deposit box at the bank where my grandmother had her accounts," Reagan said. "I decided they needed to be secured in case they turned out to be genuine."

Aiden took them to the AC unit and showed them the container that for decades had held the gems. They both gave fingerprint samples so their prints could be eliminated. Viewing the container and tape in the daylight, it was obviously extremely old.

Detective Hilliard pursed his lips. "What on earth prompted you to look in the air conditioning unit in the first place?"

"When Reagan and I searched for a secure place, we realized there were few options that wouldn't be obvious. The door in the laundry room that opens to the mechanical equipment closet isn't visible at first glance. It seemed like the best place to hide them overnight. As it turned out, someone else had the same idea years ago. Since the recent intruders never touched the AC unit, we assumed they didn't know to look there."

"And where was the period jewelry during the original break-in?" Detective Kowalski asked.

"Stored in a pink decorated boot box in my great-grandmother's old hope-chest that sits at the foot of my childhood bed," Reagan said. "Nothing was disturbed in my old bedroom during any of the break-ins. When Aiden found the gems in the air conditioner, I began to believe he may be right about my play jewelry. If you want to see my homemade jewelry box, I put it back in the chest."

When the interrogation was over, everyone got out of the way so the investigating team could work. Reagan slipped into the office hoping to get some alone time. She stiffened when Aiden strode in the room.

"Glad you're here. I wanted to show you some photos I found." He pulled out the picture of Darius, Claire, and Rosana from the desk drawer and handed it to her. His casual attitude, as if nothing had happened between them, both surprised and stung her.

"I wondered if maybe this was an old boyfriend of your mother's based on the inscription 'Love Forever.' The dark-haired girl with them resembles the boy, so she may be his sister. They appear to be Middle Eastern." He pulled out his cell and pulled up a copy of the picture of the mystery boy they found in Nana's safe deposit box and compared it to a picture of Darius. "The mystery boy could be Darius, but it's difficult to confirm with the water damage. My gut tells me there's a significance for it being kept in a secure location. There are lots of other pictures of the three of them, implying they were close friends."

Reagan reviewed the pictures closely. "I've never seen these before." She did her best to keep her voice even, overlooking the tension in the air.

"If you're interested, there are more photos in the bottom drawer in a box with your mother's name on it."

Before she could respond, Mattie walked into the room. Aiden nodded to her as he walked out to give them some privacy.

"Holding up okay?" Mattie asked, closing the door.

"Not really, but there's nothing I can do about it."

"You don't know the half of it. I overheard Tyler and Aiden talking in the kitchen this morning."

"About?"

"What a tangled web you have weaved. Sounded like Tyler thinks something happened between you and Aiden, but he doesn't want to know about it. He told Aiden he's willing to fight for you."

"Oh, my God. He said that to Aiden?"

"He did. Aiden didn't confirm or deny. Said it was your decision."

Reagan felt nauseous. Tyler hadn't made any accusation, just held her tenderly in his arms last night not expecting anything from her.

"What am I going to do?"

"Sorry, Reagan. You'll have to figure that out. Two incredible guys both wanting you. Yeah, big problem. No sympathy here."

Reagan frowned. "Thought you were my friend."

"Only you can wade through the noise and clutter to decide which one, if either of them, you want. Maybe you should give yourself a little time. I love you no matter what. Right now, I'd better see what's going on out there." Mattie gave Reagan a brief hug and left.

Reagan sat at the desk feeling restless. Getting up from the chair, she noticed recent framed pictures of Nana on the wall. In one of them, Nana was in a large industrial kitchen with several women who she didn't recognize, stirring something in a large pot. Probably the annual Chili Cook-Off at the church. Another photo was at the hospital Christmas party in the children's wing. Nana always bought coloring books and crayons for the kids during the holidays. Feelings of nostalgia swept through her. The last picture was of Nana in the backyard at the picnic table with Ellie and another little girl who Reagan didn't recognize. They were eating ice cream cones.

"Reminiscing?"

Engrossed in the photos, Reagan hadn't heard Josh come into the room. She turned around to answer.

"Good guess. Looking at the new pictures Nana hung on the wall. Do you know who this little girl is? I've never seen her."

Josh moved closer to get a better look at the photo. "Oh, that's Megan Yeager, Ellie's best friend. That's who she's staying with until things get back to normal. Megan must have spent the weekend with Ellie. They loved to come stay with Nana. She always kept them entertained."

Something nagged at the back of Reagan's mind, but she couldn't put her finger on it. "Nana never mentioned her to me."

"Probably because she came over with Ellie only when Bree and Cam went on vacation or a weekend escape." Josh laughed. "You know, the kind when you want to go to a hotel and catch up on all the sex you miss because you have kids in the house."

The thing that was tickling in Reagan's brain began to take shape. As the realization of what it might mean hit her, she turned to face Josh, clutching his sweater to steady herself.

He grasped her by her elbows, his eyes locked on hers. "What's wrong, Reagan?"

"Is Megan 5 years old?" she asked, afraid to hear the answer.

"Pretty sure. Ellie and Megan are in kindergarten together," Josh confirmed.

Reagan felt stricken. She couldn't form words. They were unthinkable.

"You're scaring me, Reagan. What's wrong?" He searched her face for answers. She could tell the instant he worked it out. "Oh, God!" he gasped. "No! No! It can't be!" He swallowed hard. "Not Camden. He would never do that … no way, Reagan!"

He wanted assurances that she couldn't give. "Josh, I…I don't know.

"Dear Christ. My daughter is at his house!"

They both rushed through the house yelling for Detective Kowalski. Josh could barely put two coherent words together as he dragged the detective by his arm into the office to see the picture of Ellie with Megan Yeager, the only other 5-year-old who Nana babysat. Hearing the commotion, Mattie and Aiden burst in just in time to see Josh hurl his breakfast into a trash can. A trembling Reagan explained the new development.

"I'm going to get my baby!" Mattie wailed.

"Calm down, Mrs. Rannell," Detective Kowalski said. "We'll get your daughter, but you can't go alone. You could be jumping to conclusions. We can't spook Camden Yeager or his wife in case he is the one who contacted Ledbetter, and right now we have no proof he was involved."

"You can't keep me from my daughter!" Mattie shot past the detective and ran down the hall, Josh on her heels.

Two policemen blocked the front door, preventing them from leaving. Mattie turned around, hellfire blazing in her eyes, and Josh shouted in outrage.

"If you didn't make that story up last night about the ring and the babysitting thing, and I know it wasn't me, then who else could it be? Mrs. Moran didn't babysit anyone else. My daughter is staying at Camden Yeager's house because I was afraid that whoever was after Reagan might find her at our house, and now Ellie may be in danger. I assumed she would be safe with Bree and Cam. Did you make that story up to get a confession out of me?"

The detectives warily exchanged looks. "No, Mr. Rannell, we didn't make it up. That was exactly what Mrs. Pane told us," Detective Kowalski confirmed.

"Then the only other 5-year-old who's been here is Megan Yeager! That means Cam did some dumbass thing that could get my daughter killed!" Josh bellowed, the veins popping out in his neck. "I don't need your permission to pick up my own daughter! Now move the fuck out of my way because you're wasting precious time!"

"Please calm down, Mr. Rannell," Detective Kowalski pleaded. "If Mr. Yeager is in fact the man who contacted Ledbetter about the ring, we have no idea what the situation is. He's probably home. It's Saturday. We have to proceed with caution. I'll have backup ready just in case. We can discuss it in the car."

Mattie squeezed Josh's arm and nodded her agreement. Josh huffed and followed the detective outside. Within minutes, Detective Kowalski was in the car with Josh and Mattie on the way to the Yeagers' home. Despite Aiden's protests, the detective wouldn't let him accompany them.

"We're finished here," Detective Hilliard said. "Ready to go to the bank and take a look at your safe deposit box?"

"Not until Ellie's safely with her parents," Reagan said firmly.

"Ms. Asher, I have a cellphone with me, and I promise I'll notify you as soon as any word comes back on the situation. We're paying a gemologist to be on call and there are two forensic specialists already on the way to the bank. The clock is ticking," he said tapping his wrist.

# Chapter 21

"I want to make one thing perfectly clear, Detective Hilliard. You are all here at the invitation of Ms. Asher," Tyler clarified in a professional, no-nonsense tone. "You have no warrant. As far as the law is concerned, the items in the lockbox are Ms. Asher's possessions. The first thing I would like done is a complete logging of the items. Gems are easily misplaced." Ethan Rowling nodded his agreement.

"That's why we have the gemologist, Mr. Hamilton," the detective said.

The gemologist, a distinguished man in a pinstripe suit, was introduced as Terrence Capshaw. He sat down at the only desk in the room and opened a black leather case, while the CSI team, the detective, Mr. Rowling, Tyler, Aiden, and Reagan waited with anticipation. Taking out his tools, he put on gloves and set up special lighting, then spread a square, one-foot cushioned pad on the desk.

He looked at Reagan. "Shall we begin?" She nodded.

"This is one of the containers," Reagan said, handing him the plastic orange. "It pulls apart."

A smile played on Mr. Capshaw's face as he carefully placed his fingers on each side of the fruit and gently pulled, allowing an array of sparkling diamonds to rain out onto the jeweler's pad. There was a collective "ah" from the small group gathered around. He handed the empty orange to a member of the CSI team.

"Jesus," Detective Hilliard muttered under his breath.

The appraisal process took longer than Reagan would have preferred, her mind focused on Ellie. Through the whole process, she had watched Aiden nervously check his watch every few minutes.

Mr. Capshaw counted 95 diamonds and 86 black pearls. Because of time constraints, only five of each were randomly selected by the CSI team for appraisal. Reagan couldn't help but wonder if there had been an even hundred of each before they were stashed in Nana's AC unit. Mr. Capshaw's appraisal results were similar to the one done by Mr. Dunbar. The five diamonds were of extremely high quality, ranging from 3.1 to 4.6 carats and were valued from the smallest at $42,000 to the largest at $96,000. That announcement was met with more astonished exclamations. Although Mr. Capshaw declared the quality of the black pearls to be exquisite in all aspects, without an x-ray machine he couldn't confirm if they were natural or cultured. For that reason, he refused to give an appraised value. Reagan considered revealing that Mr. Dunbar already confirmed with an x-ray machine that they were natural but decided against it since she had no proof. As if reading her mind, Aiden caught her attention and gave her a barely perceptible shake of his head.

The CSI team took pictures of all the evidence and collected the containers for fingerprinting and possible DNA samples. Mr. Capshaw replaced the fruit containers with black velvet bags.

After clearing more space on the desk for the jewelry, he carefully lifted each piece out of the box one at a time. Jeweled necklaces, earrings, broaches, bracelets, rings, hair barrettes, and finally the sapphire and diamond tiara. Because the jewelry had participated in countless mud-pie tea parties and trips to the playground, and hadn't been cleaned in decades, it didn't have the same dazzling effect on the group.

"Those can't be real," commented a man from the crime unit.

"That's what we are here to determine," Mr. Capshaw said, barely hiding his excitement. It was obvious he was as giddy as a kid let loose in a toy store.

For 45 minutes, he scrutinized the jewelry with his tools and tester, holding the pieces to the light and turning them over to determine how they were made, while the crime scene photographer took numerous pictures of each one.

Detective Hilliard leaned over the desk and crinkled his nose in disgust. "This is a waste of time. That stuff looks like cheap glass."

"Well, Detective Hilliard, I haven't had enough time to check every piece, but the ones I have are quite genuine precious stones." He picked up the tiara. "For example, these are sapphires and diamonds. The stones are not all the same size, which was typical of earlier time periods. They often adjusted the jewelry to the gems, not the other way around. I'll give you a few general observations: All the pieces I've had time to review are handmade, and I suspect the others are as well. According to the results of the assay test I used to determine the karats in the three pieces I tested, they are 18k gold. Some of the stones are a rose or a table cut, which were characteristic of the Georgian Period, between 1714 through 1830. Pieces from that period are quite rare. Since they are all similar in style, they are likely from the same time period. To be precise and adequately appraise all these period pieces, it will take much analysis and research, probably weeks by an expert. I wish I could do more, but period jewelry is far from my specialty and, unfortunately, my time is up. My granddaughter turns 8 today, and I'm not going to be late to her party."

"Are we talking millions?" Detective Hilliard asked.

"I would assume many are quite valuable, but as I said, I am not qualified to make any determinations."

He pulled out several more bags and covered as many of the jewelry pieces as he could and stuck them gently back into the safe deposit box. When he had packed all his tools, he handed everyone a business card and offered to help do the detailed appraisal of the diamonds and black pearls at a later date.

"Any news about Ellie?" Aiden asked Detective Hilliard for the millionth time.

"Not yet," the detective answered dismissively, his eyes fixed on the jewels. "Last I heard they were with Kowalski at the police station."

Tyler and Ethan Rowling made sure everything was securely placed back in the safe deposit box and closed the lid.

"I'll go get the manager so we can get this locked back up," Mr. Rowling said, as he followed Mr. Capshaw out the door.

Detective Hilliard cleared his throat and crossed his arms over his pot belly. "I find it interesting that the number of diamonds and pearls are so close to 100. Almost like someone skimmed a few off the top." His accusatory tone was directed at Reagan. Then his eyes cut to Aiden.

She started to defend herself, but Tyler held up his hand. "What exactly are you implying, Detective?"

Detective Hilliard took a step toward Tyler. "I'm saying the number is suspicious, and I think your client knows something about them."

While Reagan stood stunned, Aiden stepped into the detective's space, his jaw clenched. "If Reagan or I were interested in keeping the gems, we would never have told you about them. We would have either left them in the safe deposit box or headed to Bora Bora!"

Tyler touched Aiden's forearm, signaling to let him handle it.

"Are they done with us?" Reagan asked, hoping to end the questioning.

"I know I am. Ellie is my only concern right now," Aiden said.

Reagan could picture the wheels turning in the detective's head as his lips contorted. She sighed in relief when the bank manager and Mr. Rowling came back into the room.

The manager pulled her keys out of her pocket. "If you'll come with me, Ms. Asher, we'll secure your safe deposit box."

Reagan picked up the box and proceeded to the door when Detective Hilliard stepped in front of her.

"What do you think you're doing with those jewels? I'm taking them in," he said with a condescending tone. Even the CSI team seemed shocked.

"Beg your pardon?" Tyler said, moving in between the two of them. "On what grounds?"

"Evidence in a murder investigation," the detective said, placing his hand on the box.

Aiden laughed out loud. "Are you fucking kidding me?"

Tyler took the box out of Reagan's hands, pulling from the opposite direction and forcing the detective to let go.

Ethan Rowling moved closer to Tyler and faced off with the detective. "Are you out of your mind? In what universe do you think we're going to let you waltz out of here with millions of dollars' worth of jewelry and loose gems in your hands? Not happening."

"Agreed," Tyler said. "Whenever those gems do leave this bank, I guarantee it will be escorted by an armored security service, and the destination remains to be seen. Until determined otherwise, this is the inherited property of Reagan Asher."

"I could arrest both of you for obstruction and have you disbarred," Detective Hilliard threatened, his hand casually resting on his gun seemingly to coerce them into compliance.

"Let's see you try," Tyler offered. "My client had no legal obligation to show you anything you've seen today. If you find evidence that any of these items were obtained illegally, you come see us with a warrant. If I were you, I'd start looking 20 to 30 years ago."

"The gems would be safer with us," Detective Hilliard persisted.

"I just bet they would," Aiden scoffed.

# Chapter 22

When Reagan and Tyler arrived at the police station, an officer behind a Plexiglas shield directed them to Detective Kowalski's office. Mattie sat alone in front of a large desk, twisting a handkerchief in her hands.

"Oh, Mattie," Reagan said as she fell to her knees in front of her. When Mattie looked up, Reagan's heart squeezed at the sight of her colorless face with dried mascara crusted under her eyes.

Her voice was robotic. "She's gone, Reagan. He took her, and they don't know where she is." Reagan wrapped her arms around her, hugging her tightly.

"Who took her, Mattie? Did Cam take her? What are the police doing?"

Mattie just shook her head. Emotionless, in shock.

"They'll find her," Reagan said, praying she spoke the truth. She appealed helplessly to Tyler, who only shrugged. Pulling a tissue from her handbag, she dabbed the smudged makeup on Mattie's face.

"Tyler, would you find Josh so we can figure out what's going on? She's in no condition to explain," Reagan whispered.

He mouthed, "Be right back" and left.

Five minutes later, Tyler walked back into the office with a frazzled Josh trailing behind. Josh wasn't in much better shape than Mattie, but at least he was coherent.

Tyler pulled out a chair and calmly directed Josh to sit. "Can you tell us what happened when you went to get Ellie?"

Josh ran his hand over his face. "It was a fucking nightmare. When we got to Bree and Cam's house, Mattie and I went to the door while the detective waited in the car. He didn't want to panic them, at least not until we had Ellie safely in our custody. Bree greeted us all bubbly and shit, like nothing was wrong. Invited us inside right away. It was hard as hell for me not to run up the stairs screaming for my baby. Anyway, Bree told us the girls weren't home. Cam had offered to take them out to do something fun, maybe go to a movie downtown. I was so pissed, I wanted to punch something. Cam was supposed to call Bree around 1 o'clock to check in and let her know when they'd be home, but he never called. She said it so nonchalantly, like it was no big deal. Then she offered to let me know when the girls got back home, but at that point, I was so scared I didn't hear another word she said. Mattie jumped up and started screaming Ellie's name. I didn't know what the hell to do, so I grabbed her hand, and we ran back to the car to get Kowalski."

He cleared his throat, his eyes filling with tears as he continued. "Cam isn't answering his phone. The police have checked all the movie theaters within a 20-mile radius and haven't found a trace of the girls. I've called all of their friends." He wrapped his arms around himself nervously. "The police have checked the surrounding neighborhoods. Found nothing. My baby has disappeared, and I'm about to lose my shit all over this police station." Reagan fought back her own panic, her heart breaking as she saw the tears streaming down his face.

Aiden arrived a few minutes later, took in the emotional scene and pulled Josh into his arms. Reagan did her best to explain what she had heard from the distraught pair. A few minutes later, Detective Kowalski came back to his office carrying two 8-by-10 photos in his hands.

"What the hell are you doing to find my niece?" Aiden demanded.

"You can't keep us in the dark like this," Josh shouted.

"I understand you're all upset, and with good reason, but if you'll give me a minute, I'll explain what's going on," Detective Kowalski said as he sat down in his chair. "We had a lot of pieces to the puzzle, but I had to connect all the dots to secure the warrants we needed to do a thorough search for your daughter. As far as a judge was concerned, you granted custody of your daughter to the Yeagers and had not planned a scheduled time for her to be picked up. The court couldn't assume she was in jeopardy until we proved Mr. Yeager himself was the threat. That's what I've been doing while the police carried out a local search.

"Luckily, Mrs. Yeager dismissed our concerns about her husband, so she gave us permission to search his office. We found a burner phone in his desk. He received a call this morning from a number that was probably from another burner phone, because we couldn't identify an account. The call history on Mr. Yeager's burner phone showed he had received a call from the same number five days prior to Mrs. Moran's murder. We also found the same picture of the diamond and sapphire ring on Camden Yeager's burner phone that we found on Justin Pane's phone. It was sent to Pane from the same phone that Yeager received a call from this morning. A perfect loop. That was enough for me to get a search warrant for the Yeager home and for the phone provider to track the numbers from the burner phones and Yeager's personal cell to phone towers. The burner phone that called Yeager's burner phone this morning was turned off, but the last ping was from a tower in Boardman, Ohio. Mr. Yeager's personal cell phone was also turned off, but the last ping was from a tower just off Interstate 80, near the Pennsylvania border."

"What does that mean?" Mattie asked.

"My God, please no," Josh murmured.

"All law enforcement agencies have been notified as well as public announcements to the media. The Youngstown/ Boardman area is right next to the Pennsylvania border, but we can't assume he left the state with your daughter. I know this feels like it's taking forever to happen, but considering how slow justice turns sometimes, this is rocket speed. A lot of strings have been pulled to get warrants issued and searches done. Megan Yeager is an innocent in this too. We have no idea the state of mind Yeager is in. We'll continue to utilize all resources at our disposal to find the girls."

"But that man … that fence who sells stolen jewelry is from Youngstown. What if he has my baby?" Mattie cried out.

"We have no way of tying the other burner phone to Ledbetter, but we have a detective in the area on his way to talk to him. That's all we can do until we have more than secondhand information. So far, we have no evidence connecting Ledbetter to the burglary or the attack on Mrs. Moran other than Pane's wife's hearsay. That won't get us a warrant. We have Mrs. Yeager in interrogation now and hope she can shed some light on this, but I'm afraid it's going to be a dead end. We're almost certain she knows nothing about her husband's activities."

Reagan was racked with guilt. The jewelry from Nana's home had brought this madness to Mattie and her family. As she released Mattie to stand, a wave of nausea hit her.

"You all right?" Tyler whispered in her ear.

"Got to get some air. I'm suffocating." She pulled on the collar of her turtleneck sweater, struggling to breathe.

"I'll go with you," he suggested. Reagan squeezed his hand.

"Please give me a few minutes alone." He nodded.

She hadn't even reached the door, when the room erupted into chaos. Everyone shouting, pointing fingers, demanding to be heard. The noise echoed in her ears as she made her escape. If she could just get out the door without anyone noticing her unsteadiness, she would get some fresh air and regain her equanimity. Making her way through the desks in the squad room, she steadied herself with a hand on the backs of the few empty chairs she passed. The officers and detectives, busy with interviews and paperwork, were oblivious to her presence. A glance out the large-paned windows in the hall reminded her that the weather had deteriorated into the blizzard-like conditions that were expected by late afternoon. Unfortunately, she had left her coat and hat in Detective Kowalski's office. The thought of going back into the lion's den to retrieve them twisted her stomach in knots. She settled for taking a seat on a bench in the hallway to compose herself.

Although her job was in human resources, Reagan wasn't used to being in direct contact with overwrought people. Matter of fact, she avoided it at all cost. She had learned a long time ago how to compartmentalize her feelings. When people became too emotional, they often lost perspective, all rational thought, and made bad decisions. Removing herself from the turmoil allowed her to regroup and think more clearly.

She racked her brain trying to think of places Ellie and Megan might be. Where would Cam Yeager have taken them? Just because he tried to sell Nana's ring didn't necessarily mean he was the kind of man who would hurt his own daughter or Ellie. And if Josh had been friends with him for years, surely Cam had redeeming qualities. *Maybe he just dropped them off somewhere while he did business and never made it back. But there are no movie theaters in Clairmont, where both of their families live.* The only kid-friendly place she could think of in the middle of winter was the library. Nana told her last summer that the library, in an effort to expand its outreach to families, had built a new children's wing. Nana had taken Ellie there several times — for story readings, to see a children's ballet performance of *Peter and the Wolf*, and to watch black and white Three Stooges movies. *What if that's where they went to watch a children's movie?* It seemed too simple, and she knew she could be way off base, but for the moment, it gave her hope. And if the man had a shred of decency, that's what he would have done.

When she got within view of Detective Kowalski's office, she saw that Tyler had a grip on Josh's arm trying to prevent him from hitting a man in a black suit who she didn't recognize. Mattie was bent over Aiden's lap with her face in a wad of tissue, while he patted her back. Ethan sat in a chair, holding his fingers against his temples as if attempting to keep his head from exploding.

"Do you want something to drink before I take this in?" an attractive dark-haired woman in a blue police uniform asked as she carried a tray of filled coffee cups.

"No thank you, but it's nice of you to offer drinks," Reagan said, tilting her head toward the office. "Hope it's decaffeinated. They sure don't need any more stimulation."

"You're right about that, but if it was my kid, I'm pretty sure I'd be a lot worse. I've been searching movie theaters all afternoon. When I came back in to report after my shift was over, I got an up-close look at their pain. Getting these folks coffee is the least I can do," she said. "Are you a relative?"

"Ellie is my goddaughter. Mattie, her mother, and I are close friends."

"I recognize you from the papers. You've had your own share of grief. Aren't you going in?"

"Not sure. It looks like one of those caged fight clubs."

"You know it. And there's enough testosterone in that room to keep an NFL team on a winning streak for the whole season," the officer said with a grin. Reagan forced a smile.

A thought popped into her head. "Can I talk to you for a minute when you get back from delivering the beverages? I'll be in the hall."

"Sure. By the way, I'm Officer Danielle Silva, or Danni if you prefer. Nice to meet you."

"Reagan Asher. Nice to meet you too."

# Chapter 23

Five minutes later, Danni met Reagan in the hallway and took a seat beside her.

"How can I help?"

Reagan explained that when her grandmother used to babysit Ellie, she often took her to the library to participate in the children's activities in the new wing. She remembered her mentioning that the programs included old black and white movies. Reagan didn't think it was a big leap to consider Cam Yeager might have dropped the girls off to watch a movie while he finished whatever business he was involved with. To her surprise, Danni seemed to seriously consider her suggestion.

"Honestly, I think everyone was so focused on an actual movie theater, I doubt the library occurred to anyone. Why don't we go in and share your theory with Detective Kowalski?"

Reagan wrung her hands as she met Danni's eyes. "You see, I don't want to get Mattie's hopes up if it turns out to be a stupid idea. And for all I know, the police have already checked it. I thought about going to the library myself, but don't have a car. If I go in that office and ask someone to take me, Mattie will want to know where I'm going, and ..."

"You hoped I could go with you?"

"I realize you are off duty, but maybe you could just drop me off on your way home. I'll get a Lyft back."

Danni thought about it for a few seconds. "Let me talk to my sergeant and see if he'll give me a little overtime. I'll tell him I'm checking on a lead at the library. He'll also know if it's already been done. I'd prefer to go as an on-duty officer just in case we run into trouble. I'm not taking any chances. Be right back."

Ten minutes later, Reagan was in the front seat of Danni's patrol car on the way to the library. Reagan borrowed Danni's wool coat since she still had on her uniform jacket. Between the snow and the traffic, the drive took longer than usual. They had been in such a hurry,

Danni forgot to pick up the 8-by-10 pictures of the girls, so Reagan texted her a photo of Ellie from her cell phone. The only thing she remembered from Megan's picture was her long brown hair.

They split up when they got to the library. Danni went to the information desk, while Reagan headed directly to the children's wing. A teenage girl with short blond hair tucked behind her ears sat at a desk by the door doing her math homework.

She looked up with eager eyes and smiled. "Can I help you?"

Reagan stuck her cellphone in the attendant's face. "Have you seen this little girl? Her name is Ellie, and she's with her friend Megan. They may have been here earlier."

The teen took a long look at the picture, touching it with her fingers to enlarge it.

"They were here for the kid's movie. It lasted about an hour and a half. When I realized they were still here by themselves long after the movie was over, I asked them if I could call their parents. The brunette-haired girl said 'no,' her daddy would be back soon. Since they missed lunch, I gave them some juice and cookies and helped them select some books to read while they waited. When I got back from my late lunch, they were gone. Figured the dad picked them up. It's not unusual for parents to use us as babysitters."

"What time did you leave on your break?" Reagan asked, feeling a surge of optimism and panic.

"Around 3. I only get 30 minutes."

"Thank you," Reagan said, rushing out the door.

Danni and Reagan almost collided into each other in the main hall, each trying to speak at the same time.

"You go first," Danni said, holding Reagan's forearms to calm her.

"They were here by themselves! They left somewhere between 3 and 3:30," Reagan said, her words tumbling out in her excitement. "What did you find out?"

"That's good. At least we have a timeline. The woman at the front desk saw the two girls leave. They were talking about getting an ice cream cone. Couldn't remember the time. She didn't realize they were alone. Figured a parent was outside getting the car. It's 4:36 now and it'll be dark soon. There are two ice cream parlors in town. Let me make a call to the station and get some officers here. Then we'll go check ourselves."

"We can split up and each go to one. It would double our chances of getting to them faster," Reagan said, turning toward the door. Danni caught her by the hand before she could take two steps.

"Not a chance. You wait right here while I call," she said firmly. "We'll ride together." Danni radioed the station, while Reagan stewed in frustration. They were five blocks away from the downtown shops that surrounded the three-block city park. Reagan knew she could reach the shopping area faster by jaywalking and taking shortcuts between buildings long before the police cruiser got past the first traffic light. She thought about making a break for it, until she caught the stern look in Danni's eyes that said, *"I'm watching you."* Reagan let out a resigned sigh.

"Got the message to my captain, and they're on the move. We'll start at Connie's Cones on the far side of the park. Plenty of backup is on the way."

They jumped in the patrol car and screeched out into traffic, the back tires sliding on the icy road. Reagan was surprised there were still a few Saturday afternoon shoppers milling around with packages in hand, despite the increasingly heavy snow. The pace was excruciatingly slow with stops at every pedestrian crosswalk. When they finally arrived in front of Connie's Cones, Reagan jumped out of the car, almost getting run down by a honking delivery truck.

"Reagan!" Danni yelled after her. "I swear, I should have left you at the station!"

# Chapter 24

Aiden was frustrated with the police for their lack of progress, pissed at himself for not noticing Megan Yeager's picture before, and emotionally exhausted from trying to sort out his feelings about Reagan's boyfriend, who seemingly had shown up out of nowhere and now couldn't keep his hands off her. Aiden had no doubt Tyler enjoyed rubbing his displays of affection in Aiden's face every chance he got. At that very moment, Tyler appeared to be smirking at him, as if he could read Aiden's thoughts. Instinctively, Aiden turned to look at Reagan to see if she noticed the silent exchange. That's when he realized she was gone.

"Where's Reagan?" he said too loudly, not caring if Tyler heard.

"She went to get some air a while ago," Tyler replied.

Aiden gritted his teeth. With his voice tight and measured, he said, "You let her go outside alone after someone tried to kidnap her? Are you fuckin' crazy?" He was on his last nerve.

"We're in a police station, for God's sakes. Cool your jets," Tyler said defensively. "She needed some space."

While Aiden contemplated the merits of beating the shit out of him, Josh spoke up. "When I went to the restroom, I saw her talking to a woman police officer in the hall. It's been a while, though. Maybe she knows where Reagan went. She was petite … dark brown hair in a bun."

"That sounds like the officer who brought us coffee," Mattie said.

"That's Officer Silva," Detective Kowalski said as his cell phone rang. "You guys keep it down so I can hear."

Aiden didn't wait. He hurried out into the main room and asked another detective who was sitting in the squad room if he's seen Officer Silva. He shook his head, but suggested Aiden check with the sergeant, pointing the way to a conference room. When Aiden arrived, the room was buzzing. The precinct captain was putting on his jacket while he barked orders to a room full of police officers.

"I want every available law enforcement officer from surrounding townships in downtown Clairmont square! The last place the girls were seen was the library, and they were headed to an ice cream parlor. There are two in town. Officer Silva is on the scene. Now move! I want those girls found within the hour! Do you hear me?" He yelled the last part as he pushed past Aiden, almost knocking him over.

Aiden's intuition told him that Reagan had a hunch about the girls' whereabouts and asked Officer Silva to check it out with her. As usual, not considering the risk to herself. He ran full speed through the squad room and down the hall, stopping only to be buzzed out. As he opened the door, a male voice called out to him.

"I'm going with you," Tyler panted as he caught up with Aiden. "Detective Kowalski told us Reagan was with Officer Silva looking for Ellie." His voice sounded contrite, and his face softened. "You were right. It was irresponsible of me to let her leave alone. Please let me come with you."

Aiden would have preferred to put his knuckles into Tyler's perfectly sculptured nose but knew that would serve no purpose other than to vent his frustration, and the asshole did sound genuinely apologetic.

"My truck is parked out front."

Police sirens shrieked around them as they inched through traffic, the windshield wipers struggling to keep up with the snow. Aiden turned off the main route, taking backstreets to avoid the congestion. When he was within two blocks of the downtown business district, he parked in the driveway of a historic house with a "for sale" sign in the front yard. Slipping and sliding through the snow, he and Tyler sprinted the rest of the way across the front yards of houses on the periphery of the town square.

When they reached the corner of the park next to the gazebo, Aiden stopped to brush snowflakes out of his eyes so he could read the names of the businesses along Main Street. The wall of white made it impossible to distinguish anything beyond a city block.

Tyler stared at him, hands on hips. "You don't know where the ice cream parlors are located, do you?"

Aiden flipped his head toward him, unable to control his annoyance. "Hell no! I've been in the Middle East for the past 12 years. This whole area was revitalized five years ago. It doesn't look anything like I remember it. I imagine most of the shops are still around the city park, but that's about it. You go right and I'll go left."

Tyler pulled out his phone and handed it to Aiden. "Put in your cell number. I'll call you if I see them, and vice versa."

Aiden wasn't sure if he would reciprocate, but he complied rather than be a total dick.

"Good luck," Tyler said, then faded into the snow.

---

Reagan knew Danni was furious with her for hurling herself out of the police cruiser, but time was of the essence. Dodging the last of the Saturday afternoon shoppers, she rushed into the ice cream parlor, knowing there was little chance the girls would still be there. The shop, decorated in soft pastels, was empty except for an older woman in a pink-pinstripe apron behind the counter. The sign over her head guaranteed that everything was homemade.

"Good afternoon! What can I get for you today?" she said in a cheery voice.

"Nothing, thanks, but maybe you can help me. Did two small girls about 5 years old come in here alone this afternoon?" Reagan asked.

Before she could answer, Danni bolted through the door and stopped short when she saw Reagan standing at the counter.

"Don't ever do that again, or I'll leave you in the backseat of my cruiser!" she huffed.

The clerk's eyebrows rose in surprise. Reagan laughed nervously and explained, "She's just kidding."

Danni's frown said, *"No I'm not."*

"Have you seen the girls?" Reagan continued.

"Except for you and a few teenagers ordering hot chocolate, no one else has been in since noon. Going to close early. Who wants ice cream in a snowstorm?" the woman shrugged.

"Thank you, ma'am," Danni said, as she grabbed Reagan by the arm and escorted her out.

"We do this my way, or you wait in the car."

Reagan nodded and smiled innocently. "Where's the next ice cream parlor?"

"Left, at the end of the block, then a couple of doors down."

The sidewalks were covered with at least 4 to 5 inches of snow, with much more piled higher on the curb. Reagan's rubber-soled shoes were little help as she attempted to speed to the next destination. Luckily, Danni's firm hand prevented her from sliding headlong into the brick façade of a building.

Police cars began pouring into town, pulling into emergency spaces around the town square to let officers out to join the search.

"There it is!" Reagan shouted, when she caught sight of a sign that read "Icy Treats." When they reached the shop, Danni clutched the handle, but it wouldn't open. She put her face to the window, while Reagan banged on the door. A wiry, middle-aged man mopping the floor in the back of the shop waved them away. When Danni put her police badge against the window and knocked so hard that the glass vibrated, he finally opened the door.

"What can I do for you, Officer?"

Before she could open her mouth, Reagan held up the picture of Ellie on her phone. "Have you seen this little girl today? She was with a friend."

The man studied the picture for a few seconds. "Sure did. They were in here for quite a while. Hate to say it, but parents often drop their kids by to get ice cream while they shop. Doesn't matter to me as long as I'm not too busy and don't need the tables."

"Do you know where they went?" Danni asked. "It's very important."

"The weather's gotten so bad, I decided to close up. My wife offered to take them home, but one of the girls said she promised her dad she'd wait for him. That's when the other little girl, the one in your picture, suggested they go to the bookstore. It's a couple of doors down," he pointed the direction.

Danni threw one of her cards at him. "Please call if you see them and don't let them out of your sight!"

*This is so frustrating,* Reagan thought. *Why didn't somebody call the police?*

The bells on the door jingled when Danni and Reagan dashed into the old-fashioned bookstore. A heavy-set woman in her 60s greeted them with a welcoming smile.

"Good afternoon. Can I help you find something, Officer?" she asked Danni.

Reagan showed the woman Ellie's picture. "Have you seen this child? She's with another little girl the same age with long brown hair."

The lady broke out into a huge grin. "Are you her mother? She's right upstairs in the children's reading room." She waved her hand toward the stairs. "I was j…"

Before the clerk could finish her sentence, Reagan pushed herself away from the counter and charged in the direction of the stairs, dodging display tables and bookcases, with Danni right behind her. They fought for position as they stomped up the narrow staircase, almost knocking each other back down the stairs. They froze on the top step when they saw the two precious, weary girls seated at a child-sized round table with their heads laying on their open picture books, both peacefully sleeping.

"Thank God," Reagan breathed a sigh of relief. Danni patted her on the back, giving her a big grin and a thumbs up.

Not wanting to startle her, Reagan knelt on one knee and softly spoke in Ellie's ear. "You need to wake up, Sweetie. It's time to go home to Mommy and Daddy."

Ellie flinched, lifted her head, and rubbed her eyes. Upon recognizing Reagan, she threw her arms around her neck and sobbed. Reagan clutched Ellie to her chest as she heard Danni radio the station that the missing girls had been found, their location and that they were in her custody.

"Looks like Megan is still out," Danni said. "I hate to wake her up, poor thing."

"Are you okay, Ellie?" Reagan asked, searching for signs of abuse.

"So sleepy," she yawned and wiped drool from her chin on her coat sleeve. "Mr. Yeager never came back to get us at the library. Megan tried to call him on her phone, but her battery was dead. We must have played too many games. Mr. Yeager told us not to call Mommy and Daddy, because he said they were too busy, and I'd get in trouble if I bothered them. A lady at the ice cream store looked up our house phone number on the computer, even though I told her I wasn't supposed to call, but nobody answered."

"Oh, Ellie," Reagan sighed, fighting to control her rage. "Your mommy and daddy love you and can't wait to see you. They would never, ever get mad at you for calling."

*How could Cam leave two 5-year-olds unattended?* Reagan mentally fumed. *He was probably running scared, but that was no excuse. The jerk hadn't wanted Ellie to call her parents because he didn't want to tip them off that something was wrong.*

Reagan squeezed her again. "You're safe now."

Ellie's cheeks puffed out indignantly. "I wasn't scared! I'm a big girl!"

Reagan took Ellie's hands in hers and suppressed a grin. "I know, Sweetie."

"Well, not too scared," Ellie admitted. "I mean Mommy never lets me walk around downtown alone, so I knew it was wrong, but Mr. Yeager forgot all about us and Megan cried every time I wanted to call Mommy. She didn't want her daddy to get mad. We just got so tired of the library." She turned her palms up for emphasis.

"You are a really brave girl," Danni said.

Ellie looked up, not noticing the policewoman until then. "The lady downstairs said she was going to call the police to find Mommy. You sure got here fast."

"I guess I did," Danni said with a smile.

An officer radioed Danni with instructions to bring Megan Yeager to his patrol car, so he and a female officer could escort her back to the station to meet her mother. Officer Ivan Griffin was on his way to the bookstore to stay with Reagan and Ellie until Danni got back.

Danni woke Megan with a gentle pat. "Megan, honey, I'm Officer Danni, and I'm going to take you for a little walk. Then a nice policewoman will take you to your mother."

Megan jolted up straight, wide-eyed. "What?" Danni repeated it again.

"Where's Daddy? He told me not to leave until he came back. He made me promise. He'll be so mad," she said defiantly, her puffy cheeks red.

"He got delayed, honey, but your mother's going to be so glad to see you. Now let's get your hat and coat on and get you on your way," Danni said soothingly.

When they all went downstairs and stopped at the counter, Danni thanked the clerk, then handed her a business card. "You let me know if I can ever do anything for you. We appreciate you taking good care of the girls."

"It was nothing. I had just come downstairs to call the police when you showed up. It must have been fate," the woman replied earnestly.

"Maybe it was," Reagan said.

They all turned toward the door at the sound of the entrance bells jingling. A red-cheeked, young officer in his twenties stepped in the door and pulled off his winter hat, beating it against his leg to shake off the snow.

"Afternoon, folks," he said with a small wave.

"Hey, Ivan," Danni said, with the familiarity of a coworker. "This is Reagan Asher and Ellie Rannell. If you'll keep an eye on them for a few minutes, I'd appreciate it. I shouldn't be more than ten minutes."

The officer nodded to Reagan and Ellie. "Nice to meet you, ladies. Take your time, Danni. Looks like you guys saved the day."

"It was Reagan's idea, so I can't take all the credit. Is the captain still in town?" Danni asked.

"Most everyone headed back to the station as soon as they heard the girls were safe," he said.

Danni gave Reagan a semi-serious look. "Don't give Officer Griffin any trouble. I'll be right back."

"Yes, ma'am," Reagan saluted playfully.

Reagan pulled out her cell to call Mattie, but she was unable to get reception. It sometimes happened in bad weather. She caught Danni at the door. "Has anyone told Mattie and Josh that Ellie is safe and with me?"

"I'm sure they have, but I'll make check as soon as I get in the cruiser," Danni said before she closed the door.

"I have a chair right back here if you'd like to sit down," the clerk said, motioning Ellie behind the counter. "I'll show you my favorite collection of *Winnie the Pooh* figurines. Tigger's my favorite." Ellie looked at Reagan, who nodded approvingly.

"Eeyore was my favorite," the officer said, looking over the counter.

With Ellie sufficiently entertained and under the watchful eye of the police officer, Reagan walked to the front window to wait for Danni's return. The snow was so heavy, she could barely see across the street to the park. The two-lane street had never been widened to accommodate Clairmont's growing population, which resulted in constant congestion, especially at peak times and magnified in bad weather. She was so thankful that her hunch had paid off and the girls were safe. Whatever Cam Yeager had been planning to do today, she was sure he hadn't wanted to put Megan or Ellie at risk. For that, she was grateful, no matter what kind of snake he turned out to be.

The late afternoon traffic in front of the shop was practically at a standstill. A powder blue and white 1950-something Impala coming up the street made her think of her dad. He collected models of classic muscle cars when she was a child. She couldn't help but wonder if he still did, and it stung that she had no idea. It was difficult to make out the driver, who was probably an older man, she imagined.

The sound of bells ringing and the closing of a door brought Reagan out of her nostalgic moment. She was standing next to the front door and no one had entered, so where had the bells come from? When she turned around, she stared in disbelief. A man, bundled in a thick black jacket and knit hat covered with snow, was walking from the back of the shop toward the counter with a gun in his hand. *Oh, my God. There must be a back door.*

The police officer who was talking to the salesclerk looked up in surprise, obviously too late to draw his weapon. Reagan visually searched the counter for Ellie and found her back turned away from the gunman as she played with little figurines.

"You need to put the gun down before someone gets hurt," the officer said, keeping his voice low and calm. "This town is full of police officers. You'll never get away."

The man just laughed. "Where is the Asher woman?" he asked the clerk, while he kept his gun focused on the cop.

Reagan was paralyzed, unsure of what to do. How to help. She recognized the voice and the accent.

"I...I'm not sure who your t...talking about," the anxious clerk said.

The gunman looked behind the counter and noticed Ellie. "Is that the Rannell girl?" he asked, motioning to her. "And don't play stupid."

"It's not her. We haven't seen either one of them," the officer said.

"Don't lie to me. I heard it over a police car radio. I know they are here, but I will make this easy for you. Either you tell me where Ms. Asher is, or I'm going to shoot that pretty little girl," he demanded.

"No!" Reagan cried. "I'm here! Don't hurt her! Please!"

Ellie whipped her head around, saw the man holding the gun and shrieked in terror.

When the gunman turned toward Reagan, the officer grabbed for the gun. A struggle between them ensued. Reagan was running to get to Ellie when the gun went off. Officer Griffin went down, clutching his leg. The gunman swung his gun down on the back of the officer's head, knocking him out cold. Then he yanked the radio off his shoulder and smashed it with his boot.

Ellie hurried around the counter and jumped into Reagan's arms, every inch of her body trembling.

When the gunman was sure the cop was incapacitated, he stalked up to Reagan and grabbed her arm. She swallowed hard and pushed Ellie away.

"Okay. You have me. Let this woman and the child leave," Reagan said, stepping in front of Ellie. Her pulse pounded in her throat as she stood face to face with the man who had claimed to be Arturo Fuentes. She glared at him with contempt, refusing to show weakness. He smiled with a satisfied smugness, then leveled a semi-automatic pistol to her chest. It took all her willpower to stand firm.

"No!" Reagan screamed, reaching for his gun, but he caught her hand and shoved her backward, slamming her against a cabinet. Ellie screamed.

"You will be much more cooperative if I have a gun to her head."

Reagan shook so hard she could barely stay upright, her legs like rubber.

"P...please don't shoot Reagan," Ellie pleaded.

"It'll be okay, Ellie," she said, wiping the tears from her puffy little face and tucking her securely behind her. The man waved his gun, motioning for them to move to the door. The clerk stood against the wall, frozen in place. Reagan caught her eye and tilted her head slightly to the counter where Danni's business card lay.

As they approached the door, the man behind them tucked his gun into his jacket pocket, but there was no mistaking where it was aimed. A gust of frigid wind and snow blasted them as he pushed them through the door. The blue and white Impala was double parked outside, blocking traffic, while the drivers in the cars behind it honked with impatience. Her abductor shoved Reagan and Ellie into the backseat, then ran around to the passenger side and hopped in.

"Go!" he commanded the driver. All she could see of the second man was the back of his black hair and the dark tan complexion of his neck, but she had a feeling it was the man who tried to run her down at the funeral home. All she could do now was pray someone would save them.

# Chapter 25

Aiden had been around the town square and checked in almost every business but found no trace of Reagan or the girls. The sea of police officers swarming the area had been a welcome sight and increased the odds the girls would be found quickly. He was standing in front of a drugstore when he heard the scratching sounds of a police radio coming from a cruiser parked on the curb. An officer stood on the sidewalk a few feet from the police cruiser talking to a salesclerk, but the radio was turned up loud enough for Aiden to hear the broadcast. His heart leapt with the announcement that Ellie and Megan had been found at the Teacher's Pet Book Store. Officer Silva was escorting Megan Yeager to Officer Jenkins on the corner of Main and 3rd Street. *Reagan must still be there,* he guessed.

After asking a lady in a nearby store for directions, he began jogging to the bookstore. Before he got to the next block, he caught sight of an officer across the street in the park, crouched down as he maneuvered from tree to tree. The 9mm in the officer's right hand was tucked against his hip. He was moving parallel with the street and in the same direction as Aiden. The officer was in pursuit, and Aiden had a gut feeling that Reagan and Ellie were the victims.

He stayed on the sidewalk as he continued to keep pace with the officer while he scrutinized the passengers in each car that passed. Most of them were either couples or parents with kids buckled up in the backseat. He spotted an old Impala coming toward him that looked out of place among the late model vehicles moving along in traffic. His attention was drawn to the man sitting in the front passenger seat, because he was twisted sideways with his back to the car door, his attention focused on the passengers in the back seat. The man's right arm was extended over the back of his seat toward the rear, and his hand was suspiciously covered by a knit scarf. Bingo. He had to get a look into that car.

Aiden nonchalantly moved between the parked cars and into the street alongside the Impala, trying to appear to be jaywalking. Luckily, traffic was barely moving. The driver of the Impala, who wore a baseball cap covering most of his face, wasn't paying any attention to him, so Aiden casually glanced in the backseat as the car eased past. His heart skidded to a stop when he saw Reagan huddled against the door on the driver's side with Ellie cradled tightly in her arms. Reversing his direction, he began following the rear-bumper of the slow-moving car as it inched along at a snail's pace. There was no doubt in his mind that once the car made its way out of the downtown traffic, Reagan and Ellie would be gone. Older cars had no GPS, so there was no way to track its movements if they identified the owner.

The approaching dusk, coupled with the snow from the near blizzard conditions, made it increasingly difficult to see clearly. When he caught a flash of blue in the periphery of his vision, he could just make out the cop across the street who appeared to be unaware of the captives in the Impala. Besides that, the officer was about to be headed in the wrong direction. Frantically waving his hand over his head, Aiden caught the cop's attention. When they locked eyes, he pointed to the Impala and turned his finger into the universal sign for a gun. The officer nodded back in understanding and reversed course, now keeping pace and walking parallel with Aiden. He needed a plan fast. As soon as the car reached the light at the next intersection, it would be smooth sailing out of town.

When the light turned green and the cars in front of the Impala began to move forward, Aiden decided what he needed to do. With lightning speed, he maneuvered his way to the driver's window before the man had a chance to put his foot on the gas. Aiden used his left hand to knock on the glass, while he slipped his right hand inside his coat for his Colt .45. After the recent kidnapping attempt on Reagan, he had decided he needed higher-powered protection.

"Yeah! Dude! Can you help me? I'm lost!" Aiden repeatedly knocked on the glass and yelled until the driver finally acknowledged him, rolling down his window as he glared up at him with aggravation. He didn't recognize the man at the wheel, but he suspected he was the guy who attacked Reagan at the funeral home. An impatient driver in the truck behind the Impala beeped his horn a few times. Without breaking eye contact with the driver of the Impala, Aiden waved his hand dismissively at the traffic behind them.

"Move away. We cannot help you," the man sniped in a Middle Eastern accent. Before he reached the handle to roll the window back up, Aiden pressed the barrel of his .45 against the man's temple. The driver gasped when he felt the cold metal press against his skin, his eyes widening.

"Put the car in park and place your hands on the steering wheel where I can see them with your head down, or I'll blow your fuckin' brains out," Aiden said between clenched teeth.

"Bo, do something. He has a gun to my head!" he shouted. Bo. Aiden planted that in his memory.

"Don't worry. He won't shoot you, you idiot. I have a gun pointed at the kid," the passenger named Bo said confidently.

Aiden leaned down to the window to make sure the abductor who sat in the passenger seat could hear him clearly. "You're going to let the child go. You don't need her. Do you hear me?" Neither of the men responded or moved to release Ellie. Aiden wasn't low enough to actually see the Bo guy without losing sight of Reagan and Ellie, but he knew he needed another approach. "Listen, asshole, either let the girl go, or when I pull the trigger, this gun is big enough for the bullet to go right through your buddy's skull and into yours. My 12 years in special forces guarantees it."

"Bo, give him the girl," the driver begged, his hands white-knuckled on the steering wheel. "He's right, we don't need her."

"Nour, you are foolish. He is bluffing," Bo said, identifying the driver.

"Let her go!" Nour yelled.

Bo paused for a few seconds then said to Reagan, "Get her out. She was only a bonus anyway."

Reagan freed one of her arms from Ellie's grip so she could wedge the door open, but when she tried to put Ellie out of the car, Ellie refused to let go of her.

"Run, Ellie!" Reagan shrieked. She struggled to pry her loose and push Ellie out the door, but Ellie became hysterical and clung to her neck.

"No! No! No!" Ellie cried, wrapping her legs around Reagan's waist.

"Now, Ellie!" she yelled as she pried Ellie's tiny hands from her neck and roughly shoved her out on to the street as far away from the car as she could, then slammed the door shut. Ellie tumbled onto the snowy pavement too stunned to move. Although her long heavy coat and the piles of snow cushioned her fall, she let out a terrified scream at Reagan's abandonment. Aiden knew it crushed Reagan to manhandle Ellie, but a few scrapes and bruises were a small price to pay for her life. With the gun still firmly pressed against the driver's head, Aiden chanced a quick glance. Ellie's face was swollen, and snot streamed from her nose as she coughed and gasped for air. He wanted to scoop her in his arms but couldn't risk their lives.

"Ellie. It's Uncle Aiden, Sweetheart, you need to get up," he said softly but firmly, his eyes still on the driver. When she didn't move, he took another quick glance and repeated his words. She looked up and recognized him immediately, but he could tell she didn't understand what was happening or what she do. The next time he spoke to her, he used a disciplinary tone.

"Listen to me, Ellie. You're a big girl and you need to do what I say. Get up this second and run into that store with the blue door. Now! I'll come get you in a minute. I promise." With a pouty, hurt look on her face, she stumbled and slipped a few times until she got to her feet. She took one last terrified look at him, then ran crying into the store.

The Bo guy, still pointing a gun at Reagan, said, "You have the child, now go or I'll kill the woman."

Aiden's brain raced. He was making it up as he went along. Reagan sat up straight against the backseat next to the door, her eyes focused on him, silently begging him to save her. In the corner of his eye, he caught movement to his right. The officer had crossed the street and was now duck-walking from behind the car to the passenger door, the falling snow and the approach of evening masking the advance. For some reason, the cars behind them were no longer sitting on their horns, even though traffic was stalled.

As he worked through it in his mind, he realized if Reagan were on the floorboard, the man holding the gun would have to lift himself up and twist to get the right angle to shoot at her. It was Aiden's intent to make sure the man was incapacitated by then.

"I'm waiting," Bo said. "You back away from the car or I will kill her."

Pressing the gun harder against the driver's temple, Aiden leaned down to get a better read on the man holding the gun. When the guy looked up at him, he recognized him immediately. The electrician who impersonated Arturo Fuentes. Then, to his surprise, the officer who had been tracking the car peeked in the passenger window, catching his attention with a blink and a nod toward the backseat. He mentally kicked himself for his assumption. It was a woman. He was grateful for the backup. Bo's back was still to the door and his attention turned toward Reagan, totally unaware of the officer outside his window.

"If you want to see the woman live, you must back away from the car," Bo demanded, smiling maliciously at Reagan.

Aiden gave the officer a chance to surveil the situation in the front and back seats. When Bo's eyes flicked back to Reagan, Aiden mouthed to the cop, "Get ready." She disappeared without further acknowledgement. He hoped she would cooperate with his off-the-cuff plan. When he looked in the backseat, Reagan still watched him closely. Moving his eyes from hers to the floorboard, back and forth in rapid succession, he waited for a response that she understood. She slowly blinked her eyes. The driver's hands remained on the steering wheel, his head down.

It all happened in a flash. With his left hand, he slapped the roof of the car. Reagan dove for the floorboard. The startled driver sat up straight, blocking Aiden's shot of the man with the gun. As Bo lifted up to shift his position to retrain his gun on Reagan, the cop popped up and shot two rounds through the window, hitting Bo twice and forcing him to fall back down in the seat, his gun landing at his feet. Aiden's immediate priority was Reagan. He yanked the back door open and grabbed her by the arm, unceremoniously flinging her out of the car and onto the snowy street. As the officer wedged the front passenger door open to pull Bo out of the car before he could retrieve the gun, the Impala was slammed from behind with such tremendous force that it knocked the wounded man out of his seat and into the middle of the street. Because there was no longer traffic in front of the Impala, the driver took the distraction as an opportunity to escape. He threw the gearshift into drive and stomped on the gas. The wheels spun, swerved side to side, slamming into a parked car and slinging ice down the street until the tires gained traction and sped off. The passenger door clipped the female officer on the arm sending her backwards into the street as it slammed shut. Aiden thought about shooting out the tires, but better judgment prevailed, and he decided capture was best left to the police. He had a sinking feeling he would regret it later.

By the time Aiden got to the downed officer, she had already sprung to her feet and was handcuffing the man called Bo, who was lying in the street moaning. Police came running from all directions. Aiden couldn't help but wonder where the fuck they had been. An ambulance arrived at the scene within minutes for the injured abductor. As a precautionary measure, the police captain had ordered it as soon as he had gotten word the missing girls had been found. It enabled the kidnapper to get immediate attention.

When Aiden finally turned toward the sidewalk to make sure Reagan was okay, she was seated on a bench under the awning of a jewelry store with Ellie hanging on her waist and Tyler's arms draped protectively around her shoulders. *I guess the old saying "to the victor go the spoils" does not apply here,* he thought.

After Bo had been loaded into the ambulance, Aiden held his hand out to the officer who had helped save Reagan.

"Aiden Rannell. Nice work. You okay? You took a pretty hard hit from that door."

Firmly shaking his hand, she said, "A bit bruised, but fine. Officer Silva. Danni. Ex-cop or military?"

"Ex-Seal," he smiled, releasing her hand. "And yes, I do have a carry permit. I don't know how this would have gone down without your help. I thought I had it under control until that jackass hit the Impala from behind, then I lost my shot."

"Appreciate your assist too. I couldn't radio for help because the bookstore clerk told me the perps either had a police radio or heard where Reagan was over a radio, so I was afraid to give away my position. I was hoping another officer would see me and assist. Either the snow was too heavy or most of them had already headed back to the station. Guess it worked out for both of us. I recognized you from Kowalski's office. Knew you were with the family. Never forget a pretty face," she chuckled good-naturedly. *His adrenalin was pumping. Her adrenalin was pumping. What was a little harmless flirtation?*

"Ditto." He flashed her a huge grin. He was jacked up and had to move. Do something before he jumped out of his skin, but there was nothing to do but ride it out. "Do you need a lift to the hospital?"

"I'm fine, but my arm's probably going to hurt like hell in a few hours. By the way, who hit the back of the Impala?"

Two officers walked up to Danni and Aiden, catching the last of their conversation. One pointed to a black Ford truck.

"The guy in the truck behind the Impala watched the woman and the little girl get thrown into the backseat and thought it didn't look right. When he saw Office Silva approach, he decided he could help by plowing into the back of the car."

Danni shook her head. "Some help."

"Yeah. We'll be taking him to the station," the officer said.

Detective Kowalski appeared out of nowhere. He glared at Aiden and turned to Officer Silva. "Why don't you head back to the station with Captain America here so we can get this debacle sorted out? Heard one of the perps is already on the way to the hospital."

"Yeah," Danni said. "He was attempting to shoot Ms. Asher. I hit him in the left upper arm and somewhere in the side. He was conscious and talking to the paramedics."

"We'll recap in my office and begin the process for an officer involved shooting," the detective sighed and walked away.

Danni turned to Aiden. "As much as I appreciate the help, unfortunately you've caused me a ton of paperwork." She laughed. "And you owe me a drink."

*Definitely flirting, but I can use the distraction.* He gave her a mischievous smile and winked. "That's one fine I don't mind paying." Then he remembered Tyler had ridden with him, so he wouldn't have any way to get Reagan and Ellie home. "Can I catch a ride with you? I think my truck is spoken for."

"Not a problem," she said.

Walking over to Ellie, Aiden bent down and hugged her, kissing her cheek. "I'm sorry I scared you, baby girl. Just wanted to get you to safety. I'll see you tonight." She slowly nodded her head and curled farther into Reagan's arms. Tossing his keys to Tyler, he said, "The truck's parked on Church Street midway down the block. Make sure Ellie gets home as soon as possible. I'm sure Josh and Mattie are going apeshit."

Reagan didn't say a word to him, but he thought he caught a hint of disapproval or maybe a flash of jealously. Or maybe it was his imagination. At that moment, he didn't give a shit.

He put his hand on Danni's shoulder and smirked. "Lead the way. It will be my first ride in a patrol car. You going to let me play with the siren?" She rolled her eyes and shook her head.

# Chapter 26

It was 4 a.m. and Reagan was wide awake. She had barely slept all night, listening for the door to Aiden's room to click open, a signal he hadn't stayed out all night. It was irrational and hypocritical for her to fret over his whereabouts, especially as she lay in bed next to Tyler, who had fallen asleep as soon as his head hit the pillow. Tired of staring at the same spot on the ceiling, she slipped out of bed and eased out the bedroom door. The house was silent. She tiptoed down the stairs and through the darkened family room to the kitchen, still wearing her cotton nightshirt, a soothing cup of chamomile tea on her mind.

"Really? A t-shirt? I would've thought you'd bring out the La Perla for Mister GQ," a sarcastic voice startled her. "He can certainly afford it."

Aiden. She turned around to find him bare-chested in sweatpants sprawled out on the sofa. His tone irritated her, and the words were out before she could filter them.

"Don't be an ass. Where have you been?"

"None of your business … but I'm just fine, princess." He ran his hands up and down his muscular abs. "See, not a single bullet hole. Thanks for asking. You're welcome, by the way. I guess you've gotten so used to me coming to your rescue it's become mundane. One bad guy shot. One got away. I'd call that a 50% success rate. Everyone walked away in one piece, except Ellie."

Reagan winced. His comments were cruel and hit their intended mark, to make her feel responsible. As if she didn't already feel bad enough. But he was right about one thing, she hadn't thanked him.

"Where were you? I was worried?" her voice softer.

"Your concern is touching," he grimaced, running his hands over his face and through his hair trying to shake off the fog.

"You're not going to tell me?" She sat on the coffee table in front of him.

He sighed. "Out with a bunch of cops for a few drinks. Made new friends."

"Are you hungover?"

"Hungover implies some level of sobriety. I'm not sure I'm there yet." He was agitated and determined to be obstinate.

"You didn't drive home like that, did you?"

"Now how would I have done that, Reagan, when your boyfriend took *my* truck?"

She winced.

"I got a lift."

"Danni?" she asked, knowing full well she shouldn't have. She had no right, and they both knew it. He didn't answer.

"Did Danni bring you home?"

"Why do you care? You've got your own bed warmer."

She tried to ignore the comment, but it hurt. "Did you sleep with her?"

He sat up, put his elbows on his knees, and leaned within inches of her face. When she met his eyes, they were narrowed with indignation. He punctuated every word as he spoke.

"Why are you doing this? You have no damn right to ask me who I sleep with when you are across the hall screwing your boyfriend only hours after we were sucking each other's face off in the back of the movie theater!"

Tears sprung to her eyes. "I didn't … I mean I couldn't ... You have to believe me."

Studying her face for what seemed an eternity, probably giving her some kind of special ops lie detector test, he finally said, "Doesn't matter if I believe you or not. Let's look at the most important fact. He's in your bed, not me. End. Of. Story."

"Aiden. Please give me some time." He shook his head.

"You are fucking with my head, Reagan, and I'm doing my best to stop it."

Not being able to stop herself, she reached for his hand, but he quickly pulled it out of her reach.

"That's exactly what I mean. Don't fuckin' touch me, Reagan. You have a boyfriend waiting for you upstairs, in your bed. Apparently, you're missing the significance of that."

"Don't give up on me," she whispered.

"You asked for space. Now give me mine. If I decide to get laid, it's none of your fucking business." He grabbed a blanket and pillow off the sofa and stormed up the stairs.

# Chapter 27

The next morning, the house was full of activity, a scheduled meeting with Detective Kowalski in the morning and Nana's funeral in the afternoon. Josh and Aiden's parents showed up at 7 a.m. to pick up Ellie. They were taking her on a vacation to the Gulf Coast until things settled down. Reagan and Tyler stayed out of the way to give them family time. It was a short visit with lots of tears and emotions.

When Detective Kowalski arrived at 11, Reagan was astonished to see Danni Silva accompany him. Her starched navy-blue uniform had been replaced by a tailored, black pantsuit with a white silk blouse. Her dark brown hair, which had been twisted into a tight knot on the back of her head yesterday, now hung loose several inches past her shoulders. Reagan was perplexed as to why Danni was there and instantly felt uncomfortable, especially knowing Aiden had spent the evening with her. His cocky grin revealed that Danni's arrival was no surprise to him.

Once everyone had taken a seat and the introductions made, Detective Kowalski began the meeting.

"Ms. Asher, I want to apologize for Detective Hilliard's behavior yesterday at the bank. Ethan Rowling reported to us that Detective Hilliard tried to take possession of the jewels in your safe deposit box. That was totally unauthorized and against departmental policy. I assure you if we were confiscating the jewelry, you and the bank would be served warrants and security would be provided. That's why you don't see him here today. The captain removed him from the case, and he has been suspended until an investigation can be conducted. Officer Silva passed the detective exam eight months ago and has been waiting for an opening to accept a promotion. Since her intervention in the kidnapping yesterday helped secure the release of you and Ellie Rannell, the captain thought she'd be a good fit to replace Detective Hilliard."

Reagan caught Aiden's eye. He shrugged. Her stomach churned.

"Congratulations, Detective Silva," Reagan said begrudgingly. "I didn't get an opportunity to thank you last night. I'm afraid I wasn't in the best frame of mind. How did you know we were in trouble?"

"The clerk at the bookstore used the business card I left and called my cell as soon as she could. She informed me that the kidnappers learned of your location by overhearing a police radio, so I was afraid to use it to call for help. Luckily, Aiden overheard the same way," she explained.

"Let me add my deepest appreciation as well," Mattie said, wearing a sincere expression of gratitude. "Words can't express what it means to us. I heard you were injured."

"Just a deep tissue bruise on my arm. No big deal."

"Have you caught the other kidnapper or that Ledbetter guy?" Josh directed the question to Detective Kowalski. "We want to get some normalcy back in our lives. I had to pack my baby up and send her out of state with my parents, for fuck sakes!"

"Ledbetter was brought into the Youngstown Police station yesterday for questioning. We weren't surprised that he denied knowing or having any contact with Justin Pane or Camden Yeager. Without any concrete evidence linking him to either of the men or the murder of Mrs. Moran, they had to let him go. We are still trying to get information from the man referred to as Bo. He's in serious but stable condition at the hospital, but so far has refused to talk. Still don't have identification on him," Detective Kowalski said.

"Do you think the driver was the same man who tried to kidnap me at the funeral home? I'm not sure about the voice, but it seemed like the same kind of accent," Reagan said.

"It's a good chance."

"Can't you identify him from his prints?" Aiden asked. "Surely this isn't his first rodeo."

"Not yet. The FBI and the NSA are still running them through all the databases. We're hoping to hear something by tomorrow morning."

"Do you think they're connected to Gabe Ledbetter?" Aiden asked.

"We're not sure, but it doesn't feel right," Detective Kowalski said. "It's more likely they have some connection to the jewels themselves. Or learned about them from someone. It's hard to say at this point."

He turned to Reagan. "Ms. Asher, is there anything they said to you that could help us in any way?"

"Not really. Like I said yesterday, they called each other Bo and Nour. When I replayed everything in my head last night, I decided the Bo guy was the one in charge. He was older too. Gave most of the orders."

"Those guys didn't strike me as professionals," Aiden said. "Both attempts to take Reagan were opportunistic, no prior planning. And they didn't seem to be concerned about being recognized."

"What if they aren't US citizens and don't have an arrest record in the States?" Danni suggested. "They wouldn't have to worry about being recognized."

"If that's the case and the jewels are their motivation, they'd have to have a way to smuggle them out of the country or have made prior arrangements to sell them in the States," Detective Kowalski said. "That could be the connection to Ledbetter, but the FBI doesn't believe that's the case. Ledbetter isn't known to have had any prior dealings on an international level."

"Why do they need me?" Reagan asked.

"To tell them where the jewels are. Ellie would be leverage to get you to talk," Aiden suggested.

Detective Kowalski's phone rang, and he stepped into the kitchen. When he came back in the room, he wore a grave expression.

"They found Cameron Yeager a few miles over the Pennsylvania state line. He was in his car with a bullet in the back of his head."

The room went silent.

Mattie choked out a sob. "What is happening?" she exclaimed. "They were our best friends!"

Josh put his arms around her, pulling her close. "This is crazy. Why would they kill Cam? It's not like he's some sort of mastermind. Trust me, he's not that smart. I've thought a lot about it. We've known each other since college. Barbecued on weekends. Took family vacations together. I can't wrap my brain around it. Why would he do something like this? If he had money troubles, you would never know it."

"The Yeagers were having major financial issues," Detective Kowalski confirmed. "Three months behind on their mortgage and a stack of unpaid bills. According to his boss, Yeager recently lost a lot of high-profile clients due to inattention, so he was demoted to a smaller territory. Made a huge impact on his income. His wife said she wasn't aware of the money problems, but she suspected he was having an affair. We haven't confirmed it one way or the other. At least when things went south, he didn't drag the young girls along. Probably received a call from someone, my guess would be Ledbetter, before he left home with them. He must not have been too concerned, or you'd think he would have left the kids with Mrs. Yeager. He was probably the last loose end that could tie Ledbetter to Justin Pane and Mrs. Moran's murders. That's the working theory."

"You need to come home, Reagan," Tyler said, placing his hand possessively on hers.

"But Nana's funeral is in a couple of hours. I can't leave," Reagan said defiantly.

"That's not a bad idea," Danni said. "At least until the other assailant is caught, and for all we know, there could be others involved."

"There's so much that needs to be done to get Nana's house repaired and ready to sell. And what if they follow me to Chicago?"

"You already have some things at my place. Move in with me," Tyler suggested.

Reagan glanced at Aiden. His face was stoic.

"You're welcome to stay with us as long as you want," Mattie said.

"I'll think about it. For now, I need to get changed so I'm not late for the visitation," Reagan said.

Danni was assigned to accompany Reagan to the funeral for protection. They were amazed by the number of TV vans and reporters shoving microphones into the faces of mourners as they arrived. After Nana's murder, Justin Pane's murder, and now two attempted kidnappings, the press was ripe with eagerness to solve a mystery.

"Jesus Christ," Tyler said to Reagan. "This is bullshit! You're leaving with me in the morning."

Reagan was speechless. She hated when he bossed her around as if she didn't have a mind of her own, but she had to admit, this time he might be right.

# Chapter 28

After the funeral, Aiden decided he needed to distance himself from Reagan, so he accepted an invitation from Danni to go to dinner. He hated seeing Reagan internalizing her pain and wearing an emotionless mask. To people who didn't know her, she appeared removed and aloof, but he knew the truth. She had mentally shut down, and all he could do was watch Tyler play the comforting, rich boyfriend. If circumstances had been different, it might have been him, but it wasn't. Time he got the hint and removed himself emotionally. He had put his own needs on hold to keep her safe and help get the answers she needed, and despite the awkwardness, he wasn't about to renege on his promise.

On the way to the restaurant, Danni turned to him and asked, "I know Tyler is Reagan's boyfriend, but I can't help sensing something between the two of you."

He glanced at her from the driver's seat, trying to get a read on her motivation for the question. *Personal clarification or professional inquiry?* "You don't mess around with small talk, do you?"

"Sorry. Don't mean to pry, but I prefer the honest approach. Am I wrong? In case you couldn't tell, I'm interested, but I need to know if I'm wasting my time. You're not bad to look at, and you seem like a good guy. Rare qualities these days, but I'm a bit jaded."

"Huh … thanks? Appreciate your directness. I'll admit Reagan and I have a complicated relationship of sorts, but as you said, she has a boyfriend, and he's successful and loaded. Can't, nor do I want to, compete with that."

"Just checking," she said with a sly grin and quickly changed the subject. "I'm starving! There's a little Italian restaurant on the way to my house that makes the best homemade pasta you'll ever eat. What if we spend a little time getting to know each other over a carbohydrate-charged meal?"

"Sounds like a plan."

It was a typical neighborhood Italian eatery with red-checkered tablecloths and old-world photos of Italy on the walls. The food was excellent, and the conversation flowed easily. The thing he liked about Danni was that she was so comfortable in her own skin. No pretenses. She was naturally sexy without trying, easygoing, confident, and she kept him entertained with her wicked sense of humor. He was conflicted when she invited him back to her place for a drink but found himself agreeing.

As he started the car, his cell phone rang through the Bluetooth speaker. The screen flashed Mattie. He groaned and pushed the green button.

"What's up, Mattie?" He struggled not to sound annoyed.

"Where are you? Can you talk?"

"If you make it quick. Danni's in the car with me, and I'm on speaker."

"I made reservations for Reagan to fly to Spokane, Washington, tomorrow. She's going to talk to her dad."

"That's probably a good idea, don't you think? He may be able to fill in some blanks. I'm surprised the police haven't done that already." He glanced at Danni, who shrugged and turned her palms up.

"She's going alone, Aiden," Mattie said, her voice full of apprehension.

"Tyler's not going with her?"

"She told him she needed to do it by herself, and he didn't object. Said he needed to get back to work anyway."

"What's that got to do with me?"

"She can't go alone! What if those men are still following her?"

"If she didn't listen to Tyler, what makes you think she'll listen to me?"

"At this point, all she hears is white noise. She's shutting everyone out. It's scaring me, and I'm afraid she's going to do something to put her life in danger. That's why I made a reservation for you to fly to Spokane tonight at 1 a.m. I already paid for the ticket. You'll get there in the morning and meet her plane in the afternoon. That way she won't have anything to say about it, and I'll know she's safe."

He shook his head and looked at Danni, who raised an eyebrow in question.

"You made a lot of assumptions, Mattie. Our relationship is tenuous at best. It was bad timing," he said, for Danni's benefit as well.

"Since Danni is there, I'll ask her," Mattie said. "Can you guarantee that Reagan will be completely safe while she's in Washington?"

Danni looked at Aiden for confirmation that she should get involved. He nodded.

"We don't know if the guys who tried to take Reagan are connected to Gabe Ledbetter, or if they're lone wolves, or part of an international syndicate. We're hoping to get more information tomorrow, but we have no idea how far their reach is or what resources they have at their disposal. There's a lot of money at stake, and sometimes that means someone with deep pockets. Honestly, I can't tell you for sure one way or the other."

"Why don't you give Tyler the same speech you gave me?" Aiden suggested.

"I did. Seems he's not quite as concerned when you're out of the picture," Mattie said.

"Not playing the jealous game with anyone. Let it alone," Aiden practically scowled.

"Fine, I'll go with Reagan myself, even though that will mean I have to cancel my flight for tomorrow morning to join Ellie at your parents' beach house for a couple of days, because she cried all the way to the Alabama coast. But hey! Maybe your mom and dad can find her a good psychologist," Mattie hissed. "Talk to you later."

"Wait! Shit, Mattie! Guilt-tripping me doesn't help." *Making me feel like it's my fault doesn't either,* he thought. "You know I'd do anything for Ellie. Do you want me to fly down and bring her home?"

"Thanks for offering, but Ellie needs me. You know I love Reagan, and I don't want to see her get hurt. Did you see her at all during the funeral? She was almost non-responsive. Even if she's not in danger, she hasn't seen her father in years, and who knows what shit she'll find out about her crazy-ass family. He didn't even come to the funeral to support her, so she's dealing with all this shit without one actual family member!"

"She hasn't even told her father what was going on?"

"He said he broke his leg in a skiing accident, and he's in rehab or some BS excuse I'm sure he made up."

Aiden pulled over to the side of the street and stopped. He slammed his head against the headrest and ran his fingers through his hair.

"Please, Aiden," she whispered.

"Okay, Mattie. Text me the flight information."

Mattie's voice was thick with emotion when she spoke. "Thank you, Aiden. I'll never forget this."

He was pissed and didn't have any desire to fly across the country, but he couldn't in good conscious leave Reagan vulnerable, physically or emotionally. What he wanted to do was smack her *oh-so-concerned* boyfriend around for leaving her to deal with it by herself. *No wonder they have a communication problem. He doesn't step up when it counts.* Aiden was both aggravated and relieved that his evening with Danni would be cut short.

He turned in his seat to face her. She gave him a quirky smile that said, *I don't like it, but I understand.*

"I'm sorry," he said.

"It's okay. You're a good guy. That's what I admire most about you."

"Can I call you when I get back?" he asked.

"Let's see how things play out."

He nodded in agreement. "I hate to ask this, but would you mind if we dropped by Reagan's grandmother's house? If I'm going to see her father, I'd like to take some pictures I found in her grandmother's desk to refresh his memory. Reagan's mother, Claire, had two friends when she was a teenager who were Middle Eastern. It's probably a coincidence, but maybe the guys trying to abduct Reagan are connected to them in some way. Those jewels have been hidden in the A/C for a long time, and they had to come from someone who knew the family — if it wasn't someone in the family, that is. For Reagan's sake, I hope not. If it's not convenient, I'll drop you by your place first."

"Fine with me. Maybe a fresh set of eyes can offer a different perspective," Danni offered.

The yard and driveway were covered in at least a foot of new snow from yesterday's storm. Since the streetlight provided the only light, Aiden parked out front at the curb.

Unlocking the door with the key Reagan had given him, he reached inside and flipped the light switch by the door. Nothing happened. He opened the front door wide enough to allow the outside lighting to illuminate the living room so he could find a table lamp. It didn't work either. He tried one more switch on the dining room wall and got nothing.

"Power's out. Stay here, and I'll get a flashlight out of my truck."

He was back quickly.

"Why would the power be off? The storm wasn't that bad," Danni asked, stepping inside the door.

"Watch your step. This place is a mess. The cleanup service is supposed to be in this week." Aiden took Danni's arm to help her navigate the debris of slashed cushions, broken glass, and busted furniture in the dark. They hadn't gone far when a scraping sound came from somewhere in the house.

"Did you hear that?" Danni asked, holding her hand out to stop him.

"I heard something."

Danni reached in her coat and pulled out her 9mm. "Do you still have that gun you were carrying yesterday?"

"Got it right here." He pulled his Colt from his waistband.

After quickly giving her the layout of the house, he went left toward the bedrooms, while she went right toward the kitchen, taking the flashlight with her.

He carefully made his way down the hall, then stopped at the office door and eased inside. Streaks of moonlight shining in through the curtains showed that the room was clear of intruders, but he had a nagging feeling that something wasn't quite right. He would need more light to be sure. Cautiously, he moved the shower curtain in the bathroom and found nothing. Reagan's room was clear as well. By the time he reached Nana's room, he remembered his cellphone had a flashlight app and smacked himself in the forehead. A frigid breeze hit him in the face as he eased the bedroom door open. Flashing the light on the far wall, he discovered the window that had previously been broken was now once again wide open. He quietly pulled out his gun and extended the phone away from his body so he wouldn't make himself a target, then rotated the beam around the room. A newly placed blanket and pillow were thrown on the mattress. Soda cans, snacks, and a fried chicken carryout box were scattered on the floor. After a quick check of the closet and the master bathroom, he was reasonably sure the intruder had just fled the house.

He heard Danni call "Clear."

"Clear," he called back. "But we just missed them. The master bedroom at the end of the hall."

She was at the door within seconds. Aiden pointed to the open window and trash.

"A vagrant," she asked, flashing a light on the floor.

"The house hasn't been empty long enough for squatters. Aside from the guy making himself a little nest here, something seemed off in the office. The CSI team could have moved things around, but I'll need the flashlight to know for sure."

Danni walked to the window and flashed the light on the ground. "There's a set of prints from where he jumped out the window and a trail leading out of the yard to the left. I'll call it in." She handed the flashlight to Aiden and pulled out her phone.

"I'll be in the office," Aiden said.

The first odd thing he noticed was the desk drawers weren't closed all the way. He couldn't be sure the CSI team hadn't left them that way, but he didn't think so. As he scanned the desk, he realized the picture he left there of Darius and Rosana with Claire was gone. Flashing the light on the floor to see if it got knocked off, he was surprised to find stacks of photos spread out on the floor. There was no way the CSI team would have done that.

He knelt on the carpet and began shuffling through the pictures.

"I've got two patrol cars coming. Luckily, one of the officers was less than a quarter mile away from here. The heavy snow on the ground should leave a clear trail and slow the intruder down. Maybe they'll spot him. They're calling Kowalski too." She knelt on the floor beside him. "What are you doing?"

"There pictures weren't on the floor when we left yesterday," he said.

"Maybe our B&E perp is one of those weirdos who likes to look at people's photos and pretend he's part of the family," Danni suggested, looking over his shoulder.

"Doubt it," Aiden said, closely reviewing the pictures before putting them back the way he found them. "And don't worry, I'm holding them all by the edges, so I won't cover any fingerprints left by our intruder."

"What are you looking for?" she asked.

"Give me a minute, and I'll explain. Will you hold the light for me? I want to check the drawer." She took the flashlight from him. Their eyes met when they heard sirens approaching the area. "Maybe we'll catch a break, and they'll find him," Danni said. Aiden nodded in agreement.

He opened the bottom drawer to see if it still held the photo box with Reagan's pictures. It was in the same place he had left it. When he opened it up, the pictures were still there.

"Damn!" He scratched his chin.

"What?" she asked.

"The last time we were here, I left a picture of Reagan's mother with her two Middle Eastern friends from high school right on top of the desk. There were lots of other pictures of them in a photo box with Claire's name on it in the bottom drawer. As I said, it was a long shot, but I was hoping there might be a connection to the men who have been after Reagan."

"So?"

He held up the photo box on the floor. "This is Claire's photo box. I found it empty, with her pictures spread out on the carpet." He pointed to her name on the top. Then he pulled the box with Reagan's pictures out of the drawer. "Reagan's pictures are still neatly tucked away in the drawer."

"Maybe he got bored, or we interrupted him before he got a chance to look at them."

"I would agree with you if it weren't for one glaring problem. All the pictures with Claire's two Middle Eastern friends are gone.

The one I left on the desktop had 'Love Forever' written on the back. Their names were Darius and Rosana. It can't be a coincidence that those pictures are missing. Why would the intruder want those specific photos unless he recognized them? Maybe it was the Nour guy who got away. He knew the house would be empty, so maybe he thought it was a safe place to hide. Now how the hell are we going to identify Claire's friends?"

"Let's not get ahead of ourselves. If Reagan's mother went to school with them, maybe she had a yearbook with their pictures that would give us a surname. Did Reagan mention anything about her mother's personal items?"

"That's a really good idea. The only photos we found were in here or Reagan's room. She did mention a storage area over the garage, but I believe she said it was old Christmas decorations. Wouldn't hurt to check."

On the way to the garage, they heard sirens growing closer and shared a knowing look that said, *Slim chance our intruder is going to be caught at this point.*

They located the breaker box in the garage where they discovered the power had been intentionally cut off. More than likely by the intruder, so he wouldn't risk accidentally turning on a light that could be seen by the neighbors. Danni steadied the ladder as Aiden made his way up into the attic. He handed down two sealed boxes he found behind the Christmas decorations, both marked "Claire".

They each took a box to search for yearbooks. Danni found three, from 1981-1984. They searched for Darius and Rosana, assuming one of them would be in the same class as Claire.

"Got it!" Danni said excitedly, turning the pages around for Aiden to see. "They are brother and sister. In the same class. Their surname is Nader." She pulled out a notebook from her handbag and wrote it down. "Probably fraternal twins."

Aiden looked over. "That sounds like a Middle Eastern surname. See if there are any other pictures in the yearbook." Now that he had a name, he flipped to the pictures in the 1983 book, and Danni took 1982.

"Here's a picture of all three of them at a football game. His arm is around both girls," Danni said. "That's it for this yearbook other than the individual class photos. I'll try 1984. Maybe there will be more since it's their senior years."

"There are lots of pictures of Claire in her junior yearbook," Aiden said. "She was in the Homecoming Court, and guess whose arm she's holding? Darius Nader's."

Danni leaned over for a closer look. "They look pretty cozy."

They found more photos of Claire, an active and seemingly popular girl, in her junior and senior years. She was voted most likely to succeed, was on the debate team, of which Darius was a member too, and she was salutatorian of her senior class. There was also a picture of Darius and Claire dancing at their senior prom. She was breathtaking in an elegant emerald-colored gown that matched her vibrant green eyes, which reflected pure joy and elation. There was also a special senior page where they had quotes from representatives of the class about what they most wanted for their future.

*"My dream is to study art history at Oxford University in England, visit art museums around the world, and be a renowned professor,"* Claire was quoted as saying.

"Why would someone so full of life and ambitious dreams end up killing themselves and leaving a 7-year-old daughter?" Aiden mused mostly to himself.

"No idea. Something drastic had to have changed in her life. Add the millions of dollars of hidden gems and it's certainly a mystery."

"A sad one for Reagan," he said.

Danni picked up an envelope from the photo box marked "Reagan" and pulled out some pictures. "Is this Reagan's father, Stuart?" Danni asked, holding it up for Aiden to see.

"Yeah," he confirmed.

"Nice-looking guy." Blond hair, blue eyes. Not bad at all. Claire certainly didn't have a type, did she?"

"What do you mean?" Aiden asked.

"Darius is the epitome of tall, dark, slim, and handsome with an exotic bad-boy vibe. Stuart, on the other hand, is the blond, well-built, fair-skinned boy-next-door type. Total opposites." Danni reached for the yearbook and stared at the prom picture of Claire and Darius for a long moment, then glanced up at Aiden with a frown.

"What?" Aiden asked expectantly.

"Do you think Darius could be Reagan's father? I mean she looks nothing like her dad."

Aiden let out a breath. "Tossed that idea around in my head too. No resemblance to Stuart at all."

"What does any of this have to do with the jewels?" Danni asked.

"Maybe the men looking for the jewels are related to the Nader family and recognized the pictures. Why else would anyone want them? If the DNA from the man who camped out here last night matches the DNA of the man who tried to abduct Reagan from the funeral home, then there must be a connection. The Nader siblings' pics seem to be the only ones missing."

Aiden used his camera phone to get copies of what he felt were relevant pictures to show Reagan and Stuart.

"You could be right, but are you sure Reagan didn't take the pictures?"

"Positive. They were here when we left yesterday."

"What does Reagan's father do for a living?"

"Reagan said he's a vice president of human resources for the international division of some big manufacturing company, and he travels all over the world. Mattie suggested that was why Reagan went into personnel, hoping maybe it would help them connect."

"He travels internationally. That would give him access to lots of possibilities," Danni suggested.

"I'm asking myself what kind of man, who's obviously pretty well off, allows his only daughter to grow up with her grandmother, who's struggling to pay the bills."

"A man who knows Reagan isn't his daughter?" Danni suggested.

"Maybe. But if he is connected to the jewels, do you honestly think he would have left them here?" Danni's cell phone rang. "Danni Silva … What? … Thanks for letting me know." She ended the call.

"Anything on our intruder?"

"The perp's tracks led through multiple yards and ended a few streets over to a recently vacated parking space. The ice on the street is so frozen, it's impossible to tell which way he headed. A squad car is going to be parked out front until a crime scene team can get here. Maybe they'll find something helpful."

They were interrupted by a honking out front.

"That must be Josh. He's my ride to the airport," Aiden said.

He walked Danni to his truck and gave her his keys. Josh agreed to pick up the truck later.

Aiden stood at the driver's window, smiling down at Danni seated in the driver's seat. "Sorry about all this. Maybe there'll be another time for a drink and late-night dessert."

She laughed and fired up the engine. "We'll see," she said as she blew him a kiss.

# Chapter 29

The thought of seeing her dad after six years filled Reagan with tremendous anxiety. She had no idea what to expect. She wiped her clammy palms on her wool coat. *Will he be glad to see me? Or even agree to see me? Will I be an inconvenience to be dealt with?* She had to pull herself together and keep her mind out of the dark corners of her insecurities. Glancing out the window over a vast expanse of mountains, she felt a chill run up her spine. She was alone. Utterly and completely alone.

Rolling her carry-on through the automatic sliding exit doors of the Spokane Airport, she was shocked to hear someone call her name. Impossible, she thought, because the only people who knew where she was going were Mattie, Josh, and Tyler.

"Reagan!"

The overhead announcements were so loud, she had to have been mistaken, but couldn't help searching the crowd for the source. When her eyes locked on his, her heart leapt. *He's here! How?* She held her breath as he strode toward her with his confident swagger and cocky grin.

"Need a ride?" Aiden asked, as casually as he would if he'd found her at the corner Starbucks in Lancashire, rather than in an airport more than 2,000 miles away. Dropping her suitcase, she threw herself into his arms, inhaling his musky scent and sending warmth through her body. The feel of his strong arms wrapping around her waist and his large hands caressing her back gave her hope that he had missed her too, but the feeling lasted only for a few brief seconds. Like a switch had been flipped, he pulled away. His beautiful smile was gone. He'd remembered. They didn't belong to each other. Her heart fell.

"That's not why I'm here, Reagan," he said, grabbing the handle of her carry-on.

"Then why are you here?" she asked, aggravated that he pretended he didn't care.

"Mattie asked me to come. Since Tyler wasn't willing to make the trip, she was worried about your safety. Danni agreed, so here I am."

The last part was an intentional jab. *He did it for Mattie and Danni, not for me.*

She stared at him, disappointment in her eyes. "Danni, huh?"

"Yeah." No clarification, reminding her of just how screwed up things were between them.

"If you're here to be my bodyguard, I don't need you. Leave. You're off the hook. Tell Mattie you tried. Go back to your cute little detective. I'm perfectly capable of taking care of myself," she said curtly, flipping around to go a different direction, anywhere away from him and his cold demeanor. He grabbed her forearm and pulled her back, glaring at her with hard eyes.

"Let's not do this here, and don't give me that 'I am woman' bullshit. It took two of us to keep you from being kidnapped, and a man got shot, so you tell me exactly how you handled that situation by yourself."

She wedged her arm from his grasp, shocked by his attitude, but she simply didn't have it in her to fight. The thought of seeing her father was enough to wreak havoc on her emotions.

"I guess you're right," she sighed softly, mentally sealing her heart in steel. "Thank you for coming. Where's your car?" He raised his eyebrows and studied her for a few moments, then motioned toward the parking lot.

Aiden led her to a white Camry illegally parked in the pickup lane. He put her luggage in the trunk and slipped into the driver's seat. It was impossible for her to look at him. Coming out the exit doors and hearing him call her name had been a breath of fresh air that lifted her heavy heart, but less than one minute later, she felt sucker punched, and she only had herself to blame.

"Does your father know you're coming?"

She shook her head. "Didn't want to give him an excuse not to see me. Mattie called his office and pretended to be a family friend, isn't that rich? Although she didn't really believe his story about his broken leg, she asked for the address of the rehab center where he was supposed to be staying so she could send flowers. His administrative assistant readily gave her the address. Visiting hours are over at 9 p.m."

"I'm sorry."

"For what?"

"That you have to have a friend make up a story to see your father. That sucks."

Aiden waited by the elevator at the motel while she checked in and got her key card, and they went up together.

"How much time do you need?" he asked.

"Thirty minutes if that's okay."

"What's your room number?"

"206."

"Mine's 208. Leave it to Mattie. It's an adjoining room," he huffed. "I already checked in."

"Don't worry. I won't sneak over and molest you." She rolled her eyes.

He opened her door and put her luggage on the rack.

"Before you go, can you tell me what you and Danni were doing in Nana's house last night? Mattie told me the police were called."

"Yeah. Let's sit," he said, motioning to the round table in the corner. He explained what happened when he and Danni went by the house to get the pictures of Darius and Rosana. He showed her the pictures he had taken with his iPhone from her mother's yearbooks, flipping through each one without comment. When they got to the prom picture with Claire dancing with Darius, she put her fingers on the phone to expand the page, focusing more closely on the faces of Darius and her mother.

"He was a handsome guy," she commented, then traced her mother's face with her finger. "Momma was so beautiful, wasn't she? And so happy."

"She was," he said. "We're pretty sure Darius and Rosana are fraternal twins."

"Momma must have really cared about him."

"Looks that way."

"I've never seen her yearbooks before. They were over the garage?"

"There were two boxes of her things. We left them in the office if you want to look through them when you get back."

"Nana must have forgotten about them. I can't believe all of the photos of Darius and Rosana were stolen."

"I know. That's what led us to believe the man who broke into the house might have some association with your mother's old friends. Why else would those be the only photos missing? Danni's going to run background checks on them. Their last name is Nader. Ever heard of it?"

"Not that I remember." She flipped through the pictures on his phone again. There were a couple of Reagan with her mother and father before the divorce. The three of them, side by side. She wasn't sure why Aiden had included them, or maybe she was. She just didn't want to acknowledge what he was trying to tell her out loud and make it true. He was dropping breadcrumbs for her. A puzzle she was supposed to figure out, but she didn't want to, so she looked back through all the pictures from the yearbook again.

She looked at Aiden with sadness in her eyes. "I would have given anything to be this girl," she said, pointing to her mother in the emerald gown. Next, she ran her fingers over the words her mother had been quoted about her desire to go to Oxford and travel the world.

"Beautiful and smart, just like her daughter."

She smiled at Aiden's compliment, then furrowed her brow when a thought occurred to her.

"Aiden, this is like looking at a total stranger. This girl had such energy and light. She was vivacious, full of motivation and future potential. What on earth happened? Something broke her."

Aiden placed his arm across her shoulders in a gesture of comfort, but there was nothing he could say that would help her understand. It was time for her to seek the answers from the one man she knew could shed light on her past.

"I'm ready," Reagan said with a confidence she wasn't sure she possessed.

They drove to Ponderosa Pine Restoration Resort just outside of Spokane. When they pulled up to the 12-foot iron gate, a guard asked who they were visiting, took photos of their IDs, and gave them visitor passes. They followed a winding road lined with evergreens until it ended in front of a huge wood-and glass-fronted log cabin building. Although it was designed in a rustic style to blend in with the lush forest surroundings, it had all the comforts of a five-star hotel. The front doors opened into a large reception/gathering area with a three-story open ceiling and a rough-stone fireplace that covered one wall.

Reagan introduced herself to the receptionist and asked to see her father. The young man made several calls. Five minute later, a striking woman in her 50s wearing a soft, dove-gray sweater-dress came out to meet them.

"Reagan?" she asked, surprise registering on her face.

"Yes. I'm Reagan Asher and this is my friend, Aiden Rannell. I would like to see my father, Stuart Asher."

The woman held out her hand and gently clasped Reagan's. "You don't recognize me, do you? I'm Carol Asher, your father's wife. I realize this must be awkward for you. We haven't seen each other in over 20 years." Her voice was sincere, her smile open, nothing like the 'husband-stealing' woman Reagan held resentfully in her mind. "You've become such a stunning young woman. Your father will be so excited to see you."

"Nice to meet you, Mrs. Asher," Aiden said, extending his hand.

"You too, Mr. Rannell. I seem to remember one of Reagan's best friends, Mattie, I believe, was married to a Rannell. Would that be you?" Reagan was dumbfounded that Carol Asher could possibly know that.

"That's Josh, my brother."

She nodded politely. "Sorry. I know you're all like family to Reagan, so it wouldn't have surprised me to see him accompany her."

Reagan anticipated the next thing out of Carol's mouth would be an excuse for why she couldn't see her dad, but it never happened.

"If you'll follow me, Stuart is in his room. He just got back from a physical therapy session so he's a bit worn-out, but he'll be thrilled to see both of you."

They followed Carol Asher to the third floor and down a long hall to the last door at the end. The door opened to what resembled a penthouse suite. The entire back wall was floor-to-ceiling glass windows that featured a panoramic view of the scenic snow-covered valley below. Her dad sat in a brown leather lounger with his right leg propped up on an ottoman. To her surprise, he recognized her instantly, his eyes lighting up in amazement and a broad smile gleaming across his face.

"What a wonderful surprise! Come here, princess," her father said with outstretched arms. If she didn't know better, she might have thought he had tears in his eyes. *But how can that be? He's never really cared about me.* She didn't realize until she let go that she had been squeezing the blood from Aiden's hand. Hesitantly, she walked to her father, bent down, and accepted his warm embrace. She fought back the tears that stung her eyes as his arms drew her tightly into a bear-hug, just like the ones he had given her as a child. The kind that made her feel wanted and secure, a feeling that was now foreign to her. As her nose pressed against his shoulder, she reveled in the familiar smell of his earthy cedar and citrus cologne. She took a shuddering breath.

"Oh, my beautiful Reagan. I am so glad to see you," he whispered in her ear. Reagan was filled with so many dueling emotions, she thought her heart might burst.

"Let me pull up a chair so you can sit closer," Carol said, sliding a padded wooden chair near the lounger. Aiden hurried over to help, placing it within her father's reach. "The couch is so far away to have any meaningful conversations. I appreciate the desire for space and to keep the furnishings authentic, but it's not very cozy in this massive room. Aiden, there's another chair like it in the far corner. They aren't particularly comfortable, but certainly the easiest to move. Oh, how rude of me. Stuart, this is Aiden Rannell, a friend of Reagan's."

Aiden offered his hand.

"Josh's brother. Yes! I remember," Stuart said, shaking Aiden's hand. Again, Reagan was taken aback that her dad seemed to know a lot about her life.

"So nice to meet you, Sir."

"I'll leave you all alone so you can talk." Carol said. "Would anyone like something to drink?"

"No, thank you," Reagan said. Aiden shook his head. No one spoke until the door closed.

Her father took her hand in his. "I'm so glad you came. How are you, princess?"

"Not too good, Dad." His reference to her as "princess" tore at her heart.

"Mr. Asher, do you have any idea what's been going on with your daughter?" Aiden asked with a little too much judgment in his voice.

Stuart's forehead wrinkled and his face grew serious. "Not until this morning when one of the nursing attendants snuck me a newspaper. It's one of the rules for admittance here. A stress-free environment is part of the recovery process. Since Carol has been staying with me the whole time, neither of us has had any outside contact through television, newspapers, or internet for over a week. When Reagan and I spoke briefly about Fiona's death, the only information I had was a possible robbery. I felt terrible that I was unable to be with her, having only been a few days out of surgery. An article on the front page talked about a nationwide manhunt for a man wanted for attempted murder and kidnapping in Ohio. When I scanned the details and read your name, I demanded a phone, and I've been trying to call you all day."

"I didn't receive any calls," she said, mistrust in her voice.

"Check your phone. Is it still on airplane-mode?" Aiden asked. Then to Stuart, he said, "She never answers her phone."

Stuart chuckled. "Stubborn, those Moran women."

Reagan checked. There were at least 20 calls from her dad and several from Mattie and Tyler. "I see," she said apologetically.

"All that matters is that you are safe. Have they caught the assailant?" her dad asked hopefully. She shook her head.

"One of them, but the second man escaped. It's an ongoing investigation," Aiden said.

Stuart leaned forward and squeezed her hand. "What I don't understand is why they would be after you, Reagan. You haven't lived in Ohio for years."

"I'll get to that, Dad, but first I need to ask you some questions.

"Certainly."

"It's important that you answer me honestly. Can you do that? Please? I'm not a child anymore, and I deserve to know the truth. Things are happening that I can't explain. My life and those around me are in danger, and none of this has anything to do with me."

He straightened in his seat, worry apparent on his face, and nodded.

"The first thing I want to know … W…Why did you leave my mother?" She hadn't intended to ask that question, there were certainly more important ones, but for some reason it just popped out. Maybe it was because the hurt and disappointment were still burrowed in her gut after all those years, and she knew she might never get another opportunity to ask.

# Chapter 30

Stuart Asher's eyes darkened. "I guess you're going to bypass the idle chitchat and get right to the point, he said, obviously stunned by Reagan's blunt question. "You may not believe it, but I loved Claire more than anything in the world. The last thing I wanted was to leave her."

Reagan was speechless. That was not what she had expected. "Then w…why did you leave *us*?" Reagan's voice broke. "Was there someone else? For you? For her? Carol?"

Reagan watched him closely as he leaned back in his chair and ran his fingers through his thick white-blond hair. Even is his 50s, he was still a strikingly handsome man.

"It's complicated, princess. I tried desperately to make our marriage work, but ultimately it wasn't my choice." His voice was strained.

"Did you know there were precious stones hidden in the house?" Aiden interjected out of the blue, trying to catch him off guard. It worked.

Stuart's eyes flew to Aiden and held for a couple of beats before he squeezed them tightly closed, his face contorted. The unnatural silence that came afterward spoke volumes. Stuart Asher knew something. When he finally spoke, his voice remained calm, almost resigned.

"I didn't read about any gems in the newspapers. What exactly are you referring to?"

Reagan's eyes widened and her lips tightened. "What the hell, Dad? What difference does it make what kind of gems they are?"

"Cut diamonds …" Aiden paused for effect. Reagan caught a brief glimmer of recognition in her father's eyes and was sure Aiden saw it too when he cast her a sideways glance. Her heart sank.

"You know about the diamonds, Dad?" Reagan shouted. "Did you steal them? Am I being hunted by dangerous men because of you?" She jumped out of her chair, but Aiden grabbed her arm and gently pulled her back down, resting his hand on her forearm.

"No! I've never stolen anything in my life," he said emphatically, clutching the arms of his chair.

"Then tell me what's going on!" Reagan cried, back on her feet with arms flailing. The emotional dam broke. "I don't understand any of this! How you could leave us if you loved Momma and me. How could you abandon me after she died like I meant nothing to you? Where did the diamonds and black pearls come from? What about my play jewel…?" Her voice broke as a sob made its way from her throat. Her mind was a mess. A jumble of questions. Emotions. Hurt. Confusion. Everything spilled out of her mouth in random order. Nothing making sense.

Stuart Asher put his head in his hands and burst into tears. Reagan's hands flew to her mouth as her body shook from the emotional turmoil. Aiden stood, pulling her into his chest and lightly rubbed her back. The gesture helped give her a sense of calm. After a few minutes, Stuart pulled a box of tissues from an end table and blew his nose. He handed the box to Aiden to take care of Reagan.

"Where do you want me to begin?" Stuart asked, defeat in his eyes.

"From the beginning … with the truth," Reagan whispered as she sat and reached for Aiden's hand.

"Then you have to promise you'll listen and try to keep an open mind." He turned to Aiden. "Would you give me an opportunity to talk to my daughter alone?"

"Sure," Aiden said, but Reagan stopped him before he could step away.

"Dad, right now, Aiden is one of the only people alive who I trust. Josh and Mattie are the other two, so if you don't mind, I'd like him to stay." He nodded, and Aiden returned to his seat. Stuart cleared his throat.

"Your mother and I met at OSU, and we began dating our freshman year, the fall of 1984. It was love at first sight for me, not so much for her. The summer before her sophomore year, she applied to Oxford University in England with their art history program for her last two years of university. I had mixed feelings about it, mostly because I knew it was an opportunity of a lifetime for her, but I was also terrified it would be the end for us. Claire was made for greater things, and I knew it. Still, I gave my full support. She was accepted, and I was heartbroken.

"Things were always tense with her parents and had been since Claire became good friends in high school with a couple of kids from Lebanon ... Darius and I can't remember his sister's name. They lived down the street from Fiona and Daniel with their grandparents. I believe their father might have lived in the U.S. for a while but went back to Lebanon at some point. Then years later, he sent his two teenage twins to the United States to be raised by their grandparents. Your grandfather took an instant dislike to them, mostly because they were foreign. He wasn't a tolerant man, to say the least. Particularly didn't want Claire involved with Darius. Thought he was a bad influence on her. When the twins ended up going to OSU at the same time as Claire, it made matters worse. I think your grandfather thought Darius was going to whisk her away to somewhere in the Middle East and he'd never see her again.

"Claire accepted the scholarship to Oxford without consulting her parents. There was a big blowup when they found out just before she was supposed to leave. The next thing I knew, Claire was asking me if I wanted to get married. I was ecstatic. Over the moon. Believing she would be in Europe for the next two years, I had already made arrangements to transfer to the University of Dayton. Claire decided to quit school and go with me. Both sets of parents were extremely supportive. I know it was a terrible sacrifice for your mother to give up Oxford, but she said it was her decision. She had you very soon after we were married. When I graduated, we moved back to Lancashire.

"It wasn't another man or another woman that broke us up, Reagan. It was another life. A life she wanted but gave up. I should have questioned her decision at the time, but I was selfishly so elated that she chose me, I didn't look too deeply into her motivations. That was a mistake on my part. Things were fine for the first couple of years, then she began to lose interest in everything, except you. She started sleeping a lot. Was depressed. Refused counseling. I even suggested she reapply for a scholarship at Oxford. I offered to keep you with me while she went to the UK. Anything to make her happy and bring her back to me, but she insisted it was too late."

He stopped and took a sip of water, visibly shaken.

"Your grandfather asked me to come over one afternoon to talk to him. He told me he had made a horrible mistake by not allowing Claire to go to England. It was destroying her spirit, and he couldn't stand to watch it anymore. He reached in his desk and pulled out a folded handkerchief and handed it to me. When I opened it up, there were five cut diamonds. You could have knocked me over with a flick of your finger. He told me he found them hidden in the house when he was doing some work and wasn't sure where they had come from, but he didn't care. He wanted me to take them and go ... get as far away from Claire as I could. He admitted that he and Fiona had pressured her into canceling her plans to attend Oxford and convinced her to get married. The guilt was killing him. It had been selfish and the worst decision of her life. He knew I loved her, and said she probably loved me in her own way, but he hoped I could understand and do what was best for her. As long as I still was there, he didn't think she would ever leave. He told me he had a few more diamonds that he was going to sell to send her to Oxford."

"What?" Reagan breathed with shock. "He just happened to find diamonds laying around the house. Do you know how ridiculous that sounds?"

"Of course, I know how it sounds, but that's what he told me. I swear. Please let me finish."

She reluctantly nodded, tightening her arms around herself. She could hear Aiden cursing under his breath.

"I didn't want to leave Claire or you, and adamantly told your grandfather, but he refused to listen to me. He wanted me to promise I would never take you away, because Claire would never leave if she lost custody of her daughter. No amount of money would make me leave, and I told him that while I shoved the diamonds back at him. He slid them back to me and begged me to just think about it for a week, consider her best interests, not mine. He accused me of being selfish. The next day, I left on a weeklong business trip. Five days later, Claire called me to tell me her father had died of a heart attack at work, before I could give him back the diamonds and tell him no way I would ever leave either one of you."

Reagan was dazed. She let out a shaky breath. It was as if she was hearing this in her child's mind, not as an adult.

"Why did you and mother move us in with Nana?" Reagan whispered.

"Your grandmother wasn't working at the time, so when Daniel died, she was in a financial bind. I hate to say it, but she pressured your mother into us moving in with her. Claire promised it would be short-term, but every time we tried to move out, Fiona acted as if we were abandoning her financially. She played Claire like a fiddle, then when she didn't get her way, she would say it was her house. It put a lot of strain on our relationship. Claire was caught in the middle of her mother's manipulations. Since I couldn't talk Claire into going to Oxford as your grandfather wanted, I invested the diamonds in a friend's manufacturing startup in Spokane, hoping one day I could convince Claire to move to Washington for a fresh start.

"I stuck it out for three more years, hoping things would change between us. She drew further and further away from me and into herself. A few weeks before I decided to leave, I told Claire about the investments I made from the money her father had given me. I never mentioned they were diamonds. My investment had netted me over $600,000 in profit in just three years, not including my original investment. I made my case for us moving to Washington, and she seemed to like the idea a lot. Even had some of her glow back. When she told your grandmother, she hit the roof. We weren't leaving and taking her granddaughter away from her. Then Fiona wanted me out of her house. I told your mother she had to decide what she wanted to do, because we couldn't continue to live like that. It was our family, and we had to do what was best for us. Claire said there was nothing she could do and there was no more discussion, and I should go. It was the worst day of my life. She chose your grandmother over me. I packed up and left."

Reagan was stunned. This was nothing like the grandmother she knew and loved. He had to be talking about someone else.

"If you had that money, why didn't you help us?" Reagan asked, unable to believe the new revelations. "Nana said we struggled. Never had enough money."

"I did. I sent hefty amounts to your mother, but when she died, your grandmother told me she wouldn't accept a dime from me, nor would you. I continued to send support, but my checks were all returned."

"I was your daughter. Didn't you want me? Why did you leave me with Nana?" she barely whispered.

"Because that was your mother's final wish that she left in her note to me. It was the only thing she ever asked of me and it ripped my heart out," he said with fresh tears.

"What note?" Reagan asked, sitting on the edge of her seat.

"The note your mother left when she … took her life."

Reagan sat back, flabbergasted. Nana had never told her about a note. Her father had to be making it up as an excuse for his neglect. She felt Aiden's thumb rubbing her palm. "What did it say? Do you still have it?"

"I don't, princess. The police may still have it or maybe Fiona kept it. A detective sent me a copy to make sure it was her handwriting, which was flowery and very distinctive, and to see if I thought it was written under duress. It wouldn't have mattered if it had been typed, I knew it was written by h…her," his voice broke.

Aiden squeezed Reagan's hand, reminding her he was there.

"W…what did she say?" It became difficult for her to form words. To think straight.

It took Stuart a few moments to collect himself.

"She said she was sorry, but she was living with more regrets than she could continue to bear. Her life had gotten off course and there was no way to get it back on track. Her biggest regret was not coming to Washington with me. That crushed me. I should have insisted. Demanded she come. She said she didn't blame me for leaving or for Oxford. It was all her poor choices. You were her joy and her heart, but she could see she was unable to give you the emotional support you needed when she couldn't even take care of herself. I can't remember everything, but she also wrote a note to you. I assumed Fiona shared it with you … maybe not when you were 7 years old, but certainly when you were older."

"You didn't even come to Momma's funeral," Reagan said, disappointment contorting her face.

"Fiona blamed me and said she would have me physically removed if I showed up. She wanted me out of your life. I wrote to you for years, but when I mentioned something on the phone I had written to you, and you didn't know what I was talking about, I realized you weren't getting any of my letters. I eventually stopped."

Reagan was reeling. She had no note from her mother or letters from her father. *Had Nana hidden all of them from her? Was her dad lying?*

"What about Carol? She was your secretary." Her tone accusatory.

"When I left my company, the new personnel manager wanted his own staff, so they let Carol go. There had never been anything between us. She jokingly asked if we had any openings in Spokane. I called and got her a position. Why should her life be destroyed too? We gravitated to each other because we were both in a strange place. Eventually we married."

"She never liked me," Reagan said. "She wasn't even there when I came to visit the second time."

"That was because on the first visit, you told her she broke up your parents' marriage and then you threw a hairbrush that put a gash in the side of her head."

"Oh my God ... I ..." All of the air was suddenly sucked out of Reagan's lungs.

"Carol wasn't upset with you; she just didn't want to cause you any more pain or be a reminder of what you had lost. She really is a wonderful woman. We've been comfortable together, but she's not your mother, and I'm sure she has always known that."

"I have no memory of saying or doing any of that," Reagan murmured, mortified by her actions, but she had to admit to herself that she held no recollection of her visits other than the plane trips.

"You were a child who had suffered insurmountable loss," he said, reaching for her hand.

"Did Claire see Darius when she was at OSU?" Aiden asked.

"I'm sure she did," Stuart said. "They had always been close. I knew he was in love with her, but she didn't appear to feel the same way, or maybe I just didn't want to see it. It wouldn't have mattered because his parents had arranged for him to marry a woman in

Lebanon. Claire thought the whole idea of arranged marriage was archaic."

They sat in silence for a few minutes. It seemed everything Reagan had assumed or been told had a totally different side. There was one more difficult question she had to ask.

Reagan swallowed hard and watched her dad closely. She had never spoken about it to anyone, but it hung on the edges of her consciousness. Bracing herself, she asked, "Are you my biological father?"

Out of the corner of her eye, she saw Aiden's mouth open in disbelief. It shouldn't have been a surprise to him. He saw it. She realized it when they reviewed the pictures together. She looked nothing like her father. And except for her green eyes and fair skin, she had no resemblance to her mother.

Stuart Asher ran his hand over his face and leaned back in his chair. The tension in the room was palpable. Reagan knew the conversation was just as much of an emotional roller coaster for him as it was for her. Stuart squeezed Reagan's hand and pulled her close, so she could read the truth on his face. Her heart slammed wildly against her chest. *Do I really want to know?*

"You are my daughter in every sense of the word, princess."

"That's not what I mean, and you know it. Are you my biological father?"

He searched her eyes, mentally battling over what to tell her. Trying to evaluate what she could handle. It was written across his face.

"I'm not, Reagan, nor do I know or care who is. Your mother never tried to trick me. She was honest and straightforward about it. I can't say that it didn't have anything to do with us getting married, because it did, more for your mother than for me. I loved her with every beat of my heart and would have done anything to make her happy. We wanted to make a life together. Although there are many things I would have done differently in hindsight, never would I have changed one minute I spent with you."

Reagan didn't cry or shout or stomp her feet for being lied to her whole life; instead, she was astounded. And completely numb.

"Did Nana know you weren't my biological father?"

"She did," he sighed.

"Why didn't she tell me any of this? Why did she lie to me? She made you out to be a selfish man who cared only about himself. That you had abandoned me. Why would she do that?"

"Fiona was a complicated woman, and maybe that's how she perceived it in her mind. I can't say for sure."

"Do you remember the play jewelry Reagan and her friends used to wear?" Aiden asked.

"Sure, I do. Princess Reagan had her own tiara. Such a beautiful child," he said, his wide smile evidence of his fond memories.

"Do you know where the jewelry came from?" Aiden asked.

"I do. Darius' grandmother gave it to Reagan when she was just a toddler right before she and her husband moved back to Lebanon."

"Why would she do that?" Reagan asked.

"After I graduated from the University of Dayton, we moved back to Lancashire for me to find a job. Claire had developed a good relationship with Darius' grandmother when they were in high school. Unlike Claire's parents, the grandmother was supportive of the friendship Claire developed with her grandkids. When we visited your Nana, Claire would take you down the street to visit with her. Their name was Nibara or Nibber or Nader … something like that. It got to be a routine, and the elderly woman was so lonely, she loved watching you play with her colorful jewelry. After Darius and his sister graduated from OSU, their father came to move his parents permanently back to Lebanon. Before she left, she brought a box of the colorful jewelry to Fiona to give to Reagan. Why is that relevant?"

"Because it's genuine," Reagan said with emphasis. "Real diamonds, real sapphires, real rubies, real, real, real. Worth millions. We also found a container hidden in the air conditioning unit that had black pearls and loose diamonds."

"The air conditioner?" Stuart rubbed his chin absently. "Oh, my God. There was no mention of diamonds in the newspaper article I read this morning, but I couldn't help but wonder if those five diamonds Daniel gave me had anything to do with it, even though that was over 25 years ago. Do you think the gems could have come from Lebanon?"

"That's a possibility," Aiden said. "Do you think Mrs. Moran knew about the diamonds or pearls?"

"Daniel never mentioned black pearls, but I just assumed he would've told Fiona about the diamonds. When she refused to take money from me, I thought that might have been the reason. Daniel told me he had a few more diamonds. When you went to college, I called the registrar to see how much your expenses would be. I sent you a check for $200,000 with a note saying how proud I was of you and to let me know if you needed more. Fiona sent it back to me in pieces. It aggravated me, so I sent the check directly to the university registrar. They sent it back to me with a letter saying the student refused to allow access to her college records or finances. They had a copy of the form with your signature. I became more convinced Fiona had sold those diamonds Daniel told me about to pay for your education."

Reagan gasped in horror. "It wasn't my signature. I took out student loans for what wasn't covered by my scholarships. Nana really didn't have the money to help me. I took part-time jobs and struggled to make my payments. I finally paid the loans off last year."

"Oh, princess, I'm so sorry." He slowly shook his head. "This is all my fault. I should have reconnected years ago. Forced Fiona to let me see you. I thought the damage was done and you hated me."

"I didn't hate you, D…Daddy. I…I just thought you didn't want me. How could Nana do that to me?"

The regret in her father's eyes pierced her heart. When he opened his arms to her, silently pleading a thousand apologies, she leaned over and melted into his embrace. Their tears mingled as they tried to drown away the memory of all the years they had missed.

# Chapter 31

Reagan was silent on the drive back to their hotel. Aiden knew she was still reeling from her father's revelations because he certainly was. He had felt helpless watching each new reveal tear a little bit more from her psyche, crumbling the few remaining vestiges of her trust. Not even her grandmother had been the savior she had seemed. *How could her grandmother force her father out of her life, especially after she lost her mother?* It was pure selfishness and probably the act of a desperate woman trying to hold on to her only grandchild after her husband and daughter had died. The consequences to Reagan were devastating, and the realization of the betrayal by someone she loved so completely was unconscionable. Her world had shattered, and all he knew to do was help her pick up some of the pieces and fill in the blanks.

Once Reagan was safely tucked in bed, Aiden went to his room and turned on the television for background noise. He had calls to make and didn't want her to overhear through the thin walls. He made the first call to Danni, who had phoned him twice.

"What's up?" he asked.

"Has the trip been successful?" She got right to the point, all business.

"Reagan's father did clear up a few things, but most of it was not good for Reagan."

"Is she okay?" Danni's voice softened.

"Not really. She just learned that her family has deceived her for most of her life, but she's safely tucked away in her room, if that's what you're asking."

"Ouch! Not at all. Who you sleep with is none of my business. I like Reagan and am genuinely concerned."

"Sorry. Guess I'm on edge. Got any updates?"

"That's actually why I called. We got information back on the Bo guy we have in custody. His name is Borzin Nader, same last name of Claire Asher's friends. Bo must be a nickname. By the age, we think he could be a father or uncle, but that's a guess. He entered the country about a week ago with his cousin, Nour Nader, on a tourist visa supposedly to visit relatives. It says on their visa applications they have relatives in New Orleans and lists ... wait for it ... Darius and Helena Nader. Helena must be Darius' wife. There's an address." She gave it to him. "They're rushing the DNA, but we suspect it was Nour Nader who was staying in Mrs. Moran's house. Ten years ago, Nour spent five years in prison in Afghanistan, but some of the records were lost, so we aren't sure of the charge. Borzin Nader currently has charges pending in Iraq for grand theft and looting. Nothing on his charges are related to the gems or jewelry you found in Mrs. Moran's home. There are also petty thief and forgery records for both in Lebanon, their country of residence."

He filled Danni in on what they had learned from Stuart Asher.

"She's a basket case right now," Aiden said.

"To find out her grandmother lied to her all those years about her father. How do you deal with that?"

"Not well. Any hits on the jewels?"

"Nothing. If it was reported as a theft where the owners can prove ownership, we should know soon."

"If they find out the diamonds were stolen, will Stuart Asher be prosecuted for those five diamonds he sold?"

"The statute of limitations on selling stolen goods over 25 years ago more than likely expired. Let's keep it on the down-low for now. It might be a non-issue and would be difficult to prove at this point. If Asher was involved in the original theft, he would have taken more than five diamonds. His story rings true," Danni said.

"Thanks. That family has been through so much already."

"Appreciate the update, Aiden. Stay safe."

"You have a good evening."

After he hung up, he called Mattie to give her the rundown of the conversation with Reagan's dad. While she screamed in his ear, he begged her to wait until the following day to call Reagan. His last call was to his mom and dad to tell them he loved them. After the convoluted drama he had witnessed, he had a new appreciation for the happy, uncomplicated childhood his parents had given him.

He was awakened from a deep sleep by knocking on the door. Though he was in his boxers, he figured if you showed up in the middle of the night, you get what you get. Somebody probably had the wrong room. When he opened the door, no one was there. When the knocking continued, he realized it was coming from the adjoining door. Shit, he thought, opening the door. Reagan stood on the other side in a tank top and sleep shorts.

"Can't sleep?" he asked, cracking a smile.

"I woke up over an hour ago. Too many thoughts swirling around my head. Can I cuddle with you? Maybe I won't feel so alone."

He knew it was a terrible idea but didn't know how he could refuse her after the train-wreck of a day she just had.

"Okay, but that's it. I'm going back to sleep." He got in bed and opened the covers on the right side. She crawled in, curling up against his side with her arm over his bare chest and closed her eyes. He tried to ignore the heat from her thighs against his body sending arousal notices to his lower regions. Untangling himself, he fluffed his pillow and turned over on his side. She nuzzled against his back. With a sigh, he closed his eyes, letting exhaustion take over.

He awoke with a start when he felt a nibbling on his shoulder and a tickling on his lower abdomen. A rush of warmth shot through his nerve endings, forcing a groan from the back of his throat. Once he was alert and had come to his senses, he turned over to face the source of this disturbance. She smiled teasingly as her fingers feathered lightly up the inside of his leg until his hand grabbed hers before it reached its intended destination. He struggled for the right words to say when he read the hurt and rejection in her eyes.

"You're hurting right now, Reagan, but sex isn't going to make those feelings go away. It also doesn't change our situation. This isn't what either of us needs."

"Don't you want me?" she whispered.

"Wanting you is not the issue."

"Good. I want you too. And I need you. Can't you understand? I need to feel something other than lies and betrayal … and loneliness."

"Reagan, I can't …" but he never finished his thought.

When Reagan opened her eyes the next morning, she was cradled in a sleeping Aiden's arms. It was safe and warm, which was what she had craved when she slipped into his bed in the early-morning hours. She knew he'd be upset with her for her seduction. It was emotional blackmail, and she had shamelessly used it. The more he tried to pull away from her, the more she resisted. Unable to face him, she took the cowardly way out and slipped out of bed before he woke up. Best-case scenario when they saw each other again, they would act like nothing happened.

Dressed in a tan-suede jacket and brown-tweed slacks for the trip back home to Chicago, she checked herself in the hotel mirror. Except for the bags under her eyes, she would pass.

Her flight was scheduled to leave at noon. Aiden hadn't mentioned his, so she wasn't sure if they would ride to the airport together. When she spoke to Tyler that morning, he insisted on picking her up. She intentionally neglected to tell him that Aiden was in Spokane. It felt dishonest, but she was in no mood for a confrontation with him over the phone. A knock on the hall door interrupted her thoughts. It was Aiden. He was dressed in dark blue jeans and a burgundy La Costa sweater, his winter coat over his arm, ready to go. Reagan got her carry-on and followed him to the garage.

As luck would have it or Mattie's strategic planning, they both ended up at the same automated check-in for the same airline. Aiden went first while Reagan peered over his shoulder. When she read Spokane to New Orleans, LA, on the screen, she grabbed his arm and pulled him around to face her.

"Where the hell are you going?" she demanded. The man behind her looked alarmed and moved to another line. The next guy in line said, "Look, buddy. Take your drama somewhere else. I've got a plane to catch."

"Sorry," Aiden apologized to the man. Firmly removing Reagan's hand, he turned back to finish his transaction, while she stood fuming. He wasn't telling her anything, and it pissed her off. When he got away from the crowd, he stopped and faced her. "That was uncalled for."

"Why are you going to New Orleans?"

He sighed deeply and rubbed his scruffy chin in frustration. "Look, Reagan, I'm trying my best to help you get answers, but you make it so damn difficult sometimes."

"What or who is in New Orleans?" Hands on hips.

"Darius Nader. I want to get to him before the police do, and he totally clams up when he realizes what a cluster-fuck this whole thing is."

Reagan thought about it for a few seconds. "How did you find out he lives there?"

"Danni gave me the address. I doubt she thought I'd actually do anything with it, but then again, that might be why she gave it to me in the first place."

"You seem to have gotten pretty close."

"I'm not going down that road with you. Unless I miss my guess, Tyler will be waiting at the airport when you get home. Now get checked in. Get on your fuckin' plane and go home." He stormed off.

"We'll see about that!" she said to no one.

---

Fury coursed through his veins when Aiden recognized Reagan standing in front of her seat in first class, calmly waiting for him to disembark in New Orleans. He not so politely escorted her to a chair in the waiting area. Plopping down next to her, he leaned within inches of her face.

"What the hell are you doing here?" He was so mad he was sure smoke was pouring out of his ears.

She narrowed her eyes at him, her lips tight. "If you're going to see Darius Nader, I'm going with you. He could be my father, and if he is, I have every right to know."

He put his elbows on his knees, resting his face in his hands. He struggled to weigh his options. Last night had been a mistake. He wasn't sure if he was more upset with her machinations to sleep with him or finding her on the same flight to New Orleans. The only person he really had to blame was himself and his lack of willpower. He was an idiot, and obviously a hard "no" wasn't in his vocabulary when it came to her.

"I complicated things for us, didn't I?" she said rhetorically.

He pinched the bridge of his nose. "We passed complicated a long time ago. This would have been a lot less messy if you hadn't come, but now that you're here, there's not a hell of a lot I can do about it. If you're coming with me, you are going to have to respect some boundaries. You have a boyfriend. I'm doing my best to respect that, and I think you should too. I'm not going to be the other guy. I'll take responsibility for last night. Apparently, I have no self-control when it comes to you, so please back off. Do we understand each other?" His emotions were raw but restrained.

"Completely."

"Good."

Aiden knew that taking Reagan to see Darius Nader, who might be her biological father, had disaster written all over it.

# Chapter 32

It was almost 7 by the time Aiden and Reagan were in a rental car and on their way to see Darius. They knew there was a chance he might not be home, but it was one that Aiden was willing to take to prevent giving Darius advance warning. Aiden told Reagan that he couldn't rule out Darius Nader as a suspect in her attempted abductions. A quick Google search revealed his home was in the Garden District of New Orleans, best known for its elaborate houses and pricy real estate. Reagan couldn't help wondering where they had gotten the money.

The Naders lived in a spacious, two-story shrimp-colored French provincial home with a large willow tree in the front yard. Lights glowed from the windows on all levels, giving the house a welcoming appeal that Reagan hoped was a good sign. There was a late model Subaru, a Mercedes, and a Lexus in the driveway, more indications of serious wealth. Aiden parked the black Kia Optima rental on the street.

The front double doors were white with beautiful stained-glass panes. When Aiden rang the doorbell, Reagan clutched her fist with nervous anticipation. Aiden must have noticed, because he clasped her right hand in his and rubbed her knuckles with his thumb in a calming gesture. She smiled back at him with assurance that she still had her shit together, even if she was hanging by her last nerve. A couple of minutes later, a pretty, dark-haired teenage girl with almond-shaped brown eyes, wearing a gold and black band uniform, flung open the door.

She gave them both a quick up-and-down appraisal before she spoke in a slightly robotic tone. "If you're selling anything, our neighborhood has a no-solicitation policy," she said with an exaggerated sigh. "That's my spiel when strangers come to the door. So, bye bye."

When the girl started to close the door, Reagan held up her hand in a nonthreatening way, realized it was trembling, and quickly lowered it to her side. "We're not selling anything, I promise. Is Darius Nader home?"

The teenager narrowed her eyes suspiciously. "Huh? Does he know you?"

Reagan plastered on a big smile and continued. "He and your Aunt Rosana went to school with my mother when they were about your age. I'm Reagan Asher and this is my friend, Aiden Rannell."

She grinned at the mention of her aunt's name, and her demeanor instantly relaxed. "That's cool. By the way, I love your suede jacket."

"Thank you," Reagan said, momentarily caught off guard. "May we speak to your father?"

"Papa! Someone's at the door for you! They know you! Nobody's selling crap!" she screamed over her shoulder. Aiden stifled a laugh.

Reagan suddenly found it difficult to breathe. *What if this is my real father? Will I feel a connection? See a part of myself in him? Too much to ask,* she decided. Her grip tightened on Aiden's fingers.

"Paaaa Paaaa!" the teen girl yelled again, then rolled her eyes. "When he's working in his office, it's hard to get him to put stuff down."

A distinguished man, tall and slender with dark brown wavy hair graying around his hairline, bounded down a curved marble staircase and hurried to the door. Although she didn't immediately feel a zing of any kind, there was a sense of familiarity that Reagan couldn't place. Maybe her mother had introduced her to him at some point in her childhood. Darius smiled and nodded at Reagan, then spoke to his daughter.

"Lauren, baby, how many times have I told you not to use the word crap? It is unbecoming of a young lady and reflects poorly on your vocabulary usage, not to mention your upbringing." He kissed the top of her head. She blew out an irritated breath. "Now go change out of your uniform and get on your homework. You're getting a late start, and I don't want you up studying all night. You'll be cranky tomorrow."

"Oh, Papa, everybody says 'crap.' It's not half as bad as what most of my friends say." He shook his head in an *I don't want to hear it* kind of way that parents do and pointed to the stairs. She gave him a little smirk, waved goodbye to everyone, and ran up the stairs two at a time. Stopping at the top of the stairs, she called, "By the way Pops, I want a jacket just like hers for my birthday!"

Shaking his head, Darius gave Reagan a broad smile. "Sorry to make you wait. How may I help you?"

For a few moments, Reagan was speechless, her mouth filled with cotton, so Aiden stepped in.

"Mr. Nader, my name is Aiden Rannell, and this is Reagan Asher. We apologize for showing up unannounced this evening, but …"

"My mother was Claire Moran Asher," Reagan blurted out, finding her voice.

"Claire?" His face went slack, as if the mere mention of her name shocked him to his core. "My God," he whispered, scrutinizing her face for signs of recognition. "When I first saw you from the stairs, you reminded me of someone I couldn't quite put my finger on, but now I know why. Please come in," he said warmly, shaking hands with Aiden and Reagan. "My son has some of his rowdier friends in the house, so let's go to the living room for privacy. It's the one place no one uses and the quietest. My office is an embarrassing mess."

He led them through the caramel and shrimp-colored marble entryway, under a 12-foot arch to the living room. It was so spacious, there were two different seating areas. Reagan and Aiden sat at the far end on a cerulean blue velvet Queen Anne sofa. Darius took a seat on one of the twin oyster sateen accent chairs across from them, sliding it closer for a more intimate conversation.

"Your eyes are the same brilliant green as your mother's," he said with genuine emotion. "She was one of the most strikingly beautiful and vibrant women I have ever known and was my dearest friend. Her loss left a hole in my heart."

"Thank you, Mr. Nader. I know this must be a surprise to you, me showing up at your door like this, but you may be the only one who can help me. My grandmother Fiona Moran died recently … actually she was murdered." His eyes went wide. "There are things from my family's past that may be connected to what happened to her. I hoped, since you knew my mother back then, you might be able to help fill in some blanks."

His concerned expression looked real. "Of course, I will help any way I can." He settled back in his chair. "And please call me Darius. Only my students call me Mr. Nader or Dr. Nader."

"You teach?" Aiden asked.

"Professor of art history."

Reagan's brows furrowed. "That was my mother's field of interest," she said, remembering the picture Aiden had on his phone of what her mother had written in her yearbook. "Funny. I only recently found that out about her. Did she acquire the interest from you, or vice versa?"

"Neither. Bayyi — that is what I call my father — was an art history professor in Lebanon and a well-known international lecturer in his field. Retired now. He has always been a passionate man who sees the world through a kaleidoscope. We both found it contagious. I ..."

Loud laughter rang through the house, interrupting his train of thought.

"Sorry about that. My son Caleb has a couple of fraternity brothers in the kitchen making cookies for a party. He thought my wife Helena would be home to do most of the baking, but she got called into work for an emergency. She's an anesthesiologist. A smart woman and a wonderful cook. I am afraid to see what they have done to our kitchen." He laughed.

"Just the two children?" Aiden asked.

"My oldest son, Liam, is doing his residency in orthopedics in New York City. Caleb is a senior at Tulane and will start medical school in the fall. They both inherited their mother's gray cells. Lauren is 14 and a gifted musician. Definitely more like me."

"She's a lovely girl," Reagan said.

"Thank you. She is my diamond in the rough. A mind of her own." He beamed with pride.

"Let me explain what has happened to Reagan over the past week," Aiden said. "Maybe it will give you an idea of why you might be able to shed some light on a few things."

Darius listened to Aiden explain the murder of Mrs. Moran, the break-in at her home, and the two attempted abductions. He didn't mention the jewels. Reagan assumed he was holding back that information until he had a better read on Darius. There was still the question of his involvement but judging from the expression of horror on his beet-red face, if Darius was faking ignorance, he was a damn good actor.

"Why would someone do such vile things?" Darius asked indignantly.

"The police are still trying to figure that out," Aiden said.

"There is evidence leading us to believe it could involve people associated with my family many years ago," Reagan said. "Since you were one of my mother's friends and lived down the street in your school years, I hoped there was something significant you might remember."

"I'll try, but I'm not sure how much help I can be," Darius said, shrugging his shoulders.

"I was only 7 when my mother died. As you must know, as children, we only see our parents as Mom and Dad. We don't really know them as individuals. Could you tell me some things about her?" she asked, expecting him to be vague.

"What if I start from the beginning, and you can ask questions you think might be relevant?"

"Sounds good," Reagan answered with relief.

"My father, Karim, is from Lebanon, but he lived in America during his teenage years when my grandfather got a teaching appointment at a private university in Cleveland. After my father graduated from high school, my grandparents arranged for him to go back to Lebanon to marry into a wealthy family who had agreed to send him to the American University of Beirut. He married my mother as soon as he graduated. As old-fashioned as it sounds, they seem to have had a happy marriage, or at least comfortable. When I was growing up, my father grew weary of the politics and conservative views of my mother's family in Lebanon, so he decided to send my sister Rosana and me to America to live with my grandparents as he had done. We were 14 years old at the time. Rosana and I had a difficult time adjusting to western schools. Many parents didn't want their children associating with Middle Easterners. Claire and Rosana met in their freshman year when they were chemistry partners. When they realized they lived in the same neighborhood, they began hanging out and almost immediately became best friends. Rosana and I were usually joined at the hip, as twins often are, so we became a threesome."

"There is a picture in my mother's yearbook at prom. You were dancing ..."

"... and she wore the most beautiful green gown that matched her dazzling emerald eyes," he finished her sentence. "Rosana helped her pick it out. Her beauty was ethereal." His lips turned up in the most effortless smile, his eyes shining from the memory.

"Sounds like you may have been a bit more than friends," Aiden suggested.

Darius slowly shook his head. "Ah, if that had only been true, I would have been the happiest boy on the planet."

"So, you never dated?" Reagan asked.

"Only as friends, much to my dismay. Those last two years of high school, I was madly in love with Claire, but unfortunately, she didn't love me in the same way." His disappointment appeared genuine.

Reagan leaned forward, trying to analyze what he had said. *Is he sparing my feelings about having sex with my mother or is he telling me the truth?* She had to know.

"Darius, we just came from a visit with my father. He reluctantly admitted to me that he is not my biological father." She let it hang in silence.

His face went blank for a few moments while he pondered her words, then it was soon replaced with understanding. "I see. And after seeing the pictures of us in the yearbook, you thought it might be me?"

"Maybe," she whispered.

Darius coughed to clear his throat and chose his words carefully. His demeanor was serious. "I promise you, Reagan, your mother and I were never intimate. That was her decision, not mine. When I finally confronted her with my feelings, she explained to me that she loved me as a dear friend. Like a brother. As you can imagine, I was heartbroken. At first I blamed it on her father, who didn't approve of her association with Rosana and me, but then I realized Claire was the type of girl who would fight to the death for what she wanted, and it just wasn't me."

"Do you have any idea who she might have been seeing other than my dad? She had to have gotten pregnant sometime in the summer of 1986. There are missing pieces here, and I need to find them."

"And you think this might have something to do with your grandmother's death?"

"We don't know for sure," Reagan said.

Darius took a steadying breath and swallowed hard.

"You know something, don't you?" Aiden asked.

"I'm not sure. It's not something I can confirm or want to believe," he said tentatively.

Reagan had to be sure he wasn't lying to her about his relationship with her mother. Why else would Nana keep his picture in her safe deposit box for all those years? Not wanting to give it to the police, Reagan had tucked the picture in her wallet, which was now in her handbag. She had meant to show it to her father along with the yearbook photos Aiden had on his cell phone, but totally forgot about it when his revelations turned her world upside down. Putting her handbag in her lap, she fished it out and handed it to Darius. Aiden's eyes met hers. He nodded his head in agreement.

"Is that you?" she asked Darius.

He held it in his hand and stared at it for over a full minute, then hugged the picture to his chest. When he looked back at Reagan, his eyes were misty.

"Oh, Bayyi," he whispered to himself, his face reflecting an inner turmoil Reagan didn't understand, though she could tell she had struck a nerve.

"We found it in Claire's mother's safe deposit box after her death last week. Why would Fiona Moran keep this picture that bears a striking resemblance to you, in a lockbox for years, if it wasn't significant? Is that you?" Aiden asked.

Darius closed his eyes and lowered his head. "Not me," he choked out when he looked up to meet Aiden's eyes. "It's my father … Karim Nader. When he was a teenager."

Reagan and Aiden looked at each other, both baffled.

"This has to mean something, or you wouldn't be this visibly upset," Aiden said, moving to the edge of his seat. "We've come a long way to find the truth, and Reagan deserves it."

Darius sat up straight in his chair, steeling himself. "I agree. You deserve my honesty, but I am not sure I know exactly what the truth is, only assumptions on my part. Claire, Rosana, and I started OSU at the same time. When Claire received a scholarship to Oxford University for her last two years of university, she was beyond excited. She saved every dime from her summer jobs to pay for the plane ticket and the first year's living expenses. Mr. and Mrs. Moran were very controlling and vetoed any suggestion of Claire leaving the country, so she kept it a secret, using my apartment at OSU as her mailing address. While Claire spent her summers at home working a part-time job, Rosana and I worked as tutors in Columbus during the summer. Claire made several trips during the summer to visit and pick up her mail.

"The summer before Claire was supposed to leave for England in the fall, she received an assignment for an essay that had to be returned a few weeks before her classes began. Of course, her parents were still under the impression she would be returning to OSU and had no idea she would be leaving the country. Claire was desperate to make a good first impression on her Oxford professors, so she coordinated her visit with my father to Columbus in order to utilize his expertise. Bayyi was more than happy to help. He was in the States for a couple of months that summer on a lecture tour and took advantage of the weekends to visit us whenever he could work it into his schedule.

"The week before Claire was due to leave for Oxford, she called to inform me she had canceled her scholarship. She and Stuart were getting married right away, then they were moving to Dayton for him to finish school. Not her. Him. Rosana and I were dumbfounded. It was as if her dream she had worked so hard for since high school never existed. I suspected her parents found out about Oxford, but Rosana thought she might have gotten pregnant. We later learned her guess was correct."

"What does that have to do with a picture of your father in Nana's safe deposit box?" Reagan asked.

"When my father had a heart attack three weeks ago, I traveled to Lebanon to be there for his operation. We were alone while he waited for the nurses to take him to surgery. He grabbed my hand and, with tears in his eyes, said he had something important to tell me in case he didn't survive.

"Years ago, he received a letter from a woman he had had a relationship with when he was in America. She told him she was sorry for keeping it from him, but he had a 7-year-old daughter. Bayyi was so doped up on drugs, I assumed he was hallucinating. Plus, if you knew how conservative he is, you would have a hard time believing it too, though he assured me his memory was clear.

"He described her as if she were standing in front of him … 'fair and beautiful with flaming red hair like the glowing embers in a campfire.' They shared the same passions, and though he had tried to resist their attraction, their love would not be denied. He said it happened when he spent the summer lecturing in the States. He considered leaving my mother for her but decided the shame he would bring to our family was too much for them to endure. It's more likely that he was afraid that my mother's father, who was a very powerful man in Beirut, would have ruined him.

"When he came back to America for our graduation from university a couple of years later and to pack up my grandparents to go back to Lebanon, he saw his lover again. She was unhappy and struggling with her marriage, which he blamed on himself. Although he didn't know about the child at the time, he ended things for good when he saw her. It broke his heart to leave her, knowing he would never see her again. He said he never stopped loving her and wanted me to know I had a sister. He admitted that he was a coward for never attempting to contact his daughter or check on her well-being. He asked for my forgiveness, then broke down in my arms." Tears began to flow freely down Darius' cheeks.

Reagan could barely wrap her brain around what he was saying. She clasped her hands together as she began to tremble. She was too stunned to cry.

"I tried to imagine who my father had fallen in love with. It couldn't have been someone he met on his lecture tour, because he was never anywhere more than a night or two, not long enough for a meaningful affair. The only extended time he spent that summer was when he visited my grandmother in Lancashire or Rosana and me in Columbus. Then suddenly the pieces began to fall into place. Claire. Fair. Beautiful. Flaming red hair. When we were in high school, she joked about having a crush on my father. She thought he was so intelligent, handsome, and worldly. Rosana and I dismissed it as hero worship. The weekend he assisted Claire with her paper, they worked in the conference room at his hotel, or that's what he told me. When he was visiting my grandparents that summer, Claire was right down the street. All the opportunity they would need. The timing would be right."

Darius stopped to compose himself.

"When Bayyi woke up the next morning, he denied everything. I accused him of having an affair with Claire, but he adamantly denied it. She had been so innocent. Young and trusting. There was fury in his eyes as he continued to deny everything he had confessed. Said it must have been a dream."

"He didn't remember anything at all?" Aiden asked.

"Nothing, or so he claimed. It was foolish of me to bring it up at all with his condition, but I was furious and could not hold my tongue. Bayyi said the very idea that he would take advantage of a student was ludicrous. Then he asked me never to repeat such things, because it would insult the memory of my mother. He had also known her mother Fiona when they were teenagers, before he moved back to Lebanon, and it would hurt her deeply to hear such rumors about her daughter. I didn't believe him. His account had been too vivid. Maybe it was because I figured out who the girl was that made him deny it, or maybe he had expected to die."

All Reagan could do was stare. Her mouth like sawdust.

"My father's younger brother came into the room while he was asleep, and as much as I dislike him, I thought maybe he knew something. I told him what my father had said about finding out he had a daughter with a woman he had loved in America. My uncle seemed interested and wanted to know who I thought the woman was. I told him my suspicions. He was only 6 years old when he and my father lived in the States with my grandparents, and he was sent back to Lebanon to live with relatives at the same time my father left to go to university, so I doubt he remembered your mother. My uncle told me to forget it and agreed it was probably a dream."

"Is your Uncle's name Borzin Nader?" Aiden asked.

Darius looked stunned; his voice thick. "How could you possibly know that?"

It was the first time Reagan had heard that name. She began to wonder what else Aiden had kept from her.

"Borzin Nader was one of the men who attempted to abduct Reagan and her goddaughter, who is also my 5-year-old niece. He was shot in the attempt and is being held in police custody at a hospital in Akron, Ohio," Aiden explained. "Nour Nader was his accomplice and escaped. There are numerous local, state, and federal law enforcement agencies looking for him. Has he tried to contact you?"

Reagan felt her face flush with anger that she forced back down. It was the wrong time and place to confront Aiden for keeping those important details to himself, all more than likely supplied by Danni Silva.

Darius sprang to his feet. "I would never let either of those men near my family. Nour is one of my father's cousins. Borzin lived with his family in Lebanon for years, and he was a terrible influence on Nour, who is 15 years younger. Borzin was resentful that my grandparents sent him back to Lebanon. He started getting in trouble at an early age as his way of getting back at them. Those two have been in and out of trouble for years. When Borzin showed up at the hospital, I should have turned him away, but I was afraid my father would die and not letting him see his brother would have weighed on my conscience."

"So Borzin Nader knows that Claire Moran Asher may have been the mother of your father's illegitimate child?" Aiden asked.

"That's how he knows about me?" Reagan said in a shaky voice.

"It is, and I'm so sorry," Darius said, sinking back into his chair. "But why would he care? What would he have to gain by kidnapping Reagan? My father has no money to pay a ransom."

"That's what we are trying to figure out," Aiden said. "You said both men were often in trouble. What types of crimes?"

"The list is long. Theft. Looting. Assault. Coercion. Battery. Many of the charges happened in neighboring countries. They took advantage of political unrest in destabilized nations for personal gain. I'm surprised they were allowed into the United States."

Reagan had a million thoughts swirling in her head. *Could the jewels she had tucked away in a bank have come from a theft in a war-torn county? Ripped out of the hands of desperate people fleeing for their lives or stolen from an abandoned museum that had been ransacked? How much blood had been lost to obtain them? And how did they end up in my grandparents' house?* Her dad had told her the five diamonds had been given to him by her grandfather, who claimed he found them. *Was he involved?*

Darius looked up pensively. "Reagan, it just occurred to me that you may be my half-sister."

"Would you be willing to take a DNA test?" Aiden asked. "That way you both would know for sure."

The question surprised Reagan. Although she knew all the evidence was there, hearing the words spoken out loud made it too real. *How many more lies would she uncover about her life?* Everything she thought she knew about herself and her family was slowly being chipped away. Everyone lied. *What will be left of me when all the secrets are revealed?*

"Certainly. As much as I would hate to know my father took advantage of Claire, I would be honored to have Reagan in my family." Despite everything, Darius was reaching out to her, a total stranger, with compassion and openness. Reagan's heart swelled and she was in awe of the unconditional acceptance he offered her.

It all became clear when he suddenly stood up and walked to an end table on the other side of the room, picking up a framed picture of himself with his wife and children at younger ages. Bringing it back to Reagan, he spoke with unbridled emotion.

"Do you see this beautiful family? This house? My career? My life? I owe this all to Claire Moran. Everything! She taught me to be strong. Stand up for myself against my parents and bullies. When I was in college and my parents arranged for me to marry into a wealthy family like my father had done, the girl's father decided he would send me to graduate school to get my MBA so I could work for him in his business in Lebanon. Claire said, 'No, I refuse to let you go. You are going to graduate and come live with me in England. We will see the world together.' She said that to me every day, and it gave me courage. 'Bide your time,' she would preach. 'You always have a way out.'

"Then she changed everything. She lost her dream … our dream. How could I possibly fight my family without her? I felt alone and betrayed. With no way out and no support, I went along. Lost hope. Then the week before I graduated from OSU, I had plans to go to my grandmother's home for the weekend to pack up and talk about my upcoming wedding plans. I hadn't seen Claire in two years. When I arrived at my grandparents, Claire was sitting on the living room carpet with the most beautiful little girl I had ever seen toddling around on wobbly legs. Claire hugged me and acted as if I had just seen her yesterday." He looked at Reagan with tenderness. "You had pitch-black hair and huge sparkling green eyes. You radiated light.

"When she asked about my plans, I told her I was getting married as my family had arranged. She took my hands in hers and frowned, 'No, you are not,' she said. 'You are going to tell your parents that you have your own goals. You are going to get a graduate degree in art history like we always planned.' I told her I had no money of my own and no job and would probably be thrown out of the family.

"She asked me if I wanted to live in Lebanon and marry a stranger. I told her no. She said, 'You are going to get a job, two if needed, and work for a year to save money. Then you are going to send applications to universities all over the country to get a graduate scholarship and research money, even if you end up in Alaska. By next year, you will be in school doing what you want to do, not what someone else tells you to do. When you live your life by someone else's rules, you lose a little piece of yourself every day, until you finally disappear.'" Darius exuded emotion as he spoke.

"I did exactly what she gave me the courage to do. I tended bar at two different restaurants and roomed with friends. A year later, I was accepted into a graduate program at Tulane with a teaching assistant position, and then research grants, until I received my PhD. That's where I met Helena. My father eventually forgave me. If only I had done the same for Claire," he said, shaking his head. "She had no one on her side who understood her but me, and I let her down. I didn't fight for her, and eventually it destroyed her."

Reagan was thrown for a loop, dealing with a cacophony of feelings. The vivacious, strong-willed, and goal-oriented woman described by this man, who could be her half-brother, was nothing like the subdued, emotionally fragile woman she remembered.

*What happened to my mother's life that changed her course so dramatically? Did mother's pregnancy derailed everything she cared about? Was it my fault for being born? How could Nana and Grandpa have treated my mother so unfairly by putting a stop to her dreams? And how could Nana have lied to me for all those years and kept me from the only parent I had left? What did it all have to do with millions of dollars' worth of jewels?*

If she allowed herself to dwell on all the secrets and lies she had learned in the past 24 hours, she was sure to unravel. The guilt of knowing she was the unwanted pregnancy that squelched her mother's plans was overwhelming. That and her mother's love for a man she could never have, who lived halfway around the world. Who had abandoned her. *Had Mother committed suicide because he never answered her letter?*

When she looked at Darius holding the picture of his father, maybe her father too, she realized she wasn't the only one suffering. Propelled by an instinct that drew her to him, she wrapped her arms around his neck and held him tightly.

# Chapter 33

Aiden hated to interrupt the tender moment between Reagan and Darius, but there were still questions to be answered. Darius appeared to be as much a victim of the consequences of his father's bad decisions as Reagan was of her mother's. The past had come back to bite these two people in their butts, and none of it was their fault.

"Darius, I realize this is a lot for you and Reagan to take in, but I need to know if you've had any contact with your uncle or cousin since you saw them in Lebanon recently."

Darius glanced up and met Aiden's eyes, wiping his face with the back of his hand.

"I've heard from both at different times. Borzin called about a week ago. He told me that he and Nour were in the States to make a major investment. He called it a sure thing. In other words, a scam. Wanted me to invest $10,000 in a venture that would yield millions. My cut would be 10% of the profits. I assured him that I wasn't interested in any of his schemes, then made it clear he was never to contact me or my family again. I thought that was the end of it until Nour phoned me yesterday at work to tell me their plans had hit a snag. Bo had gotten himself into trouble in Cleveland. Nour needed money and a place to stay, until he could figure out a way to help him. Again, I refused. After Nour screamed obscenities, he threatened that I would be sorry. My children have been warned not to speak to either of them under any circumstances."

"Nour is a dangerous man, and I agree that you need to keep your family as far away from him as possible," Aiden said emphatically.

Darius stood up and nervously tried to straighten the wrinkles in his pants. Aiden noticed his fingers were trembling. "I'll hire a security service to guard our home until he has been apprehended."

"Good idea," Reagan said. "I've seen firsthand what he's capable of doing."

"Papa!" Lauren whined as she appeared in the archway wearing a pink t-shirt and gray sweatpants. "Caleb and his hot friends left the kitchen a disaster! There's not an empty spot in the whole kitchen for me to make a snack. And they left the oven on, which I turned off, you're welcome, so the house wouldn't burn down, and there's green icing on the floor! Mom's going to be pissed."

"Watch your language, baby," Darius replied affectionately, clearly amused. "Why don't you do your papa a favor and get the dirty dishes and pans into the sink to soak?"

"Oh, Papa. Why me?" He walked toward her with his hands outstretched. She stepped into his arms for a hug.

"Because you are my favorite daughter, and I can always depend on you to be the responsible one."

She stepped back and huffed with mock exasperation. "I'm your only daughter. One day that's not going to work anymore."

He patted her cheek and gently tweaked her ear. "Until then, habeebti (my love), please help your old Pops out." She pursed her lips and left for the kitchen.

So far, neither Aiden nor Reagan had brought up the jewels. Aiden decided it was time to broach the subject.

"Do you remember if your grandmother had any jewelry made of different colors of cut glass?" Aiden asked.

Darius rubbed his chin and thought for a few seconds. "Except for a small solitaire diamond necklace and her wedding band, my grandmother never wore jewelry. She was so tiny, anything else would overwhelm her small frame. That's the very reason why what you are asking sticks out in my mind. Many years ago when they still lived in Lancashire, Borzin mailed my grandmother a birthday gift from Lebanon that contained an assortment of secondhand colored-glass jewelry, with everything from hair pins to tiaras. It was so tacky, Rosana and I guessed he had bought the whole lot of it for a couple of pounds in an outdoor market. To be honest, I think my grandmother was insulted. For her own son to send her something so inappropriate to her tastes hurt her feelings. Why do you ask?"

"Because when your grandmother was moving back to Lebanon, she apparently gave it to my mother for me to play with," Reagan said. "This past week, on a hunch, we had it appraised. Imagine our surprise when we found out it was all genuine. Diamonds, sapphires, rubies, emeralds. Worth millions."

"You can't be serious!" Darius exclaimed. Then he broke out into a full belly laugh.

"What's so funny?" Aiden asked, perplexed.

"I assure you, Borzin would never have given it to his mother had he known its true value. So, he is not only a thief, but a stupid one as well."

"Some of it is hundreds of years old," Aiden said. "Period jewelry. Do you think your father might have known about it?"

Darius shook his head. "My dad considered period jewelry a form of art. The designs of the jewelry were a result of the specific historic times they were made in. He used slides of some very elaborate pieces in his lectures. If he had seen the jewelry, I'm sure he would have recognized its worth and insisted it go back to its rightful owners or to a museum for others to appreciate. My father may be an adulterer, but he is no thief."

"Has Borzin ever been back for a visit since he moved to Lebanon before now?" Aiden asked.

"Nour and Borzin both came with my father when Rosana and I graduated from OSU and to pack my grandparents up to move home to Lebanon. That would have been in 1988."

"Could they have smuggled something into the U.S. at that time?" Aiden asked. "Maybe gems?"

"Why do you ask?" Darius frowned.

"One of the reasons we had the jewelry appraised is because we found some valuable gems hidden in the Moran house. They had been there for well over 20 years. The mystery is how they got there," Aiden explained.

"There is no doubt Borzin and Nour were capable of smuggling something into the country all those years ago, but I'm not sure how they would have gotten it to the Moran house. Besides Rosana and me, my father was the only one who really ..." Darius was interrupted by a loud crash coming from somewhere in the house. Aiden jumped to his feet and put his hand under his sweater to reach the gun at his waist.

"Whoa!" Darius barked, eyeing Aiden's gun with disdain. "You would never have gotten into my home if I'd know you were carrying a weapon."

"It's legal. He's a retired Navy Seal," Reagan said quickly. "What was that noise?"

"Probably just Lauren banging pans to get my attention."

"Didn't sound like banging pans to me," Aiden said, flipping the safety off his 9mm. "More like broken glass."

Darius grabbed Aiden's bicep. "You're overreacting. Please put the gun away before you scare my daughter and me half to death."

"Show me the kitchen. I'll keep my gun behind my back if she's okay," Aiden said sternly. Darius didn't argue when the potential gravity of the situation hit him. As they approached the kitchen door, Aiden motioned Darius and Reagan behind him while he went in first.

Reagan gasped, her hands flying to her mouth. "Lauren." She was gone.

"Shit!" Aiden yelled, as he ran toward the wide-open backdoor with a broken jagged windowpane. Kicking the shards of glass out of his way, he stormed out the back door with Darius and Reagan trailing behind.

"Lauren!" Darius screamed, as they sprinted across the back patio and past the swimming pool. "The gate!" He pointed to the open wooden door.

As Aiden dashed through the gate of the fence surrounding the backyard, he heard the unmistakable sound of a car door slam shut. By the time he and Darius reached the driveway, Nour was sitting in the driver's seat of a white Ford Explorer, the engine revving to life. For a split second, Aiden and Nour locked eyes and recognition passed between them. After giving Aiden a sardonic grin, he stomped on the gas pedal and screeched out of the driveway to the street. Aiden felt an emptiness in the pit of his stomach as he watched Nour escape with a helpless and terrified young girl. Acting on his first impulse, he pulled the keys out of his pocket and ran to the rental car.

"Call 911 and tell them I'm in pursuit, and that I'm armed with a legal concealed carry!" he shouted over his shoulder to Darius.

Weaving out into the street, he caught a glimpse of Darius yanking his phone out of his pants pocket and punching the face frantically, while Reagan looked on in disbelief.

The white vehicle and the streetlights on St. Charles Avenue made it easier for Aiden to follow Nour. Unfortunately, Nour realized the same thing and swiftly turned off on a side street and made multiple turns, trying to get Aiden off his tail. At one point, he ghosted Aiden completely. The neighborhood was relatively quiet and free of traffic, so Aiden tucked his car in an alley and waited, hoping Nour had done the same thing. Five minutes later, he saw the white Ford inch out of the driveway of a darkened "for sale" home and onto the street. After letting Nour get a block ahead, Aiden eased his rental onto the street and resumed tailing him undetected. He needed to call Reagan to let her know he still had Nour in his sights so she could pass the information on to the police. When he felt in his pocket for his cell, it was empty. That's when he remembered putting it in his jacket pocket that was now lying on a sofa in Darius' living room.

Nour's driving patterns were erratic. Either he had no map or was having trouble interpreting the directions from his GPS. A few times Aiden turned off on adjacent streets that ran parallel to make sure he hadn't been spotted. Eventually, Nour headed up on the entrance ramp to I-10 West, making it easier for Aiden to blend in with the evening traffic.

The longer they were on the road, the more apprehensive Aiden became. At some point Nour would have to deal with a screaming Lauren, who probably had been knocked unconscious or drugged. She wasn't visible in the car, and there hadn't been enough time to tie and gag her. It felt like another opportunistic kidnapping, which seemed to be Nour's MO. More than likely, he had traveled to New Orleans out of desperation and was going to force Darius to give him money and shelter. If he had been watching the house, he would have known there were other cars out front. That presented a big unknown for him. When he saw the young men drive away, he probably felt safer approaching from the backyard. Lauren would have been visible through the kitchen windows, a young girl alone. It was the perfect opportunity to use her has leverage.

There had been a look of recognition on Nour's face when he locked eyes with Aiden in the driveway, so now he was aware Aiden was in New Orleans. It wasn't a leap for him to assume Reagan was there too, which made her an easier target. Aiden couldn't be sure Nour Nader didn't have other accomplices.

It was almost 8:30 p.m. when Nour turned off on the Metairie exit to Veterans Highway. Luckily, there was no indication he had seen Aiden following him. As soon as Lauren woke up, Nour was going to have his hands full. He would need to get her someplace out of the way to secure her.

Ten minutes later, Nour pulled into a strip mall and parked near the road, away from the few cars parked in front of a hardware store. Aiden parked a couple of rows over between a truck and a van. Easing the door open, he walked around the back of the truck and watched Nour get out of the SUV and walk into the store. Just as he thought, no planning.

Jumping back in his rental, Aiden backed out of his space and moved the car directly behind Nour's SUV, effectively blocking it in. He leaped out of the Kia and ran to the Explorer, pulling at the door handle. Locked. He reached in his holster, pulled out his 9 mm and used the handle to smash in the driver's side window open. Lauren was stretched across the backseat, out cold. Flipping the locks, Aiden opened the back door and pulled Lauren toward him by her feet. He slung her over his shoulder and carried her back to his Kia, tossing her on the back seat. There wasn't time to check for injuries. Her safety came first.

"Hey! What are you doing?" Nour yelled from the entrance of the store and began running toward him, while fumbling in his pocket for what Aiden assumed was a gun.

Just as Aiden grabbed the handle of the driver's door and threw himself in the seat, a bullet blew the side mirror off, barely missing him. He started up the engine and threw the car into drive as Nour drew nearer, firing shots in rapid succession. As he turned out of the shopping center into traffic, a bullet shattered the rear window and another burst the side window over Lauren's head. A truck driver sat on his horn when Aiden veered in front of him, barely escaping a collision. Lauren was safely tucked down in the backseat away from the spray of bullets, but not strapped in or protected from the pellets of shattered glass. Once she woke up, there was no telling what her reaction would be. She might panic and jump out of the moving car. He had to get her to a police station as quickly as possible.

The heavy traffic for that time of the evening made it difficult for Aiden to see who was coming up behind him. He'd never seen so many white vehicles in his life. "Was there a fuckin' blue light special on white SUVs?" he muttered to himself.

As he applied his brakes to slow down for the red light ahead, he felt a jolt from behind that sent him sliding forward into the intersection. He knew exactly who it was and sped through before the oncoming cars hit him. Accelerating, Aiden was determined to get through the next intersection before he was caught by the changing light. As he approached the next traffic light, another slam from behind on the left rear side of his bumper sent his rental spinning around until it stopped in the middle of the intersection, facing his pursuer head on. Vehicles screeched and skidded all around him attempting to avoid collisions.

Aiden did a quick check in the backseat to find Lauren lying in the floorboard, still unconscious. When he turned back around, he was temporarily blinded by the sudden flash of the high beams from the white SUV. The momentary distraction allowed Nour to lean out his window and fire several shots directly at Aiden, who grunted as a bullet struck his upper left bicep. Blood and muscle splattered against the driver's side window. Terrified drivers and passengers, now stranded in the intersection, scampered from their cars. They crouched for cover with cell phones in their hands, frantically calling for help, some videotaping the scene.

Keeping his head down and mentally blocking out the pain, Aiden tried unsuccessfully to start the engine. He and Lauren were sitting ducks if Nour decided to ram his car again, and this time it would be head-on. With the intersection crowded with people and possible witnesses, Aiden hoped Nour would take the opportunity to make his escape before the police arrived.

He secured his 9mm in his right hand as he watched Nour ease his car door open and slip out, using the driver's door for cover. Aiden was sure help was on the way, but he was afraid it would be too late. He had to do something before somebody got killed. Peeking over the dashboard, he saw Nour with gun in hand approaching his rental. Making a split decision, Aiden turned on his high-beams, momentarily blinding Nour. Tucking his injured arm against his chest, he rolled out of the driver's door, popped up beside the car to zero in on his target, used his peripheral vision to make sure no civilians were in his path, then fired multiple shots in rapid succession. Nour jerked twice, grabbed his upper right thigh, and went down on one knee wincing in pain. The blinding lights from both cars made it difficult to tell exactly where his bullets had hit. Within seconds, Nour pulled himself to his feet and limped back toward his SUV for cover.

One of the drivers partially blocking Nour's Explorer must have been afraid of being rammed, because he frantically whipped his car over the raised center median, knocking his back bumper completely off, as he moved into the reverse lane. That in turn opened an exit for Nour to follow suit.

Turning back toward the Kia, Aiden heard a screeching cry come from the backseat. "Maaamaaaa," Lauren screamed.

Aiden hurried back to the car to catch her before she bolted. When he opened the backseat door and leaned in, a panicked Lauren caught him off balance as she blindly slammed into his chest, sending him backward onto the asphalt. He stifled a moan as excruciating pain radiated down his left arm all the way to his fingertips. It took all his strength to jump to his feet and catch her wrist before she ran off. Her flailing arms slammed into his injured arm. He winced but held his grip.

"Lauren. Don't run. You're okay, Sweetie," Aiden said calmly, clutching his teeth in pain. "It's Aiden. We met at your house. Remember? You're safe now. The police will be here any minute. We'll get you to a hospital and call your papa." Her wild eyes locked on his as she panted, trying to catch her breath. She slowly nodded her head, finally comprehending his words. He carefully put his right arm around her shoulders, then led her to the front passenger seat of the rental.

She sat sideways on the front passenger seat with her feet dangling out the door, tears streaming down her blood-stained cheeks. When she noticed the blood covering the front of her pink t-shirt, terror spread across her face.

"I'm bleeding!" she cried.

"No, Lauren," Aiden said softly, pointing to his bicep. "You are injured, but that's my blood, not yours."

After soothing the hysterical teen enough for her to understand he was there to help, he took a quick assessment of her injuries, lightly lifting her chin with his fingertips. She immediately covered her face with her hands.

"My face hurts!" she yelled.

"I know, Lauren. Please move your hands. I just want to make sure you're okay until an ambulance arrives." Pieces of shattered glass rained from her hair when she reluctantly nodded her consent.

"Oh, no," she began to whine. Aiden inspected her scalp.

"It's going to be okay. If you lean your head out the door, we'll shake the glass out of your hair, just don't touch it." He gently used his fingers to work the pebbles out. *Thank God for safety glass*, he thought.

"I c...can't see very well," she whispered. One of the blows Nour struck had landed squarely on her left eye. It made Aiden's blood boil.

With the car door open, the overhead light allowed him to fully assess her condition. His heart sank as he took in the extent of damage Nour Nader had done to the innocent girl's face. Dried blood from a three-inch gash near her right temple covered the side of her face almost to her jaw. Her left eye was swollen shut and the whole left side of her face was so inflamed and bruised that she was almost unrecognizable from that angle. The thought of a man doing that to a child was incomprehensible.

"It looks bad, doesn't it?" Lauren choked out, fighting back more tears.

"You're going to be fine, I promise. We're going to get you back to your mama and papa as soon as we can." He patted her hand. She grabbed it and squeezed.

"Don't leave me."

"I won't," he promised.

# Chapter 34

By the time Reagan and Darius arrived at the hospital, Aiden was in surgery. They knew he had been shot, but no one had information on how bad it was. Reagan wanted to scream and force someone to give her answers, but a friendly nurse promised to notify her as soon as the doctor was finished. Thankfully, when Aiden was admitted, he'd given his consent to the hospital to share his medical condition with her.

When they found Lauren's room, Helena Nader, a lovely petite brunette, was sitting in a chair by her sleeping daughter's bed tenderly clutching her hand. Darius gasped in horror at the sight of Lauren's almost unrecognizable face and fell to his knees burying his head in his wife's lap. It broke Reagan's heart to see what Nour Nader had done to a child, his own family. She quietly slipped out of the room to give them privacy.

A couple of hours later, Darius brought Helena into the waiting room to meet Reagan and give her an update on Lauren, who had sustained a moderate concussion, a fractured clavicle, and lacerations on her face that required stitches. An excellent plastic surgeon had done the sutures and assured them that the scars would eventually be almost invisible. The emergency room doctor explained that the skin under Lauren's fingernails was collected for DNA evidence. It was obvious that Lauren had fought her attacker, and her parents were proud of her grit.

Reagan was surprised that even after Helena learned of the dishonorable affair of Claire and Karim, she still treated Reagan with warmth and respect. As an anesthesiologist with privileges in the hospital, Helena pulled some strings to have DNA tests done for Reagan and Darius. Her attitude was "let's get this done," fully understanding Darius and Reagan's need to know the truth of her parentage. Reagan took an instant liking to Helena's genuine straightforward, take-charge personality.

While Reagan settled into an uncomfortable vinyl chair in the waiting room on the surgery wing, her thoughts were of Aiden. Even though he had just met Lauren, he had put her safety above his own. It wasn't a surprise, because he had done the same thing for her, and she had been cavalier about it. Took him for granted, and he didn't deserve that. She'd gotten so wrapped up in trying to figure out where he fit into her life compared to Tyler, and how the constant upheaval of her emotions might be influencing her decisions, she never stopped to just look at him. Maybe it was time to take inventory of both relationships separately.

She had been the aggressor in her pursuit of Aiden, which was a role she had never taken before. It wasn't only his rugged good looks, it was his giving nature, his dry humor, the ease of being with him, and the comfort in sharing her most personal thoughts. Despite the hard shell he often presented, he was a good and kind man, and she loved all those things about him. She realized in the past six months she had spent with Tyler, everything they knew about each other was superficial. They had fun together, but they never seemed to let their guard down long enough to really get to know each other. Reagan knew what she wanted, and he was lying on an operating table because he took a bullet for a teenage girl he barely knew.

Reagan jumped when a young nurse touched her shoulder, startling her awake. She was escorted to a small consultation room where she met Dr. Roger McCray, the surgeon who repaired Aiden's arm. The bullet he removed was lodged 2 inches under the skin on his left bicep and had carved out a chunk of muscle. Aiden would need physical therapy but should eventually be back to at least 90% of normal usage. Dr. McCray explained that Aiden refused to stay overnight, threatening to walk out as soon they got him to a room, so the doctor had no choice but to release him. She was given instructions for his aftercare and told he needed to see a doctor within the next three days to be reevaluated. The nurse gave her a week's worth of antibiotics and three days of pain medicine.

An hour later, the nurse escorted Reagan to the recovery room where she found Aiden dozing in a chair dressed in jeans and a green scrub top. A black sling supported his left arm.

The cab was waiting outside, and the driver helped Aiden to the car. The police had retrieved their luggage from the damaged rental and left it for them at the hospital. Aiden leaned against her shoulder and fell asleep immediately. With the assistance of a wheelchair and the motel desk clerk, she got him to their room.

Aiden, his mood somber, hadn't spoken since he got out of surgery. She helped him get off his clothes, and he climbed in one of the queen-size beds without objection. After giving him pain medication, she tucked him in and turned up the air conditioner to help him sleep.

She was startled awake by loud groans. When she sat up and flipped on the bedside lamp, Aiden was moving restlessly in the other bed, mumbling something indiscernible in his sleep. A nightmare. She worried that his flailing would break open his stitches. After getting a cool wet washcloth from the bathroom sink, she sat next to him on his bed. His entire body was covered in sweat.

"Oh, baby," she said softly, rubbing her fingertips up and down his cheek. She contemplated what his dreams must be like after spending so much of his adult life in combat zones, and if the violent events of the evening had reopened old wounds or created new nightmares.

"Aiden. It's Reagan. Wake up. Everything's okay. I'm here." Gently cradling her arm around his head, she tenderly wiped the sweat from his forehead, cheeks, and neck. He opened his eyes and held her gaze. There was no terror or fear that you might expect after waking from a nightmare, only sadness. She continued to lightly wash his face while he watched her, his pale-blue eyes never leaving hers. When she moved down to his perspiration-soaked chest, he caught her hand.

"I wasn't trying to …" she began.

"I know, but I'm fine now," his voice hoarse from sleep. "Thanks."

"Would you like me to rewet the washcloth so you can cool off some more?"

"I'll take care of it. You go back to sleep," he said, taking the cloth from her hand and getting out of bed. She watched helplessly.

Not knowing exactly what to do, she decided not to push. She was there if he needed her, but she was afraid he would never ask. Aiden was one of those people who didn't want to depend on others. Climbing back into her own bed, she turned on her side to let the cool air from the air conditioning vent lull her back into a restless sleep.

# Chapter 35

While Aiden was in surgery the night before, Detective Al Benoit introduced himself to Reagan and explained he would be sending a car to their motel the following morning at 10 to bring Aiden and her to the police station for a debriefing. When they walked into a conference room, Detective Benoit, a wiry and slightly disheveled man with a heavy Cajun accent, was seated with two others at a mahogany conference table in matching straight back chairs. He stood and introduced them to Detective Louis Vincent, a middle-aged heavyset man with deep-set gray eyes, and FBI Special Agent Robert Mallard, who was tall and muscular with ruddy cheeks and a perpetual scowl.

They were dealing with a multitude of jurisdictional issues, and everyone seemed to want to run point. Aiden and Reagan each told their account of the events leading up to Lauren's kidnapping. Then Aiden recounted his pursuit of Nour Nader after he abducted Lauren. Everything seemed to jibe with other witness statements the police had been able to secure.

"Now that we have covered what happened," Agent Mallard said, "I'd like to talk about what brought you to New Orleans in the first place. When I spoke with Detective Kowalski of the Lancashire PD this morning, he informed me that it had only been a couple of days since they identified Nour Nader and Borzin Nader as the assailants in Ms. Asher's attempted kidnappings. Although their names have since been released to the media, their association to Darius Nader has not. So, Mr. Rannell, can you explain to me how you knew about Darius Nader, his association with both men, and that he lived in New Orleans?" Special Agent Mallard's question was more of an accusation.

Since Danni was the source of most of that information, and Aiden didn't want to get her fired for revealing said information, he was prepared to give a version of the truth, but Reagan beat him to it by telling her truth.

"I'll answer that," she interrupted. "I recently learned from pictures in my grandmother's home and from my mother's high school yearbook that Darius Nader had been a good friend of my mother's since she was a teenager. When we visited my father in Spokane a couple of days ago, he confirmed what I had suspected, that he is not my biological father. Because of Darius' relationship with my mother at the time, he appeared to be a likely candidate. That's why I decided to visit him. I had no idea of the names of the men who tried to abduct me, or that they had any connection to Darius. I merely wanted the truth about my parentage. Darius himself told us about his relationship to Borzin and Nour Nader, and he showed nothing but disdain for both men."

"When Reagan and I were in Spokane, I believe Mr. Asher might have mentioned that Darius Nader was a professor somewhere. Didn't take long to find him on the internet," Aiden interjected. Reagan looked at him with a blank expression. She knew it was a lie. He would have to explain why to her later.

"And you came as her protector of sorts?" Detective Vincent asked.

"That's one reason, but the trigger for me was the break-in at Mrs. Moran's home the night before we arrived in Spokane. Detective Danielle Silva and I entered the Moran home to pick up some pictures to help spark Stuart Asher's memory of Darius Nader, who from the pictures and name could have been Middle Eastern. It was a thin possibility, but I wondered about a connection to the Middle Eastern men who had attempted to kidnap Reagan. The police were unable to locate the intruder. The only things we could determine were missing from the home were the photos of Darius Nader and his sister Rosana. I had to ask myself, why would the intruder take those pictures, unless he had a connection that he didn't want uncovered? When Reagan expressed concerns that Darius might be her biological father, it was even more reason to make the trip."

"Do you think Nour Nader followed you from Cleveland?" Detective Benoit asked.

"Impossible," Aiden said, then elaborated on the short notice of the trip.

"We spoke to Darius Nader and his wife, Helena, earlier this morning. He thinks the reason his daughter was taken was to extort money from him. Do you agree, Mr. Rannell?" Special Agent Mallard asked. Aiden felt that he was angling for something.

"I do. His uncle, Borzin Nader, is in custody without much hope of being released. Nour Nader had to have figured the police and the FBI had his name by then, so he'd never be allowed to fly out of the country, and Darius had turned down his request for money on two separate occasions. A recipe for desperation. Nour must have been watching the house when he saw Lauren alone in the kitchen. The idea probably struck him that she could be leverage. Then the asshole broke into the back door, punched her out, and abducted her. He recognized me immediately and there was no doubt he was surprised. I'm confident he didn't know that Reagan and I were in New Orleans, but now that he does, it makes me very uncomfortable."

"You were a Navy Seal, Mr. Rannell. Were you ever stationed in Lebanon?" Special Agent Mallard asked. *So that's his angle. He's trying to tie me to this dirt bag.* Reagan's eyes widened.

"If you want any information about my time in special ops, you are going to have to contact the United States Navy. That's classified and above your security clearance."

Agent Mallard pursed his lips and furrowed his brows, clearly irritated. "Can you tell me if you have ever come across Nour or Borzin Nader when you were overseas and not on a special operations mission?" Agent Mallard asked.

"I have never met nor heard of either of those assholes in any circumstance until a week ago," Aiden answered with exasperation.

"What about you, Ms. Asher?" Special Agent Mallard asked.

"Same for me. I'd never even heard of Darius Nader until Aiden showed me pictures of him and his sister with my mother when they were teenagers."

After another hour of the same questions over and over, mostly from Special Agent Mallard who seemed to be convinced Aiden had some hidden association to the Naders in Lebanon when he was overseas, Aiden had had enough. Standing up, he offered Reagan his hand, pulled her to her feet, and cleared his throat.

"Well, gentlemen, we're done here. If you have any additional questions, you have our contact information. We have a plane to catch." *It doesn't leave until the evening, but they don't need to know that.*

Special Agent Mallard scrambled to his feet. "I'm not finished with you!" he pronounced. "This is all a little too coincidental for me."

"You may not be done, but we are," Aiden said. "Unless you have something you want to charge us with?" The room fell silent. "Well then, I guess we'll be on our way." Then he turned to Detective Vincent. "Will I ever see my 9mm again?"

"Not until there's an arrest, trial, conviction, possible appeals ... so probably not for a long time," Detective Vincent said. "Why? Do you think you'll need it?"

"There's a lunatic running around trying to get his hands on Reagan. He's also a danger to most of the Nader family and anyone else who gets in his way. Until we get on a plane, we're vulnerable," Aiden said.

"Want a ride to the airport? You should be safe there," Detective Benoit offered.

"Thanks. We'll take you up on that," Aiden said.

"Mr. Rannell," Agent Mallard called. Aiden turned around.

"Yeah?"

"When I check your cell phone records for the past two months you've been out of the service, will I find calls to the Middle East?"

*That son of a bitch.* Aiden knew Mallard could get his phone records if he tried hard enough, so he might as well admit it. "I've spent most of the past 12 years of my military career in the Middle East. Many of my brothers are still there, and I don't plan on ever cutting those bonds, so check till your heart's content."

The concern, or was it doubt, in Reagan's eyes troubled him as he grabbed her hand and ushered her from the room. He debated whether he should reassure her that he had no connection to the Naders, but decided he was only borrowing trouble. The fact that he would even acknowledge the possibility may cause her to distrust him more than if he treated it as ridiculous as it was.

# Chapter 36

While they were enjoying shrimp po boys at a boutique restaurant in the airport, Aiden received a call from Danni. She and Detective Kowalski had spent the past 45 minutes on a conference call with Detectives Benoit and Vincent, receiving an update on the highly eventful 24 hours in NOLA.

"Thanks for not outing me for giving you the Nader names and Darius Nader's location," Danni said. "I could've lost my job and had the shortest detective career in the history of the department."

"I would have found him on the internet whether you told me or not. Besides, who knows what would have happened to Lauren if I hadn't been there? Maybe it was fate."

"For his daughter's sake, I'm glad you were."

"Are there any new updates on the case? Anything on Gabe Ledbetter?"

"Not really. We've been waiting for Arturo Fuentes to get back from Mexico to check out his house. Borzin and Nour Nader could have used it to hide out when they figured out he and his family were out of the town. According to his boss, Arturo and his wife, Rose, should be home tomorrow."

"Rose?" Aiden asked. "His wife?" An absurd notion hit Aiden.

"Yeah."

"Do you have her full name?"

"Hold on. I'll check the file." A few minutes later, "Here it is. Rosana N. Fuentes, but she goes by Rose."

Aiden froze for a few beats. "Well, I'll be damned."

"What? What's wrong?"

"Right under our noses," he said through clenched teeth.

"Please elaborate," Danni said.

"I'd bet my first paycheck that the N stands for Nader. I think she's Darius Nader's twin sister, Rosana."

"Oh my God!" Danni shouted in his ear. "How did we miss that? Kowalski's going to shit. I need to find him."

"Wait a minute. Let's be sure." He turned to Reagan who was licking sauce off her fingers.

"What's wrong? Did I get it on my mouth?" She instinctively used her thumb to wipe the corners of her lips. He couldn't help but smile and resisted the temptation to suck her fingers. Instead, he asked Reagan to call Darius, who confirmed that his fraternal twin sister Rosana lives in Akron, Ohio, with her husband Arturo Fuentes and their two children.

Aiden shared the news. Danni let out a string of expletives that Reagan heard from the other side of the table, then Danni hung up to call Detective Kowalski. Ten minutes later, Aiden's cell rang with a call from Josh. Reluctantly, he answered, putting the phone on speaker so he could listen to Josh rail at him while he ate.

"What the hell, Aiden? You weren't going to fucking call me and tell me you got shot?" Josh was livid. "Mom and Dad just called. They're going out of their minds. It's on the national news for fuck sakes!"

While Aiden explained the events of last evening to Josh, he heard Reagan doing the same on her cell to Mattie. There was now a nationwide manhunt for Nour Nader, and the incident made all the news stations. Josh recognized Aiden's picture on the television in a pub where he was having lunch with a client and choked on his corned beef sandwich. Their parents saw the same broadcast. To make matters worse, nobody could get in touch with Aiden, because he had turned his phone off during the police interview. It took 20 minutes to get everyone calmed down and assured that they were okay.

---

As they waited at Reagan's gate for her flight, Aiden gently intertwined his fingers with hers, bringing them to his lips. Ever since she had arrived at the hospital the night before, there had been an unspoken shift in their relationship. It became natural and unencumbered, as if all complications had evaporated.

"Thanks for taking care of me last night," he said earnestly. "You've been through so much. Endured unspeakable loss and some tough truths, but you were still there for me. It means a lot."

For a few moments, she couldn't speak, her emotions on the surface, words caught in her throat. The roller coaster she had been on the past week had left her battered and spent, forcing her to deal with realities she could never have imagined. The secrets. The lies. The violence. But despite the chaos that had become her life, Aiden had been her safe haven. She had to tell him the truth. Any lingering doubts she had about him or his motives were gone.

"Aiden, you need to know …" she swallowed hard.

"Reagan, you don't have to explain." He reached for her face, but she leaned away from him. If he touched her before she got the words out, she might lose her nerve.

A few moments passed before she turned to face him, her eyes tenderly locked on his, holding sincerity and hope. "I'm sorry, Aiden. About all the mixed signals. The indecision. It wasn't fair to you or Tyler. But I was scared. There are a ton of screwed-up things going on in my life right now, but you are the one thing that makes sense. I'm tired of pretending that my feelings for you can be explained away, because they can't be. I care about you. A lot. Enough to want to see where this relationship could go. There are plenty of arguments against it. We technically barely know each other. It's lousy timing for both of us. I live in Chicago, and you're going to be halfway around the world most of the year with your new job. Just starting out in a whole new life. A lot of obstacles to be sure, but I'm willing to risk it. Are you?"

His expression held caution. "What about Tyler?"

"When he showed up at Josh and Mattie's, I was confused. I felt hollow inside, but I owed it to him to be sure. We slept in the same bed, but there was no intimacy. All I could think about was you. How I was hurting you. Hurting me. Being with you made me realize everything I was missing with him." She took a deep breath. "If you don't feel the same way, I'll fly back to Chicago and we'll remain friends, and I'll never regret a single moment we've spent together, but there is no Tyler and me, regardless."

She could feel the heat rising in her face. Laying it all out there left her exposed and completely vulnerable but being with him felt too good not to take her chance at happiness.

Aiden slowly leaned toward her, cupping her cheek with his right hand. "I'm falling for you too, Reagan, and I think I've unconsciously been fighting it since we first met. You're right about the obstacles. Different locations. Different lifestyles. Both stubborn." He chuckled at the last part. "If we are both committed enough to face those challenges, we might just have a chance. But I want us to agree to something. If things get too tough for either of us, we have to be honest with each other. Can you promise me that?" She nodded. Then he kissed her, and in that moment all the madness fell away, and they were the only two people in the world who mattered.

# Chapter 37

"I'm going to talk to Tyler tonight after he picks me up at the airport. It's not the best time, but I feel I need to end things in person. He deserves that," Reagan said, as she stood at the boarding gate for Chicago.

"Please wait to tell him when you get to your apartment. I know he's a decent guy, but you never know how people will react in break-up situations. Sometimes rational thought flies out the window."

"I promise," she said, kissing his check.

"May I have your attention, please? Flight 1991 to Chicago has been delayed due to weather concerns at O'Hare. We will update you as soon as we have more information."

"Well, at least we have a little more time together," Reagan said, looking on the bright side.

"I hope that doesn't mean a rough flight. I need to run to the restroom. Be right back. Don't move from this seat," Aiden said. She gave him a mock salute.

Fishing her phone out of her handbag, Reagan realized she hadn't turned her cell back on after lunch. It had been her attempt to finish her meal without continued interruptions. She had missed numerous calls and voicemails from Mattie, Josh, her boss, and several unknown callers, all of which she decided to deal with later. The phone was barely back in her Coach bag when it rang with an unknown number. Reluctantly, she answered it.

"Ms. Asher, this is Joe Franklin from the New Orleans Press Spot. I'd like to get some comments from you about your relationship with Darius Nader," he said.

She stared at the phone in disbelief, then put it back to her ear. "How did you get this number?"

"If you'd just give me a minute of your time …" She hit end.

It rang again. Another unknown number. "Hello, Ms. Asher, this is Jan Hulbert."

"How did you get this number?" she demanded.

"It was published in an online news article," she explained. "I thought it was a joke and didn't expect you to actually answer." Reagan cut off the call and hesitated a few minutes while she debated throwing the phone across the room. It rang again.

"I don't know how you got my number, but you can stop …"

"This is Nour Nader. Do not hang up or you will be very sorry." His now familiar voice sent chills up her arms.

She gasped for air, unconsciously rocking back and forth, like a child comforting herself. He had her number. Had. Her. Number. The monster was speaking to her, ranting in her ear. It felt as if he was there with her. Might touch her. She didn't want to listen. Wanted to hang up. Make him disappear, but she knew she couldn't. He might reveal a clue that would help the police find him.

*Force the panic down. He's not here. He can't touch you.* Wrapping her free arm around her waist for support, she put her phone back to her ear.

"Ms. Asher? Ms. Asher do you hear me?"

*Speak!* She told herself. *I am safe in an airport filled with police and security guards. He. Can't. Hurt. Me.* But the words wouldn't come. He began again, exasperation and anger seething through the phone. "I know you have my diamonds and pearls, and I want them back. I am a dangerous man you don't want to trifle with, and I know where you are. I know where you live in Chicago." His laugh was venomous. "The internet makes it so easy. The building across the street gives me an excellent view of your apartment where I can watch you go in and out. I know where you work. Where you park your car. I know where your friends live. I particularly enjoy watching your friend Mattie with that pretty little girl." Reagan felt her blood run cold. *Ellie. Please God, no.* "I think you understand me, Ms. Asher. Give me the gems or someone you love will die. My patience is gone. You will give them to me or suffer the consequences and blame yourself. I will call soon." He hung up.

"Reagan! What's wrong?" Aiden dropped to his knees in front of her and took the phone that was still pressed against her ear away from her. She stared at him blankly.

"What happened, Reagan? Talk to me. You're white as a sheet."

"H...He c...called me." Her teeth were chattering. She wondered when it had gotten so cold.

"Who called?" Aiden asked calmly, rubbing her forearms.

"Nour Nader," she breathed.

He squeezed his eyes shut and swallowed hard before he met her eyes again. "Christ. How did he get your number? What did he say?"

She told him about the calls from the reporters. "Somebody published my private number in an online article. Nour Nader must have seen it. He threatened to kill someone close to me if I don't give him the gems. He implied he knew where I was. Where I live and work, then ... oh, God, Aiden, he said he was watching Mattie and Ellie. I freaked out. Froze like an idiot. Couldn't speak. He said he'd call back. I screwed up. Didn't get any information that would help us find him" He sat beside her, pulling her into his arms.

"That's enough, Reagan. It's not your responsibility to find him. You're not going anywhere near him."

"But he said he knows where I am," she said, her thoughts racing. "And Mattie and Ellie."

"Ellie is safe in Orange Beach, Alabama, with my parents, and Mattie and Josh have around-the-clock security. He's bluffing. Trying to get in your head. Did he say he knew you were in the airport?" She shook her head. "He would have mentioned it if he'd known."

"But my apartment, my job?"

"I didn't say I wasn't concerned." He stood up and pulled her to her feet, grabbing her carry-on. "That's why you're coming to Cleveland with me. Let's go exchange your ticket. You are not going anywhere without me."

For once, not an ounce of her wanted to argue with his bossiness.

When they walked into the kitchen at 4:30 a.m., Josh sat at the breakfast bar drinking coffee, decked out in an Armani navy suit. He was stunned to see them, but he quickly recovered and gathered them into a bear hug.

"Why the hell didn't you call me to pick you up?" he demanded.

"And screw up your night too? We took a taxi. Why are you up so early?"

"Who cares what you might screw up? Next time you call me!"

"I will, bro. So why are you up?"

"Planning to pick you up at the airport before my 8 o'clock breakfast meeting. I thought your fight got in at 6."

"We were able to catch an earlier flight."

"Hate to say it, but you look like hell. How's the arm?" Josh asked.

"Hurts like a bitch."

"He needs to take his pain meds and get some sleep," Reagan said firmly.

"We both need sleep," Aiden said, pulling her close. Josh eyed the affectionate gesture, then smiled in recognition that something had changed in their relationship. He gave a barely perceptible nod to Aiden.

"Made you an appointment this morning at 11 with our internist. I was planning to swing by at 10:30 to pick you up, but if you prefer, I'll take your truck and Reagan can drive you in my car."

"That's a good idea, Josh, if you don't mind," Reagan agreed. "That truck is too big for me to maneuver."

"No problem."

"I talked to Mattie last night. She said she's still at the beach with Ellie and your parents," Reagan said.

"Yeah. She flew down to join them right after you left for Washington. Ellie is doing much better. Even asked to go play putt-putt golf. Mattie will be home late this afternoon. We feel it's much safer for Ellie to stay with my parents until that nut job is caught."

"I'm so glad Ellie is getting back to herself. I've been so worried," Reagan said, shaking her head.

Aiden could practically feel the guilt she was carrying, so he changed the subject.

"Do you have any electrical tape and plastic? I want to cover my bandage so I can take a real shower when I wake up."

"Sure."

"I'm going to head upstairs and clean up before I get some sleep. Thanks, Josh," Reagan said before running up the stairs.

"Whoa. Is this serious? With her, I mean?" Josh asked.

"It seems to be getting there. She's breaking it off with Tyler. I really like being with her, and she says she feels the same about me. We're going into this with eyes wide open. There are lots of inconvenient obstacles, my job being a huge one. I have no idea what it's going to entail and won't know the time commitment until I actually get into the position. We both want to see where it goes."

Josh gave him a pat on the back. "I'm happy for you, man, and I hope it works out. You know we love Reagan. Don't want to be a downer, but don't you think your relationship has gone warp speed?"

"No lectures. We're taking it a step at a time. Now drop it. Can you hand me a glass of water?"

Josh filled a glass while Aiden dug out his pain pills from his luggage. He popped some in his mouth and took a swig. "I'll see you tonight."

Aiden barely dragged himself out of bed when his alarm went off at 10. His catnap made him feel worse rather than better. After drinking a quick cup of coffee, he asked Reagan to tape up his arm so it wouldn't get wet, and he jumped in the shower. When he dried off, he checked his bandage. Dry except for some blood leakage. Throwing on a short-sleeve gray t-shirt and a pair of denim jeans, he met Reagan downstairs.

"Did you get any sleep?" she asked.

"Not enough." He didn't feel talkative and was bordering on cranky, so he kept the conversation short.

"Okay then. Let's get you to the doctor so we can get you back to bed."

As Aiden grabbed his coat, his cell phone rang. He immediately recognized Kowalski's number.

"What's up, Detective?" Reagan's eyebrows went up and she leaned closer to listen.

"Sorry to hear you got shot, man. Are you doing okay?"

"Fine. Thanks." Reagan shook her head and pointed toward the garage. They were going to be late, and she knew Aiden wasn't in the mood to talk to anybody, let alone Kowalski. "I was just on my way to a doctor's appointment, so you'll have to call back later." Aiden frowned.

"It can't wait. Got a call from Detective Benoit with the NOPD. They found the SUV Nour Nader used to kidnap Lauren Nader. He ditched his bloody clothes in a nearby dumpster. Looks like you shot him in the upper right thigh and somewhere on his lower left side above his hip, or that's what the holes in the shirt and pants he discarded indicated. Good job. Hopefully, that'll slow him down."

"Not good enough," Aiden mumbled.

"They found a travel atlas with red circles marked around the locations of Ms. Asher's residence and place of employment in Chicago."

"What the hell?" Aiden blurted out of frustration, rubbing his hand over his face. "Well, as much as it pisses me off, it's not unexpected. He called Reagan when we were in the New Orleans Airport and threatened her. Some news reporter got her cell phone number and published it in an online article. So why are you calling me?"

"Spoke with Mattie Rannell last night to see if she had any idea where Reagan was going after her trip to New Orleans. She said Chicago. I contacted the Chicago PD to warn them about Nader, but I haven't been able to reach Ms. Asher to give her a heads-up. Any idea how I can get in touch with her? It's impossible to determine if Nour Nader left the information intentionally to create a false trail, but we don't want to take any chances."

"After she got his call, she changed plans. She's staying at my brother's house. I'll tell her."

"That was smart. I'll let the Chicago PD know. Got to run. Have her give me a call when she gets a chance. If he called her, I need her phone."

"Right." He hung up and filled in Reagan on what she hadn't already heard.

"We made the right call bringing you back here. I'll keep you safe."

# Chapter 38

Reagan would have preferred to end her relationship with Tyler in person, but circumstances prevented her from having a face-to-face. She could have made excuses but decided to own her decision and admit that Aiden had become an important part of her life. Being the class act he was, he wished her the best and hung up without further comment. It had been easier than she had expected. No emotional scene. No attempts to change her mind. His comment to Aiden that he would fight for her had been empty words. Probably brought on by his competitive nature. It only reinforced that she had made the right decision.

Sipping on a glass of wine while Josh and Mattie prepared dinner, Reagan received a call from her boss, Peter Mitchell. She had called him earlier that morning to let him know she wouldn't be back to work as early as planned because of the threats to her life.

His call was short and to the point. Many of the employees at Rothman-Morgan Chemical had been following Reagan's plight: her grandmother's murder, the attempted kidnappings, and the most recent incident in New Orleans. Consequently, they were concerned that her troubles would follow her back to Chicago, making their company an unsafe work environment. The visit from a Chicago police detective requesting the company provide additional security for Reagan was the tipping point. The net result was an offer of a paid leave of absence until it was deemed safe for the employees to allow Reagan to return. She couldn't disagree that her presence might endanger others, so she had no choice but to accept. In her mind, everything she had worked so hard to achieve had come to a screeching halt, another devastating blow.

From the worried look on Aiden's face, Reagan knew he had heard everything her boss had said. He turned sideways to face her on the sofa and took her hands in his.

"I know it doesn't seem like it right now, but your life *will* return to normal."

She threw up her hands in mock surrender. "And what's normal, Aiden? You mean my *new* normal where my life is something I don't recognize?"

Aiden noticed Josh standing in the doorway and motioned him out. Reagan was glad. She needed time to vent her pent-up frustrations. He pulled her to him, resting his chin on her head.

"Sweetheart, I'm not sure how this nightmare will be resolved, but I can assure you none of this will erase the things you've accomplished. You will still be the strong, intelligent, and caring woman you've always been. We'll figure the rest out together."

Feeling deflated, she sank into his chest, trying to believe his words.

Later that evening, as she lay in his arms, he lifted her chin to meet his eyes. "Can I ask you something?"

"Anything." She kissed his bare chest.

"I've been tossing an idea around in my head since last night. I want to share it with you, but you'll have to be honest with me."

"I will."

"I'm supposed to close on my condo Monday, and I've scheduled the movers and the furniture company to deliver in the afternoon. How would you feel about moving in with me for a while and helping me get settled? I don't have to start my job for a couple of weeks, and it would give us some quality time together. You could also get some contractors lined up to do the renovations on your grandmother's house. I can help with that."

It caught her off guard. "So, you want me to move in for a couple of weeks? Until you leave? I appreciate the offer, but since I have no idea how long I might be here, it would be best for me to find a temporary furnished apartment with a month-to-month lease. I can still help you move your things into your new place, though. You've done so much for me, it's the least I can do."

His reminder that he was leaving in two weeks put her on edge. She didn't want to get comfortable in his home just to have to move out and find another place. It was going to be hard enough watching him leave for months at a time. Not knowing when she would see him again. The thought squeezed her heart as she found herself fighting back tears that she didn't want him to see. *Maybe I was wrong about trying to make our relationship work. Being left over and over again, not knowing when he'll be back. Will he get bored and just stop showing up? Could I survive another disappointment?*

He must have felt her tension, because he brushed his lips across her neck and began massaging her shoulder. "That's not what I meant. I wasn't thinking about a preplanned end date. Maybe you'll even decide you like being in the Cleveland area again and stay."

*What difference would it make where I live if you aren't here anyway?* she thought.

"What about finding a renter for your condo?" There was a tiny bit of sarcasm she hadn't intended in her question.

"I don't need to find a renter," he said but didn't clarify.

"So, I'll lease the condo from you while you're gone?" *Am I trying to be argumentative or am I just confused?* Aiden slid her off his chest and sat up against the headboard, running his fingers through his hair. She sat up to face him. Apparently, the conversation was making him uncomfortable and delving into territory he hadn't planned. She didn't care. She needed to know exactly where she stood.

"You're trying to make this more complicated than it has to be. You don't have to rent the place from me. Stay here as long as you want. But there's a lot of things up in the air right now. You know this," he said.

She stared at him for what seemed like forever. "For me, yes. There are plenty of unknowns, but I could move here tomorrow. I have no real attachments in Chicago except my job, and as of a few hours ago, that has gone to hell. On the other hand, your path is fixed. You bought into a company. You will leave … for who knows how long. Don't feel bad. You made it perfectly clear to me when we first met that you get bored easily staying in the same place. There was no deception on your part. I'm just no longer sure I can handle that. It's not the best situation for a new relationship … and maybe not for me. It's like I'm setting myself up to take another fall."

Aiden climbed out of bed, threw on a pair of gym shorts and began pacing the room. She turned her back to him, lying back down and shutting herself down. It was her go-to response when emotions began to take over.

"Look at me, Reagan." She didn't move. "Please. Look at me." She felt frozen. After a few minutes, he sat on the bed beside her and twirled her hair around his fingers, comforting her. His voice was raw when he spoke.

"I don't want to lose us, Reagan. You mean too much to me. I'm not going to lie and say I have all of the answers, but I do want to find them. Tomorrow morning, I'm going to call Chase and Owen, my partners. Maybe we can come up with a compromise on my role in the company. They needed an infusion of cash without taking out another loan, and I provided it. We're all equal partners now. That should give me leverage. I also have an electrical engineering degree, which was one of the reasons they wanted me in the partnership. Maybe I can do the initial assessment of the facilities for the client, and then do the design work remotely. One of the other guys could oversee the installs and implementation. That wouldn't require me to travel nearly as much. I'm not exactly sure how we can work it out, and it may take a little time, but I want to do it. I want to make time for us."

She rolled over and faced him. Not believing what she was hearing. "Are you sure? I'm not trying to manipulate you, and I don't want you resenting me because you gave up something you really wanted to do."

"It's a new company with a lot of room to grow the business. That brings exciting new challenges. There is nothing boring about that. Besides," he chuckled, "I haven't had a boring moment since I met you, Ms. Asher."

She laughed and sobbed simultaneously as hope and happiness consumed her. "Maybe I could be your human resource manager. I could work for room and board ... well, for a while anyway."

He lay beside her and drew her into his arms. "We'll find a way, Reagan. Don't give up on us."

"I won't," she whispered.

# Chapter 39

Aiden realized Reagan had drifted off when he felt her steady breath against his skin. Their conversation had been emotionally charged, and totally unexpected, but it felt right. When faced with the possibility of her walking out of his life, he couldn't picture it. He would do everything in his power to give their relationship the commitment it deserved and still have a challenging career.

He was startled by a soft knock at the door.

"Are you decent? Can I come in?" It was Josh.

When Reagan jerked awake, Aiden pulled the covers over her.

"Come on in," Aiden called.

Josh was in flannel sleep-pants, annoyance on his face. "Hate to disturb you guys, but Detective Kowalski is at the front door. Said he's here to pick up Reagan's cell phone. Does the man have any concept of boundaries? It's 10 fucking o'clock!"

Aiden jumped out of bed, completely naked, and grabbed his discarded jeans from the floor. "Shit," he said to Josh. "I forgot Kowalski called earlier today and said he'd be dropping by in the afternoon to pick up her phone. I'd say he passed his deadline."

Mattie, wrapped in a terry cloth robe, stepped out from behind Josh. "Why did he wait so late? He has a habit of popping in at night, doesn't he? Asshole."

"You're right. It's too late. I'll send him away," Aiden said, heading for the door.

"Wait. Let's just get it over with," Reagan sighed. "And since I'm not an exhibitionist like Aiden, you guys need to step out so I can get dressed."

When everyone got downstairs, the detective was sitting at the kitchen table.

"Kowalski, you were supposed to be here this afternoon. You have no respect for time," Aiden protested as he pulled a chair out for Reagan.

"I apologize. It couldn't be helped, but you are right, I should have called first. There was a major break in the case, and this is the first time I've left the station all day. We finally have Gabe Ledbetter in custody."

Everyone remained silent, waiting for the detective to explain the startling new development.

Kowalski folded his hands on the table before he spoke. "Last night, our officers pulled over a couple of guys for speeding. When they ran the plates, they found one of the guys had served time for burglary and possession of an illegal firearm. When the younger of the two guys tried to flee, it gave the police provocation to search the car. They found stolen electronics, jewelry ... the usual kind of stuff from a B&E. The kid was an 18-year-old college student, first-time offender. He'd been coerced by his sister's boyfriend to help with a break-in in Shaker Heights. It was supposed to be low risk, because the family was on vacation in Europe and there was no alarm system. Would've gotten away with it if the guy hadn't been speeding.

"The bottom line — we used that for leverage to get the kid to talk. Seems his sister's boyfriend works for Gabe Ledbetter and needed a partner to do a job. The boyfriend threatened to beat up the kid's sister if he didn't help. Kid was scared to death. There was a joint coordination of jurisdictions, but we busted Ledbetter in Youngstown this morning. We got lucky. We found the burner phone he used to call Camden Yeager and Justin Pane in his safe. That ties him to both of those murders and backs up the story Pane's wife gave us. We found ledgers, itemized lists of stolen items, a treasure trove of bad-guy contacts, and four laptops we haven't begun to have the techs check out."

"Did you find any connection to Borzin or Nour Nader?" Aiden asked.

"We didn't and doubt there is one. When we mentioned their names to Ledbetter, he genuinely looked confused. It also seems highly unlikely because the Naders had only been in the country a few days before Mrs. Moran was killed. The FBI has taken over the case, but they're willing to cooperate to a degree to help us close our murder cases. They are convinced Ledbetter has never done business on an international level.

"The call Ledbetter received from Camden Yeager looking to fence the ring is the reason we believe he targeted the Moran house. Mrs. Moran was a soft target with the possibility of a big reward. Justin Pane was hired for the job to cut Yeager out of the deal completely. Pane owed Ledbetter a ton of money, which made him desperate. When he screwed up by killing Mrs. Moran, it had to be dealt with, so Ledbetter either killed him or had him killed, probably the latter. Same thing with Camden Yeager. Either man could have gotten scared and talked, putting Ledbetter on the police radar. Of course, all of this is supposition, but the prosecutor thinks we can make the case.

"Looks like Nour and Borzin Nader might have some other connection to the jewels or heard about them somehow. We have no theories yet as to how that might have happened. Before last week, neither of the men had entered the United States within the past 10 years. We're working with the State Department to check records further back. According to the crime lab, the electrical tape used to wrap the container storing the gems is somewhere between 25 to 30 years old. Anyone have any questions so far?" His gaze fell on Reagan. She shook her head.

Aiden watched Reagan's cool expression, as the detective laid out the facts in an emotionless manner, oblivious to the internal turmoil his words were causing her. He knew she had flipped her invisible switch, distancing herself from her feelings. He intertwined his fingers with hers hoping to remind her he was there.

Kowalski continued in the same monotone voice. "We did get some news from the Mississippi State Police and New Orleans PD. The owner of the stolen white Ford Explorer that Nour Nader was driving in New Orleans was found dead along the side of I-59, about a mile from a rest stop in Mississippi. A couple of days ago, another man was found beaten to death and left in an alley behind a bar in Metairie, Louisiana. He was reported missing by his wife, and they suspected foul play. A view of the security cameras on the street outside the bar showed the victim getting out of his gray van. He was approached by a man with a ball cap and glasses, same height and body type as Nour

Nader. They found the white SUV he had been driving a couple of blocks away from the bar. That was where they found the map noting Ms. Asher's apartment and place of employment. The victim's gray van, littered with bloody bandages, was abandoned in Memphis near a bus station. So far, we have no evidence he bought a bus ticket. If he carjacked anybody else, it hasn't been reported. The bodies are piling up. After the call he made to Ms. Asher, we assume he's still looking for her. It's anyone's guess where he is now."

"He wants the diamonds and pearls," Reagan said. "Didn't mention the jewelry, so I don't think he knows about it. He's been watching Ellie and Mattie. If I don't give him the gems, he said he will kill them or someone else I care about. I can't allow that to happened. If I give you this phone, how can he contact me?"

"He won't," Aiden said, before the detective could respond. "He's bluffing because Ellie has been with my parents at the beach, and there is a security team on Josh and Mattie. Reagan, you can't possibly believe you're going to negotiate with that man."

"He's correct, Ms. Asher. If Nour Nader finds some way to contact you, you must hang up. He's a desperate man who can't be trusted. He wouldn't have any qualms about killing you whether you gave him the gems or not. Are you sure you don't have any idea where the jewelry came from?"

Aiden caught her eye and nodded. It was time to share what she had learned, although they had agreed not to mention the five diamonds her grandfather had given her father. Reagan knew Aiden told Danni, who had agreed to keep silent unless Reagan's father ended up being implicated in the theft.

Reagan cleared her throat nervously. "There could be something, but I'm not positive. When I was in New Orleans, Darius told me that his Uncle Borzin and his cousin Nour Nader came to the States to help his father move his grandparents back to Lebanon. I think he said 1988. His grandparents lived right down the street from my grandmother. Darius told us that Borzin and Nour have arrest warrants in several countries for theft and looting. He suggested the possibility that they smuggled the gems into the United States on that trip. If they did smuggle them in, I have no idea how the gems would have gotten in our home. My father told me when I was in Spokane that the period jewelry was given to me when I was a toddler by Darius's grandmother, before she moved back to Lebanon. It had originally been a gift mailed to her by Borzin for her birthday prior to his visit. Darius believes Borzin had no idea they were genuine, or he would never have given them to his mother."

"Unless it was his way of smuggling them into the country as fashion jewelry," the detective suggested.

"But if he mailed them to his mother for that purpose, surely he would have looked for them when he got there," Aiden said.

"Who says he didn't? Do you really think his mother would have admitted she had given his gift away?" He turned to Reagan. "Why didn't you tell me what you learned about the jewels before now? The NOPD said nothing about any of this."

"We figured if you wanted the New Orleans PD to know about the jewels, then you would've told them. Since we knew you were keeping it under wraps from the public and the media, we did too," Aiden answered for her.

"I guess you missed the part about me just finding this out when I was in New Orleans," Reagan interjected indignantly. "It's the first time we've spoken, and it doesn't explain what the loose gems were doing in my grandmother's home. One thing that disturbs me, Detective, is your continued implication that I knew about the jewels before my grandmother was killed, and it's starting to piss me off. I'm sure you've looked at my finances and found all the wealth I've amassed in my 30 years on earth. You can trace every dollar I've made back to my W2 forms, 401k's, and my birthday savings account! Do you really think I would have been paying off student loans all these years if I had any idea there was a fortune buried in my house? You're insulting me, and why the hell would I even tell you about them to begin with if I was trying to hide something?"

"You have a point, but there is still a question about your relationship to Darius Nader."

"I explained to the New Orleans police detectives that I had never even heard of Darius before Nana was killed. After visiting my father, Stuart Asher, in Spokane, I learned I'm not his biological daughter.

If Aiden and Detective Silva hadn't searched through my mother's pictures and yearbooks and made the connection between her and Darius Nader, I would never have known about his relationship with my mother. He seemed a likely candidate, so I made a trip to New Orleans to find out. Darius assured me they were never intimate. To my surprise, Darius suggested his father, Karim Nader, may have had an affair with my mother. The DNA test we took at the hospital in New Orleans should put that question to rest."

"Can you not see how convoluted this seems, Ms. Asher? So many interconnected parts that appear to go nowhere, but all seem to come back to your family." She said nothing. He blew out a long breath, stood up, and held his hand out to Reagan. "Your phone?"

She pulled it out of the pocket of her robe. "I want to see if there are any important calls I missed. If you want, you can watch me."

Aiden glared at the detective.

"I need to get it back to the station," he said testily.

Aiden slid back his chair and stepped into Detective Kowalski's personal space. "You do realize you don't have a warrant for that phone, right? Reagan has been completely cooperative with you. If you continue with your intimidation tactics and innuendos about her involvement, this will be the last conversation you have with her without her attorney present. Got it?"

Detective Kowalski and Aiden had a brief stare down, with the detective finally giving in. "Take all the time you need."

Reagan scrolled through the calls ignoring all but one missed call from Darius. She hit play to listen to his message. Aiden put his ear near the phone.

"Hello, Reagan. We got the results back from the DNA tests. The lab owed Helena a favor, so we got them in record time. It's not the kind of information I want to leave on a message. Give us a call when you can." She hit the delete button and handed him the phone.

"What did you delete?" the detective asked.

"It was personal."

He tightened his lips. "Don't let your guard down until we have Nour Nader in custody. We'll have a car on the street until we do. Have a good evening."

As soon as he walked out the door, Reagan asked to borrow Aiden's cell.

"What a dick," Mattie muttered.

"Let it go, baby," Josh said, rubbing her neck. She frowned and rolled her eyes.

"Darius called with the DNA results. I'll put it on speaker," Reagan said, punching Darius's number.

"Hello, Aiden," Darius said cheerfully.

"Hi, Darius, it's Reagan, but Aiden's here too. I had to turn my cell phone over to the police. I'll text you my new number when I replace it Monday morning. How is Lauren doing?"

"She's in a lot of pain, but her spirits are good. Her friends from school have been very supportive, constantly visiting and sending gifts. It will take some time, but she should make a full recovery."

"That's great. I'm so happy to hear that. You have some DNA results?"

"We do. My wife has a lot of clout at the hospital. The first test they ran against my DNA showed similar markers. You could be my half-sister, but the exact relationship was not clear. I remembered that my father gave me his gold chain bracelet when I went to see him in the hospital. It was something he never took off except to bathe, but he wanted me to have it. Helena took it to the lab to see if they could retrieve any DNA samples from it. They found usable DNA caught in the clasp." He paused. Aiden grabbed her hand. "Reagan, he is your father."

Aiden watched as the blood drained from her face. He put an arm around her waist to steady her, then led her to a chair.

"Reagan, are you still there?" Darius asked with concern.

"We're here," Aiden said, holding her to his chest. "Even though she knew it was a possibility, it's still a shock to find out after all of these years."

Mattie rushed over and sat on the other side of Reagan, holding her hands.

"For all of us." Darius paused, searching for words. "I do not understand any of this any more than you do, Reagan. We cannot be responsible for the choices our parents made. Maybe we will be able to find out the circumstances and motivations that led us here, but we may never know. My father will be a locked vault, I'm sure. All I can do now is feel blessed for the lovely sister God has brought into my life. Sometimes, it is difficult to see through the chaos but finding you has been one good thing that has come out of this. We did not choose the course that was set before us, but we can choose how we respond to it."

"Thank you, Darius, for opening your heart to me when it would be so much easier to push me away. Our parents' deception is as hard on you as it is on me. Maybe when things settle down and our psychopathic cousin is caught, you can tell me about my Lebanese family."

"I look forward to that. I'll call Rosana to give her the news. You will probably be surprised to know we come from a long line of professors and educators, but like all of us, they are fallible. Every family has its black sheep. You both take care. We will speak soon." He disconnected.

"I'd like to go to bed," Reagan said weakly.

"I'll come with you," Aiden said, folding her under his arm.

# Chapter 40

Monday morning arrived with all the promise of a busy but exciting day. Reagan chose to believe the first sunshiny day in a week was a sign of new beginnings. She and Aiden had two stops to make before going to the closing of his condo, then they had the rest of the day to get themselves moved in. The phone store had very few customers, so it didn't take long for Reagan to find a replacement for her cell. She thought about getting a temporary one but decided that even if she got her old phone back, she never wanted to see it again.

The second stop was to a gun store. She tried to convince Aiden he didn't need another gun, but he was confident he would never see the weapon the New Orleans PD confiscated from him again and wasn't willing to take chances with her safety. Nour Nader was still at large, and she had a target on her back.

While Aiden was purchasing a Glock 17 semi-automatic 9mm and a new holster, Reagan perused the cases with .22 semi-automatics. From her observations, they appeared small enough to fit her hand and light enough for her to easily carry. She had never considered owning a gun before, but the idea of being able to protect herself, especially when Aiden wasn't around, appealed to her. Without second-guessing herself, and before she lost her nerve, she quickly flagged down a salesclerk. The salesman was running the background check when Aiden found her leaning against the counter.

"You ready to go?" he asked. "We've got 45 minutes to get to my closing."

Before she could answer, the salesman came back with the receipt and paperwork in one hand and a bag in the other. "You're good to go. Just need a signature at the bottom of the slip, and she's all yours."

Aiden's eyes widened, then narrowed as she signed the receipt.

"Thank you, Ms. Asher. I included a list of certified trainers who can help you get your concealed carry permit. You have a good day."

She was afraid to meet Aiden's eyes, but she didn't have to look at him to know he was fuming. When she turned to leave, he caught her hand.

"What's in the bag, Reagan?" he asked in a no-nonsense tone.

"A present for me." She grinned impishly.

He pursed his lips. "What could you possibly need from here? Tell me it's not what I think it is."

She shrugged.

"Let me see the bag." She handed it over without hesitation. Aiden looked in the sack, then locked eyes with hers as he reached inside the Samuel's Firearms bag and pulled out the box containing her new gun.

"You bought a .22 automatic?" He didn't try to mask his irritation.

She nodded innocently, as his eyes narrowed to slits.

"And ammunition?" Another nod.

"Do you have any idea on God's green earth how to use this?"

"If by that question you mean, do I know how to load and shoot it, the answer would be a firm 'no,' but I'm pretty resourceful." She paused for a beat. "Or … you could teach me. Do you think I need one of those snazzy leather holsters? One that will strap to my thigh under my skirt like in the movies?" She smiled seductively, mostly trying to let humor calm his temper.

He shook his head and rolled his eyes. "Not happening. You don't have a concealed carry permit, nor do you need one. The only place this is going is in my gun safe as soon as my stuff gets delivered today, at least until I can take you to a range and give you some lessons. In the meantime, I don't want you shooting yourself."

"Don't you like my new gun?"

"Sweetheart, the only thing this little gun is going to do is piss somebody off unless you empty the entire clip." He sighed.

"Then show me how to empty it in all the right places."

"At least it isn't pink," he muttered. Reagan inwardly patted herself on the back for nixing that idea.

After the house closing, they stopped by to pick up sandwiches to take back to the new home and wait for the movers. When Aiden pulled into the driveway of a beautiful two-story Georgian colonial-style condo, she was blown away. It had an open floor plan with beautiful hardwood floors throughout, a spacious great room with a gray stone fireplace that went all the way up the wall and met with a vaulted ceiling with four skylights. A big archway led to the kitchen with quartz countertops, a prep island with a breakfast bar on the opposite side, built-in stainless-steel appliances, and sleek white Shaker cabinets. A nice sized yard was surrounded by a 7-foot wooden privacy fence.

As she stood on the back deck admiring what a magnificent choice he'd made, she felt his arms slip around her waist, his chest snuggled against her back.

"What do you think?" he whispered in her ear.

"It's perfect in every detail."

"I haven't seen it in several weeks, but I think is suits us perfectly."

"Us?" she smiled, turning to kiss him lightly on the lips.

"Wishful thinking. Be forewarned, I'm gonna want to keep you." He smiled devilishly.

"I hope so," she whispered, squeezing his arms.

The movers arrived shortly, followed by furniture deliverymen and cable and alarm system installers. The house was so crowded, they needed a cop to direct traffic. It was around 5 o'clock when the last person left. Reagan went to the refrigerator and pulled out a bottle of Dom Pérignon she'd bought to celebrate their first day in Aiden's new home.

He walked into the kitchen pulling his t-shirt over his head and flung it over a chair. "I think the heat's too high in here. Ah, Champagne. Time to celebrate?"

She grabbed the hem of her t-shirt, yanked it over her head, and threw it on the chair beside his, mimicking his actions. Picking up the bottle and a couple of plastic cups, she flashed him her most alluring smile.

"I think it's about time we christened your new home, don't you?" she said, batting her eyelashes playfully.

He gave her a sexy smirk and took the bottle and cups from her hands, setting them on the counter. Grabbing her around the waist, he threw her over his shoulder. "Yes, ma'am. Every room."

Reagan woke up with her head on Aiden's chest, and her legs intertwined with his on his new four-poster king-size bed, minus the linens. Two damp towels from their shower were twisted around them. Aiden was still asleep. Her heart glowed with a sense of belonging as she silently watched the rise and fall of his chest and snuggled closer. It had been an amazing day. If things worked out between them, maybe this could be her new life. She was about to drift back to sleep when Aiden's cell phone rang. The startling sound jarred him upright in bed.

"What the hell?" He scrambled out of bed and fished his phone from his jeans lying on the floor.

"It's Josh," he said, putting it on speaker. "What's up, bro?"

"Sorry to bother you guys, but I've got a message for Reagan from Kowalski."

"Why didn't he call her himself?" Aiden asked, rubbing the sleep from his eyes.

"He said he didn't have her new number, and I think he's afraid to call you. Told him she was no longer staying with us. I might have implied that I didn't know where she was."

"Good. I don't want to talk to him," Reagan said.

"What did he say?" Aiden asked.

"Said that today they contacted your new half-sister, Rosana Fuentes — she goes by Rose now — and her husband, Arturo. It looks like Nour and Borzin Nader broke into their home and spent at least a few days there while the family was in Mexico. The house was ransacked and stripped of the valuables ... even stole the kids' electronic toys. Real scum, huh? They took some of the family pictures just like they did at Nana's house. Detective Kowalski assumes they didn't want anything that could be connected to them. Arturo sent his wife and kids to stay with one of his cousins in Cincinnati. Seems they are just as afraid of Nour and Borzin Nader as everyone else. Kowalski said Rose hadn't spoken to either one of them in over 20 years. Thinks they're trash. Not sure how it came up, but I told him about the DNA test results."

"No worries. I would have told him anyway," Reagan said.

"Do they think Nour's in Cleveland?" Aiden asked.

"No sign of him in Chicago, so probably. Detective Kowalski is worried about how you're going to protect Reagan when you start work," Mattie said, popping into the conversation.

"Just won't start work," Aiden said flatly.

"Yes, you will!" Reagan stood up with hands on her hips and stomped her foot, the towel wrapped around her almost falling to the floor. She knew her current state of dress didn't scream seriousness, but she was determined to make her point. "I've disrupted your life enough."

"We'll talk about it later, Josh. I've still got some time before I have to report. Got to go. We've got a lot of unpacking to do," Aiden said, giving Reagan a wink.

# Chapter 41

"You look yummy," Reagan said, eyeing Aiden in his charcoal gray suit. She straightened his tie and rubbed up and down his chest. He grabbed one of her hands, pulling it to his lips for a quick kiss.

"Don't start that or I'll never get to my appointment on time. You wouldn't want to be responsible for my company losing one of the best security IT specialists in the country, would you?"

Reagan was so proud of him. Things seemed to be working out so much better than either of them had anticipated. Aiden had been pleasantly surprised that his new partners had been amicable to him taking on a different role in the company. The business had grown so rapidly in the past year that the bare-bones staff could no longer support it. With Aiden's leadership experience in the Seals, he was the ideal person to develop a new business plan that would bolster the current and future expansion of their security company. Since the current location in a small office in Naples, Florida, was inadequate, the guys knew they needed to be more centrally located and move into a larger facility to expand their services. It was Aiden's task to find an alternative location and hire key personnel, many of whom could work remotely. Reagan helped Aiden's recruiting efforts, but she refused their offer of a position until things were more settled in her life. Today, Aiden was meeting with a talented IT expert in a conference room he had booked for the week in Beachwood.

"No, I don't want you to be late. That's why you need to get going. I'll be right here locked in the house until you get back," Reagan declared. He hadn't let her out of his sight in the past two weeks, and she had been perfectly fine.

"No, Sweetheart. You're coming with me and waiting in the Starbucks in the lobby until my interview is over. I would ask you to join me, but you have already nixed that idea. No more arguments. There is no way I'm risking your safety. Now please get your coat so we can get moving."

Aiden's cell phone rang.

"Hello … Sure that's fine … She has a new cell number. I'll tell her … I understand. We'll do that today. Thanks."

"Who was that?"

"The service company that did the clean-up in your grandmother's house. They need a walk-through and final approval before the insurance company will pay them. Since they're a small operation with limited resources, they asked if we could do it today. We can drop by after my meeting."

"Sounds good. Let me grab my handbag out of the bedroom, and I'll be ready to tag along to work with you like a good little girl."

When the doorbell rang, Reagan stopped in the hall, curious who would be dropping in unannounced so early in the morning.

"Detective Kowalski. Didn't take you long to find me. What can I do for you?" Aiden asked.

"Can I come in?" he asked sheepishly.

"I'm on my way out for an appointment," Aiden said.

"Please. I'll make it quick."

"I'll give you five minutes."

Reagan heard the door close and footsteps heading to the kitchen.

"This is a really nice place," Detective Kowalski said.

"Before you ask, it wasn't purchased with ill-gotten gains."

"I'm aware of that," Kowalski said. Aiden frowned. "I'd be a fool if I didn't check everyone out, but that's not why I'm here. I'm trying to get in touch with Ms. Asher. And please hear me out before you show me the door."

"I'm listening," Aiden said.

"We obviously didn't start out on the right foot, and that's my fault. I'm told that sometimes I can be a dick."

"Been talking to Danni?" Aiden asked.

The detective laughed good-naturally. "As a matter of fact, I have. I just want to clear the air about a few things. We no longer consider Ms. Asher or you a suspect. I can't speak for any of the federal agencies, because they don't confide in me, but I doubt if they do either. My problem is that all my facts are coming in pieces, which isn't uncommon for most of my cases, but when it spans over decades, it makes it hard to pin down a motive and figure out the players. I know you and Ms. Asher have found out a lot on your own, and I think if she could share some of that information with me in an actual timeline, maybe I wouldn't feel like I had one hand tied behind my back.

"As I said before, we feel we've solved the murder of Mrs. Moran, and the prosecutors are putting the case together now. We have Borzin Nader in custody for attempted kidnapping, and we have a national manhunt for Nour Nader for assault, carjacking, kidnapping, and homicide in two states, but we aren't sure how this ties together. If Ms. Asher could help me fill in some of the blanks, I would be grateful."

Aiden remained silent while the detective spoke with what appeared to be a genuine plea. Reagan waved her hand and caught his attention. She nodded her head, deciding the more knowledge the detective had, the higher the probability Nour Nader would be caught. Maybe then her life would get back to normal, or a new normal, anyway.

"So, you want to talk to Reagan?"

"I don't have her new number, and I know she's not with the Rannells. Her employers told me she has taken a leave of absence. I even tried to call Tyler Hamilton, but he isn't returning my calls."

Reagan walked into the room. "I'm here."

Detective Kowalski turned around, eyebrows raised in surprise. "Good morning, Ms. Asher."

"Apparently, Reagan has decided to speak to you. In that case, I have a favor to ask. I now have less than 30 minutes to make a meeting on time. Reagan needs to walk through her grandmother's home to approve the work the cleaning company did so her insurance company will pay them. If you can take her to do the inspection, it would give you both an opportunity to talk. I'll meet you guys there as soon as my meeting is over to pick her up. That way I'll know she's safe."

Detective Kowalski glanced at Reagan for approval. She nodded.

"Fine with me. I've got nothing else on my schedule until late this afternoon," the detective said.

"I feel like a child who just got handed off to a substitute babysitter," she said.

"Sorry, Sweetheart, but for the moment that's all we've got." He glanced at his watch. "Shit! I'm going to be late. Don't forget to set the security alarm." Grabbing her around the waist, he laid a passionate kiss on her and sprinted for the door to the garage.

*He's marking his territory,* she thought. *At least he didn't pee on my leg.*

"You live here now?" the detective asked.

"For a while."

He gave her a sly grin. "Testing the waters? That was fast."

She shrugged and smiled. "I guess it was."

The traffic was stop-and-go due to a tractor-trailer wreck, but it gave them plenty of time to talk on the way to Nana's house.

"Rather than me trying to figure out what I need to ask you, why don't you start from the beginning and tell me how you got involved in this whole mess? Maybe I missed some minor detail that's important."

Starting with the first day she arrived after Nana's death, Reagan chronicled the events as they happened. The only thing she fudged on was the timeline of when the gems were found. She went into detail about how she discovered the relationships between her mother and Darius and Rosana Nader, and eventually their connections to Borzin and Nour Nader, who to her dismay, turned out to be related to her.

"What about the DNA test? Josh briefly mentioned the results to me, but maybe you can clarify."

"Karim Nader is my biological father. Darius and Rosana Nader are my half-brother and sister. Since Karim seduced my mother when she was a student at OSU, I don't have any respect for the man. If you look up my biological father on the internet as I have done, you'll find out he is a retired art history professor and lecturer who is respected in the liberal arts community. He lives in a middle-income neighborhood, not a wealthy man. On what he thought might be his deathbed, he confessed to Darius about his affair with a woman who matched a description of my mother. Being the weasel that he is, he has since denied everything and continues to do so to save face with his family. He chalked it up to an elaborate dream." She waved her hand dismissively.

"You've had a shitload dumped on you in the last few of weeks. How do you feel about it?"

"Really haven't taken time to process it all. I'll probably need intensive therapy when I do," she said with a humorless chuckle. "Maybe you could do me a favor."

"If I can," he said cautiously.

"If there is still a file on my mother's suicide at the police department, I would appreciate a copy of the notes she left. My dad, the legal one, told me that she wrote two — one specifically to me. Who knows, it might even give some clues into this whole mess, but mostly I want to know what she had to say to me. It's inconceivable that my grandmother never gave it to me, but then I've learned a lot of things about her recently I would never have believed. Like keeping my father away from me while making me believe he didn't care."

"She probably thought she had more time. Once you've kept a secret for that long, it gets harder to reveal the truth and sometimes you start to believe your own lies."

"Thank you for that," she said. "I almost wish I could believe it."

"Do you think the jewels may have had something to do with your mother's suicide?"

Reagan briefly met his eyes before he turned back to the road. "I'd like to say unequivocally 'no way in hell,' but lately I've found that my trust in the people closest to me has been misplaced. So it's safer to say, who knows?"

Kowalski was silent for a few minutes before he continued. "What are you going to do with all that money if the jewels aren't claimed?"

"Darius asked me that too. He calls it blood money and wants nothing to do with it. He feels God has blessed him with a good life and he's not planning on doing anything to mess that up."

"And you?" She stared at his profile for a few seconds before she answered, trying to read his motive for the question.

"I really haven't given it much thought. Hard to believe, huh? Probably give it away." His cocked a brow is question.

"What?" Reagan could think only in terms of the grief the jewels had brought to her life. "It feels cursed."

"You guys are a rare breed. Most people would've taken off the minute they found the gems. Sounds like you're serious."

"Want to know what matters to me? Knowing Nour Nader is behind bars for life. I'll figure the rest out."

"Do you think Karim Nader was in on the original theft? And I say theft because it's the only scenario that makes sense, not that there is actual proof," he said.

"Darius assured me that our father is extremely honest and would have immediately turned them over to the police. Apparently, his moral compass loses its direction when it comes to adultery. Darius believes it's more likely that Borzin smuggled them into the States years ago when they visited from Lebanon. Since Nour was 15 years old at the time, it's doubtful he had much involvement. How they ended up in my grandmother's house is anyone's guess at this point."

"We're still trying to identify the owners of the jewelry, but the chances of finding them are slim. They're probably going to be yours."

"That's not even on my radar right now."

"It looks like the traffic has died down. We'd better get you to the house for that walk-through. If Aiden gets there before us, he's going to push the panic button."

# Chapter 42

The cleaning service did a much better job on her childhood home than she'd expected. The broken furniture, slashed cushions, and busted houseware items had all been removed. Carpets, barely salvageable from years of wear and tear, had been vacuumed. As her eyes raked over the huge gouges left in the walls, chills rippled through her spine reminding her of the lengths the intruders had gone to find what they wanted. The sight of the untouched dining room table amid the destruction was almost laughable, but then again, what could you hide in a table?

The kitchen had basically been gutted; all appliances removed. Except for personal items packed neatly in boxes, Reagan was relieved to find Nana's bedroom and closet empty, one less thing for her to deal with. At her instruction, her old bedroom and the office were the only rooms inside the house that remained untouched.

"It looks better than it did the last time I saw it. Some new sheetrock, a little paint, and it should be sellable," the detective offered with optimism.

"Unfortunately, it's going to take a lot more than that. The carpets are originals, the air conditioning and heater are crap, and the kitchen will have to be completely remodeled. Other than that, it's perfect!" She grimaced at his well-meaning attempt to sugar-coat the situation.

Reagan walked back into the kitchen and stared out the window into the backyard. The detective came up behind her.

"I'm sorry. I wasn't trying to minimize what you'll have to do here. You're correct. It's going to cost a chunk of change to make the house sellable."

"Yeah. It's a sad little place right now. I know you might not understand this, but I want to give it a happy face before I let it go."

"I get it." His cellphone rang. He pulled it out of his coat pocket and scanned the face. "It's Danni. I'll meet you out front when you're ready."

"Danni, what ya got?" he said, walking out of the kitchen.

"Be there in a sec," Reagan said to his back. "I think I heard a car pull up outside. That's probably Aiden. Tell him I'm doing a quick check on the garage."

"Take your time," Detective Kowalski replied.

When she opened the door to the garage, her eyes were immediately drawn to the spot where Nana was killed. Thankfully, the blood stain was gone. She looked around for a few minutes making a mental note to bring Aiden back to see if he was interested in any of the lawn and gardening tools.

When she stepped back into the kitchen, she half expected to see Aiden greet her. She heard the front door open as she approached the dining room door.

"What the hell ..."

Bang! Bang!

Reagan heard Detective Kowalski's exclamation abruptly cut off when the two shots rang out. Panic and adrenalin slammed into her, momentarily blurring her vision. She felt her heart beating in her throat, forcing her to struggle to catch her breath.

Maneuvering herself into the corner of the dining room, she attempted to melt out of sight, illogically willing her body to become invisible. She clutched her handbag to her breast as if it were a security blanket. *Think clearly. Breathe. Breathe. Breathe.* Then she remembered. Taking steadying breaths, she slipped her right hand inside the leather bag that hung from her shoulder. Eyes focused on the entry to the dining room, she waited for the intruder to appear. It was inevitable. The front door opened into the living room, and she was separated only by a half wall. Her cellphone was easily identifiable. It was important, so she pulled it out and tossed it down the front of her blouse. Next, she made out her wallet, lipstick, Tampax, and then there it was ... the cool metal handle of the .22 semi-automatic. Courage. A reminder that she wasn't powerless. Her thumb slid over the hard steel until she located the safety and flipped it off. Aiden would kill her if Nour didn't do it first, but her early mornings had been spent in his office while he got dressed, watching internet videos on how to load and shoot her new weapon. She was tired of relying on others, unable to defend herself. That stopped today.

Just having her hand curled around the handle, a finger resting against the trigger, gave her a sense of control. Before she could decide her next move, Nour stood before her with a gun pointed directly at her chest. She straightened her shoulders and stared at him, defiance in her eyes.

"So here we are again, Miss Asher. But this time your hero is lying dead on the floor. There is no one to help you."

His twisted, evil grin made her think of a cartoon villain, with narrowed eyes and raised eyebrows scrunched together. She wasn't sure if she was going to burst out laughing or throw up on his shoes. The telltale signs of panic began to take over. Tightness in her throat. Shortness of breath. Blood pounding in her ears so loudly she couldn't hear a word he spewed. She fought for control. *I have a gun,* she reminded herself.

Then it occurred to her. *If his immediate plan was to kill me, I would already be dead.* That small realization gave her a boost of confidence. There had been no hesitation with Detective Kowalski. Nour was first and foremost interested in the gems, and she appeared to be his only hope, so she might have some leverage, could stall for time. She also knew he would kill her as soon as he got what he wanted. Surely, Aiden would be there soon. That thought terrified her. Aiden would be walking into a trap. Nour would shoot him in cold blood the minute he stepped through the door. She would never let that happen regardless of the consequences to her. There was only one way to stop him.

"Did you hear me, bitch!" he screamed, her brain finally processing his words.

"Yes," she choked, though it was a lie. With her handbag still clutched to her chest, she slowly angled her body sideways to him while she kept her eyes trained on his cold black pupils. Her palm felt wet with perspiration as she tightened her grip on the handle, her index finger resting lightly against the trigger felt numb. *Was it still there?*

He shouted commands. His red face contorted with contempt. She mentally blocked out everything, her entire focus on her quivering fingers wrapped around the hard metal. Her inaction inflamed his rage, but she was blind and deaf to all of it. She had to do the one thing that might buy her a chance.

Aiden's words screamed in her head. *"Sweetheart, you would have to empty the entire clip to do anything but piss him off."* As Nour stepped closer, a small wince flashed over his face, disappearing as quickly as it appeared. That reminded her that Aiden had left two bullet wounds in his body. When he reached out his shaky left arm to seize her, she didn't move away, only blinked once to clear her vision. Hoping she was applying enough pressure, she fired straight through her handbag, over and over and over again until all she heard was the metallic sounds of the empty clip.

Nour's mouth fell open and his pupils dilated with shock. His body jerked wildly with each bullet that penetrated its mark, slamming his back hard against the dining room wall. Reagan hesitated for a few moments, stunned by what she had done and simultaneously trying to assess the damage. *Would it stop him?* There were three torn holes in his jacket gushing blood from his upper right arm, under his right armpit, and near his collar bone. The remaining bullets peppered the wall behind him, evidence of her inexperience. He glared at her with pure hatred. While struggling to gain his balance, he raised his gun in his trembling right hand and fired. Reagan screamed and stumbled backward, falling against the dining room table. Luckily, his lack of strength to lift his injured arm caused him to miss his mark, shooting a hole in front of her feet.

The abrupt sound of his gun hitting the wood floor, his blood-soaked muscles no longer able to support the weight, sparked Reagan to action. She dropped her handbag and dashed toward the front door. Fear blinding her flight, she tripped over the prone body of Detective Kowalski on the living room floor and fell flat on her face. As she scrambled to her feet, she felt a hand clasp around her left ankle. A shriek escaped her lips. Glancing back to locate Nour's position, she drew up her right leg and slammed the heel of her boot into the blood stain near his collarbone. He groaned, released her ankle, and fell backward. Instinctively, she grabbed the detective's wrist searching for signs of life and was welcomed by the slight beat of his pulse against her fingers. When she tried to stand, Nour grabbed the back of her black down-filled coat and yanked. Her arms flailed in a futile attempt to loosen his grip. Unable to reach him, she threw the entire weight of her body backwards, sending him sprawling to the floor with her landing on top of him. With a quick jab of her elbow into his wounded arm, she rolled off him and sprang to her feet. When he rolled over and reached for the gun in Detective Kowalski's shoulder holster, Reagan stomped her boot heal in his groin, grinding it for extra emphasis, and dashed out the open front door. She made it just beyond the end of the yard when she heard the gun fire. *He must be using his left hand,* she thought, knowing it would give her an advantage.

Reagan tried to wiggle her cell phone out of her blouse as she ran into the icy street, hoping to use the few cars parked on the curb for cover. Aiden had been right. All she had done was piss him off, but at least it slowed him down, and he was forced to shoot with his non-dominant hand. She also had the advantage of speed. He was limping badly from the wound Aiden had inflicted on his right leg.

The sleepy street she'd grown up on had very little traffic during the day, making it difficult for her to find help. She hoped Nour would eventually bleed out from one of his wounds, but since her .22 was a small caliber, she knew it was unlikely unless she had hit a vital artery. Another shot pinged off the top of a car near her head causing her to slip down on her butt in the slushy ice. When she peeked over the trunk, she could see he had picked up his pace despite having to drag his right leg. A few blocks down the street, she spotted a tan-shingled house with rust-colored shutters on the windows. For some reason, it seemed familiar, but she wasn't sure why. She hadn't been this far down the street in years. There was a sign stuck in the front yard that read, "Work done by First Rate Painters," and another said, "For sale by Owner." She was spurred on by the possibility that the contractors might still be working in the home. The cracked-open front door had to be a good sign.

Another shot rang out, causing her to cautiously increase her speed while maintaining her balance on the slippery pavement. One fall, and he would be on top of her in no time.

Bursting through the front door, she called out frantically, as she hurried from room to room in the small home, not unlike Nana's.

Maybe that was why it seemed familiar to her. Most of the houses on the street were built by the same contractor.

"Help! Somebody, please help me!" No answer.

She searched the front rooms and jogged down the hall to what she expected to be the bedrooms. When she got to the back bedroom, the sight momentarily paralyzed her. The windows were covered with sheets, unlike the rest of the house, and on the floor was a sleeping bag, opened cans of food, four boxes of ammunition, and newspaper articles with pictures — of her. Reality struck like a brick to the side of her head. This had to be where Darius and Rosana had grown up with their grandparents. She knew she had been here sometime in her childhood. Nour had found it empty and made himself a hideout. A perfect place to bide his time, watching and waiting for her to show back up at Nana's house. Right under the noses of the police.

Bending over to catch her breath, she sucked in a foul order that sent her into a coughing fit. Gas. The house was full of it. Was it a leak? She rushed out of the room and made her way to the back door in the kitchen. Unlike the door in Nana's house opening to the garage, this one led directly to the back yard. Reagan knew all it took was one gunshot into a house filled with gas to blow her to pieces. Bending down to see what was preventing it from turning, she found the lock had been smashed with a hammer. She frantically scanned the room for something to pry it open. She gasped at the sight of a nylon rope and box of plastic ties laying on the kitchen counter.

"Oh, my God," she said aloud. "This was his plan all along. To bring me here and leave me stuck in a house full of gas. And I came of my own free will."

Her life depended on keeping a clear head, which was becoming increasingly difficult with her current consumption of gas fumes. There was nothing visible in the kitchen strong enough to break the glass panes on the door, so she balled her fist in her coat sleeve and punched through the glass, leaving uneven shards. As she hit the few jagged pieces left, her hand slipped out of the sleeve and cut a 6-inch gash down the inside of her arm. She ignored the pain radiating up her forearm to her shoulder as she reached her hand through the window to the outside handle. A scream escaped her lips when she realized the handle on the other side was jammed too. It had been a foolish waste of time. A lock was a lock on both sides. The gas was affecting her ability to reason.

"Reagan Asher! Where are you?" she heard him call from outside the house. Taunting her.

She had to get out now. With her adrenalin surging, she lifted her right leg and slammed her foot into the door by the latch. Nothing moved. Repeating the action again, she felt the door give a little and splinter. One more time with determination and it finally gave way, sending her sprawling down the back steps face into the snow. As she attempted to stand, a sharp pain shot through her right leg, buckling her knee and sending her back down.

*No! No! No! Run!* her brain commanded. Gritting her teeth, she made a few futile attempts to get up before she finally made it to her feet. She took a step, then collapsed again. Biting her lip to distract her from the searing pain, she tasted the metallic flavor of her own blood. Gathering a strength she didn't know she possessed, she repeated her actions over and over. *Get up. Step. Fall. Get up. Step. Fall.* Tears burned her eyes, but determination fueled her forward. She would not let that monster win.

"Reagan!" he shouted, as she tumbled down into the deep snow, her fingers burning from the ice. "You will pay for what you have done to me. You will never live to enjoy what you stole!"

Reagan knew he was now more dangerous than he had ever been because he had nothing left to lose. He would never see the gems again, let alone get out of the country alive. Revenge was all he had left, but she didn't care about him or his jewels. They meant nothing to her. They had turned her life upside-down. All she cared about was getting to Aiden. She groaned as she pushed herself to her feet and dragged her leg for three consecutive steps. Then, "BOOM!" An earsplitting blast and an invisible force hurled her through the air, then nothing.

# Chapter 43

Aiden mentally fist pumped the air when he left the meeting. He had secured a highly sought-after candidate for a key position who agreed to start in two weeks. The two of them hit it off so well, the guy was willing to move to their new headquarters whenever they secured it, just as long as it wasn't Alaska. No danger there, Aiden assured him. His partners were going to be breaking out the champagne on this hiring acquisition.

As soon as he cranked up the heat in the truck and pulled out into traffic, he used his hands-free command to call Reagan. It rang numerous times before it went to voicemail. Not wanting to make a pest of himself, he waited 10 minutes before he tried again but still no answer. Worst-case scenarios were always his first thoughts, but he refused to panic. Swallowing his pride, he broke down and called Detective Kowalski's cell thinking Reagan may have forgotten to charge her phone, but it went straight to voicemail.

"Shit! Shit! Shit!" Aiden growled, beating the steering wheel with his palms. Something was wrong. He could feel it in his gut. As he maneuvered through traffic on the interstate, he called Danni. If he was overreacting, he would apologize later for wasting her time.

"Danni Silva."

"Danni, it's Aiden Rannell."

"What's up?" Her voice was chipper.

"Reagan went to her grandmother's house with Detective Kowalski this morning, and I can't reach either one of them. I know it's probably nothing, but I don't want to take any chances. Can you please reach out to him and alleviate my fear that something terrible has happened?"

"Huh. I just got off the phone with him. They were finishing up and about to leave. He said he was going to call you to arrange a place we could all meet to share new information we received from the FBI. Wanted to keep you guys in the loop. That was like five minutes ago. Hold on. I'll call him back on the office phone."

Aiden's anxiety grew by the second while he waited impatiently. The congested traffic didn't help matters.

"No answer. I even texted him our emergency code and got nothing. I'll meet you at the Moran house." She clicked off. Now full-blown panic set in.

Aiden pulled in behind Detective Kowalski's car parked on the front curb and slid his Glock out of his holster. There was a silver Ford Bronco parked in the driveway that he didn't recognize. When he noticed the front door was ajar, he blew out a slow breath. He bent down and approached from the side of the house, crouching under the windows as he made his way to the front door. The house was silent. *Not a good sign,* he thought but refused to allow any other thoughts to run wild. Cautiously nudging the door farther open, he peeked into the living room and gaped in horror when he saw the bottoms of a man's shoes just inside the door. A few steps closer brought the prone, still body of Detective Kowalski into view, two bullet wounds bleeding from his torso.

"Dear God," he whispered. Fear gripped him as he thought of what it might mean for Reagan. Over the years, he'd been in some of the worst combat situations imaginable, but he couldn't remember ever being more terrified than he was at that moment. *Please God, she has to be alive.*

Easing the door fully open with the toe of his shoe, he cautiously knelt and checked the detective's neck for a pulse. A faint flutter. One of the wounds was in his chest, near his heart, the other a couple of inches above his hip. It took two minutes to clear the house, before he called to request an ambulance and police assistance for a possible kidnapping. It had taken all his composure to keep his voice steady. Disconnecting the call, he noticed Reagan's black leather handbag on the floor of the dining room. His heart sank. All the nightmare scenarios that could explain her disappearance played out in his mind on an endless loop. Thankfully, a call from Danni kicked him out of his own head. She was five minutes away.

"And Reagan?" Danni asked hesitatingly.

"S…she's not here," his voice broke.

"We'll find her."

Aiden knelt beside Kowalski and tried to wake him. The bullet could have nicked his heart, Aiden couldn't be sure. Kowalski's body was cool, his skin color ashen. Aiden ran into Reagan's old bedroom and yanked the comforter off the bed, then wrapped it around his body. He loosened the detective's tie and applied pressure with his palms to stop the bleeding in his chest. Within seconds, the comforter was soaked in blood under his hands.

Danni burst into the door, a cry escaping her lips as she fell to her knees. Tears filled her eyes.

"Oh, Brad," she whispered, her hands shaking as she reached to touch him.

Still applying pressure to his chest, Aiden sent Danni to find something else to help apply pressure to the second wound. When she came back with a blanket, Aiden remembered the linen closet had already been packed.

"Nour Nader?" she barely whispered.

"That's my guess. I need to be out looking for him." His voice thick with concern.

"I know you feel helpless, Aiden, but I promise I've made the calls. To the local police, the state police, and even my contact at the FBI. I'm so sorry. I don't know what else to do right now." She wiped her eyes on her jacket sleeve.

"I'm about to lose my fuckin' mind," he seethed. "I'm going to kill that sonofabitch!"

"Not if I get to him first," Danni said through clenched teeth. They both sighed in momentary relief when they heard a car screech to a stop out front. Danni had requested the responding officers arrive without sirens to prevent Nour Nader from being alerted if he was still in the area. Seconds later, two policemen ran in and stopped in their tracks when they saw the detective unconscious on the floor.

"Jesus Christ," one of the men muttered, then made the sign of the cross.

They took over attending to Detective Kowalski so Danni and Aiden could look around more thoroughly. Aiden picked up Reagan's handbag and handed it to Danni.

"Reagan's?"

"Yeah. She must had dropped it."

"Well, I'll be damned," Danni breathed.

"What?"

She turned the handbag around so Aiden could see. One end of the leather had a giant, ragged burn hole.

"What the hell?" Aiden said, grabbing the bag and digging his hand inside. He pulled out the Rugger .22 semi-automatic. "Shit, Reagan! What did you do?"

Danni slipped on a pair of latex gloves, took the gun from his hand and pulled the clip. She pointed to a revolver lying a few feet away, then to a bullet hole in the floor.

"He probably had that gun on her. Reagan tried to defend herself. Emptied the entire clip. Shot straight through her handbag. Pretty smart if you ask me. She'd probably be lying here dead if she'd tried to pull it out."

Aiden, stunned, nodded in agreement.

Danni surveyed the room and pointed to the wall riddled with holes.

"I count seven in the wall," she said. "This smudge looks like blood." Aiden moved in for a closer look.

"You're right. I told her if she was attacked, she'd have to empty the clip to do the most damage with that .22. We can only pray the other three bullets hit their mark, and he's bleeding out somewhere. That damn gun was supposed to be in my safe until I could teach her how to use it. I was so wrapped up in moving into my new condo and getting settled, I forgot all about it. Surprised she figured out how to load it."

"You can learn just about anything on the internet," Danni huffed. "There's no doubt even a .22 semi-automatic can do some serious damage in the right places. Don't forget you already put a few bullets in him yourself in New Orleans. If that's his blood, he fell back against the wall. May have given her a chance to get out."

"Hope you're right, but it could be her blood," Aiden said, shivering at the thought.

"Don't let that get in your head. She could be out there running. The Bronco outside is probably his ride. I'll run the plates. They may be on foot."

"Yeah. She might have gotten away." He ran for the door with Danni on his heels.

"Which way are you going?" she asked.

Aiden stopped and surveyed the yard for tracks through the snow. There were two sets leading from the front door across the yard. Based on the distance apart, it was obvious they weren't traveling together. "Shit! There are two different trails headed west. If she bought herself enough time to get away, he's not far behind her."

As he tore across the yard, Danni called after him. "Aiden! Brad's gun in missing from his holster. Be careful!"

He waved his hand over his head in acknowledgement without a backward glance.

One trail led to the street but was quickly lost in the frozen sludge and tire tracks. The other followed the icy sidewalk and was easier to follow due to the traces of blood in the footsteps that were too big to be Reagan's. Or at least that was what Aiden convinced himself. The alternative was too much to think about. With a wounded leg and maybe a few bullet holes, Nour would probably stick to the sidewalk, which was mostly salted, while Reagan would either stay in the street using parked cars for cover or dash off through somebody's yard.

He had gone a few hundred yards when he found a smudged bloody palm print on the right side of a blue SUV parked against the curb. He allowed himself a momentary sigh of relief when he realized it wasn't Reagan's. *Did Nour stop to rest?* The momentary reprieve dissipated when it occurred to him that Nour may have stopped to take aim.

The distant sound of sirens wailing broke his concentration and alerted him that help was on the way. *Shit! So much for the silent approach. If Nour is near enough to hear it, he'll be much more dangerous. Volatile.*

Aiden increased his speed as he moved into the street, using the parked cars to hide his approach. He continued to scan for signs of Reagan or the maniac who was on her trail. He refused to believe Nour had caught up to her. Crouching low to maneuver through an open space along the street, he stepped on something that caused his foot to almost slide out from under him. When he righted himself, he looked down at the offending object. It was a cell phone with an orange cover. Reagan's. Thanking God that his hunch had paid off, he broke into a full run, frantically raking his eyes down the front and side yards for any signs of her.

Aiden halted in his tracks when he heard a thick voice bellow out Reagan's name, dragging it out in a sing-song slur. The sound was close. He knew he was headed in the right direction. Aiden swiftly slipped his 9mm out of its holster and carefully picked up speed. A few moments later, he recognized who it was. Nour Nader, shouting threats about revenge, betrayal, and Reagan's impending death. The taunting tone and acerbic laughter were the unmistakable sounds of a desperate man.

As he grew close enough to pinpoint Nour's exact location, Aiden recoiled from the sound of a gunshot immediately followed by an earsplitting "boom" that shook the ground. As Aiden jumped from the slushy street onto the sidewalk, he watched in horror as a red and orange ball of fire bellowed into the air carrying smoke, debris, and splintered wood from what had once been a modest family home. Black smoke shot out from all sides, making it difficult to see anything near the blast.

When Aiden reached the house next door to the destruction, he could feel the intense heat radiating from the blazing rubble. A sob threatened to escape his throat, but he swallowed it. He refused to believe the explosion had anything to do with Reagan. If she had been inside, she would have found a way to get out. *She's smart. Determined. Too clever for a man like Nour to contain her.*

The thick smoke stung his eyes, making it difficult to see the destroyed house or front yard. Aiden cautiously approached with his gun drawn, searching for Nour, who had gone silent. *He is too much of a coward to blow himself up, but he would certainly want a front-row seat to watch the spectacle.*

Aiden caught a break when a puff of frigid breeze blew the smoke in a slightly different direction, revealing the outline of a man with his hand over his eyes. He was leaning against the wheel of a pickup truck parked on the curb in front of the burning house. Aiden's grip tightened on his Glock as he moved closer. When the man lowered his bloodied arm from his face, Aiden was met with the cold, dead eyes of Nour Nader. The gun in his left hand rested against his wet, blood-stained pants. The moment Nour recognized Aiden, he flashed a grin, revealing yellow tobacco-stained teeth and pure evil.

The man was a physical mess, covered in blood from his face to his boots. *You got him good, Sweetheart,* he said to himself, then pushed the emotions aside that threatened to overwhelm him. Even though Nour's life was already hanging by a thread, it took every ounce of Aiden's restraint not to blow his psychopathic ass straight to hell.

"You ... you are too late. She is dead. Blown to tiny little pieces," he laughed, lifting his gun just enough to wave it fancifully through the air, but not enough to provoke Aiden to fire.

Aiden didn't speak. Couldn't. Instead, he watched and listened to the man taunt him. Here he was face-to-face with one of the men who had terrorized Reagan for weeks, and he couldn't think of a thing he wanted to say to him. Or ask him. He already knew why they were after her — greed. When Nour figured out he would never get the gems back and had no hope of ever leaving the country alive with every law enforcement agency in the country after him, all he had left was revenge. The irony was that Reagan was the one person who had nothing to do with any of it, but she ended up suffering for those responsible.

As much as he despised him, Aiden wouldn't be able to explain shooting a half-dead man in the street without provocation. Then the idea came to him. He would take from Nour Nader the only thing that he thought he had won. His revenge.

"You are wrong, Nour! Reagan is very much alive and well, despite your clumsy attempts to capture her." He prayed it was true. "She made it to a neighbor's house and called the police."

Nour's eyes narrowed to slits and his jaw tightened. "You are lying!"

"Can't you hear the sirens? How do you think I made it here so quickly?"

"No!" His scream was more like the howl of a wounded animal.

Fitting, Aiden thought.

Aiden chanced a quick glance at the flaming house. Finding Reagan was his priority, but as unlikely as it was that Nour could flee in his current condition, he had to wait for back-up or someone else might get hurt.

"Aiden!" Danni's excited voice came from behind him, momentarily drawing his attention as she rushed toward him from across the street. "Look out! He's going to sho …"

Before Danni completed her sentence, Aiden caught the slow elevation of Nour's gun in the periphery of his vision. Instinct took over. He twirled around and fired three shots hitting Nour Nader dead center in the chest. Without wasting another moment, he tore off around the backyard of the neighbor's house, trying to avoid the intense heat from the explosion. He wrapped his wool scarf around his nose and face, then flung himself over the chain-link fence that surrounded the backyard of the burning house, cutting gashes through his leather gloves into his palms.

The heavy smoke flowing from the demolished home made it almost impossible to breathe or see through his watery eyes. Flinging off his coat, he waved it to clear the smoke as he frantically dug through the debris scattered around the yard. Reagan had to have gotten out of the house, he told himself, refusing to believe otherwise. More than a foot of snow covered the backyard, making it difficult to maneuver through the twisted metal, sheetrock, roof shingles, and other indistinguishable rubble, some buried and others lying on top. When he had almost reached the back fence, he spotted a patch of black nylon peering out from underneath a tattered backdoor screen. His heart squeezed, remembering Reagan had left his condo that morning in a long, black quilted-nylon coat. A mixture of fear and relief propelled him forward. Tossing the screen door aside, he fell to his knees beside her.

"Oh, Reagan!" She was lying on her stomach perfectly still, her face turned sideways, wet strands of matted hair covering her face, blood trickling from her exposed ear. A dark, damp blood stain was smeared across the back of her coat. With trembling hands, he leaned over her body. Holding his breath, he gently touched the pulse-point on her neck. He coughed to mask a sob. It was slow and steady. After a quick inspection of the blood on the back of her coat, he realized it was a surface stain, not soaked through. *Not her blood.*

He swallowed hard to compose himself and whispered in her ear. "I'm here, Reagan. You're going to be okay. He'll never hurt you again."

Aiden knew he shouldn't move her in case of internal injuries but leaving her unconscious in the snow was not an option. He carefully turned her over and scooped her into his arms. One side of her face was bright red from exposure to the hardened snow, the other side had the beginning signs of a bruise on her cheek. Her right coat sleeve was ripped and soaked in blood that trickled down to her fingertips. She needed immediate medical attention. Carrying her through the back gate, he made his way around to the front of the house. Danni rushed toward them.

"Oh, Aiden, thank God she wasn't in the house! How badly is she hurt?"

"Her breathing is shallow, but her heartbeat is steady. She hasn't regained consciousness. Probably a concussion. We need to get her to a hospital."

Danni pulled out her cell and called for another ambulance.

Aiden looked up to see a small gathering of neighbors in the street watching the house burn, taking pictures and videos of Nour Nader lying dead on the sidewalk.

A young officer ran up to them. Aiden recognized him as one of the first responders who helped attend to Detective Kowalski. "Let's get her into the backseat of my patrol car, and we can take her down to the Moran house until the ambulance gets here."

"Kowalski?" Aiden asked.

"Barely alive. Just left in an ambulance," the officer said.

Aiden nodded. He gingerly slid into the car with Reagan cradled in his arms, then briskly rubbed her hands and uninjured arm to raise her body temperature. Her eyes fluttered open, finding his. Disoriented, searching for answers, she moved her lips, but no sound emerged.

"Hey, Sweetheart. You're going to be okay." His emotions were raw as he gently kissed her forehead.

"A...Aiden," she whispered. "Am I in heaven?" He couldn't help but grin, thankful she still had a sense humor.

"No, but some *have* used that to describe being in my arms," he kidded gently.

She gave him a tired smile as he gingerly smoothed her wet hair from her neck and brushed his lips across hers. She suddenly pushed him away and tried to sit up, a look of terror across her face.

"What did you say? I can't hear you, Aiden. I can't hear you!" Her hand tightened around his arm.

He tried to mouth his words so she could understand. The blast had damaged her eardrums, but he felt sure it was temporary. It had happened to him in combat. Pointing to her ears, he mouthed his words distinctly. "Probably temporary." He prayed it was the truth.

Reagan nodded her understanding. She struggled to keep her eyes open, but unconsciousness slowly took over.

"We don't have time to wait for an ambulance," he said to the police officer. "Take us to the hospital now!"

# Chapter 44

*Three months later*

Reagan stared at the two boxes that had been sitting on the floor of the guest bedroom closet for the past eight weeks, still unopened. She knew her mother's yearbooks were there, but they didn't concern her. It was the possibility of having some other truths revealed that would unravel the remaining threads of the life she once knew.

Her physical injuries had healed within a couple of months of the explosion, but the psychological ones were still a work in progress, forgiveness being her biggest hurdle. The weekly counseling sessions helped her cope with the new truths in her life and accept that she may never understand the motivations that led to the lies and betrayal from the people she trusted most. The hardest being Nana's deceptions that had kept her father away from her. It didn't matter that Stuart wasn't her biological father, he wanted her in his life, and they had made that happen. Thanks to the love and support from Aiden, the darkest clouds seemed to have lifted. Not everything was rosy between them as they blended their lives together, but they had been determined to work through the challenges one day at a time.

Gabriel Ledbetter was charged with the murders of Justin Pane and Camden Yeager, among other crimes, but was still awaiting trial. Borzin Nader had pleaded guilty to multiple charges and was sentenced to prison without possibility of parole. Darius made several attempts to confront his father about Reagan and his years of deceit, but Karim refused to acknowledge any truth to the accusation that he was her father, despite the DNA evidence. So far, no identifications had been made of the owners of the period jewelry, the diamonds, and the black pearls.

Aiden became the VP of Operations for COA International Security, the newly renamed company he now owned with his Seal brothers, Chase and Owen. After Aiden presented the results of his extensive research on the most centralized locations, the partners all agreed on Chicago. Aiden found an ideal facility for their corporate headquarters and hired key personnel to accommodate their expanding business model. During the HQ remodel, Reagan and Aiden lived part-time in his condo in Beachwood and part-time in her condo in Chicago.

Despite her former boss's pleas for her to return to work after Nour Nader had been killed, Reagan turned in her notice. Even when the CEO personally called to offer her a promotion and a 40% increase in salary, she still declined. She had been disappointed that it took her absence for them to truly realize her worth. The company had abandoned her at one of the worst times of her life, and it wasn't something she could get past. After multiple requests from all the COA owners, Reagan finally agreed to become the Director of Human Resources. It was a fresh start and would provide her many opportunities to help grow the company. Once they got the HQ fully staffed and running smoothly, she and Aiden wanted to find a home with a lakefront view.

As she knelt beside the boxes, mustering her courage, she thought back to her last conversation with her therapist.

*"Have you opened the boxes of your mother's mementos?"* her therapist asked.

*"Not yet,"* she answered meekly. *"Should I? Maybe I should just toss them in the trash."*

*"Okay. Let's pretend you did. Last night, you threw them in the trash, rolled the bin to the street, and this morning you stood at the window and watched the trash hauler take them away. They are gone for good. Nothing in those boxes can ever hurt you. Right?"*

*Reagan pondered that for a few minutes, contemplating what that would mean.*

*"Tell me what you're thinking,"* the therapist prompted.

*Reagan had looked up with tears in her eyes. "I would always wonder if there was something important I should have known. But on the other hand, what if I find out a terrible truth?"*

*"Which would be worse?"* the therapist asked.

*"I don't know,"* Reagan said tentatively.

*"Are you happy, Reagan?"*

*"Yes,"* she answered quickly.

*"Why?" the therapist asked.*

*Talking about her new life filled her with excitement. She felt a heaviness lift and she became animated as she spoke of her love for Aiden, their two homes, her challenging job, friends, recent family connections ... all the amazing things going on in her life.*

*"What could be in that box that would change any of those wonderful things in your life?" the therapist asked. "It might hurt. You might get angry or even frustrated that you can't change what happened. But ultimately, you are in control of your life and how you respond to the challenges. Your future is yours. You can't let the past actions of others, even those you love, affect that. You are healthy and happy. Aiden and your family and friends have helped ground you, but it's your inner strength that has allowed that to happened. I am confident that you can handle whatever you decide to do with the boxes."*

In that moment, Reagan knew. If she didn't open the boxes, she would always wonder. She was also sure that nothing she found would take her future away.

The first box held four yearbooks, two scrapbooks, invitations to parties, torn concert tickets, and similar memorabilia. The second held awards and certificates of achievement, graduation programs, a sketchbook with still lifes, and report cards. On the bottom there were two envelopes. Reagan held her breath as she read "Mother" on one and "Reagan" on the other. *Could this be what I've been hoping and fearing I would find? My mother's suicide note?*

Taking a deep, steeling breath, she opened the one she knew was addressed to Fiona.

*Mother,*

*As much as I would like to blame you for my screwed-up life, I guess it isn't entirely fair. I could have made different choices. I could have believed in myself instead of giving into my insecurities and fears. But you're the one who had to maintain appearances no matter what the consequences to Dad, Stuart, Reagan, or me. One is already dead because of it, you drove another away, and now I've chosen to take the cowardly way out. You've got want you wanted ... Reagan. You've done your best to undermine me and Stuart at every turn. I pray you won't force him out of her life. He loves her as his own and is legally her father. Don't forget that. I would insist she be with him if I thought you wouldn't pull out all the*

314 | Joy York

*stops to keep her and end up destroying her and him in the process. Reagan is the best thing that ever happened to me and the only thing that has made the last seven years worthwhile. I hope you will find it in your heart to tell her the truth one day. She deserves it. I'm leaving her a letter for you to give to her when she becomes an adult. I realize I have no control over whether she sees it or not, but I pray you will do the right thing.*

 *Claire*

Reagan was stunned. The animosity her mother had for her grandmother bled through every word, shocking Reagan to her core. She realized that when her mother became pregnant, her grandmother must have insisted she marry Stuart out of propriety. To maintain appearances. Stuart was a respectable choice and was already in love with her. Would have done anything for her and didn't care that Reagan wasn't his biological child. Her mother had given up everything because Fiona had guilted and shamed her into it. Even after her mother made the sacrifice, Fiona had continued to interfere until she drove Stuart away. Claire had to have felt she was losing Reagan too. Would never have control of her life. Reagan felt a surge of rage. *How had I not realized how selfish and narcissistic my grandmother was?*

Even worse, her grandmother had ignored her mother's dying wishes. Fiona had driven a wedge between Reagan and Stuart, isolating her from her only other parent, making her feel unwanted and unloved. And she never gave Reagan the letter her mother left for her. Never told her the truth.

With trembling hands and trepidation, she picked up and opened the letter addressed to her.

*My Dearest Reagan,*

 *I hope you are reading this when you have become a young woman and have gained some understanding of how unpredictable and complicated life can be. First, I beg for your forgiveness for leaving you. I promise you it was never my intent, and I have always been watching over you to make sure you are safe, and I always will.*

 *I know it is difficult for you to understand, but for the last few years, I have been barely hanging on to the edge of a deep crevice, and it has become too much for me to bear. When I look down, all I see is a darkness that tries to consume me. When I look up, I see you, my ray of sunshine and light, my princess. You sparkle as bright as the sapphire and diamond tiara you love to wear.*

*For most of my life, I have lived with fear and uncertainly. Constantly struggling between what I wanted to do and what was expected of me. Afraid of making the wrong decisions. Over time, I learned to put on a brave face and forge ahead. Doing what was expected of me, until I couldn't. My biggest fear, my love, is that my unhappiness will eventually negatively influence your perceptions of all the things that will make life worth living. As you begin your journey as the lovely and intelligent woman I know you are, I want to impress upon you the importance of being yourself and never compromising your dreams. You can't allow others to control you. We all make mistakes and run into obstacles along the way, but you will pick yourself up and keep going. People will try to criticize you and mold you into what they think you should be, but remember it's your decision, not theirs. You have always had a mind of your own, so don't ever lose sight of that.*

*When you meet the right person, you will recognize them by their selflessness, their kindness, the way they put you first, the ease with which they fit into your life, and somehow you can't remember how you ever lived without them. I could have had that with your dad, but I let too many things interfere, and I was just not strong enough to stand up for myself. Stuart is a good man and a wonderful father. He loves you, and you can always count on him.*

*I hope your grandmother has told you the truth by now. Through all the turmoil and hurt, never doubt how much you are loved.*

*Momma*

Reagan's tears spilled on the worn pages of the faded pink stationery, smearing the ink. She carefully dabbed them with the hem of her yellow t-shirt, afraid she would lose the words that had both lifted and broken her heart. It was obvious by the creases and bent corners that the two handwritten pages had been read and reread numerous times. Most certainly by her grandmother. *Had she been conflicted about giving the letter to Reagan? Felt remorse?* It really didn't matter, because ultimately, Fiona had never felt compelled to give her the letter. Not only had she denied Reagan a relationship with her father, she prevented her from knowing how deeply her mother had loved her.

On some level, the letter gave Reagan a sense of relief. She had always believed she had somehow contributed to her mother's death, asking herself if she hadn't been good enough. Had she been too much trouble? Too loud or annoying? Not lovable? Now Reagan realized there were many dynamics to her mother's relationships and internal pain that a young girl could never have understood. She had been loved by both of her parents, and that felt good. It confirmed that her instinct about Stuart's sincerity had been correct.

Rereading her mother's words about finding the right person brought a huge smile to her lips. It was as if she was describing Aiden. Had already met him and was giving her blessing that Reagan had chosen well. She knew it in her heart. Her future was in her hands and would not be derailed by the mistakes of others.

# Chapter 45

*Five months later*

Reagan hummed as she folded her third bikini into the luggage she was packing for her destination wedding and honeymoon at an all-inclusive resort on the northeast coast of Jamaica, near Blue Mountains National Park. They had chosen an intimate gathering of friends and family to share their special moments. Family had taken on a whole new meaning recently, as if the universe had shifted beneath her feet.

Reagan heard the garage door go up while she filled her cosmetic bag with toiletries and suntan lotion. A few minutes later, she heard Aiden call from the kitchen. He had spent the afternoon teleconferencing with clients all over the world from his temporary office in Beachwood.

"Where's the most beautiful woman in the world who's about to become my wife?"

"In the bedroom packing suntan lotion so we won't burn our butts off and end up stuck in our room the whole time," she called back.

Aiden appeared at the door with his navy suit jacket in hand, loosening his tie, both of which he tossed into a chair. Slipping his arms around her waist and pulling her snuggly against him, he nibbled her ear.

"Sweetheart, I don't see being confined to a bed with you for two weeks as a bad thing," he said in his sexiest voice.

"Me either, but since I'm the one who burns easily, you wouldn't be able to touch me."

"In that case, pack as many bottles as you need," he murmured against her hair. "Don't you think it's time for a little pre-honeymoon practice just to make sure we get it right?"

She laughed and teasingly pushed him away. "You have to pack! Your luggage has been sitting in the corner completely empty for a week, and you haven't even removed the tags from your new clothes."

He kissed her again, slipping his hands in the back pockets of her denim jeans and nuzzled her closer.

"You sure we can't take a little time to ..." he stopped and traced the curve of her neck with the tip of his tongue.

"You don't play fair," she said, unbuttoning his shirt.

"I think we've already established that."

As soon as they shed their clothes and moved to the bed, the doorbell rang two consecutive times.

"Shit!" Aiden cursed. "If we ignore them, maybe they'll go away."

They cuddled and giggled as they waited. The doorbell rang another couple of times, followed by solid knocks on the door.

"Sounds persistent. We'd better get it," Reagan said. "It could be important."

"It damn well better be," Aiden grumbled, jumping out of bed and grabbing a pair of gym shorts and a t-shirt from a stack of folded laundry, while Reagan threw her clothes back on in record time.

"Maybe it's Josh and Mattie coming over to mess with us," Reagan suggested.

"If it is, I'll be looking for a new best man because this one's going to be dead!"

Reagan and Aiden reached the door at the same time. "If it is them, be nice," she laughed.

Aiden shook his head good-naturedly and flung the door open. Recognition hit Reagan like a lead pipe to her chest, all the air forced from her lungs. Suddenly, her legs felt too weak to sustain her body's weight and she grabbed Aiden's arm for support. He slipped his arm around her waist, tucking her into him. When she looked up, his eyes met hers with concern and questions, seeking a signal to indicate what she wanted to do. At that moment, the reassurance of seeing the love and support in his eyes, knowing she wasn't alone, gave her strength. Aiden would always be there, not to fight her battles, but to give her the courage she needed to do it herself.

She let go of his arm and strengthened her resolve.

"What do you want?" she asked firmly.

"I am Karim Nader," he said, focusing solely on her. "I apologize for showing up unannounced, but it's important that I speak to you, Reagan."

Several inches taller than Darius, he was slim in stature, with deep brown, intelligent eyes. His hair was mostly silver but still held on to remnants of dark chocolate streaks. His lips were the same shape and pale mauve color as Reagan's. Even in his 70s, he was a handsome man with a regal quality to his features and posture.

"I know who you are," Reagan responded coldly. "What do you want?"

"May I come in? I hate to have a private conversation on your front doorstep for your neighbors to overhear."

"Don't you think it's a bit hypocritical to be concerned about propriety?" Aiden asked.

"I'm not here to defend actions that are indefensible." His gaze remained on Reagan, his eyes pleading. "May I?"

She hesitated, then moved away from Aiden and motioned Karim Nader inside her home. It was incomprehensible that her biological father was standing before her.

When they were seated on the sofa across from him, she noticed tiny beads of perspiration on his brow. *It couldn't have been easy for him to show up here*, she thought. *Had he come to continue to refute what DNA evidence had already proven? Or had he decided to swallow his pride and do the honorable thing?*

"Why are you here?" Reagan asked.

Karim searched her face for a few moments and smiled. "You are so naturally beautiful, like your mother," he said softly.

"Thank you," she said, his words catching her off guard.

He cleared his throat. "I want to first apologize for the actions of my brother and cousin. Although I knew they were not honorable men, I would never have dreamed the evil they were capable of doing. Thankfully, they got what they deserved."

Reagan had a million questions. Many had kept her up at night. Questions she had given up hope of ever finding the answers to, but she decided to begin with less emotional inquiries. Her need to control the conversation seemed tied to her sanity, so she took the lead.

"Do you know how the diamonds and pearls ended up hidden in my grandmother's home? And if you want to speak with me, I believe you owe me complete honesty."

Karim sighed deeply. "And you will get it. If that is where you wish to begin our conversation, so be it. When Borzin and Nour came to America to help move my parents back to Lebanon, I found them in Borzin's luggage by accident when a latch broke, spilling the contents. There was no doubt in my mind that he had stolen the gems and smuggled them into the United States. With his reputation, it would have been almost impossible for him to sell them in Lebanon. His criminal actions put my family at great risk. My mother had a plastic fruit arrangement in the top of the closet of the bedroom where my brother would be sleeping, so I quickly hid the gems inside the fruit. It was dangerous to leave them in my parents' home. Once Borzin realized they were missing, he would tear the house apart looking for them, but find nothing. For all I knew, he was already under investigation and the authorities could be watching my parents' home. I hoped Borzin would assume the gems were stolen from his luggage during his trip.

"At the first opportunity Borzin and Nour were out of the house, I called your mother to see if I could drop by to say goodbye. I was going to take the fruit basket to her as a small gift. I had no plans to tell her what was hidden inside. I was in denial of my unwitting involvement in the whole mess and wanted fate to decide if the gems were ever discovered. Ideally, I would have preferred they go back to the rightful owners, but that was not possible without destroying all our lives.

"Your mother was supposed to be in the house alone with you. Although I had no idea you were my daughter at the time, I later wondered if it was her way of making sure I met you at least once before we ended our affair. Regrettably, her husband answered the door. I explained the basket was a small thank-you to his wife for being so kind to my mother and children over the years. He quickly took the arrangement from me and, with hatred in his eyes, told me to never speak to his wife again or he'd kill me with his bare hands. I have no idea what happened to the gems after that encounter."

Reagan was dumbfounded. If Karim was telling the truth, then her father Stuart had known about the affair and the gems all along. He had intercepted the fruit basket meant for her mother. *Then why had he only taken five of the diamonds? Or was that a lie too? And why had he said they came from her grandfather? Why wouldn't he have taken all the diamonds with him to Washington? Had her mother known and didn't want them for fear they were stolen?*

"How and when did you find out about Reagan?" Aiden asked.

Karim turned back to Reagan. His voice was strained as he spoke. "Years ago, I received a letter from your mother telling me we had a daughter. She said you were 7 years old, and she had never revealed your true parentage but felt it was time. She was no longer married and was hoping there was still a chance for us to finally be together."

"Did you believe her?" Reagan asked, her voice tight. "That I was your daughter?"

"There was proof enclosed in the letter. Copies of birth certificates, adoption papers, and a picture of a beautiful young girl with bright green eyes and dark brown hair. The adoptive father had moved across the country and was threatening to take you away from her. She vowed to me she would never allow that to happen. As soon as she heard from me, she was going to tell you and her family the truth. She said the lies had caused too much heartache for her family."

Reagan listened intently, trying to remain detached. "And what did you say to her?" she asked.

Karim lowered his head. His words almost a whisper. "Nothing. I loved her with all my heart, but I said nothing. I was a coward. It didn't make sense to destroy my wife, my children. They would have lived in shame if I abandoned them for another woman and moved to America. My career would have been finished, leaving me with no means to support either family. All of our reputations would have been ruined."

Aiden grabbed Reagan's hand. His face was full of fury. She couldn't tell if he was asking her to hold him back from choking her father or if it was the other way around. Her insides burned like nothing she had ever known. Bile rose in her throat. Her father had decided that his family and reputation were more important than the risk of acknowledging his bastard child. Tears stung the back of her eyes, but she refused to give him the satisfaction of seeing her shed a single tear. Then a horrible realization hit her. Had his non-response to her mother's letter been the impetus for her suicide? It became so clear. He not only rejected her mother, but he didn't even have the decency to respond.

"You couldn't be bothered to acknowledge my mother's letter?" She jumped to her feet and angrily pointed her finger. "You are the reason she killed herself!" she screamed. "She gave up everything for you! Her plans to go to Oxford! Her friends! Her life! She was forced to marry another man and had your baby, and you just let her fall apart while you lived your life! She was an empty shell when she died! Because of you!"

The blood drained from Karim's face. "I don't understand ... I thought Fiona was killed months ago in an attempted burglary. That's what Darius told me."

"I'm not talking about my grandmother!" she yelled indignantly. "I'm talking about my mother ... Claire. The student you seduced! Or were there so many women that you couldn't keep track of their names?"

He shook his head, appearing utterly confused. Maybe he was too old to remember, she thought.

"Darius said something about that misconception. I told him it was ridiculous to suggest such a thing," he said firmly.

Reagan scoffed at him, her hands on her hips. "So even in the face of a 99.7% DNA test, you are going to deny me?"

He slowly shook his head. "I have many regrets. Done things I can never take back, but I am not denying you, Reagan. But Fiona was the only other woman in my life other than my wife."

"Claire ... you mean Claire," she corrected with irritation.

"No, Reagan. You are the one who is confused. Fiona was your mother, not Claire. We had been lovers since we were teenagers, at least until my parents forced me to go to university in Lebanon and into an arranged marriage. They refused to let Fiona and me be together."

Reagan's legs collapsed underneath her as she fell back on the sofa. She looked at him in stunned silence. Saw his lips moving as he continued to speak, but her brain registered nothing after "Fiona is your mother." *No. No. No. No. No.*

Aiden pulled her into his arms, then held up his hand to Karim. "Stop! Just stop! You just landed a 10-ton bomb on her, and obviously, you didn't realize it. But you need to let Reagan process what you just told her. Claire has always been her mother. She thought Fiona was her grandmother."

"I...I had no idea," Karim said apologetically, dropping his head in his hands.

"Oh, God, Reagan. I'm so sorry," Aiden whispered, holding her against his chest. She was numb, unable to feel her arms or legs or even Aiden's arms around her. She could see them but couldn't feel them. She had to pull herself together. *This man destroyed my family. Now is not the time to fall apart.*

Reagan straightened in her seat and met her father's eyes. "Fiona was my mother? How can that be? She was too old! It can't be true!"

Karim shifted to the edge of his chair and rubbed his hand over his face. "She was 43 when she had you. Fiona and your grandfather, Daniel, had not been close for years. We resumed our affair one summer when I did a lecture tour in America. Claire had been best friends with my children, Darius and Rosana, for years. I would never have touched her. I was in love with Fiona. Always have been." The last part conveyed regret.

"You gave the fruit basket to Daniel, Fiona's husband?" Aiden asked.

"Yes. Daniel and Fiona hadn't had an intimate relationship for years, so I'm sure he realized her indiscretion was with me when she became pregnant. Reagan, I swear I never knew until that letter that you were mine. Darius told me years ago that Claire had given up her plans to attend Oxford after she had worked so hard to get accepted. I was shocked because I knew the lengths that she had gone to to hide it from Fiona and Daniel. Reluctantly, I kept Claire's secret from Fiona. A couple of months later, Rosana told me Claire had gotten married, was pregnant, and had moved with her husband to Dayton. Rosana also told me Fiona moved to Dayton and lived with Claire and Stuart for almost a year. I assumed it was to help them with the baby.

I couldn't possibly have known at the time you were actually Fiona's child."

"It wouldn't have mattered anyway, would it, Mr. Nader? Because when you found out the truth seven years later, you did nothing." Aiden's words dripped with contempt.

"This has to be a mistake," Reagan said with disbelief. And then bits and pieces began to unfold in her head. The picture in Nana's safe deposit box that she and Aiden had suspected was important. Reagan thought it was Darius until he identified it as his father. It turns out it was important — to her grandmother — not to Claire. The girl cut out of the picture must have been Fiona. Then there was the conversation Darius had with his father in the hospital. After his father's confession about having a daughter in America, which he later refuted, Darius had accused him of having an affair with Claire. His father had adamantly denied it the next day, explaining he had known her mother Fiona when they were young, and he wouldn't want that ridiculous rumor to hurt her. Her mother's suicide note to her grandmother. The words came back to her: *You insisted on maintaining appearances no matter what the consequences to Dad, Stuart, Reagan, or me.* Claire, her sister, gave up everything to claim Reagan as her own so her mother could save face. Stay in a marriage to a man she didn't even love.

"Do you have the documents you spoke of?" she asked.

Karim handed her a manila envelope. She stared at it for a few seconds before sliding it over to Aiden.

"Would you mind?" she choked.

He pulled the papers out and set them on his lap, as Reagan peered over his shoulder. He read them aloud. "Certificate of Birth. Reagan Karim Moran born May 1,1987. Mother — Fiona Aileen Moran. Father unknown."

Aiden flipped to the second document.

"Certificate of Adoption. Claire Moran Asher and Stuart Alan Asher adopted Reagan Karim Moran on June 24, 1987 from biological mother Fiona Aileen Moran. Father is listed as unknown."

"My grandfather knew I wasn't his," Reagan said tentatively. "I was really nothing at all to him, was I?"

"You know that's not true, Reagan. You've told me how good he was to you," Aiden said. He glared at Karim. "Having the same blood doesn't make family. Nurturing and love do."

Karim lowered his head, at least having the good graces to look remorseful, though Reagan didn't buy it.

"The third document is a revised birth certificate for Reagan Karim Asher born May 1, 1987. Parents Claire Moran Asher and Stuart Alan Asher. I'm not sure how they got someone to change the original birth certificate, but they did," Aiden said.

"Karim … Your name is right there on my birth certificate. The first time I saw it when I applied for my Social Security card, Nana told me my middle name was supposed to be Karen, that it was just a typo. Funny, huh? I signed my name Reagan K. Asher and never thought another thing about it. Even with the subtle clues, I didn't figure it out. Never once thought my grandmother could be responsible for any of this."

"You did nothing wrong, Reagan. Don't you dare put any of this on you," Aiden said, squeezing her hand.

"Mr. Nader, do you realize Reagan and I are getting married this weekend? Why in hell would you bring this crap down on her now?"

Karim stood up and cleared his throat. "Sorry isn't enough, my daughter. Nothing I say will ever fix the pain and betrayal you must feel. The guilt has been eating me alive. I had to come and own up to my mistakes. When I leave here, I am flying home to confess my sins to my family. My children already know. Darius is a good man and accepts you unconditionally. Rosana is more like her mother and doesn't forgive so easily. My timing is poor with your impending nuptials, but I wanted you to know exactly who you are when you make that commitment for the rest of your life. I loved Fiona with my heart and soul, and she loved you with hers. I felt I owed it to her and to you to attempt to make amends. Only time …"

Reagan pushed herself away from Aiden and stood. She quickly moved within inches from Karim standing toe-to-toe, glaring up at him. He held his ground, towering over her by a good 6 inches and didn't flinch at her aggressive stance. Her jaw clenched.

"How self-serving of you to pick my wedding weekend to relieve your guilty conscious. To finally acknowledge me as your daughter now, rather than 23 years ago when you learned of my existence. To make sure I knew that not only did you deny me, but my own mother denied me as well. Instead of taking responsibility for her actions, she chose to put that responsibility on my half-sister Claire, who gave up everything. For what? So you and my grandmother wouldn't be humiliated? Didn't want to have a scandal? I can only imagine the twisted things my grandmother said or did to guilt Claire into giving up her dreams to pretend to be my mother. The sad thing is … even after Claire made that sacrifice, my grandmother never allowed her to have her own life. She was self-centered. Ruined her own daughter's marriage rather than give up control over her. Destroying my relationship with the only father I knew so she wouldn't lose me. Fiona manipulated and isolated both of us for her own selfish motives."

Reagan could feel her body trembling. Her mind going to a dark place. A place she had spent the last six months putting behind her. Coming to terms with. She couldn't lose ground now. Not when she had the final pieces to the puzzle. Her biological father had swallowed his pride to come forward and accept responsibility. It was a huge step for a man like him. Reagan had learned a lot about forgiveness and maybe she wasn't there yet with him, but she could at least open her mind. Maybe her heart would come later. When she continued, a calm had come over her.

"Mr. Nader, do you realize that by sneaking those gems into my grandparents' home so you wouldn't be implicated in a crime of your brother's making, you transferred all the risk and danger squarely on the family of the woman you loved? You said you left it to fate if the gems would be found. Well, fate took a nasty turn. It caused the total destruction of my family. My father left us. Claire committed suicide. Fiona was murdered, and I was almost killed. I doubt you intended any of those things, but they did happen. All a consequence of your actions."

Karim squeezed his eyes closed for a few seconds, then spoke. "You are correct in your assessment. I was so caught up in saving myself and my family, I didn't stop to consider the ramifications of my actions.

Unfortunately, there is nothing I can say or do to change any of those things. I only pray that one day you and my other children will be able to forgive me."

Reagan took a deep steadying breath. "This wasn't the best timing, but I appreciate your honesty and acknowledgement. I'm not ready to accept you in my life, and I'm not sure if I ever will be. They say time heals. I guess we'll see."

Reagan and Aiden calmly walked him to the door. As soon as it was closed, she fell into Aiden's arms.

# Chapter 46

Aiden and Reagan lay on a white canvas lounger the size of a double bed, sunbathing on a secluded narrow beach in Jamaica. Their skin was tanned, and their bodies glowed with perspiration as they held hands and watched the brilliant burnt-orange sun glimmering off the crystal blue waters not far from where they said their "I do's" the week before. Friends and family had just left to fly home, leaving Aiden and Reagan to spend the second week of their honeymoon by themselves. Having quality time with loved ones had been therapeutic for them and helped forge a bond with in-laws and new family members. Mattie and Josh stood up for Reagan and Aiden as Best Man and Matron of Honor. Aiden had been thrilled for Reagan when Stuart insisted on giving her away. The arrival of Darius and Helena cemented their commitment to be an integral part of Reagan's life. Now they were ready to explore life as a couple.

"Can you pass me the suntan spray, please?" Reagan asked.

Aiden cocked an eyebrow and laughed. "It amazes me how you have managed to get a tan despite the fact that you've been covered in lotion with 50 SPF."

"Even flour can be browned. You just have to do it gradually, so it won't burn," she said.

Aiden's cell rang. He looked at Reagan for permission to pick it up. They had agreed no calls unless it was an emergency, but since their families had just left for the airport, it was a good idea to make sure someone hadn't left a passport behind.

He hit the green light.

"Aiden, it's Brad Kowalski."

"Detective Kowalski. You do realize you're interrupting my honeymoon, right?" Aiden asked, flipping the speaker on so Reagan could hear. The detective's recovery had been long and painful with months of rehab. Only recently had he been allowed to return to work on partial duty. The chances of him returning to his former position were slim, but there was talk of a promotion that wouldn't require field work. Danni Silva's continued support in his recovery had resulted in a budding romance, surprising them both more than anyone else.

"Oh, shit! Sorry. I had no idea. This was mostly for Reagan, but I haven't been able to reach her. It can wait," Kowalski said.

"She's right here, and you're on speaker so you might as well go ahead."

"Hey, detective. What's so important?" Reagan asked.

"My boss thought I might like being the one to give you some good news. Guess it will be a kind of wedding present."

"We're all ears," Aiden said.

"Actually, there are a couple of things that might help put your mind at ease. Borzin Nader finally gave us the name of the man he originally stole the jewels and gems from, and it just so happened that he was also a well-known criminal. Bad guys stealing from bad guys. We just got confirmation from the CIA that the original thief died in an Iraqi prison serving a life sentence for manslaughter. The FBI has been unable to identify the loose gems or the period jewelry. They don't appear on any international list as stolen from a museum or private collector. Many aristocratic families have held similar pieces in their family for centuries. The owner may have been killed or didn't have proof of ownership. This wouldn't be unusual in countries with unstable regimes. You would be surprised how many private citizens make questionable deals to get what they want. Regardless, they're not willing to waste any more resources to continue the search. The statute of limitations is long over for the theft anyway. You will be receiving a letter within the next few weeks relinquishing any future claims by the government to the jewels and notifying you of the inheritance taxes you will need to pay once the full appraisal is done. Want to know what their estimated value is?"

Aiden and Reagan exchanged looks. She did a thumbs-up.

"Go for it," Aiden said.

"This is rough, but around $26 million. You could possibly get twice that amount for the period pieces at auction with the right buyers."

"Seriously?" Aiden asked. He turned to look at Reagan, who merely shrugged. She had always felt the jewels were tainted and thought as little about them as possible.

"Looks like you're going to have to sell some pieces of the stuff to pay the taxes. I think the government sees you guys as cash cows. The quicker the Feds discontinue the search, the quicker they get their cut. You've got some time to think about what you want to do. Just a heads-up."

"Thanks," Aiden said.

"Any idea what you plan to do with the money?" Kowalski asked.

"We're going to set up a nonprofit with whatever is left after taxes and give it all away to children's causes. We are hoping to use it to build lives, not destroy them," Reagan said emphatically.

"That doesn't surprise me. You're good people. Again, sorry for the lousy timing. Best wishes to you both."

"Anything you want to talk about?" Aiden asked after ending the call.

"Only how amazing it is to be married to the most wonderful and supportive man on this earth. We've spent an amazing week with our true friends and family. Dad and Carol are coming to visit us for Thanksgiving with your family. We're going to New Orleans to spend Christmas with Darius and his family. I love your parents and extended family. Mattie and I are finally sisters. I can give millions of dollars away to children in need. I'd say that is an excellent foundation for a happy and fulfilling life."

"So do I, Sweetheart."

# About the Author

Joy York grew up in Alabama but has spent much of her adult life in the Midwest, currently living with her husband in Indiana with their two goldendoodles, Jake and Bailey. Inspired by a family legacy of oral storytelling, she began creating stories and adventures for her son when he was growing up. With encouragement from family and friends, she began to write them down. Her first book, *The Bloody Shoe Affair: A daring and thrilling adventure with the jailer's daughter*, a YA mystery, was published in 2015. *Genuine Deceit,* an adult suspense novel, is her second book. For more information, visit www.joyyork.com.

Made in the USA
Monee, IL
22 May 2021